Enid Blyton's
FAMOUS FIVE
T.V. SPECIAL

HODDER AND STOUGHTON
LONDON SYDNEY AUCKLAND TORONTO

Blyton, Enid
   Famous Five TV special.
   I. Title   II. Blyton, Enid.   Five go off in a caravan
III. Blyton, Enid.   Five go off to camp
IV. Blyton, Enid.   Five go to Mystery Moor
823'.9'1J   PZ7.B629

ISBN 0 340 23147 5

Five go off in a caravan first published by
Hodder and Stoughton, 1946.

Five go off to camp first published by
Hodder and Stoughton, 1948.

Five go to Mystery Moor first published by
Hodder and Stoughton, 1954.

This edition first printed 1978.
Line illustrations copyright © 1974 Hodder and Stoughton Ltd.
Colour stills copyright © 1978 Southern Television.

ISBN 0 340 23147 5

Printed and bound by Henri Proost and Cie, Turnhout,
Belgium for Hodder and Stoughton Children's Books,
a division of Hodder and Stoughton Ltd,
Mill Road, Dunton Green, Sevenoaks, Kent TN13 2YJ
(Editorial Office: 47 Bedford Square, London WC1B 3DP).
Typeset by Trident Graphics Ltd, Reigate, Surrey.
Colour reproduction by Colourcraftsmen Ltd, Chelmsford,
Essex.

Contents

Five go off to camp

1 Holiday time

'Two jolly fine tents, four groundsheets, four sleeping-bags – I say, what about Timmy? Isn't he going to have a sleeping-bag, too?' said Dick, with a grin.

The other three children laughed, and Timmy, the dog, thumped his tail hard on the ground.

'Look at him,' said George. 'He's laughing, too! He's got his mouth stretched wide open.'

They all looked at Timmy. He really did look as if a wide grin stretched his hairy mouth from side to side.

'He's a darling,' said Anne, hugging him. 'Best dog in the world, aren't you, Timmy?'

'Woof!' said Timmy, agreeing. He gave Anne a wet lick on her nose.

The four children, Julian, tall and strong for his age, Dick, George and Anne were busy planning a camping holiday. George was a girl, not a boy, but she would never answer to her real name, Georgina. With her freckled face and short, curly hair she really did look more like a boy than a girl.

'It's absolutely wizard, being allowed to go on a camping holiday all by ourselves,' said Dick. 'I never thought our parents would allow it, after the terrific adventure we had last summer, when we went off in caravans.'

'Well – we shan't be *quite* all by ourselves,' said Anne. 'Don't forget we've got Mr Luffy to keep an eye on us. He'll be camping quite near.'

'Pooh! Old Luffy!' said Dick, with a laugh. 'He won't know if we're there or not. So long as he can study his precious moorland insects, he won't bother about us.'

'Well, if it hadn't been that he was going to camp, too, we wouldn't have been allowed to go,' said Anne. 'I heard Daddy say so.'

Mr Luffy was a master at the boys' school, an elderly, dreamy fellow with a passion for studying all kinds of insect-life. Anne avoided him when he carried about boxes of insect specimens, because sometimes they escaped and came crawling out. The boys liked him and thought him fun, but the idea of Mr Luffy keeping an eye on them struck them as very comical.

'It's more likely we'll have to keep an eye on *him*,' said Julian. 'He's the sort of chap whose tent will always be falling down on top of him, or he'll run out of water, or sit down on his bag of eggs. Old Luffy seems to live in the world of insects, not in our world!'

'Well, he can go and live in the world of insects if he likes, so long as he doesn't interfere with *us*,' said George, who hated interfering people. 'This sounds as if it will be a super holiday – living in tents on the high moors, away from everybody, doing exactly what we like, when we like and how we like.'

'Woof!' said Timmy, thumping his tail again.

'That means he's going to do as *he* likes, too,' said Anne. 'You're going to chase hundreds of rabbits, aren't you, Timmy, and bark madly at anyone who dares to come within two miles of us!'

'Now be quiet a minute, Anne!' said Dick, picking up his list again. 'We really must check down our list and find out if we've got every single thing we want. Where did I get to – oh, four sleeping-bags.'

'Yes, and you wanted to know if Timmy was to have one,' said Anne, with a giggle.

'Of course he won't,' said George. 'He'll sleep where he always does – won't you, Timmy? On my feet.'

'Couldn't we get him just a *small* sleeping-bag?' asked Anne. 'He'd look sweet with his head poking out of the top.'

'Timmy hates looking sweet,' said George. 'Go on, Dick. I'll tie my hanky round Anne's mouth if she interrupts again.'

Dick went on down his list. It was a very interesting one. Things like cooking-stoves, canvas buckets, enamel plates and drinking-cups were on it and each item seemed to need a lot of discussion. The four children enjoyed themselves very much.

'You know, it's almost as much fun planning a holiday like this as having it,' said Dick. 'Well – I shouldn't think we've forgotten a thing, have we?'

'No. We've probably thought of too much!' said Julian. 'Well, old Luffy says he'll take all our things on the trailer behind his car, so we'll be all right. I shouldn't like us to carry them ourselves!'

'Oh, I wish next week would come!' said Anne. 'Why is it that the time seems so long when you're waiting for something nice to happen, and so short when something nice *is* happening?'

'Yes – it seems the wrong way round, doesn't it?' said Dick, with a grin. 'Anyone got the map? I'd like to take another squint at the spot where we're going.'

Julian produced a map from his pocket. He opened it and the four children sprawled round it. The map showed a vast and lonely stretch of moorland, with very few houses indeed.

'Just a few small farms, that's all,' said Julian pointing to one or two. 'They can't get much of a living out of such poor land, though. See, that's about the place where we're going – just there – and on the opposite slope is a small farm where we shall get milk, eggs and butter when we need them. Luffy's been there before. He says it's a rather small farm, but jolly useful to campers.'

'These moors are awfully high, aren't they?' said George. 'I guess they'll be freezing cold in the winter.'

'They are,' said Julian. 'And they may be jolly windy and cold in the summer, too, so Luffy says we'd better take sweaters and things. He says in the winter they are covered with snow for months. The sheep have to be dug out when they get lost.'

Dick's finger followed a small winding road that made its way over the wild stretch of moorland. 'That's the road we go,' he said. 'And I suppose we strike off here, look, where a cart-track is shown. That would go to the farm. We shall have to carry our stuff from wherever Luffy parks his car, and take it to our camping-place.'

'Not too near Luffy, I hope,' said George.

'Oh, no. He's agreed to keep an eye on us, but he'll forget all about us once he's settled down in his own tent,' said Julian. 'He will, really. Two chaps I know once went out in his car with him for a day's run, and he came back without them in the evening. He'd forgotten he had them with him, and had left them wandering somewhere miles and miles away.'

'Good old Luffy,' said Dick. 'That's the sort of fellow we want! He won't come sprinting up to ask if we've cleaned our teeth or if we've got our warm jerseys on!'

The others laughed, and Timmy stretched his doggy mouth into a grin again. His tongue hung out happily. It was good to have all four of his friends with him again, and to hear them planning a holiday. Timmy went to school with George and Anne in term time, and he missed the two boys very much. But he belonged to George, and would not dream of leaving her. It was a good thing that George's school allowed pets, or George would certainly not have gone!

Julian folded up the map again. 'I hope all the things we've ordered will come in good time,' he said. 'We've got about six days to wait. I'd better keep on reminding Luffy that we're going with him, or he's quite likely to start without us!'

It was difficult to have to wait so long now that everything was planned. Parcels came from various stores and were eagerly opened. The sleeping-bags were fine.

'Super!' said Anne.

'Smashing!' said George, crawling into hers. 'Look! I can lace it up at the neck – and it's got a hood thing to come right over my head. Golly, it's warm! I shan't mind the coldest night if I'm sleeping in this. I vote we sleep in them tonight.'

'What? In our bedrooms?' said Anne.

'Yes. Why not? Just to get used to them,' said George, who felt that a sleeping-bag was a hundred times better than an ordinary bed.

So that night all four slept on the floor of their bedrooms in their sleeping-bags, and voted them very comfortable and as warm as toast.

'The only thing is, Timmy kept wanting to come right inside mine,' said George, 'and honestly there isn't enough room. Besides, he'd be cooked.'

'Well, he seemed to spend half the night on my tummy,' grumbled Julian. 'I shall jolly well keep the bedroom door shut if Timmy's going to spend the night flopping on everyone's bag in turn.'

'I don't mind the flopping, so much as the frightful habit he's got of turning himself round and round and round before he flops down,' complained Dick. 'He did that on me last night. Silly habit of his.'

'He can't help it,' said George at once. 'It's a habit that wild dogs had centuries and centuries ago – they slept in reeds and rushes, and they got into the way of turning themselves round and round in them, to trample them down and make themselves a good sleeping-place. And our dogs go

Timmy was as excited as the four children.

on turning themselves round now, before they go to sleep, even though there aren't any rushes to trample down.'

'Well! I wish Timmy would forget his doggy ancestors were wild dogs with rushy beds, and just remember he's a nice tame dog with a basket of his own,' said Dick. 'You should see my tummy today! It's all printed over with his foot-marks.'

'Fibber!' said Anne. 'You do exaggerate, Dick. Oh, I do wish Tuesday would come. I'm tired of waiting.'

'It'll come all right,' said Julian. And so it did, of course. It dawned bright and sunny, with a sky that was a deep blue, flecked with tiny white clouds.

'Good-weather clouds,' said Julian, pleased. 'Now let's hope old Luffy has remembered it's today we're starting off. He's due here at ten o'clock. We're taking sandwiches for the whole party. Mother thought we'd better, in case Luffy forgot his. If he's remembered them it won't matter, because we're sure to be able to eat them ourselves. And there's always Timmy to finish things up!'

Timmy was as excited as the four children. He always knew when something nice was going to happen. His tail was on the wag the whole time, his tongue hung out, and he panted as if he had been running a race. He kept getting under everyone's feet, but nobody minded.

Mr Luffy arrived half an hour late, just when everyone was beginning to feel he had forgotten to come. He was at the wheel of his big old car, beaming. All the children knew him quite well, because he lived not far away and often came to play bridge with their father and mother.

'Hallo, hallo!' he cried. 'All ready, I see! Good for you! Pile the things on the trailer, will you? Mine are there too but there's plenty of room. I've got sandwiches for everyone, by the way. My wife said I'd better bring plenty.'

'We'll have a fine feast today then,' said Dick, helping Julian to carry out the folded-up tents and sleeping-bags, while the girls followed with the smaller things. Soon everything was on the trailer and Julian made them safe with ropes.

They said good-bye to the watching grown-ups and climbed excitedly into the car. Mr Luffy started up his engine and put the lever into first gear with a frightful noise.

'Good-bye!' called all the grown-ups, and Julian's mother added a last word. 'DON'T get into any awful adventure this time!'

'Of course they won't!' called back Mr Luffy cheerfully. 'I'll see to that. There are no adventures to be found on a wild and deserted moor. Good-bye!'

Off they went, waving madly, and shouting good-bye all the way down the road. 'Good-bye! Good-byeeeeee! Hurrah, we're off at last!'

The car raced down the road, the trailer bumping madly after it. The holiday had begun!

11

2 Up on the moors

Mr Luffy was not a good driver. He went too fast, especially round the corners, and many times Julian looked behind at the trailer in alarm, afraid that everything would suddenly leap off it at some sharp bend.

He saw the bundle of sleeping-bags jump high into the air, but fortunately they remained on the trailer. He touched Mr Luffy on the shoulder.

'Sir! Could you go a bit slower, please? The trailer will be empty by the time we arrive, if the luggage leaps about on it much more.'

'My word! I forgot we had a trailer,' said Mr Luffy, slowing down at once. 'Remind me if I go over thirty-five miles an hour, will you? Last time I took the trailer with me, I arrived with only half the goods on it. I don't want that to happen again.'

Julian certainly hoped it wouldn't. He kept a sharp eye on the speedometer, and when it veered towards forty he tapped Mr Luffy on the arm.

Mr Luffy looked supremely happy. He didn't like term time, but he loved holidays. Term time interfered with the study of his beloved insect-world. Now he was off with four nice children he liked, for a holiday on a moorland he knew was alive with bees, beetles, butterflies and every other kind of insect he wanted. He looked forward to teaching the four children quite a lot. They would have been horrified if they had guessed this, but they didn't.

He was an odd-looking fellow. He had very untidy, shaggy eyebrows over kind and gentle brown eyes that always reminded Dick of a monkey's. He had a rather large nose, which looked fiercer than it was because, unexpectedly, it had quite a forest of hairs growing out of the nostrils. He had an untidy moustache, and a round chin with a surprising dimple in the middle of it.

His ears always fascinated Anne. They were large and turned rather forward, and Mr Luffy could waggle the right one if he wanted to. To his great sorrow he had never been able to waggle the left one. His hair was thick and untidy, and his clothes always looked loose, comfortable and rather too big for him.

The children liked him. They couldn't help it. He was so odd and gentle and untidy and forgetful – and yet sometimes unexpectedly fierce. Julian had often told them the story of Tom Killin the bully.

Mr Luffy had once found Tom bullying a small new boy in the cloakroom, dragging him round and round it by his belt. With a roar like an angry bull, Mr Luffy had pounced on the big bully, got him by the belt, lifted him up and stuck him firmly on a peg in the cloakroom.

'There you stay till you get someone to lift you down!' Mr Luffy had thundered. '*I* can get hold of a belt too, as you can see!'

And then he had stalked out of the cloakroom with the small, terrified boy beside him, leaving the bully hung up high on the peg, quite unable to free himself. And there he had to stay, because not one of the boys who came pouring in from a game of football would lift him down.

'And, if the peg hadn't given way under his weight, he'd be stuck up there still,' Julian had said with a grin. 'Good old Luffy! You'd never think he could be fierce like that, would you?'

Anne loved that story. Mr Luffy became quite a hero to her after that. She was pleased to sit next to him in the car, and chatter about all kinds of things. The other three were squashed at the back with Timmy on their feet. George firmly prevented him from climbing up on her knee because it was so hot. So he contented himself with trying to stand up with his paws on the window-ledge and his nose over the side.

They stopped about half past twelve for lunch. Mr Luffy had indeed provided sandwiches for everyone. And remarkably fine ones they were too, made the evening before by Mrs Luffy.

'Cucumber, dipped in vinegar! Ham and lettuce! Egg! Sardine! Oooh, Mr Luffy, your sandwiches are much nicer than ours,' said Anne, beginning on two together, one cucumber and the other ham and lettuce.

They were all very hungry. Timmy had a bit from everyone, usually the last bite, and watched each sandwich eagerly till his turn came. Mr Luffy didn't seem to understand that Timmy had to have the last bite of any sandwich, so Timmy simply took it out of his hand, much to his surprise.

'A clever dog,' he said, and patted him. 'Knows what he wants and takes it. Very clever.'

That pleased George, of course. She thought that Timmy was the cleverest dog in the world, and indeed it did seem like it at times. He understood every word she said to him, every pat, every stroke, every gesture. He would be much, much better at keeping an eye on the four children and guarding them than forgetful Mr Luffy.

They drank ginger-beer and then ate some ripe plums. Timmy wouldn't have any plums, but he licked up some spilt ginger-beer. Then he snuffled up a few odd crumbs and went to drink at a little stream near by.

The party set off again in the car. Anne fell asleep. Dick gave an enormous yawn and fell asleep too. George wasn't sleepy, nor was Timmy, but Julian was. He didn't dare to take his eye off the speedometer, though, because Mr Luffy seemed to be very much inclined to speed along too fast again, after his good lunch.

'We won't stop for tea till we get there,' said Mr Luffy suddenly, and Dick woke up with a jump at the sound of his booming voice. 'We should be there about half past five. Look, you can see the moorland in the distance now – all ablaze with heather!'

Everybody looked ahead, except Anne, who was still fast asleep. Rising up to the left for mile upon mile was the heather-covered moorland, a lovely sight to see. It looked wild and lonely and beautiful, blazing with heather, and shading off into a purple-blue in the distance.

'We take this road to the left, and then we're on the moors,' said Mr Luffy, swinging violently to the left, and making the luggage in the trailer jump high again. 'Here we go.'

The car climbed the high moorland road steadily. It passed one or two small houses, and in the distance the children could see little farms in clearings. Sheep dotted the moorland, and some of them stood staring at the car as it drove by.

'We've got about twenty miles to go, I should think,' said Mr Luffy, jamming on his brakes suddenly to avoid two large sheep in the middle of the road. 'I wish these creatures wouldn't choose the centre of the road to gossip in. Hi, get on there! Let me pass!'

Timmy yelped and tried to get out of the car. The sheep hurriedly decided to move, and the car went on. Anne was thoroughly awake by now, having been almost jerked out of her seat by the sudden stop.

'What a shame to wake you!' said Mr Luffy, gazing down at her kindly, and almost running into a ditch by the side of the road. 'We're nearly there, Anne.'

They climbed steadily, and the wind grew a little cold. All around the children the moors stretched for mile upon mile, never-ending. Little streams sometimes splashed right down to the roadway, and ran beside it.

'We can drink the water in these streams,' said Mr Luffy. 'Crystal clear, and cold as ice! There's one quite near where we're going to camp.'

That was good news. Julian thought of the big canvas buckets they had brought. He didn't particularly want to carry those for miles. If there was a stream near their camping place it would be easy to get the buckets filled with washing-water.

The road forked into two. To the right was a good road, leading on and on. To the left it became not much more than a cart-track. 'That's the one we take,' said Mr Luffy, and the car jerked and jolted over it. He was forced to go slowly, and the children had time to see every little thing they passed.

'I shall leave the car here,' said Mr Luffy, bringing it to a standstill beside a great rock that stood up bare and grey out of the moor. 'It will be sheltered from the worst winds and rain. I thought we'd camp over yonder.'

There was a little slope just there, backed by some enormous gorse bushes. Thick heather grew everywhere. Julian nodded. It was a good place for camping. Those thick gorse bushes would provide fine shelter from the winds.

'Right sir,' he said. 'Shall we have tea first, or unpack now?'

'Tea first,' said Mr Luffy. 'I've brought a very good little stove for boiling and cooking things. Better than a wood fire. That makes kettles and saucepans so black.'

'We've got a stove, too,' said Anne. She scrambled out of the car and looked all round. 'It's lovely here – all heather and wind and sun! Is that the farm over there – the one we shall go to for eggs and things?'

She pointed to a tiny farmhouse on the hill opposite. It stood in a small clearing. In a field behind it were three or four cows and a horse. A small orchard stood at the side, and a vegetable garden lay in front. It seemed odd to see such a trim little place in the midst of the moorland.

'That's Olly's Farm,' said Mr Luffy. 'It's changed hands, I believe, since I was here three years ago. I hope the new people are nice. Now – did we leave something to eat for our tea?'

They had, because Anne had wisely put away a

good many sandwiches and bits of cake for tea-time. They sat in the heather, with bees humming all round them, and munched solidly for fifteen minutes. Timmy waited patiently for his bits, watching the bees that hummed round him. There were thousands of them.

'And now I suppose we'd better put up our tents,' said Julian. 'Come on, Dick – let's unpack the trailer. Mr Luffy, we don't intend to camp on top of you, sir, because you won't want four noisy children too near. Where would you like your tent put?'

Mr Luffy was about to say that he would like to have the four children and Timmy quite close, when it suddenly occurred to him that perhaps they might not want him too near. They might want to make a noise, or play silly games, and if he were near it would stop them enjoying themselves in their own way.

So he made up his mind not to be too close. 'I'll pitch my tent down here, where that old gorse bush is,' he said. 'And if you'd like to put yours up here, where there's a half-circle of gorse bushes keeping off the wind, you'd be well sheltered. And we shan't interfere with one another at all.'

'Right, sir,' said Julian, and he and Dick began to tackle the tents. It was fun. Timmy got under everyone's feet as usual, and ran off with an important rope, but nobody minded.

By the time that dusk came creeping up the heather-covered moorland, all three tents were up, the groundsheets were put down, and the

sleeping-bags unrolled on them, two in each of the children's tents, and one in Mr Luffy's.

'I'm going to turn in,' said Mr Luffy. 'My eyes are almost shut. Good-night all of you. Sleep well!'

He disappeared into the dusk. Anne yawned widely, and that set the others off too. 'Come on – let's turn in, too,' said Julian. 'We'll have a bar of chocolate each, and a few biscuits. We can eat those in our sleeping-bags, Good-night, girls. Won't it be grand to wake up tomorrow morning?'

He and Dick disappeared into their tent. The girls crawled into theirs with Timmy. They undressed, and got into their warm, soft sleeping-bags.

'This is super!' said George, pushing Timmy to one side. 'I never felt so cosy in my life. *Don't* do that, Timmy. Don't you know the difference between my feet and my middle? That's better.'

'Good-night,' said Anne, sleepily. 'Look, George, you can see the stars shining through the opening of the tent. Don't they look enormous?'

But George didn't care whether they were enormous or not. She was fast asleep, tired out with the day's run. Timmy cocked one ear when he heard Anne's voice, and gave a little grunt. That was his way of saying good-night. Then he put his head down and slept.

'Our first night of camping,' thought Anne, happily. 'I shan't go to sleep. I shall lie awake and look at the stars and smell that heathery smell.'

But she didn't. In half a second she was sound asleep, too!

'I'm going to turn in,' said Mr Luffy.

3 Anne's volcano

Julian awoke first in the morning. He heard a strange and lonely sound floating overhead. 'Coor-lie! Coor-lie!'

He sat up and wondered where he was and who was calling. Of course! He was in his tent with Dick – they were camping on the moors. And that wild cry overhead came from a curlew, the bird of the moorlands.

He yawned and lay down again. It was early in the morning. The sun put its warm fingers in at his tent opening, and he felt the warmth on his sleeping-bag. He felt lazy and snug and contented. He also felt hungry, which was a nuisance. He glanced at his watch.

Half past six. He really was too warm and comfortable to get up yet. He put out his hand to see if there was any chocolate left from the night before, and found a little piece. He put it into his mouth and lay there contentedly, listening to more curlews, and watching the sun climb a little higher.

He fell asleep again, and was awakened by Timmy busily licking his face. He sat up with a start. The girls were peering in at his tent, grinning. They were fully dressed already.

'Wake up, lazy!' said Anne. 'We sent Timmy in to get you up. It's half past seven. We've been up for ages.'

'It's a simply heavenly morning,' said George. 'Going to be a frightfully hot day. Do get up. We're going to find the stream and wash in it. It seems silly to lug heavy buckets of water to and fro for washing, if the stream's near by.'

Dick awoke too. He and Julian decided to go and take a bathe in the stream. They wandered out into the sunny morning, feeling very happy and very hungry. The girls were just coming back from the stream.

'It's over there,' said Anne, pointing. 'Timmy, go with them and show them. It's a lovely little brown stream, awfully cold, and it's got ferns along its banks. We've left the bucket there. Bring it back full, will you?'

'What do you want us to do that for, if you've already washed?' asked Dick.

'We want water for washing-up the dishes,' said Anne. 'I suddenly remembered we'd need water for that. I say, do you think we ought to wake up Mr Luffy? There's no sign of him yet.'

'No, let him sleep,' said Julian. 'He's probably tired out with driving the car so slowly! We can easily save him some breakfast. What are we going to have?'

'We've unpacked some bacon rashers and tomatoes,' said Anne, who was a very good little housewife and loved cooking. 'How do you light the stove, Julian?'

'George knows,' said Julian. 'I say, did we pack a frying-pan?'

'Yes. I packed it myself,' said Anne. 'Do go and bathe if you're going to. Breakfast will be ready before you are!'

Timmy gravely trotted off with the boys and showed them the stream. Julian and Dick at once lay down in the clear brown bed, and kicked wildly. Timmy leapt in too, and there were yells and shrieks.

'Well – I should think we've woken up old Luffy now!' said Dick, rubbing himself down with a rough towel. 'How lovely and cold that was. The trouble is it's made me feel twice as hungry!'

'Doesn't that frying bacon smell good?' said Julian, sniffing the air. They walked back to the girls. There was still no sign of Mr Luffy. He must indeed sleep very soundly!

They sat down in the heather and began their breakfast. Anne had fried big rounds of bread in the fat, and the boys told her she was the best cook in the world. She was very pleased.

'I shall look after the food side for you,' she said. 'But George must help with the preparing of the meals and washing-up. See, George?'

George didn't see. She hated doing all the things that girls had to do, such as making beds and washing-up. She looked sulky.

'Look at old George! Why bother about the washing-up when there's Timmy only too pleased to use his tongue to wash every plate?' said Dick.

Everyone laughed, even George. 'All right,' she said, 'I'll help of course. Only let's use as few plates as possible, then there won't be much washing-up. Is there any more fried bread, Anne?'

'No. But there are some biscuits in that tin,' said Anne. 'I say, boys, who's going to go to the farm each day for milk and things? I expect they can let us have bread, too, and fruit.'

'Oh, one or other of us will go,' said Dick. 'Anne, hadn't you better fry something for old Luffy now? I'll go and wake him. Half the day will be gone if he doesn't get up now.'

'I'll go and make a noise like an earwig outside his tent,' said Julian, getting up. 'He might not wake with all our yells and shouts, but he'd certainly wake at the call of a friendly earwig!'

He went down to the tent. He cleared his throat and called politely: 'Are you awake yet, sir?'

There was no answer. Julian called again. Then, puzzled, he went to the tent opening. The flap was closed. He pulled it aside and looked in.

The tent was empty! There was nobody there at all.

'What's up, Ju?' called Dick.

'He's not here,' said Julian. 'Where can he be?'

There was a silence. For a panic-stricken moment Anne thought one of their queer adventures was beginning. Then Dick called out again: 'Is his bug-tin gone? You know, the tin box with straps that he takes with him when he goes insect-hunting? And what about his clothes?'

Julian inspected the inside of the tent again. 'Okay!' he called, much to everyone's relief. 'His clothes are gone, and so has his bug-tin. He must have slipped out early before we were awake. I bet he's forgotten all about us and breakfast and everything!'

'That would be just like him,' said Dick. 'Well, we're not his keepers. He can do as he likes! If he doesn't want breakfast, he needn't have any. He'll come back when he's finished his hunting, I suppose.'

'Anne! Can you get on with the doings if Dick and I go to the farmhouse and see what food they've got?' asked Julian. 'The time's getting on, and if we're going for a walk or anything today, we don't want to start too late.'

'Right,' said Anne. 'You go too, George. I can manage everything nicely, now that the boys have

brought me a bucketful of water. Take Timmy. He wants a walk.'

George was only too pleased to get out of the washing-up. She and the boys, with Timmy trotting in front, set off to the farmhouse. Anne got on with her jobs, humming softly to herself in the sunshine. She soon finished them, and then looked to see if the others were coming back. There was no sign of them, or of Mr Luffy either.

'I'll go for a walk on my own,' thought Anne. 'I'll follow that little stream uphill and see where it begins. That would be fun. I can't possibly lose my way if I keep by the water.'

She set off in the sunshine and came to the little brown stream that gurgled down the hill. She scrambled through the heather beside it, following its course uphill. She liked all the little green ferns and the cushions of velvety moss that edged it. She tasted the water – it was cold and sweet and clean.

Feeling very happy all by herself, Anne walked on and on. She came at last to a big mound of a hill-top. The little stream began there, half-way up the mound. It came gurgling out of the heathery hillside, edged with moss, and made its chattering way far down the hill.

'So that's where you begin, is it?' said Anne. She flung herself down on the heather, hot with her climb. It was nice there, with the sun on her face, and the sound of the trickling water near by.

She lay listening to the humming bees and the water. And then she heard another sound. She took no notice of it at all at first.

Then she sat up, frightened. 'The noise is underground! Deep, deep underground! It rumbles and roars. Oh, what is going to happen? Is there going to be an earthquake?'

The rumbling seemed to come nearer and nearer. Anne didn't even dare to get up and run. She sat there and trembled.

Then there came an unearthly shriek, and not far off a most astonishing thing happened. A great cloud of white smoke came right out of the ground and hung in the air before the wind blew it away. Anne was simply horrified. It was so sudden, so very unexpected on this quiet hillside. The rumbling noise went on for a while and then gradually faded away.

Anne leapt to her feet in a panic. She fled down the hill, screaming loudly: 'It's a volcano! Help! Help! I've been sitting on a volcano. It's going to burst, it's sending out smoke. Help, help, it's a VOLCANO!'

She tore down the hillside, caught her foot on a tuft of heather and went rolling over and over, sobbing. She came to rest at last, and then heard an anxious voice calling:

'Who's that? What's the matter?'

It was Mr Luffy's voice. Anne screamed to him in relief. 'Mr Luffy! Come and save me! There's a volcano here!'

There was such terror in her voice that Mr Luffy came racing to her at once. He sat down beside the trembling girl and put his arm round her. 'Whatever's the matter?' he said. 'What's frightened you?'

Anne told him again. 'Up there – do you see? That's a volcano, Mr Luffy. It rumbled and rumbled and then it shot up clouds of smoke. Oh quick, before it sends out red hot cinders!'

'Now, now!' said Mr Luffy, and to Anne's surprise and relief he actually laughed. 'Do you mean to tell me you don't know what that was?'

'No, I don't,' said Anne.

'Well,' said Mr Luffy, 'under this big moor run two or three long tunnels to take trains from one valley to another. Didn't you know? They make the rumbling noise you heard, and the sudden smoke you saw was the smoke sent up by a train below. There are big vent-holes here and there in the moor for the smoke to escape from.'

'Oh, good gracious me!' said Anne, going rather red. 'I didn't even *know* there were trains under here. What an extraordinary thing! I really did think I was sitting on a volcano, Mr Luffy. You won't tell the others, will you? They would laugh at me dreadfully.'

'I won't say a word,' said Mr Luffy. 'And now I think we'll go back. Have you had breakfast? I'm terribly hungry. I went out early after a rather rare butterfly I saw flying by my tent.'

'We've had breakfast *ages* ago,' said Anne. 'But if you'd like to come back with me now I'll cook you some bacon, Mr Luffy. And some tomatoes and fried bread.'

'Aha! It sounds good,' said Mr Luffy. 'Now – not a word about volcanoes. That's our secret.'

And off they went to the tents, where the others were wondering what in the world had become of Anne. Little did they know she had been 'sitting on a volcano!'

4 Spook-trains

The boys and George were full of talk about the farm. 'It's a nice little place,' said Julian, sitting down while Anne began to cook breakfast for Mr Luffy. 'Pretty farmhouse, nice little dairy, well-kept sheds. And even a grand piano in the drawing-room.'

'Gracious! You wouldn't think they'd make enough money to buy a thing like that, would you?' said Anne, turning over the bacon in the pan.

'The farmer's got a fine new car,' went on Julian. 'Brand new. Must have cost him a pretty penny. His boy showed it to us. And he showed us some jolly good new farm machinery too.'

'Very interesting,' said Mr Luffy. 'I wonder how they make their money, farming that bit of land. The last people were hard-working folk, but they certainly couldn't have afforded a new car or a grand piano.'

'And you should have seen the lorries they've got!' said Dick. 'Beauties! Old army ones, I should think. The boy said his father's going to use them for carting things from the farm to the market.'

'What things?' said Mr Luffy, looking across at the little farmhouse. 'I shouldn't have thought they needed an army of lorries for that! An old farm wagon would carry all *their* produce.'

'Well – that's what he told us,' said Dick. 'Everything certainly looked very prosperous, I must say. He must be a jolly good farmer.'

'We got eggs and butter and fruit, and even some bacon,' said George. 'The boy's mother didn't seem worried about how much we had, and she hardly charged us anything. We didn't see the farmer.'

Mr Luffy was now eating his breakfast. He was certainly very hungry. He brushed away the flies that hung round his head, and when one settled on his right ear he waggled it violently. The fly flew off in surprise.

'Oh, do that again!' begged Anne. 'How do you do it? Do you think if I practised hard for weeks I could make my ear move?'

'No, I don't think so,' said Mr Luffy, finishing

his breakfast. 'Well, I've got some writing to do now. What are you going to do? Go for a walk?'

'We might as well take a picnic lunch and go off somewhere,' said Julian. 'How about it?'

'Yes,' said Dick. 'Can you pack us dinner and tea, Anne? We'll help. What about hard-boiled eggs?'

It wasn't long before they had a picnic meal packed in greaseproof paper.

'You won't get lost, will you?' said Mr Luffy.

'Oh no, sir,' said Julian, with a laugh. 'I've got a compass, anyway, and a jolly good bump of locality, too. I usually know the way to go. We'll see you this evening, when we get back.'

'*You* won't get lost, Mr Luffy, will you?' said Anne, looking worried.

'Don't be cheeky, Anne,' said Dick, rather horrified at Anne's question. But she really meant it. Mr Luffy was so absent-minded that she could quite well picture him wandering off and not being able to find his way back.

He smiled at her. 'No,' he said. 'I know my way about here all right – I know every stream and path and er – volcano!'

Anne giggled. The others stared at Mr Luffy, wondering what in the world he meant, but neither he nor Anne told them. They said goodbye and set off.

'It's heavenly walking today,' said Anne. 'Shall we follow a path if we find one or not?'

'Might as well,' said Julian. 'It'll be a bit tiring scrambling through heather all the day.'

So when they did unexpectedly come across a path they followed it. 'It's just a shepherd's path, I expect,' said Dick. 'I bet it's a lonely job, looking after sheep up on these desolate heathery hills.'

They went on for some way, enjoying the stretches of bright heather, the lizards that darted quickly away from their feet and the hosts of butterflies of all kinds that hovered and fluttered. Anne loved the little blue ones best and made up her mind to ask Mr Luffy what all their names were.

They had their lunch on a hill-top overlooking a vast stretch of heather, with grey-white blobs in it here and there – the sheep that wandered everywhere.

And, in the very middle of the meal, Anne heard the same rumbling she had heard before – and then, not far off, out spouted some white smoke from the ground. George went quite pale. Timmy leapt to his feet, growling and barking, his tail down. The boys roared with laughter.

'It's all right, Anne and George. It's only the trains underground here. We knew they ran under the moors and we thought we'd see what you did

. . . Anne heard the same rumbling she had heard before.

when you first heard them rumbling, and saw the smoke.'

'I'm not a bit frightened,' said Anne, and the boys looked at her, astonished. It was George who was the scared one! Usually it was quite the other way round.

George got back her colour and laughed. She called Timmy. 'It's all right, Tim. Come here. You know what trains are, don't you?'

The children discussed the trains. It really did seem queer to think of trains in those hollowed-out tunnels down below the moors – with people in them, reading their newspapers and talking – down in tunnels where the sun never shone at all.

'Come on,' said Julian, at last. 'Let's go on. We'll walk to the top of the next slope, and then I think we ought to turn back.'

They found a little path that Julian said must be a rabbit-path, because it was so narrow, and set off, chattering and laughing. They climbed through the heather to the top of the next slope. And at the top they got quite a surprise.

Down in the valley below was a silent and deserted stretch of railway lines! They appeared out of the black hole of a tunnel-mouth, ran for about half a mile, and then ended in what seemed to be a kind of railway yard.

'Look at that,' said Julian. 'Old derelict lines – not used any more, I should think. I suppose that tunnel's out of date, too.'

'Let's go down and have a squint,' said Dick. 'Come on! We've got plenty of time, and we can easily go back a shorter way.'

They set off down the hill to the lines. They arrived some way from the tunnel-mouth, and followed the lines to the deserted railway yard. There seemed to be nobody about at all.

'Look,' said Dick, 'there are some old wagons on that set of lines over there. They look as if they haven't been used for a hundred years. Let's give them a shove and set them going!'

'Oh, no!' said Anne, afraid. But the two boys and George, who had always longed to play about with real railway trucks, ran over to where three or four stood on the lines. Dick and Julian shoved hard at one. It moved. It ran a little way and crashed into the buffers of another. It made a terrific noise in the silent yard.

A door flew open in a tiny hut at the side of the yard, and a terrifying figure came out. It was a one-legged man, with a wooden peg for his other leg, two great arms that might quite well belong to a gorilla, and a face as red as a tomato, except where grey whiskers grew.

He opened his mouth and the children expected a loud and angry yell. Instead out came a husky, hoarse whisper:

'What you doing? Ain't it bad enough to hear spook-trains a-running at night, without hearing them in the daytime, too?'

The four children stared at him. They thought he must be quite mad. He came nearer to them, and his wooden leg tip-tapped queerly. He swung his great arms loosely. He peered at the children as if he could hardly see them.

'I've bruck me glasses,' he said, and to their astonishment and dismay two tears ran down his cheeks. 'Poor old Wooden-Leg Sam, he's bruck his glasses. Nobody cares about Wooden-Leg Sam now, nobody at all.'

There didn't seem anything to say to all this. Anne felt sorry for the queer old man, but she kept well behind Julian.

Sam peered at them again. 'Ain't you got no tongues in your 'eads? Am I seeing things again, or are you there?'

'We're here and we're real,' said Julian. 'We happened to see this old railway yard and we came down to have a look at it. Who are you?'

'I've told you – I'm Wooden-Leg Sam,' said the old man impatiently. 'The watchman, see? Though what there is to watch here, beats me. Does they think I'm a-going to watch for them spook-trains? Well, I'm not. Not me, Sam Wooden-Leg. I've seed many queer things in my life, yes, and bin scared by them too, and I'm not watching for any spook-trains no more.'

The children listened curiously. 'What spook-trains?' asked Julian.

Wooden-Leg Sam came closer. He looked all round as if he thought there might be someone listening, and then spoke in a hoarser whisper than usual.

'Spook-trains, I tell 'ee. Trains what come outa that tunnel by nights all by theirselves, and go back all by theirselves. Nobody in them. One night they'll come for old Sam Wooden-Leg – but, ee, I'm smart, I am. I lock myself into my hut and get under the bed. And I blows my candle out so those spook-trains don't know I'm there.'

Anne shivered. She pulled at Julian's hand. 'Julian! Let's go. I don't like it. It sounds all queer and horrid. What does he mean?'

The old man seemed suddenly to change his

mood. He picked up a large cinder and threw it at Dick, hitting him on the head. 'You clear out! I'm watchman here, ain't I? And what did they tell me? They told me to chase away anyone that came. Clear out, I tell you!'

In terror Anne fled away. Timmy growled and would have leapt at the queer old watchman, but George had her hand on his collar. Dick rubbed his head where the cinder had hit him.

'We're going,' he said soothingly to Sam. It was plain that the old fellow was queer in his mind. 'We didn't mean to trespass. You look after your spook-trains. We won't interfere with you!'

The boys and George turned away, and caught

5 Back at camp again

The children and Timmy left the deserted railway yard behind them and climbed up the heathery slope to find their way back to their camping-place. The boys could not stop talking about Wooden-Leg Sam and the queer things he said.

'It's a funny business altogether,' said Julian. 'I wonder why that yard isn't used any more – and where that tunnel leads to – and if trains ever do run there?'

'I expect there's quite an ordinary explanation,' said Dick. 'It's just that Wooden-Leg Sam made it all seem so queer. If there had been a proper watchman we shouldn't have thought there was anything queer about it at all.'

'Perhaps the boy at the farm would know,' said Julian. 'We'll ask him tomorrow. I'm afraid there aren't any spook-trains really – but, gosh, I'd love to go and watch for one, if there were any.'

'I wish you wouldn't talk like that,' said Anne, unhappily. 'You know, it makes me feel as if you want another adventure. And I don't.'

'Well, there won't be any adventure, so don't worry,' said Dick, comfortingly. 'And, anyway, if there was an adventure you could always go and hold old Luffy's hand. He wouldn't see an adven-

up with Anne. 'What did he mean?' she asked, scared. 'What are spook-trains? Trains that aren't real? Does he really see them at night?'

'He just imagines them,' said Julian. 'I expect being there all alone in that deserted old railway yard has made him think queer things. Don't worry, Anne. There are no such things as spook-trains.'

'But he spoke as if there were,' said Anne, 'he did really. I'd hate to see a spook-train. Wouldn't you, Ju?'

'No. I'd love to see one,' said Julian, and he turned to Dick. 'Wouldn't you, Dick? Shall we come one night and watch? Just to see?'

ture if it was right under his nose. You'd be quite safe with him.'

'Look – who's that up there?' said George, seeing Timmy prick up his ears, and then hearing him give a little growl.

'Shepherd or something, I should think,' said Julian. He shouted out cheerfully: 'Good after-noon! Nice day it's been!'

The old man on the path just above them nod-ded his head. He was either a shepherd or farm labourer of some sort. He waited for them to come up.

'You seen any of my sheep down along there?' he asked them. 'Got a cross on them in red they have.'

'No. There aren't any down there,' said Julian. 'But there are some further along the hill. We've been down to the railway yard and we'd have seen any sheep on the slope below.'

'Don't you go down there,' said the old shepherd, his faded blue eyes looking into Julian's. 'That's a bad place, that is.'

'Well, we've been hearing about spook-trains!' said Julian with a laugh. 'Is that what you mean?'

'Ay. There's trains that nobody knows of a-running out of that tunnel,' said the shepherd. 'Many's the time I've heard them when I've been up here of a night with my sheep. That tunnel's not been used for thirty years – but the trains, they still come out of it, just as they used to.'

'How do you know? Have you seen them?' asked Julian, a cold shiver creeping down his spine quite suddenly.

'No. I've only heard them,' said the old man. 'Choo, choo, they go, and they jangle and clank. But they don't whistle no more. Old Wooden-Leg

Sam, he reckons they's spook-trains, with nobody to drive them and nobody to tend them. Don't you go down to that place. It's bad and skeery.'

Julian caught sight of Anne's scared face. He laughed loudly. 'What a tale! I don't believe in spook-trains – and neither do you, shepherd. Dick, have you got the tea in your bag? Let's find a nice place and have some sandwiches and cake. Will you join us, shepherd?'

'No, thankee kindly,' said the old man, moving off. 'I be after my sheep. Always wandering they are, and they keep me wandering, too. Good-day, sir, and don't ee go down to that bad place.'

Julian found a good spot out of sight of 'that bad place', and they all sat down. 'All a lot of non-sense,' said Julian, who wanted Anne to feel happier again. 'We can easily ask the farmer's boy about it tomorrow. I expect it's all a silly tale made up by that old one-legged fellow, and passed on to the shepherd.'

'I expect so,' said Dick. 'You noticed that the shepherd had never actually *seen* the trains, Julian? Only heard them. Well, sound travels far at night, and I expect what he heard was simply the rumblings of the trains that go underground here. There's one going somewhere now! I can feel the ground trembling!'

They all could. It was a queer feeling. The rumbling stopped at last and they sat and ate their tea, watching Timmy scraping at a rabbit-hole and trying his hardest to get down it. He covered them with sandy soil as he burrowed, and nothing would stop him. He seemed to have gone completely deaf.

'Look here, if we don't get Timmy out of that hole now he'll be gone down so far that we'll have to drag him out by his tail,' said Julian, getting up. 'Timmy! TIM-MY! The rabbit's miles away. Come on out.'

It took both George and Julian to get him out. He was most indignant. He looked at them as if to say: '*Well*, what spoil-sports! Almost got him and you drag me out!'

He shook himself, and bits of grit and sand flew out of his hair. He took a step towards the hole again, but George caught hold of his tail. 'No, Timmy. Home now!'

'He's looking for a spook-train,' said Dick, and that made everyone laugh, even Anne.

They set off back to the camping-place, pleasantly tired, with Timmy following rather sulkily at their heels. When they at last got back they saw Mr Luffy sitting waiting for them. The blue smoke from his pipe curled up into the air.

'Hallo, hallo!' he said, and his brown eyes looked up at them from under his shaggy eyebrows. 'I was beginning to wonder if you'd got lost. Still, I suppose that dog of yours would always bring you back.'

Timmy wagged his tail politely. 'Woof,' he agreed, and went to drink out of the bucket of water. Anne stopped him just in time.

'No, Timmy! You're not to drink out of our washing-up water. There's yours, in the dish over there.'

Timmy went to his dish and lapped. He thought Anne was very fussy. Anne asked Mr Luffy if he would like any supper.

'We're not having a proper supper,' she said. 'We had tea so late. But I'll cook you something if you like, Mr Luffy.'

'Very kind of you. But I've had an enormous tea,' said Mr Luffy. 'I've brought up a fruit cake for you, from my own larder. Shall we share it for supper? And I've got a bottle of lime juice, too, which will taste grand with some of the stream water.'

The boys went off to get some fresh stream water for drinking. Anne got out some plates and cut slices of the cake.

'Well,' said Mr Luffy. 'Had a nice walk?'

'Yes,' said Anne, 'except that we met a queer one-legged man who told us he saw spook-trains.'

Mr Luffy laughed. 'Well, well! He must be a cousin of a little girl I know who thought she was sitting on a volcano.'

Anne giggled. 'You're not to tease me. No, honestly, Mr Luffy, this old man was a watchman at a sort of old railway yard – not used now – and he said when the spook-trains came he blew out his light and got under his bed so that they shouldn't get him.'

'Poor old fellow,' said Mr Luffy. 'I hope he didn't frighten you.'

'He did a bit,' said Anne. 'And he threw a cinder at Dick and hit him on the head. Tomorrow we're going to the farm to ask the boy there if he's heard of the spook-trains, too. We met an old shepherd who said he'd heard them but not seen them.'

'Well, well – it all sounds most interesting,' said Mr Luffy. 'But these exciting stories usually have a very tame explanation, you know. Now would you like to see what I found today? A very rare and interesting little beetle.'

He opened a small square tin and showed a shiny beetle to Anne. It had green feelers and a red fiery spot near its tail-end. It was a lovely little thing.

'Now that's much more exciting to me than half a dozen spook-trains,' he told Anne. 'Spook-trains won't keep me awake at night – but thinking of this little beetle-fellow here certainly will.'

'I don't very much like beetles,' said Anne. 'But this one certainly is pretty. Do you really like hunting about all day for insects, and watching them, Mr Luffy?'

'Yes, very much,' said Mr Luffy. 'Ah, here come the boys with the water. Now we'll hand the cake round, shall we? Where's George? Oh, there she is, changing her shoes.'

George had a blister, and she had been putting a strip of plaster on her heel. She came up when the boys arrived and the cake was handed round. They sat in a circle, munching, while the sun gradually went down in a blaze of red.

'Nice day tomorrow again,' said Julian. 'What shall we do?'

'We'll have to go to the farm first,' said Dick. 'The farmer's wife said she'd let us have some more bread if we turned up in the morning. And we could do with more eggs if we can get them. We took eight hard-boiled ones with us today and we've only one or two left. And who's eaten all the tomatoes, I'd like to know?'

'All of you,' said Anne at once. 'You're perfect pigs over the tomatoes.'

'I'm afraid I'm one of the pigs,' apologised Mr Luffy. 'I think you fried me six for my breakfast, Anne.'

'That's all right,' said Anne. 'You didn't have as many as the others, even so! We can easily get some more.'

It was pleasant sitting there, eating and talking, and drinking lime juice and stream water. They were all tired, and it was nice to think of the cosy sleeping-bags. Timmy lifted his head and gave a vast yawn, showing an enormous amount of teeth.

'Timmy! I could see right down to your tail then!' said George. 'Do shut your mouth up. You've made us all yawn.'

So he had. Even Mr Luffy was yawning. He got up. 'Well, I'm going to turn in,' he said. 'Good night. We'll make plans tomorrow morning. I'll bring up some breakfast for you, if you like. I've got some tins of sardines.'

'Oh, thanks,' said Anne. 'And there's some of

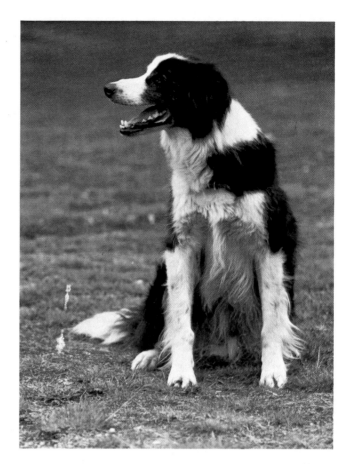

Timmy yawned enormously again.

this cake left. I hope you won't think that's too funny a breakfast, Mr Luffy – sardines and fruit cake?'

'Not a bit. It sounds a most sensible meal,' came Mr Luffy's voice from down the hillside. 'Goodnight!'

The children sat there a few minutes longer. The sun went right out of sight. The wind grew a little chilly. Timmy yawned enormously again.

'Come on,' said Julian. 'Time we turned in. Thank goodness Timmy didn't come into our tent and walk all over me last night. Good night, girls. It's going to be a heavenly night – but as I shall be asleep in about two shakes of a duck's tail, I shan't see much of it!'

The girls went into their tent. They were soon in their sleeping-bags. Just before they went to sleep Anne felt the slight shivering of the earth that meant a train was running underground somewhere. She could hear no rumbling sound. She fell asleep thinking of it.

The boys were not asleep. They, too, had felt the trembling of the earth beneath them, and it had reminded them of the old railway yard.

'Funny about those spook-trains, Dick,' said Julian, sleepily. 'Wonder if there *is* anything in it?'

'No. How could there be?' said Dick. 'All the same we'll go to the farm tomorrow and have a chat with that boy. He lives on the Moors and he ought to know the truth.'

'The real truth is that Wooden-Leg Sam is potty, and imagines all he says, and that the old shepherd, like all country people, is ready to believe in anything strange,' said Julian.

'I expect you're right,' said Dick. 'Oh my goodness, what's that?'

A dark shape stood looking in at the tent-flap. It gave a little whine.

'Oh, it's you, Timmy. Would you mind *not* coming and pretending you're a spook-train or something?' said Dick. 'And if you dare to put so much as half a paw on my middle, I'll scare you down the hill with a roar like a man-eating tiger. Go away.'

Timmy put a paw on Julian. Julian yelled out to George. 'George! Call this dog of yours, will you? He's just about to turn himself round twenty times on my middle, and curl himself up for the night'n'

There was no answer from George. Timmy, feeling that he was not wanted, disappeared. He went back to George and curled himself up on her feet. He put his nose down on his paws and slept.

'Spooky Timmy,' murmured Julian, re-arranging himself. 'Timmy spooky – no, I mean – oh dear, what do I mean?'

'Shut up,' said Dick. 'What with you and Timmy messing about, I can't get – to – sleep!' But he could and he did – almost before he had finished speaking. Silence fell on the little camp, and nobody noticed when the next train rumbled underground – not even Timmy!

6 Day at the farm

The next day the children were up very early, as early as Mr Luffy, and they all had breakfast together. Mr Luffy had a map of the moorlands, and he studied it carefully after breakfast.

'I think I'll go off for the whole day,' he said to Julian, who was sitting beside him. 'See that little valley marked here – Crowleg Vale – well, I have heard that there are some of the rarest beetles in Britain to be found there. I think I'll take my gear and go along. What are you four going to do?'

'Five,' said George at once. 'You've forgotten Timmy.'

'So I have. I beg his pardon,' said Mr Luffy, solemnly. 'Well – what are you going to do?'

'We'll go over to the farm and get some more food,' said Julian. 'And ask that farm-boy if he's heard the tale of the spook-trains. And perhaps look round the farm and get to know the animals there. I always like a farm.'

'Right,' said Mr Luffy, beginning to light his pipe. 'Don't worry about me if I'm not back till dusk. When I'm bug-hunting I lose count of the time.'

'You're sure you won't get lost?' said Anne, anxiously. She didn't really feel that Mr Luffy could take proper care of himself.

'Oh yes. My right ear always warns me if I'm losing my way,' said Mr Luffy. 'It waggles hard.'

He waggled it at Anne and she laughed. 'I wish you'd tell me how you do that,' she said. 'I'm sure you know. You can't think how thrilled the girls at school would be if I learnt that trick. They'd think it was super.'

Mr Luffy grinned and got up. 'Well, so long,' he said. 'I'm off before Anne makes me give her a lesson in ear-waggles.'

He went off down the slope to his own tent. George and Anne washed-up, while the boys tightened some tent ropes that had come loose, and generally tidied up.

'I suppose it's quite all right leaving everything unguarded like this,' said Anne, anxiously.

'Well, we did yesterday,' said Dick. 'And who's likely to come and take anything up here in this wild and lonely spot, I'd like to know? You don't imagine a spook-train will come along and bundle everything into its luggage-van, do you, Anne?'

Anne giggled. 'Don't be silly. I just wondered if we ought to leave Timmy on guard, that's all.'

'Leave Timmy!' said George, amazed. 'You don't really think I'd leave Timmy behind every time we go off anywhere, Anne? Don't be an idiot.'

'No, I didn't really think you would,' said Anne. 'Well, I suppose nobody will come along here. Throw over that tea-cloth, George, if you've finished with it.'

Soon the tea-cloths were hanging over the gorse bushes to dry in the sun. Everything was put away neatly in the tents. Mr Luffy had called a loud good-bye and gone. Now the five were ready to go off to the farm.

Anne took a basket, and gave one to Julian too. 'To bring back the food,' said she. 'Are you ready to go now?'

They set off over the heather, their knees brushing through the honeyed flowers, and sending scores of busy bees into the air. It was a lovely day again, and the children felt free and happy.

They came to the trim little farm. Men were at work in the fields, but Julian did not think they were very industrious. He looked about for the farm-boy.

The boy came out of a shed and whistled to them. 'Hallo! You come for some more eggs? I've collected quite a lot for you.'

He stared at Anne. 'You didn't come yesterday. What's your name?'

'Anne,' said Anne. 'What's yours?'

'Jock,' said the boy, with a grin. He was rather a nice boy, Anne thought, with straw-coloured hair, blue eyes, and rather a red face which looked very good-tempered.

'Where's your mother?' said Julian. 'Can we get some bread and other things from her today? We ate an awful lot of our food yesterday, and we want to stock up our larder again!'

She's busy just now in the dairy,' said Jock. 'Are you in a hurry? Come and see my pups.'

They all walked off with him to a shed. In there, right at the end, was a big box lined with straw. A collie dog lay there with five lovely little puppies. She growled at Timmy fiercely, and he backed hurriedly out of the shed. He had met fierce mother-dogs before, and he didn't like them!

The four children exclaimed over the fat little puppies, and Anne took one out very gently. It cuddled into her arms and made funny little whining noises.

'I wish it was mine,' said Anne. 'I should call it Cuddle.'

'What a frightful name for a dog,' said George scornfully. 'Just the kind of silly name you *would* think of, Anne. Let me hold it. Are they all yours, Jock?'

'Yes,' said Jock, proudly. 'The mother's mine, you see. Her name's Biddy.'

Biddy pricked up her ears at her name and looked up at Jock out of bright, alert eyes. He fondled her silky head.

'I've had her for four years,' he said. 'When we were at Owl Farm, old Farmer Burrows gave her to me when she was eight weeks old.'

'Oh – were you at another farm before this one, then?' asked Anne. 'Have you always lived on a farm? Aren't you lucky!'

'I've only lived on two,' said Jock. 'Owl Farm and this one. Mum and I had to leave Owl Farm when Dad died, and we went to live in a town for a year. I hated that. I was glad when we came here.'

'But I thought your father was here!' said Dick, puzzled.

'That's my stepfather,' said Jock. 'He's no farmer, though!' He looked round and lowered his voice. 'He doesn't know much about farming. It's my mother that tells the men what to do. Still, he gives her plenty of money to do everything well, and we've got fine machinery and wagons and things. Like to see the dairy? It's slap up-to-date and Mum loves working in it.'

Jock took the four children to the shining, spotless dairy. His mother was at work there with a girl. She nodded and smiled at the children. 'Good morning! Hungry again? I'll pack you up plenty of food when I've finished in the dairy. Would you like to stay and have dinner with my Jock? He's lonely enough here in the holidays, with no other boy to keep him company.'

'Oh, *yes* – do let's!' cried Anne, in delight. 'I'd like that. Can we, Ju?'

'Yes. Thank you very much, Mrs – er – Mrs . . .' said Julian.

'I'm Mrs Andrews,' said Jock's mother. 'But Jock is Jock Robins – he's the son of my first husband, a farmer. Well, stay to dinner all of you, and I'll see if I can give you a meal that will keep you going for the rest of the day!'

This sounded good. The four children felt thrilled, and Timmy wagged his tail hard. He liked Mrs Andrews.

'Come on,' said Jock, joyfully. 'I'll take you all round the farm, into every corner. It's not very big, but we're going to make it the best little farm on the moorlands. My stepfather doesn't seem to take much interest in the work of the farm, but he's jolly generous when it comes to handing out money to Mum to buy everything she wants.'

It certainly seemed to the children that the machinery on the farm was absolutely up-to-date. They examined the combine, they went into the little cowshed and admired the clean stone floor with white brick walls, they climbed into the red-painted wagons, and they wished they could try the two motor-tractors that stood side by side in a barn.

'You've got plenty of men here to work the farm,' said Julian. 'I shouldn't have thought there was enough for so many to do on this small place.'

'They're not good workers,' said Jock, his face creasing into frowns. 'Mum's always getting wild

with them. They just don't know what to do. Dad gives her plenty of men to work the farm, but he always chooses the wrong ones! They don't seem to like farm-work, and they're always running off to the nearest town whenever they can. There's only one good fellow and he's old. See him over there? His name's Will.'

The children looked at Will. He was working in the little vegetable garden, an old fellow with a shrivelled face, a tiny nose and a pair of very blue eyes. They liked the look of him.

'Yes. He *looks* like a farm-worker,' said Julian. 'The others don't.'

'He won't work with them,' said Jock. 'He just says rude things to them, and calls them ninnies and idjits.'

'What's an idjit?' asked Anne.

'An idiot, silly,' said Dick. He walked up to old Will. 'Good morning,' he said. 'You're very busy. There's always a lot to do on a farm, isn't there?'

The old fellow looked at Dick out of his very blue eyes, and went on with his work. 'Plenny to do and plenny of folkses to do it, and not much done,' he said, in a croaking kind of voice. 'Never thought as I'd be put to work with ninnies and idjits. No, that I didn't. Ninnies and idjits!'

'There! What did I tell you?' said Jock, with a grin. 'He's always calling the other men that, so we just have to let him work right away from them. Still, I must say he's about right – most of the fellows here don't know the first thing about work on a farm. I wish my stepfather would let us have a few proper workers instead of these fellows.'

'Where's your stepfather?' said Julian, thinking he must be rather peculiar to pour money into a little moorland farm like this, and yet choose the wrong kind of workers.

'He's away for the day,' said Jock. 'Thank goodness!' he added, with a sideways look at the others.

'Why? Don't you like him?' asked Dick.

'He's all right,' said Jock. 'But he's not a farmer, though he makes out he's always wanted to be – and what's more he doesn't like me one bit. I try to like him for Mum's sake. But I'm always glad when he's out of the way.'

'Your mother's nice,' said George.

'Oh, yes – Mum's grand,' said Jock. 'You don't know what it means to her to have a little farm of her own again, and to be able to run it with the proper machinery and all.'

They came to a large barn. The door was

They spent a very pleasant morning poking about the little farm.

locked. 'I told you what was in here before,' said Jock. 'Lorries! You can peek through that hole there at them. Don't know why my stepfather wanted to buy up so many, but I suppose he got them cheap – he loves to get things cheap and sell them dear! He did say they'd be useful on the farm, to take goods to the market.'

'Yes – you told us that when we were here yesterday,' said Dick. 'But you've got heaps of wagons for that!'

'Yes. I reckon they weren't bought for the farm at all, but for holding here till prices went high and he could make a lot of money,' said Jock, lowering his voice. 'I don't tell Mum that. So long as she gets what she wants for the farm, I'm going to hold my tongue.'

The children were very interested in all this. They wished they could see Mr Andrews. He must be a queer sort of fellow, they thought. Anne tried to imagine what he was like.

'Big and tall and dark and frowny,' she thought. 'Rather frightening and impatient, and he certainly won't like children. People like that never do.'

They spent a very pleasant morning poking about the little farm. They went back to see Biddy the collie and her pups. Timmy stood patiently outside the shed, with his tail down. He didn't like George to take so much interest in other dogs.

A bell rang loudly. 'Good! Dinner!' said Jock. 'We'd better wash. We're all filthy. Hope you feel hungry, because I guess Mum's got a super dinner for us.'

'I feel terribly hungry,' said Anne. 'It seems ages since we had breakfast. I've almost forgotten it!'

They all felt the same. They went into the farmhouse and were surprised to find a very nice little bathroom to wash in. Mrs Andrews was there, putting out a clean roller towel.

'Fine little bathroom, isn't it?' she said. 'My husband had it put in for me. First proper bathroom I've ever had!'

A glorious smell rose up from the kitchen downstairs. 'Come on!' said Jock, seizing the soap. 'Let's hurry. We'll be down in a minute, Mum!'

And they were. Nobody was going to dawdle over washing when a grand meal lay waiting for them downstairs!

7 Mr Andrews comes home

They all sat down to dinner. There was a big meat-pie, a cold ham, salad, potatoes in their jackets, and home-made pickles. It really was difficult to know what to choose.

'Have some of both,' said Mrs Andrews, cutting the meat-pie. 'Begin with the pie and go on with the ham. That's the best of living on a farm, you know – you do get plenty to eat.'

After the first course there were plums and thick cream, or jam tarts and the same cream. Everyone tucked in hungrily.

'I've never had such a lovely dinner in my life,' said Anne, at last. 'I wish I could eat some more, but I can't. It was super, Mrs Andrews.'

'Smashing,' said Dick. That was his favourite word these holidays. 'Absolutely smashing.'

'Woof,' said Timmy, agreeing. He had had a fine plateful of meaty bones, biscuits and gravy, and he had licked up every crumb and every drop. Now he felt he would like to have a snooze in the sun and not do a thing for the rest of the day.

The children felt rather like that, too. Mrs Andrews handed them a chocolate each and sent them out of doors. 'You go and have a rest now,' she said. 'Talk to Jock. He doesn't get enough company of his own age in the holidays. You can stay on to tea, if you like.'

'Oh, thanks,' said everyone, although they all felt that they wouldn't even be able to manage a biscuit. But it was so pleasant at the farm that they felt they would like to stay as long as they could.

'May we borrow one of Biddy's puppies to have with us?' asked Anne.

'If Biddy doesn't mind,' said Mrs Andrews, beginning to clear away. 'And if Timmy doesn't eat it up!'

'Timmy wouldn't dream of it!' said George at once. 'You go and get the puppy, Anne. We'll find a nice place in the sun.'

Anne went off to get the puppy. Biddy didn't seem to mind a bit. Anne cuddled the fat little thing against her, and went off to the others, feeling very happy. The boys had found a fine place against a haystack, and sat leaning against it, the sun shining down warmly on them.

'Those men of yours seem to take a jolly good lunch-hour off,' said Julian, not seeing any of them about.

Jock gave a snort. 'They're bone lazy. I'd sack the lot if I were my stepfather. Mum's told him how badly the men work, but he doesn't say a word to them. I've given up bothering. I don't pay their wages – if I did, I'd sack the whole lot!'

'Let's ask Jock about the spook-trains,' said George, fondling Timmy's ears. 'It would be fun to talk about them.'

'Spook-trains? Whatever are they?' asked Jock, his eyes wide with surprise. 'Never heard of them!'

'Haven't you really?' asked Dick. 'Well, you don't live very far from them, Jock!'

'Tell me about them,' said Jock. 'Spook-trains – no, I've never heard of one of those.'

'Well, I'll tell you what we know,' said Julian. 'Actually we thought you'd be able to tell us much more about them than we know ourselves.'

He began to tell Jock about their visit to the deserted railway yard, and Wooden-Leg Sam, and his peculiar behaviour. Jock listened, enthralled.

'Coo! I wish I'd been with you. Let's all go there together, shall we?' he said. 'This was quite an adventure you had, wasn't it? You know, I've never had a single adventure in all my life, not even a little one. Have you?'

The four children looked at one another, and Timmy looked at George. Adventures! What didn't they know about them? They had had so many.

'Yes. We've had heaps of adventures – real ones – smashing ones,' said Dick. 'We've been down in dungeons, we've been lost in caves, we've found secret passages, we've looked for treasure – well, I can't tell you what we've done! It would take too long.'

'No, it wouldn't,' said Jock eagerly. 'You tell me. Go on. Did you all have the adventures? Little Anne, here, too?'

'Yes, all of us,' said George. 'And Timmy as well. He rescued us heaps of times from danger. Didn't you, Tim?'

'Woof, woof,' said Timmy, and thumped his tail against the hay.

They began to tell Jock about their many adventures. He was a very, very good listener. His eyes almost fell out of his head, and he went brick-red whenever they came to an exciting part.

'My word!' he said at last. 'I've never heard such things in my life before. Aren't you lucky? You just go about having adventures all the time, don't you? I *say* – do you think you'll have one here, these hols?'

Julian laughed. 'No. Whatever kind of adventure would there be on these lonely moorlands? Why, you yourself have lived here for three years, and haven't even had a tiny adventure.'

Jock sighed. 'That's true. I haven't.' Then his eyes brightened again. 'But see here – what about those spook-trains you've been asking me about? Perhaps you'll have an adventure with those?'

'Oh, no, I don't want to,' said Anne, in a horrified voice. 'An adventure with spook-trains would be simply horrid.'

'I'd like to go down to that old railway yard with you and see Wooden-Leg Sam,' said Jock longingly. 'Why, that would be a real adventure to me, you know – just talking to a queer old man like that, and wondering if he was suddenly going to throw cinders at us. Take me with you next time you go.'

'Well – I don't know that we meant to go again,' said Julian. 'There's really nothing much in his story except imagination – the old watchman's gone queer in the head through being alone there so much, guarding a yard where nothing and nobody ever comes. He's just remembering the trains that used to go in and out before the line was given up.'

'But the shepherd said the same as Sam,' said Jock. 'I *say* – what about going down there one night and watching for a spook-train?'

'NO!' said Anne, in horror.

'You needn't come,' said Jock. 'Just us three boys.'

'And me,' said George at once. 'I'm as good as any boy, and I'm not going to be left out. Timmy's coming, too.'

'Oh, please don't make these awful plans,' begged poor Anne. 'You'll *make* an adventure come if you go on like this.'

Nobody took the least notice of her. Julian looked at Jock's excited face. 'Well,' he said, 'if we do go there again, we'll tell you. And if we think we'll go watching for spook-trains, we'll take you with us.'

Jock looked as if he could hug Julian. 'That's wizard of you,' he said. 'Thanks most frightfully. Spook-trains! I *say*, just suppose we really did see one! Who'd be driving it? Where would it come from?'

'Out of the tunnel, Wooden-Leg Sam says,' said Dick. 'But I don't see how we'd spot it, except by the noise it made, because apparently the spook-trains only arrive in the dark of the night. Never in the daytime. We wouldn't *see* much, even if we were there.'

It was such an exciting subject to Jock that he persisted in talking about it all the afternoon. Anne got tired of listening, and went to sleep with Biddy's puppy in her arms. Timmy curled up by George and went to sleep too. He wanted to go for a walk, but he could see that there was no hope with all this talking going on.

It was tea-time before any of them had expected it. The bell rang, and Jock looked most surprised.

'Tea! Would you believe it? Well, I *have* had an exciting afternoon talking about all this. And look here, if you don't make up your minds to go spook-train hunting I'll jolly well go off by myself. If only I could have an adventure like the kind you've had, I'd be happy.'

They went in to tea, after waking Anne up with difficulty. She took the puppy back to Biddy, who received it gladly and licked it all over.

Julian was surprised to find that he was quite hungry again. 'Well,' he said, as he sat down at the table. 'I didn't imagine I'd feel hungry again for a week – but I do. What a wizard tea, Mrs Andrews. Isn't Jock lucky, to have meals like this always!'

There were home-made scones with new honey. There were slices of bread thickly spread with butter, and new-made cream cheese to go with it. There was sticky brown gingerbread, hot from the oven, and a big solid fruit cake that looked almost like a plum pudding when it was cut, it was so black.

'Oh dear! I wish now I hadn't had so much dinner,' sighed Anne. 'I don't feel hungry enough to eat a bit of everything and I would so like to!'

Mrs Andrews laughed. 'You eat what you can, and I'll give you some to take away, too,' she said. 'You can have some cream cheese, and the scones and honey – and some of the bread I made this morning. And maybe you'd like a slab of the gingerbread. I made plenty.'

'Oh, thanks,' said Julian. 'We'll be all right tomorrow with all that. You're a marvellous cook, Mrs Andrews. I wish I lived on your farm.'

There was the sound of a car coming slowly up the rough track to the farmhouse, and Mrs Andrews looked up. 'That's Mr Andrews come back,' she said. 'My husband, you know, Jock's stepfather.'

Julian thought she looked a little worried. Perhaps Mr Andrews didn't like children and wouldn't be pleased to see them sitting round his table when he came home tired.

'Would you like us to go, Mrs Andrews?' he asked politely. 'Perhaps Mr Andrews would like a bit of peace for his meal when he comes in – and we're rather a crowd, aren't we?'

Jock's mother shook her head. 'No, you can stay. I'll get him a meal in the other room if he'd like it.'

Mr Andrews came in. He wasn't in the least like Anne or the others had imagined him to be. He was a short, dark little man, with a weak face and a nose much too big for it. He looked harassed and bad-tempered, and stopped short when he saw the five children.

'Hallo, dear,' said Mrs Andrews. 'Jock's got his friends here today. Would you like a bit of tea in your room? I can easily put a tray there.'

'Well,' said Mr Andrews, smiling a watery kind of smile, 'perhaps it would be best. I've had a worrying kind of day, and not much to eat.'

'I'll get you a tray of ham and pickles and bread,' said his wife. 'It won't take a minute. You go and wash.'

Mr Andrews went out. Anne was surprised that he seemed so small and looked rather stupid. She had imagined someone big and burly, strong and clever, who was always going about doing grand deals and making a lot of money. Well, he must be cleverer than he looked, to make enough money to give Mrs Andrews all she needed for her farm.

Mrs Andrews bustled about with this and that, laying a tray with a snow-white cloth, and plates of food. Mr Andrews could be heard in the bathroom, splashing as he washed. Then he came downstairs and put his head in at the door. 'My meal ready? he asked. 'Well, Jock – had a good day?'

'Yes, thanks,' said Jock, as his stepfather took the tray from his mother and turned to go. 'We went all round the farm this morning – and we talked and talked this afternoon. And oh, I say – do you know anything about spook-trains, sir?'

Mr Andrews was just going out of the door. He turned in surprise. 'Spook-trains? What are you talking about?'

'Well, Julian says there's an old deserted railway yard a good way from here, and spook-trains are supposed to come out of the tunnel there in the dark of night,' said Jock. 'Have you heard of them?'

Mr Andrews stood stock still, his eyes on his stepson. He looked dismayed and shocked. Then he came back into the room and kicked the door shut behind him.

'I'll have my tea here after all,' he said. 'Well, to think you've heard of those spook-trains! I've been careful not to mention them to your mother or to you, Jock, for fear of scaring you!'

'Gee!' said Dick. 'Are they really true then? They can't be.'

'You tell me all you know, and how you know about it,' said Mr Andrews, sitting down at the table with his tray. 'Go on. Don't miss out a thing. I want to hear everything.'

Julian hesitated. 'Oh – there's nothing really to tell, sir – just a lot of nonsense.'

'You tell it me!' almost shouted Mr Andrews. 'Then I'll tell *you* a few things. And I tell you, you won't go near that old railway yard again – no, that you won't!'

8 A lazy evening

The five children and Mrs Andrews stared in surprise at Mr Andrews, when he shouted at them. He repeated some of his words again.

'Go on! You tell me all you know. And then I'll tell *you*!'

Julian decided to tell, very shortly, what had happened at the old railway yard, and what Wooden-Leg Sam had said. He made the tale sound rather bald and dull. Mr Andrews listened to it with the greatest interest, never once taking his eyes off Julian.

Then he sat back and drank a whole cup of strong tea at one gulp. The children waited for him to speak, wondering what he had to say.

'Now,' he said, making his voice sound important and impressive, 'you listen to me. Don't any of you ever go down to that yard again. It's a bad place.'

'Why?' asked Julian. 'What do you mean – a bad place?'

'Things have happened there – years and years ago,' said Mr Andrews. 'Bad things. Accidents. It was all shut up after that and the tunnel wasn't used any more. See? Nobody was allowed to go there, and nobody did, because they were scared. They knew it was a bad place, where bad things happen.'

Anne felt frightened. 'But Mr Andrews – you don't mean there really are spook-trains, do you?' she asked, her face rather pale.

Mr Andrews pursed up his lips and nodded very solemnly indeed. 'That's just what I do mean. Spook-trains come and go. Nobody knows why. But it's bad luck to be there when they come. They might take you away, see?'

Julian laughed. 'Oh – not as bad as that, sir, surely! Anyway, you're frightening Anne, so let's change the subject. I don't believe in spook-trains.'

But Mr Andrews didn't seem to want to stop talking about the trains. 'Wooden-Leg Sam was right to hide himself when they come along,' he said. 'I don't know how he manages to stay on in a bad place like that. Never knowing when a train is going to come creeping out of that tunnel in the darkness.'

Julian was not going to have Anne frightened any more. He got up from the table and turned to Mrs Andrews.

'Thank you very much for a lovely day and lovely food!' he said. 'We must go now. Come along, Anne.'

'Wait a minute,' said Mr Andrews. 'I just want to warn you all very solemnly that you mustn't go down to that railway yard. You hear me, Jock? You might never come back. Old Wooden-Leg Sam's mad, and well he may be, with spook-trains coming along in the dead of night. It's a bad and dangerous place. You're not to go near it!'

'Well – thank you for the warning, sir,' said Julian, politely, suddenly disliking the small man with the big nose very much indeed. 'We'll be going. Good-bye, Mrs Andrews. Good-bye, Jock. Come along tomorrow and have a picnic with us, will you?'

'Oh, thanks! Yes, I will,' said Jock. 'But wait a minute – aren't you going to take any food with you?'

'Yes, of course they are,' said Mrs Andrews, getting up from her chair. She had been listening to the conversation with a look of puzzled wonder on her face. She went out into the scullery, where there was a big, cold larder. Julian followed her. He carried the two baskets.

'I'll give you plenty,' said Mrs Andrews, putting loaves, butter, and cream cheese into the baskets. 'I know what appetites you youngsters get. Now don't you be too scared at what my husband's just been saying – I saw that little Anne was frightened. I've never heard of the spook-trains, and I've been here for three years. I don't reckon there's much in the tale, you know, for all my husband's so set on warning you not to go down to the yard.'

Julian said nothing. He thought that Mr Andrews had behaved rather queerly about the whole story. Was he one of the kind of people who believed in all sorts of silly things and got scared himself? He looked weak enough! Julian found himself wondering how a nice woman like Mrs Andrews could have married such a poor specimen of a man. Still, he was a generous fellow, judging by all Jock had said, and perhaps Jock's mother felt grateful to him for giving her the farm and the money to run it with. That must be it.

Julian thanked Mrs Andrews, and insisted on paying her, though she would have given him the food for nothing. She came into the kitchen with him and he saw that the others had already gone outside. Only Mr Andrews was left, eating ham and pickles.

'Good-bye, sir,' said Julian politely.

'Good-bye. And you remember what I've told you, boy,' said Mr Andrews. 'Bad luck comes to people who see the spook-trains – yes, terrible bad luck. You keep away from them.'

Julian gave a polite smile and went out. It was evening now and the sun was setting behind the moorland hills, though it still had a long way to go before it disappeared. He caught up with the others. Jock was with them.

'I'm just coming half-way with you,' said Jock. 'I say! My stepfather was pretty scary about those trains, wasn't he?'

'I felt pretty scary too, when he was warning us about them,' said Anne. 'I shan't go down to that yard again, ever. Will you, George?'

'If the boys did, I would,' said George, who didn't look very much as if she wanted to, all the same.

'*Are* you going to the yard again?' asked Jock, eagerly. 'I'm not scared. Not a bit. It would be an adventure to go and watch for a spook-train.'

'We might go,' said Julian. 'We'll take you with us, if we do. But the girls aren't to come.'

'Well, I like that!' said George angrily. 'As if you could leave me behind! When have I been scared of anything? I'm as brave as any of you.'

'Yes, I know. You can come as soon as we find out it's all a silly story,' said Julian.

'I shall come whenever you go,' flashed back George. 'Don't you dare to leave me out. I'll never speak to you again if you do.'

Jock looked most surprised at this sudden flare-up of temper from George. He didn't know how fierce she could be!

'I don't see why George shouldn't come,' he said. 'I bet she'd be every bit as good as a boy. I thought she was one when I first saw her.'

George gave him one of her sweetest smiles. He couldn't have said anything she liked better! But Julian would not change his mind.

'I mean what I say. The girls won't come if we do go, so that's that. For one thing, Anne certainly wouldn't want to come, and if George came without her she'd be left all alone up at the camp. She wouldn't like that.'

'She could have Mr Luffy's company,' said George, looking sulky again.

'Idiot! As if we'd want to tell Mr Luffy we were going off exploring deserted railway yards watched over by a mad, one-legged fellow who swears there are spook-trains!' said Julian. 'He'd stop us going. You know what grown-ups are. Or he'd come with us, which would be worse.'

'Yes. He'd see moths all the time, not spook-trains,' said Dick, with a grin.

'I'd better go back now,' said Jock. 'It's been a grand day. I'll come up tomorrow and picnic with you. Good-bye.'

They called good-bye to Jock, and went on their way to the camp. It was quite nice to see it again, waiting for them, the two tents flapping a little in the breeze. Anne pushed her way through the tent-flap, anxious to see that everything was untouched.

Inside the tent it was very hot. Anne decided to put the food they had brought under the bottom of the big gorse bush. It would be cooler there. She was soon busy about her little jobs. The boys went down to see if Mr Luffy was back, but he wasn't.

'Anne! We're going to bathe in the stream!' they called. 'We feel hot and dirty. Are you coming? George is coming too.'

'No, I won't come,' Anne called back. 'I've got lots of things to do.'

The boys grinned at one another. Anne did so enjoy 'playing house'. So they left her to it, and went to the stream, from which yells and howls and shrieks soon came. The water was colder than they expected, and nobody liked to lie down in it – but everyone was well and truly splashed, and the icy-cold drops falling on their hot bodies made them squeal and yell. Timmy didn't in the least mind the iciness of the water. He rolled over and over in it, enjoying himself.

'Look at him, showing off!' said Dick. 'Aha, Timmy, if I could bathe in a fur coat like you, I wouldn't mind the cold water either.'

'Woof,' said Timmy, and climbed up the shallow bank. He shook himself violently and thousands of icy-cold silvery drops flew from him and landed on the three shivering children. They yelled and chased him away.

It was a pleasant, lazy evening. Mr Luffy didn't appear at all. Anne got a light meal of bread and cream cheese and a piece of gingerbread. Nobody felt like facing another big meal that day. They lay in the heather and talked comfortably.

'This is the kind of holiday I like,' said Dick.

'So do I,' said Anne. 'Except for the spook-trains. That's spoilt it a bit for me.'

'Don't be silly, Anne,' said George. 'If they are not real it's just a silly story, and if they are real, well, it might be an adventure.'

There was a little silence. 'Are we going down to that yard again?' asked Dick lazily.

'Yes, I think so,' said Julian. 'I'm not going to be scared off it by weird warnings from Pa Andrews.'

'Then I vote we go one night and wait to see if a spook-train does come along,' said Dick.

'I shall come too,' said George.

'No, you won't,' said Julian. 'You'll stay with Anne.'

George said nothing, but everyone could feel mutiny in the air.

'Do we tell Mr Luffy, or don't we?' said Dick.

'You know we've said we wouldn't,' said Julian. He yawned. 'I'm getting sleepy. And the sun has gone, so it will soon be dark. I wonder where old Luffy is?'

'Do you think I'd better wait up and see if he wants something to eat?' said Anne, anxiously.

'No. Not unless you want to keep awake till midnight!' said Julian. 'He'll have got some food down in his tent. He'll be all right. I'm going to turn in. Coming, Dick?'

The boys were soon in their sleeping-bags. The girls lay in the heather for a little while longer, listening to the lonely-sounding cry of the curlews going home in the dusk. Then they, too, went into their own tent.

Once safely in their sleeping-bags, the two boys felt suddenly wide awake. They began to talk in low voices.

'Shall we take Jock down to see the yard in the daytime? Or shall we go one night and watch for the Train from Nowhere?' said Julian.

'I vote we go and watch at night,' said Dick. 'We'll never see a spook-train in the daytime. Wooden-Leg Sam is an interesting old chap, especially when he chucks cinders about – but I don't know that I like him enough to go and visit him again!'

'Well – if Jock badly wants to go and have a snoop round tomorrow morning when he comes, we'd better take him,' said Julian. 'We can always go one night, too, if we want to.'

'Right. We'll wait and see what Jock says,' said Dick. They talked a little longer and then felt sleepy. Dick was just dropping off when he heard something coming wriggling through the heather. A head was stuck through the opening of the tent.

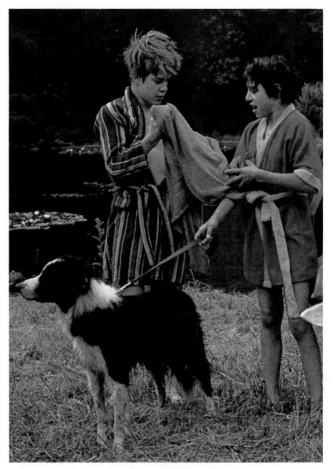

Everyone was well and truly splashed.

'If you dare to come in, I'll smack your silly face,' said Dick, thinking it was Timmy. 'I know what you want, you perfect pest – you want to flop down on my tummy. You just turn yourself round and go away! Do you hear?'

The head in the opening moved a little but didn't go away. Dick raised himself up on one elbow.

'Put one paw inside my tent and you'll be sent rolling down the hill!' he said. 'I love you very much in the daytime, but I'm not fond of you at night – not when I'm in a sleeping-bag anyway. Scoot!'

The head made a peculiar apologetic sound. Then it spoke. 'Er – you're awake, I see. Are all of you all right – the girls too? I'm only just back.'

'Gosh! It's Mr Luffy,' said Dick, filled with horror. 'I say, sir – I'm most awfully sorry – I thought you were Timmy, come to flop himself down on top of me, like he often does. So sorry, sir.'

'Don't mention it!' said the shadowy head with a chuckle. 'Glad you're all right. See you tomorrow!'

9 Night visitor

Mr Luffy slept very late the next morning and nobody liked to disturb him. The girls yelled with laughter when they heard how Dick had spoken to him the night before, thinking he was Timmy the dog.

'He was very decent about it,' said Dick. 'Seemed to think it was quite amusing. I hope he'll still think so this morning!'

They were all sitting eating their breakfast – ham, tomatoes, and the bread Mrs Andrews had given them the day before. Timmy collected the bits as usual, and wondered if George would let him have a lick of the cream cheese she was now putting on her bread. Timmy loved cheese. He looked at the lump in the dish and sighed all over George. He could easily eat that in one mouthful! How he wished he could.

'I wonder what time Jock will come up,' said George. 'If he came up pretty soon, we could go for a nice long walk over the moors, and picnic somewhere. Jock ought to know some fine walks.'

'Yes. We'll mess about till he comes, and then tell him he's to be our guide and take us to the nicest walk he knows,' said Anne. 'Oh Timmy, you beast – you've taken my nice lump of cream cheese right out of my fingers!'

'Well, you were waving it about under his nose, so what could you expect?' said George. 'He thought you were giving it to him.'

'Well, he shan't have any more, it's too precious,' said Anne. 'Oh, dear – I wish we didn't eat so much. We keep bringing in stacks of food, and it hardly lasts any time.'

'I bet Jock will bring some more,' said Dick. 'He's a sensible sort of fellow. Did you get a peep into that enormous larder of his mother's? It's like a great cave, goes right back into the wall, with dozens of stone shelves – and all filled with food. No wonder Jock's tubby.'

'Is he? I never noticed,' said Anne. 'Is that him whistling?'

It wasn't. It was a curlew, very high up. 'Too early for him yet,' said Julian. 'Shall we help you to clear up, Anne?'

'No. That's my job and George's,' said Anne firmly. 'You go down and see if Mr Luffy is awake. He can have a bit of ham and a few tomatoes, if he likes.'

They went down to Mr Luffy's tent. He was awake, sitting at the entrance, eating some kind of breakfast. He waved a sandwich at them.

'Hallo, there! I'm late this morning. I had a job getting back. I went much too far. Sorry I woke you up last night, Dick.'

'You didn't. I wasn't asleep,' said Dick, going rather red. 'Did you have a good day, Mr Luffy?'

'Bit disappointing. Didn't find quite all the creatures I'd hoped,' said Mr Luffy. 'What about you? Did you have a good day?'

'Fine,' said Dick, and described it. Mr Luffy seemed very interested in everything, even in Mr Andrews's rather frightening warning about the railway yard.

'Silly chap he sounds,' said Mr Luffy, shaking the crumbs off his front. 'All the same – I should keep away from the yard, if I were you. Stories don't get about for nothing, you know. No smoke without fire!'

'Why, sir – surely *you* don't believe there's anything spooky about the trains there?' said Dick, in surprise.

'Oh, no – I doubt if there *are* any trains,' said Mr Luffy. 'But when a place has got a bad name it's usually best to keep away from it.'

'I suppose so, sir,' said Dick and Julian together. Then they hastily changed the subject, afraid that Mr Luffy, like Mr Andrews, might also be going to forbid them to visit the railway yard. And the more they were warned about it and forbidden to go, the more they felt that they really must!

'Well, we must get back,' said Dick. 'We're expecting Jock – that's the boy at the farm – to come up for the day, and we thought we'd go out walking and take our food with us. Are you going out, too, sir?'

'Not today,' said Mr Luffy. 'My legs are tired and stiff with so much scrambling about yesterday, and I want to mount some of the specimens I found. Also I'd like to meet your farm friend – what's his name – Jock?'

'Yes, sir,' said Julian. 'Right. We'll bring him along as soon as he comes, then off we'll go. You'll be left in peace all day!'

But Jock didn't come. The children waited for him all the morning and he didn't turn up. They held up their lunch until they were too hungry to

'Funny,' said Julian, 'He knows where the camp is . . .'

wait any longer, and then they had it on the heather in front of their tents.

'Funny,' said Julian. 'He knows where the camp is, because we pointed it out to him when he came half-way home with us yesterday. Perhaps he'll come this afternoon.'

But he didn't come in the afternoon either, nor did he come after tea. Julian debated whether or not to go and see what was up, but decided against it. There must be some good reason why Jock hadn't come, and Mrs Andrews wouldn't want them all visiting her two days running.

It was a disappointing day. They didn't like to leave the tents and go for even a short stroll in case Jock came. Mr Luffy was busy all day long with his specimens. He was sorry Jock had disappointed them. 'He'll come tomorrow,' he said. 'Have you got enough food? There's some in that tin over there if you want it.'

'Oh, no, thank you, sir,' said Julian. 'We've plenty really. We're going to have a game of cards. Like to join us?'

'Yes, I think I will,' said Mr Luffy, getting up and stretching himself. 'Can you play rummy?'

They could – and they beat poor Mr Luffy handsomely, because he couldn't play at all. He blamed his luck on his bad cards, but he enjoyed the game immensely. He said the only thing that really put him off was the way that Timmy stood behind him

and breathed down his neck all the time.

'I kept feeling certain that Timmy thought he knew how to play my cards better than I could,' he complained. 'And whenever I did something wrong, he breathed down my neck harder than usual.'

Everyone laughed, and George privately thought that Timmy would probably play very much better than Mr Luffy if only he could hold the cards.

Jock didn't come at all. They put the cards away when they could no longer see them, and Mr Luffy announced that he was going to bed. 'It was very late when I got back last night,' he said. 'I really must have an early night.'

The others thought they would go to bed too. The thought of their cosy sleeping-bags was always a nice one when darkness came on.

The girls crept into their bags and Timmy flopped down on George. The boys were in their bags about the same time and Dick gave a loud yawn.

'Good night, Ju,' he said, and fell fast asleep. Julian was soon asleep too. In fact, everyone was sound asleep when Timmy gave a little growl. It was such a small growl that neither of the girls heard it, and certainly Dick and Julian didn't, away in their tent.

Timmy raised his head and listened intently. Then he gave another small growl. He listened again. Finally he got up, shook himself, still without waking George, and stalked out of the tent, his ears cocked and his tail up. He had heard somebody or something, and although he thought it was all right, he was going to make sure.

Dick was sound asleep when he felt something brushing against the outside of his tent. He awoke at once and sat up. He looked at the tent opening. A shadow appeared there and looked in.

Was it Timmy? Was it Mr Luffy? He mustn't make a mistake this time. He waited for the shadow to speak. But it didn't. It just stayed there as if it were listening for some movement inside the tent. Dick didn't like it.

'Timmy!' he said at last, in a low voice.

Then the shadow spoke: 'Dick? Or is it Julian? It's Jock here. I've got Timmy beside me. Can I come in?'

'*Jock!*' said Dick, in surprise. 'Whatever have you come at this time of night for? And why didn't you come today? We waited ages for you.'

'Yes. I know. I'm awfully sorry,' said Jock's voice, and the boy wriggled himself into the tent.

Dick poked Julian awake.

'Julian! Here's Jock – and Timmy. Get off me, Timmy. Here, Jock, see if you can squeeze inside my sleeping-bag – there's room for us both, I think.'

'Oh, thanks,' said Jock, and squeezed inside with difficulty. 'How warm it is! I say, I'm terribly sorry I didn't come today – but my stepfather suddenly announced he wanted me to go somewhere with him for the whole day. Can't think why. He doesn't bother about me as a rule.'

'That was mean of him, seeing that he knew you were to come on a picnic with us,' said Julian. 'Was it something important?'

'No. Not at all,' said Jock. 'He drove off to Endersfield – that's about forty miles away – parked me in the public library there, saying he'd be back in a few minutes – and he didn't come back till past tea-time! I had some sandwiches with me, luckily. I felt pretty angry about it, I can tell you.'

'Never mind. Come tomorrow instead,' said Dick.

'I can't,' said Jock in despair. 'He's gone and arranged for me to meet the son of some friend of his – a boy called Cecil Dearlove – what a name! I'm to spend the day with this frightful boy. The worst of it is Mum's quite pleased about it. She never thinks my stepfather takes enough notice of me – good thing he doesn't, *I* think.'

'Oh blow – so you won't be able to come tomorrow either,' said Julian. 'Well – what about the next day?'

'It should be all right,' said Jock. 'But I've a feeling I'll have dear love of a Cecil planked on me for the day – to show him the cows and the puppies, dear pet! Ugh! When I could be with you four and Timmy.'

'It's bad luck,' said Julian. 'It really is.'

'I thought I'd better come and tell you,' said Jock. 'It's the first chance I've had, creeping up here tonight. I've brought some more food for you, by the way. I guessed you'd want some. I feel down in the dumps about that adventure – you know, going to see the railway yard. I was going to ask you to take me today.'

'Well – if you can't come tomorrow either – and perhaps not the next day – what about going one night?' said Dick. 'Would you like to come up tomorrow night, about this time? We won't tell the girls. We'll just go off by ourselves, we three boys – and watch!'

Jock was too thrilled to say a word. He let out a deep breath of joy. Dick laughed.

'Don't get too thrilled. We probably shan't see a thing. Bring a torch if you've got one. Come to our tent and jerk my toe. I'll probably be awake, but if I'm not, that'll wake me all right! And don't say a word to anyone of course.'

'Rather not,' said Jock, overjoyed. 'Well – I suppose I'd better be going. It was pretty weird coming over the moorland in the dark. There's no moon, and the stars don't give much light. I've left the food outside the tent. Better look out that Timmy doesn't get it.'

'Right. Thanks awfully,' said Julian. Jock got out of Dick's sleeping-bag and went backwards out of the tent, with Timmy obligingly licking his nose all the way. Jock then found the bag of food and rolled it in to Julian, who put it safely under the groundsheet.

'Good night,' said Jock, in a low voice, and they heard him scrambling over the heather. Timmy went with him, pleased at this unexpected visitor, and the chance of a midnight walk. Jock was glad to have the dog's company. Timmy went right to the farm with him and then bounded back over the moorland to the camping-place, longing to pounce on the rabbits he could smell here and there, but wanting to get back to George.

In the morning Anne was amazed to find the food in her 'larder' under the gorse bush. Julian had popped it there to surprise here. 'Look at this!' she cried, in astonishment. 'Meat-pies – more tomatoes – eggs, wherever did they come from?'

'Spook-train brought them in the night,' said Dick, with a grin.

'Volcano shot them up into the air,' said Mr Luffy, who was also there. Anne threw a tea-cloth at him.

'Tell me how it came here,' she demanded. 'I was worried about what to give you all for breakfast – and now there's more than we can possibly eat. Who put it there? George, do you know?'

But George didn't. She glanced at the smiling faces of the two boys. 'I bet Jock was here last night,' she said to them. 'Wasn't he?' And to herself she said: 'Yes – and somehow I think they've planned something together. You won't trick *me*, Dick and Julian. I'll be on the lookout from now on! Wherever you go, I go too!'

10 Hunt for a spook-train

That day passed pleasantly enough. The children, Timmy, and Mr Luffy all went off to a pool high up on the moorlands. It was called 'The Green Pool' because of its cucumber-green colour. Mr Luffy explained that some curious chemicals found there caused the water to look green.

'I hope we shan't come out looking green, too,' said Dick, getting into his bathing trunks. 'Are you going to bathe, Mr Luffy?'

Mr Luffy was. The children expected him to be a very poor swimmer and to splash about at the edge and do very little – but to their surprise he was magnificent in the water, and could swim faster even than Julian.

They had great fun, and when they were tired they came out to bask in the sun. The high road ran alongside the green pool, and the children watched a heard of sheep being driven along, then a car or two came by, and finally a big army lorry. A boy sat beside the driver, and to the children's surprise he waved wildly at them.

'Who was that?' said Julian astonished. 'Surely he doesn't know us?'

George's sharp eye had seen who it was. 'It was Jock! Sitting beside the driver. And, look, here comes his stepfather's fine new car. Jock's preferred to go with the lorry-driver instead of his stepfather! I don't blame him, either!'

The bright new car came by, driven by Mr Andrews. He didn't glance at the children by the wayside, but drove steadily on after the lorry.

'Going to market, I suppose,' said Dick, lying back again. 'Wonder what they're taking?'

'So do I,' said Mr Luffy. 'He must sell his farm produce at very high prices to be able to buy that fine car and all the machinery and gear you've told me about. Clever fellow, Mr Andrews!'

'He doesn't look at all clever,' said Anne. 'He looks rather a weak, feeble sort of man, really, Mr Luffy. I can't even imagine him being clever enough to beat anyone down, or get the better of them.'

'Very interesting,' said Mr Luffy. 'Well, what about another dip before we have our dinner?'

It was a very nice day, and Mr Luffy was very good company. He could make fine jokes very solemnly indeed, and only the fact that his ear waggled violently showed the others that he, too, was enjoying the joke. His right ear seemed to love to join in the joke, even if Mr Luffy's face was as solemn as Timmy's.

They arrived home at the camp about tea-time and Anne got a fine tea ready. They took it down to eat in front of Mr Luffy's tent. As the evening came on Julian and Dick felt excitement rising in them. In the daytime neither of them really believed a word about the 'spook-trains', but as the sun sank and long shadows crept down the hills they felt pleasantly thrilled. Would they really see anything exciting that night?

It was a very dark night at first, because clouds lay across the sky and hid even the stars. The boys said good night to the girls and snuggled down into their sleeping-bags. They watched the sky through the tent opening.

Gradually the big clouds thinned out. A few stars appeared. The clouds thinned still more and fled away in rags. Soon the whole sky was bright with pin-points of light, and a hundred thousand stars looked down on the moorlands.

'We shall have a bit of starlight to see by,' whispered Julian. 'That's good. I don't want to stumble about over the heather and break my ankle in rabbit-holes in the pitch darkness. Nor do I want to use my torch on the way to the yard in case it's seen.'

'It's going to be fun!' Dick whispered back. 'I hope Jock comes. It will be maddening if he doesn't.'

He did come. There was a scrambling over the heather and once again a shadow appeared at the tent opening.

'Julian! Dick! I've come. Are you ready?'

It was Jock's voice, of course. Dick's thumb pressed the switch of his torch and for a moment its light fell on Jock's red, excited face, and then was switched off again.

'Hallo, Jock! So you were able to come,' said Dick. 'I say, was that you in the lorry this morning, going by the green pool?'

'Yes. Did you see me? I saw you and waved like mad,' said Jock. 'I wanted to stop the lorry and get down and speak to you, but the driver's an awful bad-tempered sort of fellow. He wouldn't hear of stopping. Said my stepfather would be wild with him if he did. Did you see *him* – my stepfather, I mean? He was in his car behind.'

'Were you off to market or something?' asked Julian.

'I expect that's where the lorry was going,' said Jock. 'It was empty, so I suppose my stepfather was going to pick up something there. I came back in the car. The lorry was supposed to come later.'

'How did you like Cecil Dearlove?' asked Dick, grinning in the darkness.

'Awful! Worse than his name,' groaned Jock. 'Wanted me to play soldiers all the time! The frightful thing is I've got to have him at the farm for the day tomorrow. Another day gone west. What shall I do with him?'

'Roll him in the pig-sty,' suggested Dick. 'Or put him with Biddy's puppies and let him sleep there. Tell him to play soldiers with them.'

Jock chuckled. 'I wish I could. The worst of it is Mum is awfully pleased that my stepfather's got this Cecil boy for me to be friends with. Don't let's talk about it. Are you ready to start off?'

'Yes,' said Julian, and began to scramble quietly out of his bag. 'We didn't tell the girls. Anne doesn't want to come, and I don't want George to leave Anne by herself. Now, let's be very, very quiet till we're out of hearing.'

Dick got out of his bag too. The boys had not undressed that night, except for their coats, so all they had to do was to slip these on, and then crawl out of the tent.

'Which is the way – over there?' whispered Jock. Julian took his arm and guided him. He hoped he wouldn't lose his way in the starlit darkness. The moorland looked so different at night!

'If we make for that hill you can dimly see over there against the starlit sky, we should be going in the right direction,' said Julian. So on they went, keeping towards the dark hill that rose up to the west.

It seemed very much farther to the railway yard at night than in the daytime. The three boys stumbled along, sometimes almost falling as their feet caught in tufts of heather. They were glad when they found some sort of path they could keep on.

'This is about where we met the shepherd,' said Dick, in a low voice. He didn't know why he spoke so quietly. He just felt as if he must. 'I'm sure we can't be very far off now.'

They went on for some way, and then Julian pulled Dick by the arm. 'Look,' he said. 'Down

there, I believe that's the old yard. You can see the lines gleaming faintly here and there.'

They stood on the heathery slope above the old yard, straining their eyes. Soon they could make out dim shapes. Yes, it was the railway yard all right.

Jock clutched Julian's sleeve. 'Look – there's a light down there! Do you see it?'

The boys looked – and, sure enough, down in the yard towards the other side of it, was a small yellow light. They stared at it.

'Oh – I think I know what it is,' said Dick, at last. 'It's the light in the watchman's little hut – old Wooden-Leg Sam's candle. Don't you think so, Ju?'

'Yes. You're right,' said Julian. 'I tell you what we'll do – we'll creep right down into the yard, and go over to the hut. We'll peep inside and see if old Sam is there. Then we'll hide somewhere about – and wait for the spook-train to come!'

They crept down the slope. Their eyes had got used to the starlight by now, and they were beginning to see fairly well. They got right down to the yard, where their feet made a noise on some cinders there.

They stopped. 'Someone will hear us if we make a row like this,' whispered Julian.

'Who will?' whispered back Dick. 'There's no one here except old Sam in his hut?'

'How do you know there isn't?' said Julian. 'Good heavens, Jock, don't make such a row with your feet!'

They stood there, debating what was the best thing to do. 'We'd better walk right round the edge of the yard,' said Julian at once. 'As far as I remember, the grass has grown there. We'll walk on that.'

So they made their way to the edge of the yard. Sure enough, there was grass there, and they walked on it without a sound. They went slowly and softly to where the light shone dimly in Sam's little hut.

The window was high and small. It was just about at the level of their heads, and the three boys cautiously eased themselves along to it and looked in.

Wooden-Leg Sam was there. He sat sprawled in a chair, smoking a pipe. He was reading a newspaper, squinting painfully as he did so. He obviously had not had his 'bruck' glasses mended yet. On a chair beside him was his wooden leg. He had unstrapped it, and there it lay.

'He's not expecting the spook-train tonight, or he wouldn't have taken off his wooden leg,' whispered Dick.

The candlelight flickered and shadows jumped about the tiny hut. It was a poor, ill-furnished little place, dirty and untidy. A cup without saucer or handle stood on the table, and a tin kettle boiled on a rusty stove.

Sam put down his paper and rubbed his eyes. He muttered something. The boys could not hear it, but they felt certain it was something about his 'bruck' glasses.

'Are there many lines in this yard?' whispered Jock, tired of looking in at old Sam. 'Where do they go to?'

'About half a mile or so up there is a tunnel,' said Julian, pointing past Jock. 'The lines come from there and run here, where they break up in many pairs – for shunting and so on, in the old days, I suppose, when this place was used.'

'Let's go up the lines to the tunnel,' said Jock. 'Come on. There's nothing to be seen here. Let's walk up to the tunnel.'

'All right,' said Julian. 'We may as well. I don't expect we'll see much up there either! I think these spook-trains are all a tall story of old Sam's!'

They left the little hut with its forlorn candle-

light, and made their way round the yard again. Then they followed the single-track line away from the yard and up towards the tunnel. It didn't seem to matter walking on cinders now, and making a noise. They walked along, talking in low voices.

And then things began to happen! A far-off muffled noise came rumbling out of the tunnel, which was now so near that the boys could see its black mouth. Julian heard it first. He stood still and clutched Dick.

'I say! Listen! Can you hear that?'

The others listened. 'Yes,' said Dick. 'But it's only a train going through one of the underground tunnels – the noise is echoing out through this one.'

'It isn't. That noise is made by a train coming through this tunnel!' said Julian. The noise grew louder and louder. A clanking made itself heard too. The boys stepped off the lines and crouched together by the side, waiting, hardly daring to breathe.

Could it be the spook-train? They watched for the light of an engine-lamp to appear like a fiery eye in the tunnel. But none came. It was darker than night in there! But the noise came nearer and nearer and nearer. Could there be the noise of a train without a train? Julian's heart began to beat twice as fast, and Dick and Jock found themselves clutching one another without knowing it.

The noise grew thunderous, and then out from the tunnel came something long and black, with a dull glow in front that passed quickly and was gone. The noise deafened the boys, and then the clanking and rumbling grew less as the train, or whatever it was, passed by. The ground trembled and then was still.

'Well, there you are,' said Julian, in a rather trembly voice. 'The spook-train – without a light or a signal! Where's it gone? To the yard, do you think?'

'Shall we go and see?' asked Dick. 'I didn't see anyone in the cab, even in the glow of what must have been the fire there – but there must be *some-one* driving it! I say, what a weird thing, isn't it? It *sounded* real enough anyway.'

'We'll go to the yard,' said Jock, who, of the three, seemed the least affected. 'Come on.'

They made their way very slowly – and then Dick gave a sharp cry. 'Blow! I've twisted my ankle. Half a minute!'

He sank down to the ground in great pain. It was only a sharp twist, not a sprain, but for a few minutes Dick could do nothing but groan. The others dared not leave him. Julian knelt by him, offering to rub the ankle, but Dick wouldn't let him touch it. Jock stood by anxiously.

It took about twenty minutes for Dick's ankle to be strong enough for him to stand on again. With the help of the others he got to his feet and tested his ankle. 'It's all right, I think. I can walk on it – slowly. Now we'll go to the yard and see what's happening!'

But even as they started to walk slowly back, they heard a noise coming up the lines from the far-away yard, 'Rumble, rumble, rumble, jangle, clank!'

11 Mostly about Jock

The three boys stood rather close together, glad to feel each other in the darkness. They couldn't believe that they had found what they had come looking for so doubtfully! What kind of a train was this that had come rumbling out of the tunnel so mysteriously, and then, after a pause at the yard, had gone just as mysteriously back again?

'If only I hadn't twisted my ankle, we could have followed the train down the lines to the yard, and have gone quite close to it there,' groaned Dick. 'What an ass I am, messing things up at the most exciting moment!'

'You couldn't help it,' said Jock. 'I *say*! We've seen the spook-train! I can hardly believe it. Does it go all by itself, with nobody to drive it? Is it a real train?'

'Judging by the noise it made, it's real all right,' said Julian. 'And it shot out smoke, too. All the same – it's jolly queer. I can't say I like it much.'

'Let's go and see what's happened to Wooden-Leg Sam,' said Dick. 'I bet he's under his bed!'

They made their way slowly back to the yard, Dick limping a little, though his ankle was practically all right again. When they came to the yard they looked towards Sam's hut. The light was there no longer.

'It's coming back again!' said Julian. 'Stand still. Watch! It'll be going back into the tunnel!'

They stood still and watched and listened. Again the noise came nearer and grew thunderous. They saw the glow of what might be the fire in the cab, and then it passed. The train disappeared into the blackness of the tunnel mouth and they heard the echo of its rumblings for some time.

'Well, there you are! There *is* a spook-train!' said Julian, trying to laugh, though he felt a good deal shaken. 'It came and it went – where from or where to, nobody knows! But – we've heard it and seen it, in the darkness of the night. And jolly creepy it was, too!'

'He's blown it out and got under the bed!' said Dick. 'Poor Sam! It really must be terrifying for him. Let's go and peep into his hut.'

They went over to it and tried to see in at the window. But there was nothing to be seen. The hut was in complete darkness. Then suddenly a little flare flashed out somewhere near the floor.

'Look – there's Sam! He's lighting a match,' said Julian. 'See – he's peeping out from under the bed. He looks scared stiff. Let's tap on the window and ask him if he's all right.'

But that was quite the wrong thing to do! As soon as Julian tapped sharply on the window, Sam gave an anguished yell and retired hurriedly under the bed again, his wavering match-light going out.

'It's come for to take me!' they heard him wailing. 'It's come for to take me! And me with my wooden leg off too.'

'We're only frightening the poor old fellow,' said Dick. 'Come on. Let's leave him. He'll have a fit or something if we call out to him. He honestly thinks the spook-train's come to get him.'

They wandered round the dark yard for a few minutes, but there was nothing to find out in the darkness. No more rumbling came to their ears. The spook-train was evidently not going to run again that night.

'Let's go back,' said Julian. 'That really was exciting! Honestly, my hair stood on end when that train came puffing out of the tunnel. Where on earth did it come from? And what's the reason for it?'

They gave it up, and began to walk back to the camp. They scrambled through the heather, tired but excited. 'Shall we tell the girls we've seen the train?' said Dick.

'No,' said Julian. 'It would only scare Anne, and

George would be furious if she knew we'd gone without her. We'll wait and see if we discover anything more before we say anything, either to the girls or to old Luffy.'

'Right,' said Dick. 'You'll hold your tongue, too, won't you, Jock?'

''Course,' said Jock, scornfully. 'Who would I tell? My stepfather? Not likely! How furious he'd be if he knew we'd all pooh-poohed his warnings and gone down to see the spook-train after all!'

He suddenly felt something warm against his legs, and gave a startled cry: 'What's this? Get away!'

But the warm thing turned out to be Timmy, who had come to meet the three boys. He pressed against each of them in turn and whined a little.

'He says, "Why didn't you take me with you?"' said Dick. 'Sorry, old thing, but we couldn't. George would never have spoken to us again if we'd taken you, and left her behind! How would you have liked spook-trains, Timmy? Would you have run into a corner somewhere and hidden?'

'Woof,' said Timmy, scornfully. As if he would be afraid of anything!

They reached their camping-place and began to speak in whispers. 'Good-bye, Jock. Come up tomorrow if you can. Hope you don't have that Cecil boy to cope with!'

'Good-bye! See you soon,' whispered Jock, and disappeared into the darkness, with Timmy at his heels. Another chance of a midnight walk? Good, thought Timmy, just what he'd like! It was hot in the tent, and a scamper in the cool night air would be fine.

Timmy growled softly when they came near to Olly's Farm, and stood still, the hackles on his neck rising up a little. Jock put his hand on the dog's head and stopped.

'What's the matter, old boy? Burglars or something?'

He strained his eyes in the darkness. Big clouds now covered the stars and then was no light at all to see by. Jock made out a dim light in one of the barns. He crept over to it to see what it was. It went out as he came near, and then he heard the sound of footsteps, the quiet closing of the barn door, and the click of a padlock as it was locked.

Jock crept nearer – too near, for whoever it was must have heard him and swung round, lashing out with his arm. He caught Jock on the shoulder, and the boy over-balanced. He almost fell, and the man who had struck him clutched hold of him. A

flash-light was put on and he blinked in the sudden light.

'It's you, Jock!' said an astonished voice, rough and impatient. 'What are you doing out here at this time of night?'

'Well, what are *you* doing?' demanded Jock, wriggling free. He switched on his own torch and let the light fall on the man who had caught him. It was Peters, one of the farm men, the one in whose lorry he had ridden that very day.

'What's it to do with you?' said Peters, angrily. 'I had a breakdown, and I've only just got back. Look here – you're fully dressed! Where have you been at this time of night? Did you hear me come in, and get up to see what was happening?'

'You never know!' said Jock cheekily. He wasn't going to say anything that might make Peters suspicious of him. 'You just never know!'

'Is that Biddy?' said Peters, seeing a dark shadow slinking away. 'Do you mean to say you've been out with Biddy? What in the world have you been doing?'

Jock thanked his lucky stars that Peters hadn't spotted it was Timmy, not Biddy. He moved off without saying another word. Let Peters think what he liked! It was bad luck, though, that Peters had had a breadown and come in late. If the man told his stepfather he'd seen Jock, fully dressed in the middle of the night, there'd be questions asked by both his mother and his stepfather, and Jock, who was a truthful boy, would find things very difficult to explain.

He scuttled off to bed, climbing up the pear-tree outside his window, and dropping quietly into his room. He opened his door softly to hear if anyone was awake in the house, but all was dark and silent.

'Blow Peters!' thought Jock. 'If he splits on me, I'm for it!'

He got into bed, pondered over the curious happenings of the night for a few minutes, and then slid into an uneasy sleep, in which spook-trains, Peters, and Timmy kept doing most peculiar things. He was glad to awake in the bright, sunny morning and find his mother shaking him.

'Get up, Jock? You're very late. Whatever's made you so sleepy? We're half-way through breakfast!'

Peters, apparently, didn't say anything to Jock's stepfather about seeing Jock in the night. Jock was very thankful. He began to plan how to slip off to the others at the camp. He'd take them some food! That would be a fine excuse.

'Mum, can I take a basket of stuff to the campers?' he said, after breakfast. 'They must be running short now.'

'Well – that boy is coming,' said the mother. 'What's his name – Cecil something? Your stepfather says he's such a nice boy. You did enjoy your day with him yesterday, didn't you?'

Jock would have said quite a lot of uncomplimentary things about dear Cecil if his stepfather had not been there, sitting by the window reading the paper. As it was, he shrugged his shoulders and made a face, hoping that his mother would understand his feelings. She did.

'What time is Cecil coming?' she said. 'Perhaps there's time for you to run to the camp with a basket.'

'I don't want him running off up there,' said Mr Andrews, suddenly butting into the conversation, and putting down his newspaper. 'Cecil may be here at any minute – and I know what Jock is! He'd start talking to those kids and forget all about coming back. Cecil's father is a great friend of mine, and Jock's got to be polite to him, and be here to welcome him. There's to be no running off to that camp today.'

Jock looked sulky. Why must his stepfather suddenly interfere in his plans like this? Rushing him off to the town, making him take Cecil for a friend! Just when some other children had come into his rather lonely life and livened it up, too! It was maddening.

'Perhaps I can go up to the camp myself with some food,' said his mother, comfortingly. 'Or maybe the children will come down for some.'

Jock was still sulky. He stalked out into the yard and went to look for Biddy. She was with her pups who were now trying to crawl round the shed after her. Jock hoped the campers would come to fetch food themselves that day. Then at least he would get a word with them.

Cecil arrived by car. He was about the same age as Jock, though he was small for twelve years old. He had curly hair which was too long, and his grey flannel suit was very, very clean and well-pressed.

'Hallo!' he called to Jock. 'I've come. What shall we play at? Soldiers?'

'No. Red Indians,' said Jock, who had suddenly remembered his old Red Indian head-dress with masses of feathers round it, and a trail of them falling down the back. He rushed indoors, grinning. He changed into the whole suit, and put on his head-dress. He took his paint-box and hurriedly painted a frightful pattern of red, blue and green on his face. He found his tomahawk and went downstairs. He would play at Red Indians, and scalp that annoying Pale-Face!

Cecil was wandering round by himself. To his enormous horror, as he turned a corner, a most terrifying figure rose up from behind a wall, gave a horrible yell and pounced on him, waving what looked like a dangerous chopper.

Cecil turned and fled, howling loudly, with Jock leaping madly after him, whooping for all he was worth, and thoroughly enjoying himself. He had had to play at soldiers all the day before with dear Cecil. He didn't see why Cecil shouldn't play Red Indians all day with him today!

Just at that moment, the four campers arrived to fetch food, with Timmy running beside them. They stopped in amazement at the sight of Cecil running like the wind, howling dismally, and a fully-dressed and painted Red Indian leaping fiercely after him.

Jock saw them, did a comical war-dance all round them, much to Timmy's amazement, yelled dramatically, pretended to cut off Timmy's tail and then tore after the vanishing Cecil.

The children began to laugh helplessly. 'Oh dear!' said Anne, with tears of laughter in her eyes, 'that must be Cecil he's after. I suppose this is Jock's revenge for having to play soldiers all day with him yesterday. Look, there they go round the pig-sty. Poor Cecil. He really thinks he's going to be scalped!'

Cecil disappeared into the farm kitchen, sobbing, and Mrs Andrews ran to comfort him. Jock made off back to the others, grinning all over his war-painted face.

'Hallo,' he said. 'I'm just having a nice quiet time with dear Cecil. I'm so glad to see you. I wanted to come over, but my stepfather said I wasn't to – I must play with Cecil. Isn't he frightful?'

'Awful,' everyone agreed.

'I say – will your mother be wild with you for frightening Cecil like that? Perhaps we'd better not ask her for any food yet?' said Julian.

'Yes – you'd better wait a bit,' said Jock, leading them to the sunny side of the haystack they had rested by before. 'Hallo, Timmy! Did you get back all right last night?'

Jock had completely forgotten that the girls didn't know of the happenings of the night before. Both Anne and George at once pricked up their ears. Julian frowned at Jock, and Dick gave him a secret nudge.

12 George loses her temper

Jock made a face at Cecil and got up. He went slowly off round the haystack, and the others listened in silence for whacks and yells. But none came.

'He frightened me,' said Cecil, sitting down by the others.

'Poor ickle ting,' said Dick at once.

'Darling baby,' said George.

'Mother's pet,' said Julian. Cecil glared at them all. He got up again, very red.

'What's up?' said George, seeing all this by-play. 'What happened last night?'

'Oh, I just came up to have a little night-talk with the boys – and Timmy walked back with me,' said Jock, airily. 'Hope you didn't mind him coming, George.'

George flushed an angry red. 'You're keeping something from me,' she said to the boys. 'Yes, you are. I know you are. I believe you went off to the railway yard last night! Did you?'

There was an awkward silence. Julian shot an annoyed look at poor Jock, who could have kicked himself.

'Go on – tell me,' persisted George, an angry frown on her forehead. 'You beasts! You did go! And you never woke me up to go with you! Oh, I do think you're mean!'

'Did you see anything?' said Anne, her eyes going from one boy to another. Each of the girls sensed that there had been some kind of adventure in the night.

'Well,' began Julian. And then there was an interruption. Cecil came round the haystack, his eyes red with crying. He glared at Jock.

'Your father wants you,' he said. 'You're to go at once. You're a beast, and I want to go home. Can't you hear your father yelling for you? He's got a stick – but I'm not sorry for you! I hope he whacks you hard!'

'If I didn't know my manners, I'd smack your faces,' he said, and marched off hurriedly, before his own could be smacked.

The four sat in silence. They were sorry for Jock. George was angry and sulky because she knew the others had gone off without her the night before. Anne was worried.

They all sat there for about ten minutes. Then round the haystack came Jock's mother, looking distressed. She carried a big basket of food.

The children all stood up politely. 'Good morning, Mrs Andrews,' said Julian.

'I'm sorry I can't ask you to stop today,' said Mrs Andrews. 'But Jock has really behaved very foolishly. I wouldn't let Mr Andrews give him a hiding because it would only make Jock hate his stepfather, and that would never do. So I've sent him up to bed for the day. You won't be able to see him, I'm afraid. Here is some food for you to take. Oh, dear – I'm really very sorry about all this. I can't think what came over Jock to behave in such a way. It's not a bit like him.'

Cecil's face appeared round the haystack, looking rather smug. Julian grinned to himself.

'Would you like us to take Cecil for a nice long walk over the moors?' he said. 'We can climb hills and jump over streams and scramble through the heather. It would make such a nice day for him.'

Cecil's face immediately disappeared.

'Well,' said Mrs Andrews, 'that really would be very kind of you. Now that Jock's been sent upstairs for the day there's no one for Cecil to play with. But I'm afraid he's a bit of a mother's boy, you know. You'll have to go carefully with him. Cecil! Cecil! Where are you? Come and make friends with these children.'

But Cecil had gone. There was no answer at all. He didn't want to make friends with 'these children'. He knew better than that! Mrs Andrews went in search of him, but he had completely disappeared.

The four children were not at all surprised. Julian, Dick and Anne grinned at one another. George stood with her back to them, still sulky.

Mrs Andrews came back again, out of breath. 'I can't find him,' she said. 'Never mind. I'll find something for him to do when he appears again.'

'Yes. Perhaps you've got some beads for him to thread? Or a nice easy jigsaw puzzle to do?' said Julian, very politely. The others giggled. A smile appeared on Mrs Andrews's face.

'Bad boy!' she said. 'Oh dear – poor Jock. Well, it's his own fault. Now good-bye, I must get on with my work.'

She ran off to the dairy. The children looked round the haystack. Mr Andrews was getting into his car. He would soon be gone. They waited a few minutes till they heard the car set off down the rough cart-track.

'That's Jock's bedroom – where the pear-tree is,' said Julian. 'Let's just have a word with him before we go. It's a shame.'

They went across the farmyard and stood under the pear-tree – all except George, who stayed behind the haystack with the food, frowning. Julian called up to the window above: 'Jock!'

A head came out, the face still painted terrifyingly in streaks and circles. 'Hallo! He didn't whack me. Mum wouldn't let him. All the same, I'd rather he had – it's awful being stuck up here this sunny day. Where's dear Cecil?'

'I don't know. Probably in the darkest corner of

one of the barns,' said Julian. 'Jock, if things are difficult in the daytime, come up at night. We've got to see you somehow.'

'Right,' said Jock. 'How do I look? Like a real Red Indian?'

'You look frightful,' grinned Julian. 'I wonder old Timmy knew you.'

'Where's George?' asked Jock.

'Sulking behind the haystack,' said Dick. 'We shall have an awful day with her now. You let the cat properly out of the bag, you idjit!'

'Yes. I'm a ninny and an idjit,' said Jock, and Anne giggled. 'Look – there's Cecil. You might tell him to beware of the bull, will you?'

'Is there a bull?' said Anne, looking alarmed.

'No. But that's no reason why he shouldn't beware of one,' grinned Jock. 'So long! Have a nice day!'

The three left him, and strolled over to Cecil,

who had just appeared out of a dark little shed. He made a face at them, and stood ready to run to the dairy where Mrs Andrews was busy.

Julian suddenly clutched Dick and pointed behind Cecil. 'The bull! Beware of the bull!' he yelled suddenly.

Dick entered into the joke. 'The bull's loose! Look out! Beware of the bull!' he shouted.

Anne gave a shriek. It all sounded so real that, although she knew it was a joke, she felt half-scared. 'The bull!' she cried.

Cecil turned green. His legs shook. 'W-w-w-where is it?' he stammered.

'Look out behind you!' yelled Julian, pointing. Poor Cecil, convinced that a large bull was about to pounce on him from behind, gave an anguished cry and tore on tottering legs to the dairy. He threw himself against Mrs Andrews.

'Save me, save me! The bull's chasing me.'

'But there's no bull here,' said Mrs Andrews, in surprise. 'Really, Cecil! Was it a pig after you, or something?'

Helpless with laughter, the three children made their way back to George. They tried to tell her about the make-believe bull, but she turned away and wouldn't listen. Julian shrugged his shoulders. Best to leave George to herself when she was in one of her rages! She didn't lose her temper as often as she used to, but when she did she was very trying indeed.

They went back to the camp with the basket of food. Timmy followed soberly. He knew something was wrong with George and he was unhappy. His tail was down, and he looked miserable. George wouldn't even pat him.

When they got back to the camp, George flared up.

'How dare you go off without me when I told you I meant to come? Fancy taking Jock and not letting me go! I think you're absolute beasts. I never really thought you'd do a thing like that, you and Dick.'

'Don't be silly, George,' said Julian. 'I told you we didn't mean to let you and Anne go. I'll tell you all that happened – and it's pretty thrilling!'

'What? Tell me quickly!' begged Anne, but George obstinately turned away her head as if she was not interested.

Julian began to relate all the curious happenings of the night. Anne listened breathlessly. George was listening too, though she pretended not to. She was very angry and very hurt.

'Well, there you are,' said Julian, when he had finished. 'If that's what people mean by spook-trains, there was one puffing in and out of that tunnel all right! I felt pretty scared, I can tell you. Sorry you weren't there too, George – but I didn't want to leave Anne alone.'

George was not accepting any apologies. She still looked furious.

'I suppose Timmy went with you,' she said. 'I think that was horrid of him – to go without waking me, when he knew I'd like to be with you on the adventure.'

'Oh, don't be so silly,' said Dick, in disgust. 'Fancy being angry with old Tim, too! You're making him miserable. And anyway, he *didn't* come with us. He just came to meet us when we got back, and then went off to keep Jock company on his way back to the farm.'

'Oh,' said George, and she reached out her hand to pat Timmy, who was filled with delight. 'At least Timmy was loyal to me then. That's something.'

There was a silence. Nobody ever knew quite how to treat George when she was in one of her moods. It was really best to leave her to herself, but they couldn't very well go off and leave the camp just because George was there, cross and sulky.

Anne took hold of George's arm. She was miserable when George behaved like this. 'George,' she began. 'There's no need to be cross with me, too. *I* haven't done anything!'

'If you weren't such a little coward, too afraid to go with us, I'd have been able to go too,' said George unkindly, dragging her arm away.

Julian was disgusted. He saw Anne's hurt face and was angry with George.

'Shut up, George,' he said. 'You're behaving like a girl, for all you think you're as good as a boy! Saying catty things like that! I'm astonished at you.'

George was ashamed of herself, but she was too proud to say so. She glared at Julian.

'And *I'm* astonished at *you*,' she said. 'After all the adventures we've had together, you try to keep me out of this one. But you *will* let me come next time, won't you, Julian?'

'What! After your frightful behaviour today?' said Julian, who could be just as obstinate as George when he wanted to. 'Certainly not. This is my adventure and Dick's – and perhaps Jock's. Not yours or Anne's.'

He got up and stalked down the hill with Dick.

George sat pulling bits of heather off the stems, looking mutinous and angry. Anne blinked back tears. She hated this sort of thing. She got up to get dinner ready. Perhaps after a good meal they would all feel better.

Mr Luffy was sitting outside his tent, reading. He had already seen the children that morning. He looked up, smiling.

'Hallo! Come to talk to me?'

'Yes,' said Julian, an idea uncurling itself in his mind. 'Could I have a look at that map of yours, Mr Luffy? The big one you've got showing every mile of these moorlands?'

'Of course. It's in the tent somewhere,' said Mr Luffy.

The boys found it and opened it. Dick at once guessed why Julian wanted it. Mr Luffy went on reading.

'It shows the railways that run under the moorlands too, doesn't it?' said Julian. Mr Luffy nodded.

'Yes. There are quite a few lines. I suppose it was easier to tunnel under the moors from valley to valley rather than make a permanent way over the top of them. In any case, a railway over the moors would probably be completely snowed up in the winter-time.'

The boys bent their heads over the big map; it showed the railways as dotted lines when they went underground, but by long black lines when they appeared in the open air, in the various valleys.

They found exactly where they were. Then Julian's finger ran down the map a little and came to where a small line showed itself at the end of a dotted line.

He looked at Dick, who nodded. Yes – that showed where the tunnel was, out of which the 'spook-train' had come, and the lines to the deserted yard. Julian's finger went back from the yard to the tunnel, where the dotted lines began. His finger traced the dotted lines a little way till they became whole lines again. That was where the train came out into another valley!

Then his finger showed where the tunnel that led from the yard appeared to join up with another one, that also ran for some distance before coming out into yet another valley. The boys looked at one another in silence.

Mr Luffy suddenly spotted a day-flying moth and got up to follow it. The boys took the chance of talking to one another.

'The spook-train either runs through its own tunnel to the valley beyond – or it turns off into this fork and runs along to the other valley,' said Julian, in a low voice. 'I tell you what we'll do, Dick. We'll get Mr Luffy to run us down to the nearest town to buy something – and we'll slip along to the station there and see if we can't make a few inquiries about these two tunnels. We may find out something.'

'Good idea,' said Dick, as Mr Luffy came back. 'I say, sir, are you very busy today? Could you possibly run us down to the nearest town after dinner?'

'Certainly, certainly,' said Mr Luffy, amiably. The boys looked at one another in delight. *Now* they might find out something! But they wouldn't take George with them. No – they would punish her for her bad temper by leaving her behind!

13 A thrilling plan

Anne called them to dinner. 'Come along!' she cried. 'I've got it all ready. Tell Mr Luffy there's plenty for him, too.'

Mr Luffy came along willingly. He thought Anne was a marvellous little camp-housekeeper. He looked approvingly at the spread set out on a white cloth on the ground.

'Hm! Salad. Hard-boiled eggs. Slices of tongue. And what's this? – apple-pie! My goodness! Don't tell me you cooked that here, Anne.'

Anne laughed. 'No. All this came from the farm, of course. Except the lime juice and water.'

George ate with the others, but said hardly a word. She was brooding over her wrongs, and Mr Luffy looked at her several times, puzzled.

'Are you quite well, George?' he said, suddenly. George went red.

'Yes, thank you,' she said, and tried to be more herself, though she couldn't raise a smile at all. Mr Luffy watched her, and was relieved to see that she ate as much as the others. Probably had some sort of row, he guessed correctly. Well, it would blow over! He knew better than to interfere.

They finished lunch and drank all the lime juice. It was a hot day and they were very thirsty indeed. Timmy emptied all his dish of water and went and gazed longingly into the canvas bucket of washing-water. But he was too well-behaved to drink it, now that he knew he mustn't. Anne laughed, and poured some more water into his dish.

'Well,' said Mr Luffy, beginning to fill his old brown pipe, 'if anyone wants to come into town with me this afternoon, I'll be starting in fifteen minutes.'

'I'll come!' said Anne, at once. 'It won't take George and me long to wash-up these things. Will you come too, George?'

'No,' said George, and the boys heaved a sigh of relief. They had guessed she wouldn't want to come with them – but, if she'd known what they were going to try and find out, she would have come all right!

'I'm going for a walk with Timmy,' said George, when all the washing-up had been done.

'All right,' said Anne, who secretly thought that George would be much better left on her own to work off her ill-feelings that afternoon. 'See you later.'

George and Timmy set off. The others went with Mr Luffy to where his car was parked beside the great rock. They got in.

'Hi! The trailer's fastened to it,' called Julian. 'Wait a bit. Let me get out and undo it. We don't want to take an empty trailer bumping along behind us for miles.'

'Dear me. I always forget to undo the trailer,' said Mr Luffy, vexed. 'The times I take it along without meaning to!'

The children winked at one another. Dear old Luffy! He was always doing things like that. No wonder his wife fussed round him like an old hen with one foolish chicken when he was at home.

They went off in the car, jolting over the rough road till they came to the smooth highway. They stopped in the centre of the town. Mr Luffy said he would meet them for tea at five o'clock at the hotel opposite the parking-place.

The three of them set off together, leaving Mr Luffy to go to the library and browse there. It seemed funny to be without George. Anne didn't much like it, and said so.

'Well, we don't like going off without George either,' said Julian. 'But honestly, she can't behave

like that and get away with it. I thought she'd grown out of that sort of thing.'

'Well, you know how she adores an adventure,' said Anne. 'Oh dear – if I hadn't felt so scared you'd have taken me along, and George would have gone too. It's quite true what she said about me being a coward.'

'You're not,' said Dick. 'You can't help being scared of things sometimes – after all, you're the youngest of us – but being scared doesn't make you a coward. I've known you to be as brave as any of us when you've been scared stiff!'

'Where are we going?' asked Anne. The boys told her, and her eyes sparkled.

'Oh – are we going to find out where the spook-train comes from? It might come from one of two valleys then, judging from the map.'

'Yes. The tunnels aren't really very long ones,' said Julian. 'Not more than a mile, I should think. We thought we'd make some inquiries at the station and see if there's anyone who knows anything about the old railway yard and the tunnel beyond. We shan't say a word about the spook-train, of course.'

They walked into the station. They went up to a railway plan and studied it. It didn't tell them much. Julian turned to a young porter who was wheeling some luggage along.

'I say! Could you help us? We're camping up on the moorlands, and we're quite near a deserted railway yard with lines that run into an old tunnel. Why isn't the yard used any more?'

'Don't know,' said the boy. ''Ee should ask old Tucky there – see him? He knows all the tunnels under the moors like he knows the back of his hand. Worked in them all when he was a boy.'

'Thanks,' said Dick, pleased. They went over to where an old whiskered porter was sitting in the sun, enjoying a rest till the next train came in.

'Excuse me,' said Julian politely. 'I've been told that you know all about the moorland tunnels like the back of your hand. They must be very, very interesting.'

'Me feyther and me grandfeyther built they tunnels,' said the old porter, looking up at the children out of small faded eyes that watered in the strong sunlight. 'And I've bin guard on all the trains that ran through they.'

He mumbled a long string of names, going through all the list of tunnels in his mind. The children waited patiently till he had finished.

'There's a tunnel near where we're camping on

the moorlands,' said Julian, getting a word in at last. 'We're not far from Olly's Farm. We came across an old deserted railway yard, with lines that led into a tunnel. Do you know it?'

'Oh ay, that's an old tunnel,' said Tucky, nodding his grey head, on which his porter's cap sat all crooked. 'Hasn't been used for many a long year. Nor the yard either. Weren't enough traffic there, fur as I remember. Shut the yard they did. Tunnel baint used no more.'

The boys exchanged glances. So it wasn't used any more! Well, they knew better.

'The tunnel joins another, doesn't it?' said Julian. The porter, pleased at their interest in the old tunnels he knew so well, got up and went into an office behind. He came out with a dirty, much-used map, which he spread out on his knee. His black fingernail pointed to a mark on the map.

'That's the yard, see? It was called Olly's Yard, after the farm. Them's the lines to the tunnel. Here's the tunnel. It runs right through to Kilty Vale – there 'tis. And here's where it used to join the tunnel to Roker's Vale. But that were bricked up years ago. Summat happened there – the roof fell in, I think it was – and the company decided not to use the tunnel to Roker's Vale at all.'

The children listened with the utmost interest. Julian reasoned things out in his mind. If that spook-train came from anywhere then it must come from Kilty Vale, because that was the only place the lines went to now, since the way to Roker's Vale had been bricked up where the tunnels joined.

'I suppose no trains run through the tunnel from Kilty Vale to Olly's Yard now, then?' he said.

Tucky snorted. 'Didn't I tell 'ee it's not bin used for years? The yard at Kilty Vale's been turned into summat else, though the lines are still there. There's bin no engine through that tunnel since I were a young man.'

This was all very, very interesting. Julian bought old Tucky a packet of cigarettes which gave him such a pleasant shock that he wanted to tell the children everything all over again. He even gave them the old map.

'Oh, thanks,' said Julian, delighted to have it. He looked at the others. 'This'll be jolly useful!' he said, and they nodded.

They left the pleased old man and went out into the town. They found a little park and sat down on a seat. They were longing to discuss all that Tucky had told them.

'It's most mysterious. I can't understand it.'

'It's jolly queer,' said Dick. 'No trains run there now – the tunnel's not been used for ages – and Olly's Yard must have been derelict for years.'

'And yet – there appear to be trains that come and go!' said Julian.

'Then – they *must* be spook-trains,' said Anne, her eyes wide and puzzled. 'Julian – they must be, mustn't they?'

'Looks like it,' said Julian. 'It's most mysterious. I can't understand it.'

'Ju,' said Dick, suddenly. 'I know what we'll do! We'll wait one night again till we see the spook-train come out of the tunnel to the yard. Then one of us can sprint off to the *other* end of the tunnel – it's only about a mile long – and wait for it to come out the other side! Then we'll find out why a train still runs from Kilty Vale to Olly's Yard through that old tunnel.'

'Jolly good idea,' said Julian, thrilled. 'What about tonight? If Jock comes, he can go, too. If he doesn't, just you and I will go. *Not* George.'

They all felt excited. Anne wondered if she would be brave enough to go too, but she knew that when the night came she wouldn't feel half as brave as she did now! No, she wouldn't go. There was really no need for her to join in this adventure at present. It hadn't even turned out to be a proper one yet – it was only an unsolved mystery!

George hadn't come back from her walk when they reached the camp. They waited for her, and at last she appeared with Timmy, looking tired out.

'Sorry I was an ass this morning,' she said at once. 'I've walked my temper off! Don't know what came over me.'

'That's all right,' said Julian amiably. 'Forget it.'

They were all very glad that George had recovered her temper, for she was a very prickly person indeed when she was angry. She was rather subdued and said nothing at all about spook-trains or tunnels. So they said nothing either.

The night was fine and clear. Stars shone out brilliantly again in the sky. The children said good night to Mr Luffy at ten o'clock and got into their sleeping-bags. Julian and Dick did not mean to go exploring till midnight, so they lay and talked quietly.

About eleven o'clock they heard somebody moving cautiously outside. They wondered if it was Jock, but he did not call out to them. Who could it be?

Then Julian saw a familiar head outlined against the starlit sky. It was George. But what in the world was she doing? He couldn't make it out at all. Whatever it was, she wasn't making any noise over it, and she obviously thought the boys were asleep. Julian gave a nice little snore or two just to let her go on thinking so.

At last she disappeared. Julian waited a few minutes and then put his head cautiously out of the tent opening. He felt about, and his fingers brushed against some string. He grinned to himself and got back into the tent.

'I've found out what George was doing,' he whispered. 'She's put string across the entrance of our tent, and I bet it runs to her tent – and she's tied it to her big toe or something, so that if we go out without her she'll feel the pull of the string when we go through it – and wake up and follow us!'

'Good old George,' chuckled Dick. 'Well, she'll be unlucky. We'll squeeze out under the sides of the tent!'

Which was what they did do at about a minute past twelve! They didn't disturb George's string at all. They were out on the heather and away down the slope while George was sleeping soundly in her tent beside Anne, waiting for the pull on her toe which didn't come. Poor George!

The boys arrived at the deserted railway yard and looked to see if Wooden-Leg Sam's candle was alight. It was. So the spook-train hadn't come along *that* night, yet.

They were just scrambling down to the yard when they heard the train coming. There was the same rumbling noise as before, muffled by the tunnel – and then out of the tunnel, again with no lamps, came the spook-train, clanking on its way to the yard!

'Quick, Dick! You sprint off to the tunnel opening and watch for the train to go back in again. And I'll find my way across the moor to the other end of the tunnel. There was a path marked on that old map, and I'll follow that!' Julian's words tumbled over each other in his excitement. 'I'll jolly well watch for the spook-train to complete its journey, and see if it vanishes into thin air or what!'

And off he went to find the path that led over the moors to the other end of the tunnel. He meant to see what happened the other end if he had to run all the way!

14 Jock comes to camp

Julian found the path quite by chance and went along it as fast as he could. He used his torch, for he did not think he would meet anyone out on such a lonely way at that time of night. The path was very much overgrown, but he could follow it fairly easily, even running at times.

'If that spook-train stops about twenty minutes in the yard again, as if did before, it will give me just about time to reach the other end of the tunnel,' panted Julian. 'I'll be at Kilty's Yard before it comes.'

It seemed a very long way. But at last the path led downwards, and some way below him Julian could see what might be a railway yard. Then he saw that big sheds were built there – or what looked like big sheds in the starlight.

He remembered what the old porter had said. Kilty's Yard was used for something else now – maybe the lines had been taken up. Maybe even the tunnel had been stopped up, too. He slipped quickly down the path and came into what had once been the old railway yard. Big buildings loomed up on every side. Julian thought they must be workshops of some kind. He switched his torch on and off very quickly, but the short flash had shown him what he was looking for – two pairs of railway lines. They were old and rusty, but he knew they must lead to the tunnel.

He followed them closely, right up to the black mouth of the dark tunnel. He couldn't see inside at all. He switched his torch on and off quickly. Yes – the lines led right inside the tunnel. Julian stopped and wondered what to do.

'I'll sneak into the tunnel a little way and see if it's bricked up anywhere,' he thought. So in he went, walking between one pair of lines. He put on his torch, certain that no one would see its light and challenge him to say what he was doing out so late at night.

The tunnel stretched before him, a great yawning hole, disappearing into deep blackness. It was certainly not bricked up. Julian saw a little niche in the brickwork of the tunnel and decided to crouch in it. It was one of the niches made for workmen to stand in when trains went by in the old days.

Julian crouched down in the dirty old niche and waited. He glanced at the luminous face of his watch. He had been twenty minutes getting here. Maybe the train would be along in a few minutes. He would be very, very close to it! Julian couldn't help wishing that Dick was with him. It was so eerie waiting there in the dark for a mysterious train that apparently belonged to no one and came and went from nowhere to nowhere!

He waited and he waited. Once he thought he heard a rumble far away down the tunnel, and he held his breath, feeling certain that the train was coming. But it didn't come. Julian waited for half an hour and still the train had not appeared. What had happened to it?

'I'll wait another ten minutes and then I'm going,' Julian decided. 'I've had about enough of hiding in a dark, dirty tunnel waiting for a train that doesn't come! Maybe it has decided to stay in Olly's Yard for the night.'

After ten minutes he gave it up. He left the tunnel, went into Kilty's Yard and then up the path to the moors. He hurried along it, eager to see if Dick was at the other end of the tunnel. Surely he would wait there till Julian came back!

Dick was there, tired and impatient. When he saw a quick flash from Julian's torch he answered it with his own. The two boys joined company thankfully.

'You *have* been ages!' said Dick, reproachfully. 'What happened? The spook-train went back into the tunnel ages and ages ago. It only stayed about twenty minutes in the yard again.'

'Went back into the tunnel!' exclaimed Julian. 'Did it really? Well, it never came out the other side! I waited for ages. I never even heard it – though I did hear a very faint rumble once, or thought I did.'

The boys fell silent, puzzled and mystified. What sort of a train was this that puffed out of a tunnel at dead of night, and went back again, but didn't appear out of the other end?

'I suppose the entrance to that second tunnel the porter told us about *is* really bricked up?' said Julian at last. 'If it wasn't, the train could go down there, of course.'

'Yes. That's the only solution, if the train's a real one and not a spook one,' agreed Dick. 'Well, we can't go exploring the tunnels now – let's wait and do it in the daytime. I've had enough tonight!'

Julian had had enough too. In silence the two boys went back to camp. They quite forgot the string in front of their tent, and scrambled right through it. They go into the sleeping-bags thankfully.

The string, fastened to George's big toe through a hole she had cut in her sleeping-bag, pulled hard, and George woke up with a jump. Timmy was awake, having heard the boys come back. He licked George when she sat up.

George had not undressed properly. She slipped quickly out of her bag and crawled out of her tent. Now she would catch the two boys going off secretly and follow them!

But there was no sign or sound of them anywhere around. She crawled silently to their tent. Both boys had fallen asleep immediately, tired out with their midnight trip. Julian snored a little, and Dick breathed so deeply that George could quite well hear him as she crouched outside, listening. She was very puzzled. Someone had pulled at her toe – so somebody must have scrambled through that string. After listening for a few minutes, she gave it up and went back to her tent.

In the morning, George was furious! Julian and Dick related their night's adventure, and George could hardly believe that once again they had gone without her – and that they had managed to get away without disturbing the string! Dick saw George's face and couldn't help laughing.

'Sorry, old thing. We discovered your little trick and avoided it when we set out – but blessed if we didn't forget all about it coming back. We must have given your toe a frightful tug. Did we? I suppose you *did* tie the other end of the string to your toe?'

George looked as if she could throw all the breakfast things at him. Fortunately for everyone, Jock arrived at that moment. He didn't wear his usual beaming smile but seemed rather subdued.

'Hallo, Jock!' said Julian. 'Just in time for a spot of breakfast. Sit down and join us.'

'I can't,' said Jock. 'I've only a few minutes.

And she walked off with Timmy, not saying where she was going.

Listen. Isn't it rotten? – I'm to go away and stay with my stepfather's sister for two weeks! Two weeks! You'll be gone when I come back, won't you?'

'Yes. But, Jock – *why* have you got to go away?' said Dick, surprised. 'Has there been a row or something?'

'I don't know,' said Jock. 'Mum won't say, but she looks pretty miserable. My stepfather's in a frightful temper. It's my opinion they want me out of the way for some reason. I don't know this sister of my stepfather's very well – only met her once – but she's pretty awful.'

'Well – come over here and stay with us, if they want to get rid of you,' said Julian, sorry for Jock. Jock's face brightened.

'I *say* – that's a fine idea!' he said.

'Smashing,' agreed Dick. 'Well, I don't see what's to stop you. If they want to get rid of you, it can't matter where you go for a fortnight. We'd love to have you.'

'Right. I'll come,' said Jock. 'I'll not say a word about it, though, to my stepfather. I'll let Mum into the secret. She was going to take me away today, but I'll just tell her I'm coming to you instead. I don't think she'll split on me, and I hope she'll square things with my step-aunt.'

Jock's face beamed again now. The others beamed back, even George, and Timmy wagged his tail. It would be nice to have Jock – and what a lot they had to tell him.

He went off to break the news to his mother, while the others washed up and cleared things away. George became sulky again when Jock was gone. She simply could not or would not realise that Julian meant what he said!

When they began to discuss everything that had happened the night before, George refused to listen. 'I'm not going to bother about your stupid spook-trains any more,' she said. 'You wouldn't let me join you when I wanted to, and now I shan't take any interest in the matter.'

And she walked off with Timmy, not saying where she was going.

'Well – let her go,' said Julian, exasperated and cross. 'What does she expect me to do? Climb down and say we'll let her come the next night we go?'

'We said we'd go in the daytime,' said Dick. 'She could come then, because if Anne doesn't want to come it won't matter leaving her here alone in the daytime.'

'You're right,' said Julian. 'Let's call her back and tell her.' But by that time George was out of hearing.

'She's taken sandwiches,' said Anne. 'She means to be gone all day. Isn't she an idiot?'

Jock came back after a time, with two rugs and an extra jersey and more food. 'I had hard work to persuade Mum,' he said. 'But she said yes at last. Though mind you, I'd have come anyhow! I'm not going to be shoved about by my stepfather just out of spite. I *say* – isn't this sport! I never thought I'd be camping out with you. If there isn't room in your tent for me, Julian, I can sleep out on the heather.'

'There'll be room,' said Julian. 'Hallo, Mr Luffy! You've been out early!'

Mr Luffy came up and glanced at Jock. 'Ah, is this your friend from the farm? How do you do? Come to spend a few days with us? I see you have an armful of rugs!'

'Yes. Jock's coming to camp a bit with us,' said Julian. 'Look at all the food he's brought. Enough to stand a siege!'

'It is indeed,' said Mr Luffy. 'Well, I'm going to go through some of my specimens this morning. What are you going to do?'

'Oh, mess about till lunchtime,' said Julian. 'Then we might go for a walk.'

Mr Luffy went back to his tent and they could hear him whistling softly as he set to work. Suddenly Jock sat up straight and looked alarmed.

'What's the matter?' asked Dick. Then he heard what Jock had heard. A shrill whistle blown loudly by somebody some way off.

'That's my stepfather's whistle,' said Jock. 'He's whistling for me. Mum must have told him, or else he's found out I've come over here.'

'Quick – let's scoot away and hide,' said Anne. 'If you're not here he can't take you back! Come on! Maybe he'll get tired of looking for you, and go.'

Nobody could think of a better idea, and certainly nobody wanted to face a furious Mr Andrews. All four shot down the slope and made their way to where the heather was high and thick. They burrowed into it and lay still, hidden by some high bracken.

Mr Andrew's voice could soon be heard, shouting for Jock, but no Jock appeared. Mr Andrews came out by Mr Luffy's tent. Mr Luffy, surprised at the shouting, put his head out of his tent to see what it was all about. He didn't like the look of Mr Andrews at all.

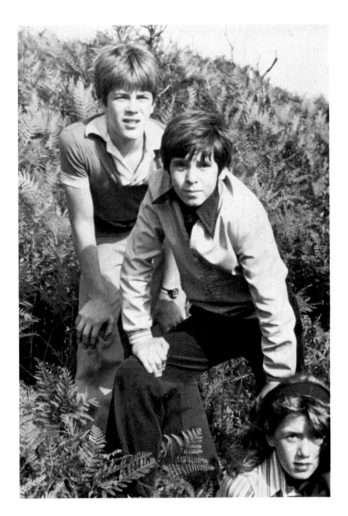

Mr Andrews' voice could soon be heard, shouting for Jock . . .

'Where's Jock?' Mr Andrews demanded, scowling at him.

'I really do not know,' said Mr Luffy.

'He's got to come back,' said Mr Andrews, roughly. 'I won't have him hanging about here with those kids.'

'What's wrong with them?' inquired Mr Luffy. 'I must say I find them very well-behaved and pleasant-mannered.'

Mr Andrews stared at Mr Luffy, and put him down as a silly, harmless old fellow who would probably help him to get Jock back if he went about it the right way.

'Now look here,' said Mr Andrews. 'I don't know who you are, but you must be a friend of the children's. And if so, then I'd better warn you they're running into danger. See?'

'Really? In what way?' asked Mr Luffy, mildly and disbelievingly.

'Well, there's bad and dangerous places about these moorlands,' said Mr Andrews. 'Very bad. I know them. And those children have been messing about in them. See? And if Jock comes here, he'll start messing about too, and I don't want him to get into any danger. It would break his mother's heart.'

'Quite,' said Mr Luffy.

'Well, will you talk to him and send him back?' said Mr Andrews. 'That railway yard now – that's a most dangerous place. And folks do say that there's spook-trains there. I wouldn't want Jock to be mixed up in anything of that sort.'

'Quite,' said Mr Luffy again, looking closely at Mr Andrews. 'You seem very concerned about this – er – railway yard.'

'Me? Oh, no,' said Mr Andrews. 'Never been near the horrible place. I wouldn't want to see spook-trains – make me run a mile! It's just that I don't want Jock to get into danger. I'd be most obliged if you'd talk to him and send him home, when they all come back from wherever they are.'

'Quite,' said Mr Luffy again, most irritatingly. Mr Andrews gazed at Mr Luffy's bland face and suddenly wished he could smack it. 'Quite, quite, quite!' Gr-r-r-r-r-r!

15 George has an adventure

George had gone off with one fixed idea in her mind. She was going to find out something about that mysterious tunnel! She thought she would walk over the moorlands to Kilty's Yard, and see what she could see there. Maybe she could walk right back through the tunnel itself!

She soon came to Olly's Yard. There it lay below her, with Wooden-Leg Sam pottering about. She went down to speak to him. He didn't see or hear her coming and jumped violently when she called to him.

He swung round, squinting at her fiercely. 'You clear off!' he shouted. 'I've been told to keep you children outa here, see? Do you want me to lose my job?'

'Who told you to keep us out?' asked George, puzzled as to who could have known they had been in the yard.

He turned and went away. When he had gone for some time, and was a small speck in the distance, Mr Luffy called loudly.

'He's gone! Please send Jock here so that I can – er – address a few words to him.'

Four children appeared from their heathery hiding-place. Jock went over to Mr Luffy, looking mutinous.

'I just wanted to say,' said Mr Luffy, 'that I quite understand why you want to be away from your stepfather, and that I consider it's no business of mine where you go in order to get away from him!'

Jock grinned. 'Oh, thanks awfully,' he said. 'I thought you were going to send me back!' He rushed over to the others. 'It's all right,' he said. 'I'm going to stay. And, I say – what about going and exploring down that tunnel after lunch? We *might* find that spook-train then!'

'Good idea!' said Julian. 'We will! Poor old George – she'll miss that little adventure too!'

'*He* did, see?' said the old man. He rubbed his eyes, and then peered at George short-sightedly again. 'Bruck me glasses,' he said.

'Who's "he" – the person who told you to keep us out?' said George.

But the old watchman seemed to have one of his sudden queer changes of temper again. He bent down and picked up a large cinder. He was about to fling it at George when Timmy gave a loud and menacing growl. Sam dropped his arm.

'You clear out,' he said. 'You don't want to get a poor old man like me into trouble, do you? You look a nice kind boy you do. You wouldn't get Wooden-Leg Sam into trouble, would you?'

George turned to go. She decided to take the path that led to the tunnel and peep inside. But when she got there there was nothing to see. She didn't feel that she wanted to walk all alone inside that dark mouth, so she took the path that Julian had taken the night before, over the top of the tunnel. But she left it half-way to look at a curious bump that jutted up from the heather just there.

She scraped away at the heather and found something hard beneath. She pulled at it but it would not give. Timmy, thinking she was obligingly digging for rabbits, came to help. He scrambled below the heather – and then he suddenly gave a bark of fright and disappeared!

George screamed: 'Timmy! What have you done? Where are you?'

To her enormous relief she heard Timmy's bark some way down. Where *could* he be? She called again, and once more Timmy barked.

George tugged at the tufts of heather, and then suddenly she saw what the curious mound was. It was a built-up vent-hole for the old tunnel – a place where the smoke came curling out in the days when trains ran there often. It had been barred across with iron, but the bars has rusted and fallen in, and heather had grown thickly over them.

'Oh, Timmy – you must have fallen down the vent,' said George, anxiously. 'But not very far down. Wait a bit and I'll see what I can do. If only the others were here to help!'

But they weren't, and George had to work all by herself to try and get down to the broken bars. It took her a very long time, but at last she had them exposed, and saw where Timmy had fallen down.

He kept giving short little barks, as if to say: 'It's all right. I can wait. I'm not hurt!'

George had to sit down and take a rest after her efforts. She was hungry, but she said to herself that she would *not* eat till she had somehow got down to Timmy, and found out where he was. Soon she began her task again.

She climbed down through the fallen-in vent. It was very difficult, and she was terrified of the rusty old iron bars breaking off under her weight. But they didn't.

Once down in the vent she discovered steps made of great iron nails projecting out. Some of them had thin rungs across. There had evidently once been a ladder up to the top of the vent. Most of the rungs had gone, but the iron nails that supported them still stood in the brick walls of the old round vent. She heard Timmy give a little bark. He was quite near her now.

Cautiously she went down the great hole. Her foot touched Timmy. He had fallen on a collection of broken iron bars, which, caught in part of the old iron ladder, stuck out from it, and made a rough landing-place for the dog to fall on.

'Oh, Timmy,' said George, horrified. 'However am I going to get you out of here? This hole goes right down into the tunnel.'

She couldn't possibly pull Timmy up the hole. It was equally impossible to get him down. He could never climb down the iron ladder, especially as it had so many rungs missing.

George was in despair. 'Oh, Timmy! Why did I lose my temper and walk out on the others to do some exploring all by myself? Don't fall, Timmy. You'll break your legs if you do.'

Timmy had no intention of falling. He was frightened, but so far his curious landing-place felt firm. He kept quite still.

'Listen, Tim,' said George, at last. 'The only thing I can think of is to climb down round it somehow and see how far it is to the tunnel itself. There might even be someone there to help! No, that's silly. There can't be. But I might find an old rope – anything – that I could use to help you down with. Oh, dear, what a horrible nightmare!'

George gave Timmy a reassuring pat, and then began to feel about for the iron rungs with her feet. Further down they were all there, and it was easy to climb lower and lower. She was soon down in the tunnel itself. She had her torch with her and switched it on. Then she nearly gave a scream of horror.

Just near to her was a silent train! She could almost touch the engine. Was it – could it be – the spook-train itself? George stared at it, breathing fast.

It looked very, very old and out-of-date. It was smaller than the trains she was used to – the engine was smaller and so were the trucks. The funnel was longer and the wheels were different from those of ordinary trains. George stared at the silent train by the light of her torch, her mind in a muddle. She really didn't know *what* to think!

It *must* be the spook-train! It had come from this tunnel the night before, and had gone back again – and it hadn't run all the way through to Kilty's Yard, because Julian had watched for it, and it hadn't come out there. No – it had run here, to the middle of the dark tunnel, and there it stood, waiting for night so that it might run again.

George shivered. This train belonged to years and years ago! Who drove it at night? Did anybody? Or did it run along without a driver, remembering its old days and old ways? No – that was silly. Trains didn't think or remember. George shook herself and remembered Timmy.

And just at that very moment, poor Timmy lost his foot-hold on the iron bars, and fell! He had stretched out to listen for George, his foot had slipped – and now he was hurtling down the vent! He gave a mournful howl.

He struck against part of the ladder and that stopped his headlong fall for a moment. But down he went again, scrabbling as he fell, trying to get hold of something to save himself.

George heard him howl and knew he was falling. She was so horror-stricken that she simply couldn't move. She stood there at the bottom of the vent like a statue, not even breathing.

Timmy fell with a thump beside her, and a groan was jerked out of him. In a trice George was down by him on her knees. 'Timmy! Are you hurt? Are you alive? Oh, Timmy, say something!'

'Woof,' said Timmy, and got up rather unsteadily on his four legs. He had fallen on a pile of the softest soot! The smoke of many, many years had sooted the walls of the vent, and the weather had sent it down to the bottom, until quite a pile had collected at one side. Timmy had fallen plump in the middle of it, and almost buried himself. He shook himself violently, and soot flew out all over George.

She didn't know or care. She hugged him, and her face and clothes grew as black as soot! She felt about and found the soft pile that had saved Timmy from being hurt.

'It's soot! I came down the other side of the vent, so I didn't know the soot was there. Oh, Timmy, what a bit of luck for you! I thought you'd be killed – or at least badly hurt,' said George.

He licked her sooty nose and didn't like the taste of it.

George stood up. She didn't like the idea of climbing up that horrid vent again – and, anyway, Timmy couldn't. The only thing to do was to walk out of the tunnel. She wouldn't have fancied walking through the tunnel before, in case she met the spook-train – but here it was, close beside her, and she had been so concerned about Timmy that she had quite forgotten it.

Timmy went over to the engine and smelt the wheels. Then he jumped up into the cab. Somehow the sight of Timmy doing that took away all George's fear. If Timmy could jump up into the spook-train, there couldn't be much for her to be afraid of!

She decided to examine the trucks. There were four of them, all covered trucks. Shining her torch, she climbed up into one of them, pulling Timmy up behind her. She expected to find it quite empty, unloaded many, many years ago by long-forgotten railwaymen.

But it was loaded with boxes! George was surprised. Why did a spook-train run about with boxes in it? She shone her torch on to one – and then quickly switched it out!

She had heard a noise in the tunnel. She crouched down in the truck, put her hand on Timmy's collar, and listened. Timmy listened, too, the hackles rising on his neck.

It was a clanging noise. Then there came a bang. Then a light shone out, and the tunnel was suddenly as bright as day!

The light came from a great lamp in the side of the tunnel. George peeped cautiously out through a crack in the truck. She saw that this place must be where the tunnel forked. One fork went on to Kilty's Yard – but surely the other fork was supposed to be bricked up? George followed the lines with her eyes. One set went on down the tunnel to Kilty's Yard, the other set ran straight into a great wall, which was built across the second tunnel, that once led to Roker's Yard.

'Yes – it *is* bricked up, just as the old porter told Julian,' said George to herself. And then she stared in the greatest amazement, clutching the side of the truck, hardly believing her eyes.

Part of the wall was opening before her! Before her very eyes, a great mass of it slid back in the centre of the wall – back and back – until a queer-shaped opening, about the size of the train itself, showed in the thick wall. George gasped. Whatever could be happening?

A man came through the opening. George felt sure she had seen him before somewhere. He came up to the engine of the train and swung himself into the cab.

There were all sorts of sounds then from the cab. What was the man doing? Starting the fire to run the train? George did not dare to try and see. She was trembling now, and Timmy pressed himself against her to comfort her.

Then came another set of noises – steam noises. The man must be going to start the engine moving. Smoke came from the funnel. More noises, and some clanks and clangs.

It suddenly occurred to George that the man might be going to take the train through that little opening in the bricked-up wall. Then – supposing he shut the wall up again – George would be a prisoner! She would be in the truck, hidden behind that wall, and the wall would be closed so that she couldn't escape.

'I must get out before it's too late,' thought George, in a panic. 'I only hope the man doesn't see me!'

But just as she was about to try and get out, the engine gave a loud 'choo-choo', and began to move backwards! It ran down the lines a little way, then forward again, and this time its wheels were on the set of lines that led to the second tunnel, where the small opening now showed so clearly in the wall.

George didn't dare to get out of the moving train. So there she crouched as the engine steamed quickly to the hole in the wall that stretched right across the other tunnel. That hole just fitted it! It must have been made for it, thought George, as the train moved through it.

The train went right through and came out in another tunnel. Here there was a bright light, too. George peered out through the crack. There was more than a tunnel here! What looked like vast caves stretched away on each side of the tunnel, and men lounged about in them. Who on earth were they, and what were they doing with that old train?

There was a curious noise at the back of the train. The hole in the stout brick wall closed up once more! Now there was no way in or out. 'It's like the Open-Sesame trick in Ali Baba and the Forty Thieves,' thought George. 'And, like Ali Baba, I'm in the cave – and don't know the way to get myself out! Thank goodness Timmy is with me!'

The train was now at a standstill. Behind it was the thick wall – and then George saw that in front of it was a thick wall, too! This tunnel must be bricked up in two places – and in between was this extraordinary cavern, or whatever it was. George puzzled her head over the strange place, but couldn't make head or tail of it.

'Well! Whatever would the others say if they knew you and I were actually in the spook-train itself, tucked away in its hiding-place where nobody in the world can find it?' whispered George to Timmy. 'What are we to do, Timmy?'

Timmy wagged his tail cautiously. He didn't understand all this. He wanted to lie low for a bit and see how things turned out.

'We'll wait till the men have gone away, Timmy,' whispered George. 'That is, if they ever do! Then we'll get out and see if we can manage that Open-Sesame entrance and get away. We'd better tell Mr Luffy about all this. There's something very queer and very mysterious here – and we've fallen headlong into it!'

16 In the tunnel again

Jock was really enjoying himself at the camp. He had a picnic lunch with the others, and ate as much as they did, looking very happy. Mr Luffy joined them, and Jock beamed at him, feeling that he was a real friend.

'Where's George?' asked Mr Luffy.

'Gone off by herself,' said Julian.

'Have you quarrelled, by any chance?' said Mr Luffy.

'A bit,' said Julian. 'We have to let George get over it by herself, Mr Luffy. She's like that.'

'Where's she gone?' said Mr Luffy, helping himself to a tomato. 'Why isn't she back to dinner?'

'She's taken hers with her,' said Anne. 'I feel a bit worried about her, somehow. I hope she's all right.'

Mr Luffy looked alarmed. 'I feel a bit worried myself,' he said. 'Still, she's got Timmy with her.'

'We're going off on a bit of exploring,' said Julian, when they had all finished eating. 'What are *you* going to do, Mr Luffy?'

'I think I'll come with you,' said Mr Luffy, unexpectedly. The children's hearts sank. They couldn't possibly go exploring for spook-trains in the tunnel if Mr Luffy was with them.

'Well – I don't think it will be very interesting for you, sir,' said Julian, rather feebly. However, Mr Luffy took the hint and realised he wasn't wanted that afternoon.

'Right,' he said. 'In that case I'll stay here and mess about.'

The children sighed with relief. Anne cleared up, with Jock helping her, and then they called good-bye to Mr Luffy and set off, taking their tea with them.

Jock was full of excitement. He was so pleased to be with the others, and he kept thinking of sleeping in the camp that night – what fun it would be! Good old Mr Luffy, taking his side like that. He bounded after the others joyfully as they went off to the old railway yard.

Wooden-Leg Sam was pottering about there as

usual. They waved to him, but he didn't wave back. Instead he shook his fist at them and tried to bawl in his husky voice: 'You clear out! Trespassing, that's what you are. Don't you come down here or I'll chase you!'

'Well, we won't go down then,' said Dick, with a grin. 'Poor old man – thinking of chasing us with that wooden leg of his. We won't give him the chance. We'll just walk along here, climb down the lines and walk up them to the tunnel.'

Which is what they did, much to the rage of poor Sam. He yelled till his voice gave out, but they took no notice, and walked quickly up the lines. The mouth of the tunnel looked very round and black as they came near.

'Now we'll jolly well walk right through this tunnel and see where that spook-train is that came out of it the other night,' said Julian. 'It didn't come out the other end, so it *must* be somewhere in the middle of the tunnel.'

'If it's a real spook-train, it might completely disappear,' said Anne, not liking the look of the dark tunnel at all. The others laughed.

'It won't have disappeared,' said Dick. 'We shall come across it somewhere, and we'll examine it thoroughly and try and find out exactly what it is, and why it comes and goes in such a mysterious manner.'

They walked into the black tunnel, and switched on their torches, which made little gleaming paths in front of them. They walked up the middle of one pair of lines, Julian in front keeping a sharp look-out for anything in the shape of a train!

The lines ran on and on. The children's voices sounded queer and echoing in the long tunnel. Anne kept close to Dick, and half wished she hadn't come. Then she remembered that George had called her a coward, and she put up her head determined not to show that she was scared.

Jock talked almost without stopping. 'I've never done anything like this in my life. I call this a proper adventure, hunting for spook-trains in a dark tunnel. It makes me feel nice and shivery all over. I do hope we find the train. It simply *must* be here somewhere!'

They walked on and on and on. But there was no sign of any train. They came to where the tunnel forked into the second one, that used to run to Roker's Vale. Julian flashed his torch on the enormous brick wall that stretched across the second tunnel.

'Yes, it's well and truly bricked up,' he said. 'So that only leaves this tunnel to explore. Come on.'

They went on again, little knowing that George and Timmy were behind that brick wall, hidden in a truck of the spook-train itself! They walked on and on down the lines, and found nothing interesting at all.

The saw a little round circle of bright light some way in front of them. 'See that?' said Julian. 'That must be the end of this tunnel – the opening that goes into Kilty's Yard. Well – if the train isn't between here and Kilty's Yard, it's gone!'

In silence they walked down the rest of the tunnel, and came out into the open air. Workshops were built all over Kilty's Yard. The entrance to the tunnel was weed-grown and neglected. Weeds grew even across the lines there.

'Well, no train has been out of this tunnel here for years,' said Julian, looking at the thick weeds. 'The wheels would have chopped the weeds to bits.'

'It's extraordinary,' said Dick, puzzled. 'We've been right through the tunnel – and there's no train there at all – yet we know it goes in and out of it. What's happened to it?'

'It *is* a spook-train,' said Jock, his face red with excitement. 'Must be. It only exists at night, and then comes out on its lines, like it used to do scores of years ago.'

'I don't like thinking that,' said Anne, troubled. 'It's a horrid thought.'

'What are we going to do now?' said Julian. 'We seem to have come to a blank. No train – nothing to see – empty tunnel. What a dull end to an adventure.'

'Let's walk back all the way again,' said Jock – he wanted to squeeze as much out of this adventure as he could. 'I know we shan't see the train this time any more than we did the last time – but you never know!'

'I'm not coming through that tunnel again,' said Anne. 'I want to be out in the sun. I'll walk over the top of the tunnel, along the path there that Julian took the other night – and you three can walk back, and meet me at the other end.'

'Right,' said Julian, and the three boys disappeared into the dark tunnel. Anne ran up the path that led alongside the top of it. How good it was to be in the open air again! That horrid tunnel! She ran along gaily, glad to be out in the sun.

She got to the other end of the tunnel quite quickly, and sat down on the path above the yard to wait for the others. She looked for Wooden-Leg

Sam. He was nowhere to be seen. Perhaps he was in his little hut.

She hadn't been there for more than two minutes when something surprising happened. A car came bumping slowly down the rough track to the yard! Anne sat up and watched. A man got out – and Anne's eyes almost fell out of her head. Why, it was – surely it was Mr Andrews, Jock's stepfather!

He went over to Sam's hut and threw open the door. Anne could hear the sound of voices. Then she heard another noise – the sound of a heavy lorry coming. She saw it come cautiously down the steep, rough track. It ran into an old tumble-down shed and stayed there. Then three men came out and Anne stared at them. Where had she seen them before?

'Of course! They're the farm labourers at Jock's farm!' she thought. 'But what are they doing here? How very queer!'

Mr Andrews joined the men and, to Anne's dismay, they began to walk up the lines to the tunnel! Her heart almost stopped. Goodness, Julian, Dick and Jock were still in that tunnel, walking through it. They would bump right into Mr Andrews and his men – and then what would happen? Mr Andrews had warned them against going there, and had ordered Jock not to go.

Anne stared at the four men walking into the far-off mouth of the tunnel. What could she do? How could she warn the boys? She couldn't! She would just have to stay there and wait for them to come out – probably chased by a furious Mr Andrews and the other men. Oh dear, dear – if they were caught they would probably all get an awful whacking! What *could* she do?

'I can only wait,' thought poor Anne. 'There's nothing else to do. Oh, do come, Julian, Dick and Jock. I daren't do anything but wait for you.'

She waited and waited. It was now long past tea-time. Julian had the tea, so there was nothing for Anne to eat. Nobody came out of the tunnel. Not a sound was heard. Anne at last decided to go down and ask Wooden-Leg Sam a few questions. So, rather afraid, the little girl set off down to the yard.

Sam was in his hut, drinking cocoa, and looking very sour. Something had evidently gone wrong. When he saw Anne's shadow across the doorway he got up at once, shaking his fist.

'What, you children again! Didn't you go into that there tunnel this afternoon, and didn't I go up

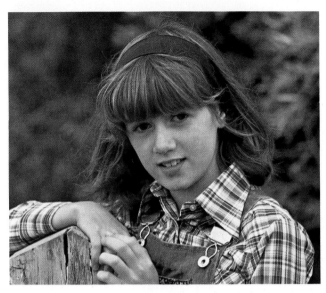

'I can only wait,' thought poor Anne.

and telephone to Mr Andrews to come and catch you all, poking your noses in all the time? How did you get out of that tunnel? Are the others with you? Didn't Mr Andrews catch you, eh?'

Anne listened to all this in horror. So old Sam had actually managed to telephone Mr Andrews, and tell tales of them – so that Jock's stepfather and his men had come to catch them. This was worse then ever.

'You come in here,' said Sam suddenly, and he darted his big arm at her. 'Come on. I don't know where the others are, but I'll get one of you!'

Anne gave a scream and ran away at top speed. Wooden-Leg Sam went after her for a few yards and then gave it up. He bent down and picked up a handful of cinders. A shower of them fell all round Anne, and made her run faster than ever.

She tore up the path to the heather, and was soon on the moors again, panting and sobbing. 'Oh, Julian! Oh, Dick! What's happened to you? Oh, where's George? If only she would come home, she'd be brave enough to look for them, but I'm not. I must tell Mr Luffy. He'll know what to do!'

She ran on and on, her feet catching continually in the tufts of thick heather. She kept falling over and scrambling up again. She now had only one idea in her mind – to find Mr Luffy and tell him every single thing! Yes, she would tell him about the spook-trains and all. There was something queer and important about the whole thing now, and she wanted a grown-up's help.

She staggered on and on. 'Mr Luffy! Oh, Mr Luffy, where are you? MR LUFFY!'

But no Mr Luffy answered her. She came round the gorse bushes she thought were the ones sheltering the camp – but, alas, the camp was not there. Anne had lost her way!

'I'm lost,' said Anne, the tears running down her cheeks. 'But I mustn't get scared. I must try to find the right path now. Oh, dear, I'm quite lost! MR LUFFY!'

Poor Anne. She stumbled on blindly, hoping to come to the camp, calling every now and again. 'Mr Luffy. Can you hear me? MR LUUUUUUFFY!'

17 An amazing find

In the meantime, what had happened to the three boys walking back through the tunnel? They had gone slowly along examining the lines to see if a train could have possibly run along them recently. Few weeds grew in the dark airless tunnel, so they could not tell by those.

But, when they came about half-way, Julian noticed an interesting thing. 'Look,' he said, flashing his torch on to the lines before and behind them. 'See that? The lines are black and rusty behind us now – but here this pair of lines is quite bright – as if they had been used a lot.'

He was right. Behind them stretched black and rusty lines, sometimes buckled in places – but in front of them, stretching to the mouth of the tunnel leading to Olly's Yard, the lines were bright, as if train-wheels had run along them.

'That's queer,' said Dick. 'Looks as if the spook-train ran only from here to Olly's Yard and back. But why? And where in the world is it now? It's vanished into thin air!'

Julian was as puzzled as Dick. Where *could* a train be if it was not in the tunnel? It had obviously run to the middle of the tunnel, and then stopped – but where had it gone now?

'Let's go to the mouth of the tunnel and see if the lines are bright all the way,' said Julian at last. 'We can't discover much here – unless the train suddenly materialises in front of us!'

They went on down the tunnel, their torches flashing on the lines in front of them. They talked earnestly as they went. They didn't see four men waiting for them, four men who crouched in a little niche at the side of the tunnel, waiting there in the dark.

'Well,' said Julian, 'I think –' and then he stopped, because four dark figures suddenly pounced on the three boys and held them fast. Julian gave a shout and struggled, but the man who had hold of him was far too strong to escape from. Their torches were flung to the ground. Julian's broke, and the other two torches lay there, their beams shining on the feet of the struggling company.

It didn't take more than twenty seconds to make each boy a captive, his arms behind his back. Julian tried to kick, but his captor twisted his arm so fiercely that he groaned in pain and stopped his kicking.

'Look here! What's all this about?' demanded Dick. 'Who are you, and what do you think you're doing? We're only three boys exploring an old tunnel. What's the harm in that?'

'Take them all away,' said a voice that everyone recognised at once.

'Mr Andrews! Is it you? cried Julian. 'Set us free. You know us – the boys at the camp. And Jock's here too. What do you think you're doing?'

Mr Andrews didn't answer, but he gave poor Jock a box on the right ear that almost sent him to the ground.

Their captors turned them about, and led them roughly up the tunnel, towards the middle. Nobody had a torch so it was all done in the darkness and the three boys stumbled badly, though the men seemed surefooted enough.

They came to a halt after a time. Mr Andrews left them and Julian heard him go off somewhere to the left. Then there came a curious noise – a bang, a clank, and then a sliding, grating sound. What could be happening? Julian strained his eyes in the darkness, but he could see nothing at all.

He didn't know that Mr Andrews was opening the bricked-up wall through which the train had gone. He didn't know that he and the others were being pushed out of the first tunnel into the other one, through the curious hole in the wall. The three boys were shoved along in the darkness, not daring to protest.

Now they were in the curious place between the two walls which were built right across the place where the second tunnel forked from the first one. The place where the spook-train stood in silence – the place where George was, still hidden in one of the trucks with Timmy! But nobody knew that, of course; not even Mr Andrews guessed that a girl and a dog were listening in a truck near by!

He put on a torch and flashed it in the faces of the three boys, who, although they were not showing any fear, felt rather scared all the same. This was so weird and unexpected, and they had no idea where they were at all.

'You were warned not to go down to that yard,' said the voice of one of the men. 'You were told it was a bad and dangerous place. So it is. And you've got to suffer for not taking heed of the warning! You'll be tied up and left here till we've finished our business. Maybe that'll be three days, maybe it'll be three weeks!'

'Look here – you can't keep us prisoner for all that time!' said Julian, alarmed. 'Why, there will be search parties out for us all over the place! They will be sure to find us.'

'Oh, no they won't,' said the voice. 'Nobody will find you here. Now, Peters – tie 'em up!'

Peters tied the three boys up. They had their legs tied, and their arms too, and were set down roughly against a wall. Julian protested again.

'What are you doing this for? We're quite harmless. We don't know a thing about your business, whatever it is.'

'We're not taking any chances,' said the voice. It was not Mr Andrews's voice, but a firm, strong one, full of determination and a large amount of annoyance.

'What about Mum?' said Jock suddenly, to his stepfather. 'She'll be worried.'

'Well, let her be worried,' said the voice again, answering before Mr Andrews could say a word. 'It's your own fault. You were warned.'

The feet of the four men moved away. Then there came the same noises again as the boys had heard before. They were made by the hole in the wall closing up, but the boys didn't know that. They couldn't imagine what they were. The noises stopped and there was dead silence. There was also pitch darkness. The three boys strained their ears, and felt sure that the men had gone.

'Well! The brutes! Whatever are they up to?' said Julian in a low voice, trying to loosen the ropes round his hands.

'They've got some secret to hide,' said Dick. 'Gosh, they've tied my feet so tightly that the rope is cutting into my flesh.'

'What's going to happen?' came Jock's scared voice. This adventure didn't seem quite so grand to him now.

'Sh!' said Julian suddenly. 'I can hear something!'

They all lay and listened. What was it they could hear?

'It's – it's a dog whining,' said Dick, suddenly.

It was. It was Timmy in the truck with George. He had heard the voices of the boys he knew, and he wanted to get to them. But George, not sure yet that the men had gone, still had her hand on his collar. Her heart beat for joy to think she was alone no longer. The three boys – and Anne, too, perhaps – were there, in the same queer place as she and Timmy were.

The boys listened hard. The whining came again. Then, George let go her hold of Timmy's collar, and he leapt headlong out of the truck. His feet pattered eagerly over the ground. He went straight to the boys in the darkness, and Julian felt a wet tongue licking his face. A warm body pressed against him, and a little bark told him who it was.

'Timmy! I say, Dick – it's Timmy!' cried Julian, in joy. 'Where did he come from? Timmy, is it really you?'

'Woof,' said Timmy, and licked Dick next and then Jock.

'Where's George then?' wondered Dick.

'Here,' said a voice, and out of the truck scrambled George, switching on her torch as she did so. She went over to the boys. 'Whatever's happened? How did you come here? Were you captured or something!'

'Yes,' said Julian. 'But, George – where are we? And what are *you* doing here too? It's like a peculiar dream!'

'I'll cut your ropes first, before I stop to explain anything,' said George, and she took out her sharp knife. In a few moments she had cut the boys' bonds, and they all sat up, rubbing their sore ankles and wrists, groaning.

'Thanks, George! Now I feel fine,' said Julian, getting up. 'Where *are* we? Gracious, is that an engine there? What's it doing here?'

'That, Julian, is the spook-train!' said George, with a laugh. 'Yes, it is, really.'

'But we walked all the way down the tunnel and out of the other end, without finding it,' said

Julian puzzled. 'It's most mysterious.'

'Listen, Ju,' said George. 'You know where that second tunnel is bricked up, don't you? Well, there's a way in through the wall – a whole bit of it moves back in a sort of Open-Sesame manner! The spook-train can run in through the hole, on the rails. Once it's beyond the wall it stops, and the hole is closed up again.'

George switched her torch round to show the astonished boys the wall through which they had come. Then she swung her torch to the big wall opposite. 'See that?' she said. 'There are *two* walls across this second tunnel, with a big space in between – where the spook-train hides! Clever, isn't it?'

'It would be, if I could see any sense in it,' said Julian. 'But I can't. Why should anyone mess about with a silly spook-train at night?'

'That's what we've got to find out,' said George. 'And now's our chance. Look, Julian – look at all the caves stretching out on either side of the tunnel here. They would make wonderful hiding-places!'

'What for?' said Dick. 'I can't make head or tail of this!'

George swung her torch on the three boys and then asked a sudden question: 'I say – where's Anne?'

'Anne! She didn't want to come back with us

through the tunnel, so she ran over the moorlands to meet us at the other end, by Olly's Yard,' said Julian. 'She'll be worried stiff, won't she, when we don't turn up? I only hope she doesn't come wandering up the tunnel to meet us – she'll run into those men if she does.'

Everyone felt worried. Anne hated the tunnel and she would be very frightened if people pounced on her in the darkness. Julian turned to George.

'Swing your torch round and let's see these caves. There doesn't seem to be anyone here now. We could have a snoop round.'

George swung her torch round, and Julian saw vast and apparently fathomless caves stretching out on either side, cut out of the sides of the tunnel. Jock saw something else. By the light of the torch he caught sight of a switch on the wall. Perhaps it opened the hole in the wall.

He crossed to it and pulled it down. Immediately the place was flooded with a bright light. It was a lightswitch he had found. They all blinked in the sudden glare.

'That's better,' said Julian, pleased. 'Good for you, Jock! Now we can see what we're doing.'

He looked at the spook-train standing silently near them on its rails. It certainly looked very old and forgotten – as if it belonged to the last century, not to this.

'It's quite a museum piece,' said Julian, with interest. 'So that's what we heard puffing in and out of the tunnel at night – old Spooky!'

'I hid in that truck there,' said George, pointing, and she told them her own adventure. The boys could hardly believe she had actually puffed into this secret place, hidden on the spook-train itself!

'Come on – now let's look at these caves,' said Dick. They went over to the nearest one. It was packed with crates and boxes of all kinds. Julian pulled one open and whistled.

'All black market stuff, I imagine. Look here – crates of tea – crates of whisky and brandy – boxes and boxes of stuff – goodness knows what! This is a real black market hiding-place!'

The boys explored a little further. The caves were piled high with valuable stuff, worth thousands of pounds.

'All stolen, I suppose,' said Dick. 'But what do they *do* with it? I mean – how do they dispose of it? They bring it here in the train, of course, and hide it – but they must have some way of getting rid of it.'

'Would they repack it on the train and run it back to the yard when they had enough lorries to take it away?' said Julian.

'No!' said Dick. 'Of course not. Let me see – they steal it – pile it on to lorries at night, take it somewhere temporarily . . .'

'Yes – to my mother's farm!' said Jock, in a scared voice. 'All those lorries there in the barn – that's what they're used for! And they come down to Olly's Yard at night and the stuff is loaded in secret on the old train that comes puffing out to meet them – and then it's taken back here and hidden!'

'Wheeeee-ew!' Julian whistled. 'You're right, Jock! That's just what happens. What a cunning plot – to use a perfectly honest little farm as a hiding-place – to stock the farm with black-market men for labourers – no wonder they are such bad workers – and to wait for dark nights to run the stuff down to the yard and load it on the train!'

18 A way of escape

The four children and Timmy went into the big cave. They made their way round piles of boxes, chests and crates, marvelling at the amount the men must have stolen from time to time.

'These aren't man-made caves,' said Julian. 'They're natural. I expect the roof did perhaps fall in where the two tunnels met, and the entrance between them was actually blocked up.'

'But were *two* walls built then?' said Dick.

'Oh, no. We can't guess how it was that this black market hiding-place came into existence,' said Julian, 'but it might perhaps have been known there were caves here – and when someone came prospecting along the tunnel one day, maybe they even found an old train buried under a roof-fall or something like that.'

'And resurrected it, and built another wall secretly for a hiding-place – and used the train for their own purposes!' said Dick. 'Made that secret entrance, too. How ingenious!'

'Or it's possible the place was built during the last war,' said Julian. 'Maybe secret experiments

'Your stepfather must make a lot of money at this game,' said Dick to Jock.

'Yes. That's why he can afford to pour money into the farm,' said Jock, miserably. 'Poor Mum. This will break her heart. All the same, I don't think my stepfather's the chief one in this. There's somebody behind him.'

'Yes,' said Julian, thinking of the mean little Mr Andrews, with his big nose and weak chin. 'There probably is. Now – I've thought of something else. If this stuff is got rid of in any other way except down the tunnel it came up, there must somewhere be a way out of these caves!'

'I believe you're right,' said George. 'And if there is – we'll find it! And what's more, we'll escape that way!'

'Come on!' said Julian, and he switched off the glaring light. 'Your torch will give enough light now. We'll try this cave first. Keep your eyes open, all of you!'

were carried on here – and given up afterwards. The place might have been discovered by the black marketeers then, and used in this clever way. We can't tell!'

They had wandered for a good way in the cave by now, without finding anything of interest beyond the boxes and chests of all kinds of goods. Then they came to where a pile was very neatly arranged, with numbers chalked on boxes that were built up one on top of another. Julian halted.

'Now this looks as if these boxes were about to be shifted off somewhere,' he said. 'All put in order and numbered. Surely the exit must be somewhere here?'

He took George's torch from her and flashed it all round. Then he found what he wanted. The beam of light shone steadily on a strong roughly-made wooden door, set in the wall of the cave. They went over to it in excitement.

'This is what we want!' said Julian. 'I bet this is the exit to some very lonely part of the moors, not far from a road that lorries can come along to collect any goods carried out of here! There are some very deserted roads over these moors, running in the middle of miles of lonely moorland.'

'It's a clever organisation,' said Dick. 'Lorries stored at an innocent farm, full of goods for hiding in the tunnel-caves at a convenient time. The train comes out in the dark to collect the goods, and takes them back here, till the hue and cry after the goods has died down. Then out they go through this door on to the moorlands, down to the lorries which come to collect them and whisk them away to the black market!'

'I told you how I saw Peters late one night, locking up the barn, didn't I?' said Jock, excitedly. 'Well, he must have got the lorry full of stolen goods then – and the next night he loaded them on to the spook-train!'

'That's about it,' said Julian, who had been trying the door to see if he could open it. 'I say, this door's maddening. I can't make it budge an inch. There's no lock that I can see.'

They all shoved hard, but the door would not give at all. It was very stout and strong, though rough and unfinished. Panting and hot, the four of them at last gave it up.

'Do you know what I think?' said Dick. 'I think the beastly thing has got something jammed hard against it on the outside.'

'Sure to have, when you come to think of it,' said Julian. 'It will be well hidden too – heather and bracken and stuff all over it. Nobody would ever find it. I suppose the lorry-drivers come across from the road to open the door when they

want to collect the goods. And shut it and jam it after them.'

'No way of escape there, then?' said George in disappointment.

''Fraid not,' said Julian. George gave a sigh.

'Tired, old thing?' Julian asked kindly. 'Or hungry?'

'Both,' said George.

'Well, we've got some food somewhere, haven't we?' said Julian. 'I remember one of the men slinging my bag in after me. We've not had what we brought for tea yet. What about having a meal now? We can't seem to escape at the moment.'

'Let's have it here,' said George. 'I simply can't go a step further!'

They sat down against a big crate. Dick undid his kit-bag. There were sandwiches, cake and chocolate. The four of them ate thankfully, and wished they had something to wash down the food with. Julian kept wondering about Anne.

'I wonder what she did?' he said. 'She'd wait and wait, I suppose. Then she might go back to camp. But she doesn't know the way very well, and she might get lost. Oh dear – I don't know which would be worse for Anne, being lost on the moor or a prisoner down here with us!'

'Perhaps she's neither,' said Jock, giving Timmy his last bit of sandwich. 'I must say I'm jolly glad to have Timmy. Honest, George, I couldn't believe it when I heard Tim whine, and then heard your voice, too. I thought I must be dreaming.'

They sat where they were for a little longer and then decided to go back to the tunnel where the train was. 'It's just possible we might find the switch that works the Open-Sesame bit,' said Julian. 'We ought to have looked before, really, but I didn't think of it.'

They went back to where the train stood silently on its pair of lines. It seemed such an ordinary old train now, that the children couldn't imagine why they had ever thought it was queer and spooky.

They switched on the light again, then they looked about for any lever or handle that might perhaps open the hole in the wall. There didn't seem to be anything at all. They tried a few switches, but nothing happened.

Then George suddenly came across a big lever low down in the brick wall itself. She tried to move it and couldn't. She called Julian.

'Ju! Come here. I wonder if this has got anything to do with opening that hole?'

The three boys came over to George. Julian

tried to swing the lever down. Nothing happened. He pulled it but it wouldn't move. Then he and Dick pushed it upwards with all their strength.

And hey presto, there came a bang from somewhere, as something heavy shifted, and then a clanking as if machinery was at work. Then came the sliding, grating noise and a great piece of the brick wall moved slowly back, and then swung round sideways and stopped. The way of escape was open!

'Open Sesame!' said Dick, grandly, as the hole appeared.

'Better switch off the light here,' said Julian. 'If there's anyone still in the tunnel they might see the reflection of it on the tunnel-wall beyond, and wonder what it was.'

He stepped back and switched it off, and the place was in darkness again. George put on her torch, and its feeble beam lighted up the way of escape.

'Come on,' said Dick, impatiently, and they all crowded out of the hole. 'We'll make for Olly's Yard.' They began to make their way down the dark tunnel.

'Listen,' said Julian, in a low voice. 'We'd better not talk at all, and we'd better go as quietly as we can. We don't know who may be in or out of this tunnel this evening. We don't want to walk bang into somebody.'

So they said nothing at all, but kept close to one another in single file, walking at the side of the track.

They had not gone more than a quarter of a mile before Julian stopped suddenly. The others bumped into one another, and Timmy gave a little whine as somebody trod on his paw. George's hand went down to his collar at once.

The four of them and Timmy listened, hardly daring to breathe. Somebody was coming up the tunnel towards them! They could see the pin-point of a torch, and hear the distant crunch of footsteps.

'Other way, quick!' whispered Julian, and they all turned. With Jock leading them now, they made their way as quickly and quietly as they could back to the place where the two tunnels met. They passed it and went on towards Kilty's Yard, hoping to get out that way.

But alas for their hopes, a lantern stood some way down the tunnel there, and they did not dare to go on. There might be nobody with the lantern – on the other hand there might. What were they to do?

'They'll see that hole in the wall is open!' suddenly said Dick. 'We left it open. They'll know we've escaped then. We're caught again! They'll come down to find us, and here we'll be!'

They stood still, pressed close together, Timmy growling a little in his throat. Then George remembered something!

'Julian! Dick! We could climb up that vent that I came down,' she whispered. 'The one poor old Timmy fell down. Have we time?'

'Where is the vent?' said Julian, urgently. 'Quick – find it.'

George tried to remember. Yes, it was on the other side of the tunnel – near the place where the two tunnels met. She must look for the pile of soot. How she hoped the little light from her torch would not be seen. Whoever was coming up from Olly's Yard must be almost there by now!

She found the pile of soot that Timmy had fallen into. 'Here it is,' she whispered. 'But, oh Julian! How can we take Timmy?'

'We can't,' said Julian. 'We must hope he'll manage to hide and then slink out of the tunnel by himself. He's quite clever enough.'

He pushed George up the vent first and her feet found the first rungs. Then Jock went up, his nose almost on George's heels. Then Dick – and last of all, Julian. But before he managed to climb the first steps, something happened.

A bright glare filled the tunnel, as someone switched on the light that hung there. Timmy slunk into the shadows and growled in his throat. Then there came a shout.

'Who's opened the hole in the wall? It's open! Who's there?'

It was Mr Andrews's voice. Then came another voice, angry and loud: 'Who's here? Who's opened this place?'

'Those kids can't have moved the lever,' said Mr Andrews. 'We bound them up tightly.'

The men, three of them, went quickly through the hole in the wall. Julian climbed up the first few rungs thankfully. Poor Timmy was left in the shadows at the bottom.

Out came the men at a run. 'They've gone! Their ropes are cut! How could they have escaped? We put Kit down one end of the tunnel and we've been walking up this end. Those kids must be about here somewhere.'

'Or hiding in the caves,' said another voice. 'Peters, go and look, while we hunt here.'

The men hunted everywhere. They had no idea

that the vent was nearby in the wall. They did not see the dog that slunk by them like a shadow, keeping out of their way, and lying down whenever the light from a torch came near him.

George climbed steadily, feeling with her feet for the iron nails whenever she came to broken rungs. Then she came to a stop. Something was pressing on her head. What was it? She put up her hand to feel. It was the collection of broken iron bars that Timmy had fallen on that morning. He had dislodged some of them, and they had then fallen in such a way that they had lodged across the vent, all twined into each other. George could climb no higher. She tried to move the bars, but they were heavy and strong – besides, she was afraid she might bring the whole lot on top of her and the others. They might be badly injured then.

'What's up, George? Why don't you go on?' asked Jock, who was next.

19 What an adventure!

And now, what had happened to Anne? She had stumbled on and on for a long time, shouting to Mr Luffy. And outside his tent Mr Luffy sat, reading peacefully. But, as the evening came, and then darkness, he became very worried indeed about the five children.

He wondered what to do. It was hopeless for one man to search the moors. Half a dozen or more were needed for that! He decided to get his car and go over to Olly's Farm to get the men from there. So off he went.

But when he got there he found no one at home except Mrs Andrews and the little maid. Mrs Andrews looked bewildered and worried.

'What is the matter?' said Mr Luffy gently, as she came running out to the car, looking very troubled.

'Oh, it's you, Mr Luffy,' she said, when he told her who he was. 'I didn't know who you were. Mr Luffy, something queer is happening. All the men

'There's some iron bars across the vent – ones that must have fallen when Timmy fell,' said George. 'I can't go any higher! I daren't pull too hard at the bars.'

Jock passed the message to Dick, and he passed it down to Julian. The four of them came to a full-stop!

'Blow!' said Julian. 'I wish I'd gone up first. What are we to do now?'

What, indeed? The four of them hung there in the darkness, hating the smell of the sooty old vent, miserably uncomfortable on the broken rungs and nails.

'How do you like adventures now, Jock?' asked Dick. 'I bet you wish you were in your own bed at home!'

'I don't!' said Jock. 'I wouldn't miss this for worlds! I always wanted an adventure – and I'm not grumbling at this one!'

have gone – and all the lorries, too. My husband has taken the car – and nobody will tell me anything. I'm so worried.'

Mr Luffy decided not to add to her worries by telling her the children were missing. He just pretended he had come to collect some milk. 'Don't worry,' he said comfortingly to Mrs Andrews. 'You'll find things are all right in the morning, I expect. I'll come and see you then. Now I must be off on an urgent matter.'

He went bumping along the road in his car, puzzled. He had known there was something queer about Olly's Farm, and he had puzzled his brains a good deal over Olly's Yard and the spook-trains. He hoped the children hadn't got mixed up in anything dangerous.

'I'd better go down and report to the police that they're missing,' he thought. 'After all, I'm more or less responsible for them. It's very worrying indeed.'

He told what he knew at the police station, and the sergeant, an intelligent man, at once mustered six men and a police car.

'Have to find those kids,' he said. 'And we'll have to look into this Olly's Farm business, sir, and these here spook-trains, whatever they may be. We've known there was something funny going on, but we couldn't put our finger on it. But we'll find the children first.'

They went quickly up to the moors and the six

men began to fan out to search, with Mr Luffy at the head. And the first thing they found was Anne!

She was still stumbling along, crying for Mr Luffy, but in a very small, weak voice now. When she heard his voice calling her in the darkness she wept for joy.

'Oh, Mr Luffy! You must save the boys,' she begged him. 'They're in that tunnel – and they've been caught by Mr Andrews and his men. I'm sure. They didn't come out and I waited and waited! Do come!'

'I've got some friends here who will certainly come and help,' said Mr Luffy gently. He called the men, and in a few words told them what Anne had said.

'In the tunnel?' said one of them. 'Where the spook-trains run? Well, come on, men, we'll go down there.'

'You stay behind, Anne,' said Mr Luffy. But she wouldn't. So he carried her as he followed the men who were making their way through the heather, down to Olly's Yard. They did not bother with Wooden-Leg Sam. They went straight to the tunnel and walked up it quietly. Mr Luffy was a good way behind with Anne. She refused to stay with him in the yard.

'No,' she said, 'I'm not a coward. Really I'm not. I want to help to rescue the boys. I wish George was here. Where's George?'

Mr Luffy had no idea. Anne clung to his hand, scared but eager to prove that she was not a coward. Mr Luffy thought she was grand!

Meanwhile, Julian and the others had been in the vent for a good while, tired and uncomfortable. The men had searched in vain for them and were now looking closely into every niche at the sides of the tunnel.

And, of course, they found the vent! One of the men shone his light up it. It shone on to poor Julian's feet! The man gave a loud shout that almost made Julian fall off the rung he was standing on.

'Here they are! Up this vent. Who'd have thought it? Come on down or it'll be worse the for you!'

Julian didn't move. George pushed desperately at the iron bars above her head, but she could not move them. One of the men climbed up the vent and caught hold of Julian's foot.

He dragged so hard at it that the boy's foot was forced off the rung. Then the man dragged off the other foot, and Julian found himself hanging by his arms with the man tugging hard at his feet. He could hang on no longer. His tired arms gave way and he fell heavily down, landing half on the man and half on the pile of soot. Another man pounced on Julian at once, while the first climbed up the vent to find the next boy. Soon Dick felt his feet being tugged at, too.

'All right, all right. I'll come down!' he yelled, and climbed down. Then Jock climbed down, too. The men looked at them angrily.

'Giving us a chase like this! Who undid your ropes?' said Mr Andrews, roughly. One of the men put a hand on his arm and nodded up towards the vent. 'Someone else is coming down,' he said. 'We only tied up three boys, didn't we? Who's this, then?'

It was George, of course. She wasn't going to desert the three boys. Down she came, as black as a nigger with soot.

'Another boy!' said the men. 'Where did he come from?'

'Any more up there?' asked Mr Andrews.

'Look and see,' said Julian, and got a box on the ears for his answer.

'Treat 'em rough now,' ordered Peters. 'Teach 'em a lesson, the little pests. Take 'em away.'

The children's hearts sank. The men caught hold of them roughly. Blow! Now they would be made prisoners again.

Suddenly a cry came from down the tunnel: 'Police! Run for it!'

The men dropped the children's arms at once and stood undecided. A man came tearing up the tunnel. 'I tell you the police are coming!' he gasped. 'Are you stone deaf? There's a whole crowd of them. Run for it! Somebody's split on us.'

'Get along to Kilty's Yard!' shouted Peters. 'We can get cars there. Run for it!'

To the children's dismay, the men tore down the tunnel to Kilty's Yard. They would escape! They heard the sound of the men's feet as they ran along the line.

George found her voice. 'Timmy! Where are you? After them, Timmy! Stop them!'

A black shadow came streaking by out of the hole in the wall, where Timmy had been hiding and watching for a chance to come to George. He had heard her voice and obeyed. He raced after the men like a greyhound, his tongue hanging out, panting as he went.

These were the men who had ill-treated George and the others, were they? Aha, Timmy knew how to deal with people like that!

The policemen came running up, and Mr Luffy and Anne came up behind them.

'They've gone down there, with Timmy after them,' shouted George. The men looked at her and gasped. She looked like a black boy. The others were filthy dirty too, with sooty-black faces in the light of the lamp that still shone down from the wall of the tunnel.

'George!' shrieked Anne in delight. 'Julian! Oh, are you all safe? I went back to tell Mr Luffy about you and I got lost. I'm so ashamed!'

'You've nothing to be ashamed of, Anne,' said Mr Luffy. 'You're a grand girl! Brave as a lion!'

From down the tunnel came shouts and yells and loud barks. Timmy was at work! He had caught up the men and launched himself on them one after another, bringing each one heavily to the ground. They were terrified to find a big animal growling and snapping all around them. Timmy held them at bay in the tunnel, not allowing them to go one step further, snapping at any man who dared to go near.

The police ran up. Timmy growled extra fiercely just to let the men know that it was quite impossible to get by him. In a trice each of the men was imprisoned by a pair of strong arms, and they were being told to come quietly.

They didn't go quietly. For one thing Mr Andrews lost his nerve and howled dismally. Jock felt very ashamed of him.

'Shut up,' said a burly policeman. 'We know you're only the miserable little cat's-paw – taking money from the big men to hold your tongue and obey orders.'

Timmy barked as if to say, 'Yes – don't you dare call him a *dog's* paw! That would be too good a name for him!'

'Well, I don't think I ever in my life saw dirtier children,' said Mr Luffy. 'I vote we all go back to my car and I drive the lot of you over to Olly's Farm for a meal and a bath!'

So back they all went, tired, dirty, and also feeling very thrilled.

What a night! They told Anne all that had happened, and she told them her story, too. She almost fell asleep in the car as she talked, she was so tired.

Mrs Andrews was sensible and kind, though upset to hear that her husband had been taken off by the police. She got hot water for baths, and laid a meal for the hungry children.

'I wouldn't worry overmuch, Mrs Andrews,'

said kindly Mr Luffy. 'That husband of yours needs a lesson, you know. This will probably keep him going straight in future. The farm is yours, and you can now hire proper farm-workers who will do what you want them to do. And I think Jock will be happier without a stepfather for the present.'

'You're right, Mr Luffy,' said Mrs Andrews, wiping her eyes quickly. 'Quite right. I'll let Jock help me with the farm, and get it going beautifully. To think that Mr Andrews was in with all those black marketeers! It's that friend of his, you know, who makes him do all this. He's so weak. He knew Jock was snooping about in that tunnel, and that's why he wanted him to go away – and kept making him have a boy here or go out with him. I knew there was something queer going on.'

'No wonder he was worried when Jock took it into his head to go and camp with our little lot,' said Mr Luffy.

'To think of that old yard and tunnel being used again!' said Mrs Andrews. 'And all those tales about spook-trains – and the way they hid that train, and hid all the stuff, too. Why, it's like a fairy tale, isn't it!'

She ran to see if the water was hot for the baths. It was, and she went to call the children, who were in the big bedroom next door. She opened it and looked in. Then she called Mr Luffy upstairs.

He looked in at the door, too. The five, and Timmy, were lying on the floor in a heap, waiting for the bath-water. They hadn't liked to sit on chairs or beds, they were so dirty. And they had fallen asleep where they sat, their faces as black as a sweep's.

'Talk about black marketeers!' whispered Mrs Andrews. 'Anyone would think we'd got the whole lot of them here in the bedroom!'

They all woke up and went to have a bath one by one, and a good meal after that. Then back to camp with Mr Luffy, Jock with them too.

It was glorious to snuggle down into the sleeping-bags. George called out to the three boys.

'Now don't you dare to go off without me tonight, see?'

'The adventure is over,' called back Dick. 'How did you like it, Jock?'

'Like it?' said Jock, with a happy sigh. 'It was simply – smashing!'

Five go to Mystery Moor

1 At the stables

'We've been here a week and I've been bored every single minute!' said George.

'You haven't,' said Anne. 'You've enjoyed all the rides we've had, and you know you've enjoyed messing about the stables when we haven't been out riding.'

'I tell you, I've been bored every single *minute*,' said George, quite fiercely. 'I ought to know, oughtn't I? That awful girl Henrietta too. Why do we have to put up with her?'

'Oh – Henry!' said Anne, with a laugh. 'I should have thought you'd find a lot in common with another girl like yourself, who would rather be a boy, and tries to act like one!'

The two girls were lying by a haystack eating sandwiches. Round them in a field were many horses, most of which the girls either rode or looked after. Some way off was an old rambling building, and by the front entrance was a great board,

Captain Johnson's Riding School

Anne and George had been staying there for a week, while Julian and Dick had gone to camp with other boys from their school. It had been Anne's idea. She was fond of horses, and had heard so much from her friends at school what fun it was to spend day after day at the stables, that she had made up her mind to go herself.

George hadn't wanted to come. She was sulky because the two boys had gone off somewhere without her and Anne, for a change. Gone to camp! George would have liked that, but girls

were not allowed to go camping with the boys from Julian's school, of course. It was a camp just for the boys alone.

'You're silly to keep feeling cross because you couldn't go camping too,' said Anne. 'The boys don't want us girls round them all the time. We couldn't do the things they do.'

George thought differently. 'I can do *anything* that Dick and Julian do,' she said. 'I can climb, and bike for miles, can walk as far as they can, I can swim, I can beat a whole lot of boys at most things.'

'That's what Henry says!' said Anne, with a laugh. 'Look, there she is, striding about as usual, hands in her jodhpur pockets, whistling like the stable boy!'

George scowled. Anne had been very much amused to see how Henrietta and George hated one another at sight – and yet both had so very much the same ideas. George's real name was Georgina, but she would only answer to George. Henry's real name was Henrietta, but she would only answer to Henry, or Harry to her *very* best friends!

She was about as old as George, and her hair was short too, but it wasn't curly. 'It's a pity yours is curly,' she said to George, pityingly. 'It looks so *girlish*, doesn't it?'

'Don't be an ass,' George said, curtly. 'Plenty of boys have curly hair.'

The maddening part was that Henrietta was a wonderful rider, and had won all kinds of cups. George hadn't enjoyed herself a bit during that week at the stables, because for once in a way another girl had outshone her. She couldn't bear to see Henrietta striding about, whistling, doing everything so competently and quickly.

Anne had had many a quiet laugh to herself, especially when the two girls had each made up their minds not to call one another Henry and

George, but to use their full names, Henrietta and Georgina! This meant that neither of them would answer the other when called, and Captain Johnson, the big burly owner of the riding-stables, got very tired of both of them.

'What are you behaving like this for?' he demanded one morning, seeing their sulky looks at one another at breakfast-time. 'Behaving like a couple of idiotic schoolgirls!'

That made Anne laugh! A couple of idiotic school-*girls*. My goodness, how annoyed both girls were with Captain Johnson. Anne was a bit scared of him. He was hot-tempered, outspoken, and stood no nonsense at all, but he was a wonder with the horses, and loved a good, hearty laugh. He and his wife took either boys or girls for the holidays, and worked them hard, but the children always enjoyed their stay immensely.

'If it hadn't been for Henry, you'd have been perfectly happy this week,' said Anne, leaning back against the haystack. 'We've had heavenly April weather, the horses are lovely, and I like Captain and Mrs Johnson very much.'

'I wish the boys were here,' said George. 'They would soon put that silly Henrietta in her place. I wish I'd stayed at home now.'

'Well, you had the choice,' said Anne, rather cross. 'You could have stayed at Kirrin Cottage with your father and mother, but you chose to come here with me, till the boys came back from camp. You shouldn't make such a fuss if things

aren't exactly to your liking. It spoils things for *me*.'

'Sorry,' said George. 'I'm being a pig, I know, but I do miss the boys. We can only be with them in the hols and it seems funny without them. There's just *one* thing that pleases me here, you'll be glad to know . . .'

'You needn't tell me, I know what it is!' said Anne, with a laugh. 'You're glad that Timmy won't have anything to do with Henry!'

'With Henrietta,' corrected George. She grinned suddenly. 'Yes, old Timmy's got some sense. He just can't stick her. Here, Timmy boy, leave those rabbit-holes alone and come and lie down for a bit. You've run for miles this morning when we took the horses out, and you've snuffled down about a hundred rabbit-holes. Come and be peaceful.'

Timmy left his latest rabbit-hole reluctantly and came to flop down beside Anne and George. He gave George a hearty lick and she patted him.

'We're just saying, Timmy, how sensible you are not to make friends with that awful Henrietta,' said George. She stopped suddenly at a sharp nudge from Anne. A shadow fell across them as someone came round the haystack.

It was Henrietta. By the annoyed look on her face it was clear that she had heard George's remark. She held out an orange envelope to George.

'A telegram for you, Georgina,' she said, stiffly. 'I thought I'd better bring it in case it was important.'

'Oh, thanks, Henrietta,' said George, and took the telegram. She tore it open, read it and groaned.

'Look at that!' she said to Anne and passed it to her. 'It's from Mother.'

Anne took the telegram and read it. 'Please stay another week. Your father is not well. Love from Mother.'

'What bad luck!' said George, a familiar scowl on her face. 'Just when I thought we'd be going home in a day or two, and the boys would join us at Kirrin. Now we'll be stuck here by ourselves for ages! What's the matter with Father? I bet he's only got a headache or something, and doesn't want us stamping about in and out of the house and making a noise.'

'We could go to *my* home,' said Anne. 'That's if you don't mind its being a bit upside down because of the decorating we're having done.'

'No. I know you want to stay here with the

horses,' said George. 'Anyway your father and mother are abroad, we'd only be in the way. Blow, blow, blow! Now we'll have to do without the boys for another week. They'll stay on in camp, of course.'

Captain Johnson said yes, certainly the two girls could stay on. It was possible that they might have to do a bit of camping out if one or two extra children came, but they wouldn't mind that, would they?

'Not a bit,' said George. 'Actually we'd rather like to be on our own, Anne and I. We've got Timmy, you see. So long as we could come in to meals and do a few jobs for you, we'd love to go off on our own.'

Anne smiled to herself. What George really meant was that she wanted to see as little of Henrietta as possible! Still, it *would* be fun to camp out if the weather was fine. They could easily borrow a tent from Captain Johnson.

'Bad luck, Georgina!' said Henry, who was listening to all this. 'Very bad luck! I know you're

terribly bored here. It's a pity you don't really like horses. It's a pity that you —'

'Shut up,' said George rudely, and went out of the room. Captain Johnson glared at Henrietta, who stood whistling at the window, hands in pockets.

'You two girls!' he said. 'Why don't you behave yourselves? Always aping the boys, pretending you're so mannish! Give me Anne here, any day! What you want is your ears boxing. Did you take that bale of straw to the stables?'

'Yes,' said Henrietta, without turning.

'Yes, *sir*,' said Captain Johnson. 'If you want to act like a boy, *be* one, and say "sir" when you speak to me, if you can't bother to remember I've got a name. It's . . .'

He broke off as a small boy came running in. 'Sir, there's a gypsy kid outside with a horse, a skewbald, a mangy looking thing. He says can you help him – the horse has got something wrong with its leg.'

'Those gypsies again!' said Captain Johnson. 'All right, I'll come.'

'What have you done to your horse this time?'

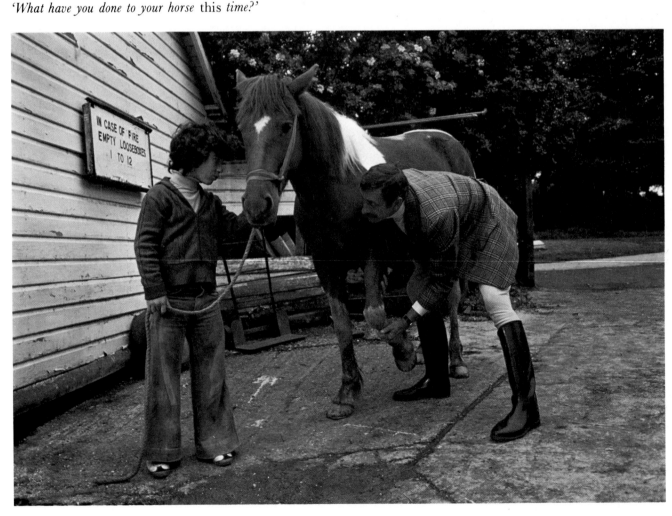

He went out and Anne went with him, not wanting to be left alone with the angry Henrietta. She found George outside with a small dirty gypsy boy and a patient little skewbald horse, its brown and white coat looking very flea-bitten.

'What have you done to your horse *this* time?' said Captain Johnson, looking at its leg. 'You'll have to leave it here, and I'll see to it.'

'Can't do that, sir,' said the boy. 'We're off to Mystery Moor again.'

'Well, you'll have to,' said Captain Johnson. 'It's not fit to walk. Your caravan can't go with the others, this horse isn't fit to pull it. I'll get the police to your father if you try to work this horse before it's better.'

'Don't do that!' said the boy. 'It's just that my Dad says we've *got* to go on tomorrow.'

'What's the hurry?' said Captain Johnson. 'Can't your caravan wait a day or two? Mystery Moor will still be there in two days' time! It beats me why you go there, a desolate place like that, not even a farm or a cottage for miles!'

'I'll leave the horse,' said the boy, and stroked the skewbald's nose. It was clear that he loved the ugly little horse. 'My father will be angry, but the other caravans can go on without us. We'll have to catch them up.'

He gave a kind of half-salute to the captain and disappeared from the stable-yard, a skinny little sunburnt figure. The skewbald stood patiently.

'Take it round to the small stable,' said Captain Johnson to George and Anne. 'I'll come and see to it in a minute.'

The girls led the little horse away. 'Mystery Moor!' said George. 'What a queer name! The boys would like that, they'd be exploring it at once, wouldn't they?'

'Yes. I do wish they were coming here,' said Anne. 'Still, I expect they'll like the chance of staying on in camp. Come on, you funny little creature, here's the stable!'

The girls shut the door on the gypsy's pony and turned to go back. William, the boy who had brought the message about the horse, yelled to them.

'Hey, George and Anne! There's *another* telegram for you!'

The two hurried into the house at once. 'Oh, I hope Father is better and we can go home and join the boys at Kirrin!' said George. She tore open the envelope and then gave a yell that made Anne jump.

'Look, see what it says. They're coming *here*!' Anne snatched the telegram and read it.

'Joining you tomorrow. We'll camp out if no room. Hope you've got a nice juicy adventure ready for us! Julian and Dick.'

'They're coming! They're coming!' said Anne, as excited as George. '*Now* we'll have some fun!'

'It's a pity we've no adventure to offer them,' said George. 'Still, you simply never know!'

2 Julian, Dick and Henry!

George was quite a different person now that she knew her two cousins were coming the next day. She was even polite to Henrietta!

Captain Johnson scratched his head when he heard that the boys were arriving. 'We can't have them in the house, except for meals,' he said. 'We're full up. They can either sleep in the stables or have a tent. I don't care which.'

'There will be ten altogether then,' said his wife. 'Julian, Dick, Anne, George, Henry – and John, Susan, Alice, Rita and William. Henry may have to camp out too.'

'Not with us,' said George, at once.

'I think you're rather unkind to Henry,' said Mrs Johnson. 'After all, you and she are very alike, George. You both think you ought to have been boys, and . . .'

'I'm not a *bit* like Henrietta!' said George, indignantly. 'You wait till my cousins come, Mrs Johnson. *They* won't think she's like me. I don't expect they'll want anything to do with her.'

'Oh well, you'll just have to shake down together somehow, if you want to stay here,' said Mrs Johnson. 'Let me see, I'd better get some rugs out. The boys will want them, whether they sleep in the stables or in a tent. Come and help me to look for them, Anne.'

Anne, George and Henry were a good bit older than the other five children staying at the stables, but all of them, small or big, were excited to hear about the coming of Julian and Dick. For one thing George and Anne had related so many of the adventures they had had with them, that everyone was inclined to think of them as heroes.

Henrietta disappeared after tea that day and could not be found. 'Wherever have you been?' demanded Mrs Johnson when she at last turned up.

'Up in my room,' said Henrietta. 'Cleaning my shoes and my jods, and mending my riding-jacket. You keep telling me to, and now I've done it!'

'Aha! Preparing for the heroes!' said Captain Johnson, and Henry immediately put on a scowl very like the one George often wore.

'Nothing of the sort!' she said. 'I've been meaning to do it for a long time. If Georgina's cousins are anything like *her* I shan't be very interested in them.'

'But you might like my brothers,' said Anne, with a laugh. 'If you don't there'll be something wrong with you.'

'Don't be silly,' said Henrietta. 'Georgina's cousins and your brothers are the same people!'

'How clever of you to work that out,' said George. But she felt too happy to keep up the silly bickering for long. She went out with Timmy, whistling softly.

'They're coming tomorrow, Tim,' she said. 'Julian and Dick. We'll all go off together, like we always do, the five of us. You'll like that, won't you, Timmy?'

'Woof,' said Timmy approvingly and waved his plumy tail. He knew quite well what she meant.

Next morning George and Anne looked up the trains that arrived at the station two miles away. 'This is the one they'll come by,' said George, her finger on the timetable. 'It's the only one this morning. It arrives at half past twelve. We'll go and meet them.'

'Right,' said Anne. 'We'll start at ten minutes to twelve – we'll be in plenty of time then. We can help them with their things. They won't bring much.'

'Take the ponies up to Hawthorn Field, will you?' called Captain Johnson. 'Can you manage all four of them?'

'Oh yes,' said Anne, pleased. She loved the walk to Hawthorn Field, up a little narrow lane set with celandines, violets and primroses, and the fresh green of the budding hawthorn bushes. 'Come on, George, let's catch the ponies and take them now. It's a heavenly morning.'

They set off with the four frisky ponies, Timmy

at their heels. He was quite a help with the horses at the stable, especially when any had to be caught.

No sooner had they left the stables and gone on their way to Hawthorn Field than the telephone rang. It was for Anne.

'Oh, I'm sorry, she's not here,' said Mrs Johnson, answering it. 'Who is it speaking? Oh, Julian her brother? Can I give her a message?'

'Yes, please,' said Julian's voice. 'Tell her we are arriving at the bus-stop at Milling Green at half past eleven, and is there a little hand-cart she and George could bring, because we've got our tent with us and other odds and ends?'

'Oh, we'll send the little wagon,' said Mrs Johnson. 'The one that always goes to meet the train or the bus. I'll get George to meet you with Anne, they can drive it in. We're pleased you are coming. The weather's very good and you'll enjoy yourselves!'

'Rather!' said Julian. 'Thanks awfully for putting us up. We won't be any trouble, in fact we'll help all we can.'

Mrs Johnson said good-bye and put down the receiver. She saw Henrietta passing outside the window, looking much cleaner and tidier than usual. She called to her.

Soon Winkie was in the shafts.

73

'Henry! Where are George and Anne? Julian and Dick are arriving at the bus-stop at Milling Green at eleven-thirty and I've said we'll meet them in the little wagon. Will you tell George and Anne? They can put Winkie into the cart and trot him down to the bus-stop.'

'Right,' said Henry. Then she remembered that George and Anne had been sent up to Hawthorn Field with the four ponies.

'I say, they won't be back in time!' she called. 'Shall I take the wagon and meet them?'

'Yes, do. That would be kind of you, Henry,' said Mrs Johnson. 'You'd better hurry, though. Time's getting on. Where's Winkie? In the big field?'

'Yes,' said Henry and hurried off to get him. Soon he was in the wagon shafts, and Henry was in the driving-seat. She drove off smartly, grinning to herself to think how cross George and Anne would be to find they had missed meeting the two boys after all.

Julian and Dick had already arrived at the bus-stop when Henry drove up. They looked hopefully at the wagon, thinking that perhaps one of the girls was driving in to meet them.

'No go,' said Dick. 'It's somebody else, driving into the village. I wonder if the girls got our message? I thought they would meet us at the bus-stop here. Well, we'll wait a few minutes more.'

They had just sat down on the bus-stop seat again when the wagon stopped near by. Henry saluted them.

'Are you Anne's brother?' she called. 'She didn't get your telephone message, so I've come with the wagon instead. Get in!'

'Oh, jolly nice of you,' said Julian, dragging his things to the wagon. 'Er – I'm Julian – and this is Dick. What's your name?'

'Henry,' said Henrietta, helping Julian with his things. She heaved them in valiantly, then clicked to Winkie to stand still and not fidget. 'I'm glad you've come. There are rather a lot of small kids at the stables. We'll be glad of you two! I say, Timmy will be pleased to see you, won't he?'

'Good old Tim,' said Dick, heaving his things in. Henry gave them a shove too. She wasn't very fat but she was wiry and strong. She grinned round at the boys. 'All set! Now we'll get back to the stables. Or do you want to have an ice-cream or anything before we start? Dinner's not till one.'

'No. We'll get on, I think,' said Julian. Henry leapt into the driver's seat, took the reins and clicked to Winkie. The boys were behind in the wagon. Winkie set off at a spanking pace.

'Nice boy!' said Dick to Julian, in a low voice, as they drove off. 'Decent of him to meet us.'

Julian nodded. He was disappointed that Anne and George hadn't come with Timmy, but it was good to be met by *someone*! It wouldn't have been very funny to walk the long road to the farm carrying their packs by themselves.

They arrived at the stables and Henry helped them down with their things. Mrs Johnson heard them arriving and came to the door to welcome them.

'Ah, there you are. Come along in. I've a mid-morning snack for you, because I guessed you'd have had breakfast early. Leave the things there, Henry. If the boys sleep in one of the stables, there's no sense in bringing them into the house. Now, are George and Anne still not back? What a pity!'

Henry disappeared to put away the wagon. The boys went into the pleasant house and sat down to lemonade and home-made biscuits. They had hardly taken a bite before Anne came running in. 'Henry told me you'd come! Oh, I'm sorry we didn't meet you! We thought you'd come by train!'

Timmy came racing in, his tail waving madly. He leapt at the two boys, who were just giving Anne a hug each. Then in came George, her face one big beam.

'Julian! Dick! I *am* so glad you've come! It's been dull as ditch-water without you! Did anyone meet you?'

'Yes. An awfully nice boy,' said Dick. 'Gave us quite a welcome, and dragged our packs into the wagon, and was very friendly. You never told us about him.'

'Oh, was that William?' said Anne. 'Well, he's only little. We didn't bother about telling you of the juniors here.'

'No, he wasn't little,' said Dick. 'He was quite big, very strong too. You didn't mention him at all.'

'Well, we told you about the other *girl* here,' said George. 'Henrietta, awful creature! Thinks she's like a boy and goes whistling about everywhere. She makes us laugh! You'll laugh too.'

A sudden thought struck Anne. 'Did the – er – boy who met you, tell you his name?' she asked.

'Yes, what was it now? Henry,' said Dick. 'Nice chap. I'm going to like him.'

George stared as if she couldn't believe her ears. '*Henry!* Did *she* meet you?'

'No – not she – *he*,' corrected Julian. 'Fellow with a big grin.'

'But that's *Henrietta*!' cried George, her face flaming red with anger. 'The awful girl I told you about, who tries to act like a boy, and whistles and strides about all over the place. Don't tell me she took you in! She calls herself Henry, instead of Henrietta, and wears her hair short, and . . .'

'Gosh, she sounds very like *you*, George,' said Dick. 'Well, I never! It never occurred to me that he was a girl. Jolly good show she put up. I must say I liked him – her, I mean.'

'*Oh!*' said George really furious. 'The beast! She goes and meets you and never says a word to us, and makes you think she's a boy – and – and – spoils everything!'

3 Sniffer

As soon as George had gone out of the room, a scowl on her face, Henry walked in, hands in jodhpur pockets.

'Hallo!' said Dick, at once. '*Henrietta!*'

Henry grinned. 'Oh, so they've told you, have they? I was tickled pink when you took me for a boy.'

'You've even got your riding jacket buttons buttoning up the wrong way,' said Anne, noticing for the first time. 'You really are a fathead, Henry. You and George are a pair!'

'Well, I look more like a real boy than George does, anyway,' said Henry.

'Only because of your hair,' said Dick. 'It's straight.'

'Don't say that in front of George,' said Anne. 'She'll immediately have hers cut like a convict or something, all shaven and shorn.'

'Well, anyway, it was jolly decent of Henry to come and meet us and lug our things about,' said Julian. 'Have a biscuit, anyone?'

'No thanks,' said Anne and Henry.

'Are we supposed to leave any for politeness sake?' said Dick, eyeing the plate. 'They're home-made and quite super. I could wolf the lot.'

'We aren't frightfully polite here,' said Henry, with a grin. 'We aren't frightfully clean and tidy,

'Hold your horses, George, old thing,' said Julian, surprised. 'After all, you've often been pleased when people take *you* for a boy, though goodness knows why. I thought you'd grown out of it a bit. Don't blame us for thinking Henry was a boy, and liking him – her, I mean.'

George stamped out of the room. Julian scratched his head and looked at Dick. 'Now we've put our foot in it,' he said. 'What an ass George is! I should have thought she'd have liked someone like Henry, who had exactly the same ideas as she has. Well, she'll get over it, I suppose.'

'It's going to be a bit awkward,' said Anne, soberly.

She was right. It was going to be *very* awkward!

either. We have to change out of our jods at night for supper, which is an awful nuisance, especially as Captain Johnson never bothers to change his.'

'Any news?' asked Julian, drinking the last of the lemonade. 'Anything exciting happened?'

'No, nothing,' said Anne. 'The only excitement is the horses, nothing more. This is quite a lonely place, really, and the only exciting thing we've heard is the name of the big, desolate moor that stretches from here to the coast. Mystery Moor it's called.'

'Why?' asked Dick. 'Some long-ago mystery gave it that name, I suppose?'

'I don't know,' said Anne. 'I think only gypsies go there now. A little gypsy boy came in with a lame horse yesterday, and said his people had to go to Mystery Moor. Why they wanted to go to such a deserted stretch of land I don't know – no farms there, not even a cottage.'

'Gypsies have peculiar ideas sometimes,' said Henry. 'I must say I like the way they leave messages for any gypsy following – patrins, they're called.'

'Patrins? Yes, I've heard of those,' said Dick. 'Sticks and leaves arranged in certain patterns, or something, aren't they?'

'Yes,' said Henry. 'I know our gardener at home showed me an arrangement of sticks outside our back gate once, which he said was a message to any gypsy following. He told me what it meant, too!'

'What did it mean?' asked Julian.

'It meant "Don't beg here. Mean people. No good!"' said Henry, with a laugh. 'That's what he *said*, anyway!'

'We might ask the little gypsy boy who came with the skewbald horse,' said Anne. 'He'll probably show us some messages. I'd like to learn some. You never know when anything like that could come in useful!'

'Yes. And we'll ask him why the gypsies go to Mystery Moor,' said Julian, getting up and dusting the crumbs off his coat. 'They don't go there for nothing, you may be sure!'

'Where's old George gone?' asked Dick. 'I do hope she's not going to be silly.'

George was in one of the stables, grooming a horse so vigorously that it was most surprised. Swish-swish-swish-swish! What a brushing! George was working her intense annoyance out of herself. She mustn't spoil things for the boys and Anne! But oh, that horrible Henrietta, meeting them like that, pretending to be a boy. Heaving their luggage about, playing a joke on them! But surely they might have guessed!

'Oh, there you are, George, old thing,' said Dick's voice at the stable-door. 'Let me help. Gosh, aren't you brown! Just as many freckles as ever!'

George grinned unwillingly. She tossed Dick the brush. 'Here you are, then! Do you and Ju want to go riding at all? There are plenty of horses to choose from here.'

Dick was relieved to see that George appeared to have got over her rage. 'Yes. It might be fun to go off for the day. What about tomorrow? We might explore a little of Mystery Moor.'

'Right,' said George. She began to heave some straw about. 'But not with That Girl,' she announced, from behind the straw she was carrying.

'What girl?' asked Dick, innocently. 'Oh, Henry, you mean? I keep thinking of her as a boy. No, we won't have her with us. We'll be just the five as usual.'

'That's all right then,' said George happily. 'Oh, here's Julian. Give a hand, Ju!'

It was lovely to have the two boys again, joking, laughing, teasing. They all went out in the fields that afternoon and heard the tales of the camp. It was just like old times, and Timmy was as pleased as anyone else. He went first to one of the four, then to another, licking each one as he went, his tail wagging vigorously.

'That's three times you've smacked me in the face with your tail, Timmy,' said Dick, dodging it. 'Can't you look behind yourself and see where my face is?'

'Woof,' said Timmy happily, and turned round to lick Dick, wagging his tail in Julian's face this time!

Somebody squeezed through the hedge behind them. George stiffened, feeling sure that it was Henrietta. Timmy barked sharply.

It wasn't Henrietta. It was the little gypsy boy. He came up to them. There were pale streaks down his dirty little face, made by tears that had run through the dirt!

'I've come for the horse,' he said. 'Do you know where he is?'

'He's not ready for walking yet,' said George. 'Captain Johnson told you he wouldn't be. What's the matter? Why have you been crying?'

'My father hit me,' said the boy. 'He cuffed me and knocked me right over.'

'Whatever for?' asked Anne.

'Because I left the horse,' said the boy. 'My father said all it wanted was a bit of ointment and a bandage. He has to start off with the other caravans today, you see.'

'Well, you really *can't* have the horse yet,' said Anne. 'It isn't fit to walk, let alone drag a caravan. You don't want Captain Johnson to tell the police you're working it when it's not fit, do you? You know he means what he says?'

'Yes. But I must have the horse,' said the small gypsy. 'I daren't go back without it. My father would half kill me.'

'I suppose he doesn't care to come himself, so he sends you instead,' said Dick, in disgust.

The boy said nothing, and rubbed his dirty sleeve across his face. He sniffed.

'Get your hanky,' said Dick. 'Don't you ever wash your face?'

'No,' said the boy, looking quite surprised. 'Let me have my horse. I tell you, I'll be half killed if I go back without it.' He began to cry again.

The children felt sorry for him. He was such a thin, skinny misery of a boy, and goodness, how he sniffled all the time!

'What's your name?' asked Anne.

'Sniffer,' said the boy. 'That's what my father calls me.'

It was certainly a good name for him; but what a horrid father he must have!

'Haven't you got a proper name?' asked Anne.

'Yes. But I've forgotten it,' said Sniffer. 'Let me have my horse. I tell you, my father's waiting.'

Julian got up. 'I'll come and see your father and put some sense into him. Where is he?'

'Over yonder,' said Sniffer with a big sniff, and he pointed over the hedge. 'I'll come too,' said Dick. In the end everyone got up and went with Sniffer. They walked through the gate and saw a dark-faced, surly-looking man standing motionless not far off. His thick, oily hair was curly, and he wore enormous gold rings hanging from his ears. He looked up as the little company came near.

'Your horse isn't fit to walk yet,' said Julian. 'You can have it tomorrow or the next day, the Captain says.'

'I'll have it now,' said the man, in a surly tone. 'We're starting off tonight or tomorrow over the moor. I can't wait.'

'But what's the hurry?' said Julian. 'The moor will wait for you!'

The man scowled and shifted from one foot to another. 'Can't you stay for another night or two and then go after the others?' said Dick.

'Listen, Father! You go with the other caravans,' said Sniffer, eagerly. 'Go in Moses' caravan and leave ours here. I can put our horse into the shafts tomorrow, or maybe the next day, and follow after!'

'But how would you know the way?' said George.

Sniffer made a scornful movement with his hand. 'Easy! They'll leave me patrins to follow,' he said.

'Oh yes,' said Dick, remembering. He turned to the silent gypsy fellow. 'Well, what about it? It seems that Sniffer here has quite a good idea, and you most certainly can't have the horse today anyway.'

The man turned and said something angry and scornful to poor Sniffer, who shrank away from the words as if they were blows. The four children couldn't understand a word, for it was all poured out in some gypsy talk that they could not follow. Then the man turned on his heel and without so much as a look at them, slouched away, his earrings gleaming as he went.

'What did he say?' asked Julian.

Sniffer gave one of his continual sniffs. 'He was very angry. He said he'd go with the others, and I could come on with Clip, the horse, and drive our caravan,' he said. 'I'll be all right there tonight with Liz.'

'Who's Liz?' asked Anne, hoping that it was someone who would be kind to this poor little wretch.

'My dog,' said Sniffer, smiling for the first time. 'I left her behind because she sometimes goes for hens, and Captain Johnson, he doesn't like that.'

'I bet he doesn't,' said Julian. 'All right, that's settled then. You can come for Clip, or Clop, or whatever your horse is called, tomorrow, and we'll see if it's fit to walk.'

'I'm glad,' said Sniffer, rubbing his nose. 'I don't want Clip to go lame, see? But my father, he's fierce, he is.'

'So we gather,' said Julian, looking at a bruise on Sniffer's face. 'You come tomorrow and you can show us some of the patrins, the messages, that you gypsies use. We'd like to know some.'

'I'll come,' promised Sniffer, nodding his head vigorously. 'And you will come to see my caravan? I shall be all alone there, except for Liz.'

'Well, I suppose it would be something to do,' said Dick. 'Yes, we'll come. I hope it's not too smelly.'

'Smelly?' said Sniffer, surprised. 'I don't know. I will show you patrins there and Liz will show you her tricks. She is very very clever. Once she belonged to a circus.'

'We must certainly take Timmy to see this clever dog,' said Anne, patting Timmy, who had been hunting for rabbits and had only just come back. 'Timmy, would you like to go and visit a very clever dog called Liz?'

'Woof,' said Timmy, wagging his tail politely.

'Right,' said Dick. 'I'm glad you approve, Tim. We'll all try and come tomorrow, Sniffer, after you've been to see how Clip is getting on. I don't somehow think you'll be able to have him then, though. We'll see!'

4 A bed in the stable

The boys slept in one of the stables that night. Captain Johnson said they could either have mattresses sent out, or could sleep in the straw, with rugs.

'Oh, straw and rugs, please,' said Julian. 'That's fine. We'll be as snug as anything with those.'

'I wish Anne and I could sleep in a stable too,' said George, longingly. 'We never have. Can't we, Captain Johnson?'

'No. You've got beds that you're paying for,' said the Captain. 'Anyway, girls can't do that sort of thing, not even girls who try to be boys, George!'

'I've *often* slept in a stable,' said Henrietta. 'At home when we've too many visitors, I always turn out and sleep in the straw.'

'Bad luck on the horses!' said George.

'Why?' demanded Henry at once.

'Because you must keep them awake all night with your snoring!' said George.

Henry snorted crossly and went out. It was maddening that she should snore at night, but she simply couldn't help it.

'Never mind!' George called after her. 'It's a nice *manly* snore, Henrietta!'

'Shut up, George,' said Dick, rather shocked at this sudden display of pettiness on George's part.

'Don't tell *me* to shut up,' said George. 'Tell Henrietta!'

'George, don't be an ass,' said Julian. But George didn't like that either, and stalked out of the room in just the same stiff, offended way that Henry had done!

'Oh dear!' said Anne. 'It's been like this all the time. First Henry, then George, then George, then Henry! They really are a couple of idiots!'

She went to see where the boys were to sleep. They had been told to use a small stable, empty except for the gypsy's horse that lay patiently down, its bandaged leg stretched out on the floor. Anne patted it and stroked it. It was an ugly little thing but its patient brown eyes were lovely.

The boys had heaps of straw to burrow into, and some old rugs. Anne thought it all looked lovely. 'You can wash and everything at the house,' she said. 'Then just slip over here to sleep. Doesn't it smell nice? All straw and hay and horse! I hope that gypsy's horse won't disturb you. He may be a bit restless if his leg hurts him.'

'Nothing will disturb *us* tonight!' said Julian. 'What with camp-life and open-air and wind-on-the-hills and all that kind of thing, we're sure to sleep like logs. I think we're going to enjoy it here, Anne, very quiet and peaceful!'

George looked in at the door. 'I'll lend you Timmy, if you like,' she said, anxious to make up for her display of temper.

'Oh, hallo, George! No, thanks. I don't particularly want old Tim climbing over me all night long, trying to find the softest part of me to sleep on!' said Julian. 'I say, look, he's showing me how to make a good old burrow to sleep in! Hey, Tim, come out of my straw!'

Timmy had flung himself into the straw and was turning vigorously round and round in it as if he were making a bed for himself. He stood and looked up at them, his mouth open and his tongue hanging out at one side.

'He's laughing,' said Anne, and it did indeed look as if Timmy was having a good old laugh at them. Anne gave him a hug and he licked her lavishly, and then began to burrow round and round in the straw again.

Someone came up, whistling loudly, and put her head in at the door. 'I've brought you a couple of old pillows. Mrs Johnson said you'd better have something for your heads.'

'Oh thanks awfully, Henry,' said Julian, taking them.

'How kind of you, Henri*etta*,' said George.

'It's a pleasure, Geor*gina*,' said Henry, and the boys burst out laughing. Fortunately the supper-bell went just then and they all went across the yard at once. Somehow everyone was always hungry at the stables!

The girls looked very different in the evening, because they had to change out of their dirty, smelly jodhpurs or breeches and put on dresses. Anne, Henry and George hurried to change before Mrs Johnson rang the supper-bell again. She always gave them ten minutes' grace, knowing that they might sometimes have a job to finish with the horses, but everyone was supposed to be at the table when the second supper-bell had finished ringing.

George looked nice, because her curly hair went with a skirt and blouse quite well, but Henry looked quite wrong somehow, in her frilly dress.

'You look like a boy dressed up!' said Anne, and this pleased Henry, but not George. The talk at the supper table was mainly about all the wonderful things that Henry had done in her life. Apparently she had three brothers and did everything with them, and according to her own tales, she was considerably better than they were!

They had sailed a ship up to Norway. They had hiked from London to York.

'Was Dick Turpin with you?' inquired George, sarcastically. 'On his horse, Black Bess? I expect you got there long before *him*, didn't you?'

Henry took no notice. She went on with wonderful tales of her family's exploits, swimming across wide rivers, climbing Snowdon to the top, goodness, there wasn't a single thing she didn't seem to have done!

'You certainly ought to have been a boy, Henry,' said Mrs Johnson, which was exactly what Henry wanted everyone to say!

'Henry, when you've told us the story of how you climbed Mount Everest and got there before anyone else, perhaps you would finish your plateful,' said Captain Johnson, who got very tired of Henry's tongue.

George roared with laughter, not that she thought it was very funny, but because she loved any chance to laugh at Henry. Henry tackled the rest of her food at top speed. How she did love to hold everyone spellbound with her extraordinary tales! George didn't believe a word, but Dick and Julian thought it quite likely that his tall, wiry girl *could* do things just as well as her brothers.

There were a few jobs to be done after supper, and Henry kept well away from George, knowing quite well that she would have a few cutting things to say. Well, *she* didn't care! Everyone else thought she was marvellous! She tore off her frilly dress and put on jodhpurs again, although it would only be a short time before they all went to bed.

George and Anne went with the boys to their stable. They were in pyjamas and dressing-gowns, both yawning as they went. 'Got your torches?' said George. 'We're not allowed to have candles in the stables, because of the straw, you know. Good night! Sleep well! And I hope that that fathead of a Henry doesn't come along early in the morning, whistling like a paper-boy, and wake you up!'

'Nothing will wake me up tonight, nothing at all!' said Julian, with a huge yawn. He lay down in the straw and pulled an old rug over him. 'Oh,

what a bed! Give me stable straw every time to sleep in!'

The girls laughed. The boys really *did* look very comfortable. 'Sleep tight,' said Anne, and walked off with George to the house.

Soon all the lights were out everywhere. Henry was asleep and snoring as usual. She had to have a separate room, otherwise she kept everyone awake! But even so, Anne and George could hear her, snoring away – rrrumph – rrrumph! rrrumph – RRRRUMPH!

'Blow Henrietta!' said George, sleepily. 'What a row she makes. Anne, she's not to come with us when we go riding tomorrow. Do you hear, Anne?'

'Not very well,' murmured Anne, trying to open her eyes. 'G'night, George!'

Timmy was on George's feet as usual. He lay snuggled there, eyes shut and ears asleep too. He got as tired as everyone else, running over the hills all day, scrabbling at scores of rabbit-holes, chasing dozens of remarkably fleet-footed rabbits. But at night he too slept like a log.

Out in the stable the two boys slept peacefully, covered by the old rug. Near by the little skewbald horse moved restlessly, but they heard nothing. An owl came swooping over the stable, looking for mice down below. It screeched loudly, hoping to scare a mouse into sudden flight. Then it would swoop down and take it into its talons.

Not even the screech awakened the boys. They slept dreamlessly, tired out.

The door of the stable was shut and latched. Clip, the horse, suddenly stirred and looked round at the door. The latch was moving! Someone was lifting it from the outside. Clip's pricked ears heard the sound of a little shuffle.

He watched the door. Who was coming? He hoped it was Sniffer, the boy he liked so much. Sniffer was always kind to him. He didn't like being away from Sniffer. He listened for the sniff-

sniff that always went with the little gypsy boy, but he didn't hear it.

The door opened very slowly indeed. It gave no creak. Clip saw the night sky outside, set with stars. He made out a figure outlined against the darkness of the starry night, a black shadow.

Someone came into the stable, and whispered 'Clip!'

The horse gave a little whinny. It wasn't Sniffer's voice. It was his father's. Clip did not like him, he was too free with cuffs and kicks, and slashes with the whip. He lay still, wondering why the gypsy had come.

The man had no idea that Dick and Julian were sleeping in the stable. He had come in quietly because he had thought there might be other horses there, and he did not want to startle them and make them stamp about in fright. He had no torch, but his keen gypsy's eyes made out Clip at once, lying in his straw.

He tiptoed across to him and fell over Julian's feet, sticking out from the straw bed he was lying on. He fell with a thud, and Julian sat up very suddenly indeed, awake at once.

'Who's there! What is it?'

The gypsy shrank down beside Clip, keeping silent. Julian began to wonder if he had been dreaming. But his foot distinctly hurt him. Surely somebody had trodden on it, or fallen over it? He woke Dick.

'Where's the torch? Hallo, look, the stable door is open! Quick, Dick, where on earth is the torch?'

They found it at last and Julian clicked it on. At first he saw nothing, for the gypsy was in Clip's stall, lying down behind the horse. Then the torch picked him out.

'Hallo! Look there – it's that gypsy, Sniffer's father!' said Julian. 'Get up, you! What on earth are you doing here, in the middle of the night?'

5 George gets a headache!

The man got up sullenly. His ear-rings shone in the light of the torch. 'I came to get Clip,' he said. 'He's my horse, isn't he?'

'You were told he wasn't fit to walk yet,' said Julian. 'Do you want him to go lame for life? You ought to know enough about horses to know when one can be worked or not!'

'I've got my orders,' said the man. 'I've got to take my caravan with the others.'

'Who said so?' said Dick, scornfully.

'Barney Boswell,' said the man. 'He's boss of our lot here. We've got to start off together tomorrow.'

'But why?' said Julian, puzzled. 'What's so urgent about all this? What's the mystery?'

'There ain't no mystery,' said the man, still sullen. 'We're just going to the moor.'

'What are you going to do there?' asked Dick, curiously. 'It doesn't seem to me to be the place to

take a lot of caravans to. There's nothing there at all, is there? Or so I've heard.'

The man shrugged his shoulders and said nothing. He turned to Clip as if to get him up. But Julian rapped out at him at once.

'Oh no, you don't! If you don't care about injuring a horse, I do! You've only got to be patient for a day or two more, and he'll be quite all right. You're not to take him tonight. Dick, go and wake Captain Johnson. He'll know what to do.'

'No,' said the man, scowling. 'Don't go waking anybody. I'll go. But just you see that Clip is given to Sniffer as soon as it's possible, or I'll know the reason why! See?'

He looked at Julian in a threatening way.

'Take that scowl off your face,' said Julian. 'I'm glad you've seen sense. Clear out now. Go off with the others tomorrow and I'll see that Sniffer has the horse in a short time.'

The man moved to the door and slid out like a shadow. Julian went to watch him across the yard, wondering whether, out of spite, the man might try to steal a hen, or one of the ducks sleeping beside the pond.

But there was no sudden clucking, no loud quack. The man had gone as silently as he had come.

'Most peculiar, all this!' said Julian, latching the door again. He tied a piece of thick string over it his side, so that it could not be lifted from outside. 'There! Now if the gypsy comes again, he'll find he can't get in. What a nerve, coming here in the middle of the night like that!'

He got back into the straw. 'He must have fallen right over my foot,' he said, snuggling down. 'He woke me up with an awful jump. Good thing for Clip that we were sleeping out here tonight, or he'd be dragging along a heavy cart tomorrow, and going lame again. I don't like that fellow!'

He fell asleep again and so did Dick. Clip slept too, his leg feeling easier. How glad he had been that day not to have to drag along the heavy caravan!

The boys told Captain Johnson next morning about the gypsy's midnight visit. He nodded. 'Yes, I ought to have warned you that he might come. They're not always very good to their horses. Well, I'm glad you sent him off. I don't reckon Clip's leg will be ready for walking on till the day after tomorrow. There's no harm in giving the poor creature a few days' rest. Sniffer can easily take the caravan on after the others.'

It looked as if that day was going to be fun. After all the horses had been seen to, and many odd jobs done, the four, with Timmy, planned to set out for a day's ride. Captain Johnson said he would let Julian ride his own sturdy cob and Dick took a bonny chestnut horse with four white socks. The girls had the horses they usually rode.

Henry hung about, looking very mournful. The boys felt quite uncomfortable. 'We *really* ought to tell her to come along too,' said Dick to Julian. 'It seems jolly mean to leave her behind with those little kids.'

'Yes, I know. I agree with you,' said Julian. 'Anne, come here! Can't you suggest to George that we take Henry too? She's longing to come, I know.'

'Yes. She is,' said Anne. 'I feel awful about it. But George will be mad if we ask Henry. They really do get across one another. I simply daren't ask George to let Henry come, Ju.'

'But this is *silly*!' said Julian. 'To think we don't *dare* to ask George to let somebody come! George will have to learn sense. I like Henry. She's boastful, and I don't believe half the tales she tells, but she's a sport and good fun. Hey, Henry!'

'Coming!' yelled Henry, and came running, looking very hopeful.

'Would you like to come with us?' said Julian. 'We're all going off for the day. Have you got any jobs to do, or can you come?'

'Can I *come*! Rather,' said Henry, joyfully. 'But – does George know?'

'I'll soon tell her,' said Julian, and went in search of George. She was helping Mrs Johnson to get saddlebags ready, full of food.

'George,' said Julian, boldly. 'Henry is coming too. Will there be enough food for everyone?'

'Oh! How *nice* of you to ask her!' said Mrs Johnson, sounding very pleased. 'She's dying to come. She's been so good this week, too, while we've been short-handed. She deserves a treat. Isn't that *nice*, George?'

George muttered something peculiar and went out of the room, her face scarlet. Julian stared after her, his eyebrows cocked in a comical manner.

'I don't somehow feel that George thinks it's nice,' he said. 'I feel as if we are in for an awkward day, Mrs Johnson.'

'Oh, don't take any notice of George when she's silly,' said Mrs Johnson, comfortably, filling another paper bag with delicious-looking sandwiches. 'And don't take any notice of Henry, either, when she's idiotic. There! If you get through all this food, I shall be surprised!'

William, one of the younger ones, came in just then. 'What a lot of food you've given them,' he said. 'Will there be enough left for *us* to have today?'

'Good gracious, yes!' said Mrs Johnson. 'You think of nothing but your tummy, William! Go and find George and tell her the food is ready for her to put into the saddle-bags.'

William disappeared and then came back. 'George says she's got a headache and doesn't think she'll go on the ride,' he announced.

Julian looked startled and upset. 'Now you listen to me, Julian,' said Mrs Johnson, beginning to insert the parcels of food carefully into the saddle-bags, 'just you leave her to her imaginery headache. Don't go fussing round her, and begging her to come and saying you won't have Henry. Just believe quite firmly in her headache, and go off by yourselves. It's the quickest way to make George see sense, believe *me*!'

'Yes. I think you're right,' said Julian, frowning. To think that George should behave like a sulky little girl, after all the adventures they had been through together! Just because of Henry. It really was absurd.

'Where *is* George!' he said to William.

'Up in her room,' said William, who had been engrossed in picking up and eating all the crumbs he could. Julian went out of the room and into the yard. He knew which window belonged to the room where George and Anne slept. He yelled up.

'I say, George! Sorry about your headache, old thing! Sure you don't feel like coming?'

'No!' came back an answering shout, and the window was shut down with a slam.

'Righto! Awfully disappointed and all that!' shouted Julian. 'Do hope your head will soon be better! See you later!'

No other reply came from the window, but, as Julian went across the yard to the stables, a very surprised face watched him go, from behind the bedroom curtains. George was extremely astonished to have been taken at her word, shocked at being left behind after all, and angry with Henry and everyone else for putting her into this fix!

Julian told the others that George had a headache and wasn't coming. Anne was most concerned and wanted to go and comfort her but Julian forbade her to.

'No. She's up in her room. Leave her alone, Anne. That's an order – see?'

'All right,' said Anne, half-relieved. She felt sure that George's headache was mostly temper, and she didn't at all want to go and argue with her for half an hour. Henry hadn't said a word. She had flushed with surprise when Julian had announced that George was not coming, and she knew at once that there was no real headache! *She* was George's headache, she knew that!

She went up to Julian. 'Look, I guess it's because you've asked *me* to come, that Georgina won't come with us. I don't want to spoil things. You go and tell her I'm not going after all.'

Julian looked at Henry gratefully. 'That's jolly nice of you,' he said. 'But we're taking George at her word. Anyway, we didn't ask you out of politeness. We *wanted* you to come!'

'Thanks,' said Henry. 'Well, let's go before anything else happens! Our horses are ready. I'll fix the saddle-bags.'

Soon all four were on their horses, and were walking over the yard to the gate. George heard the clippity-clop-clippity-clop of the hooves and peeped out of the window again. They were going after all! She hadn't thought they really *would* go without her. She was horrifed.

Why did I behave like that? I've put myself in the wrong! thought poor George. Now Henrietta will be with them all day and will be as nice as possible, just to show me up. What an ass I am! 'Timmy, I'm an ass and an idiot, and a great big fathead! Aren't I?'

Timmy didn't think so. He had been puzzled to hear the others going off without him and George, and had gone to the door and whined. Now he came back to George and put his head on her knee. He knew George was not happy.

'*You* don't care how I behave, do you, Tim?' said George, stroking the soft, furry head. 'That's the best of a dog! You don't care if I'm in the wrong or not, you just love me all the same, don't you? Well, you shouldn't love me today, Tim. I've been an idiot!'

There was a knock at her door. It was William again. 'George! Mrs Johnson says, if your headache is bad, undress and get into bed. But if it's better, come down and help with Clip, the gypsy's horse.'

'I'll come down,' said George, flinging away her sulks at one go. 'Tell Mrs Johnson I'll go to the stable at once.'

'All right,' said the stolid William, and trotted off like a reliable little pony.

George went downstairs with Timmy, and into the yard. She wondered how far the others had gone. She couldn't see them in the distance. Would they have a good day together, with that horrid Henry? Ugh!

The others were almost a mile away, cantering easily. What *fun*! A whole day before them, on Mystery Moor!

82

6 A grand day

'I think it's got a jolly good name, Mystery Moor,' said Dick, as the four of them went along. 'Look at it stretching for miles, all blazing with gorse.'

'I don't think it looks at all mysterious,' said Henry, surprised.

'Well, it's got a sort of quietness and broodiness,' said Anne. 'As if something big happened long ago in the past and it's waiting for something to happen again.'

'Quiet and broody? It sounds like one of the farmyard hens sitting on her eggs!' said Henry with a laugh. 'I think it might be a bit frightening and mysterious at night, but it's just an ordinary stretch of country in the day-time, fine for riding over. I can't think why it's called Mystery Moor.'

'We'll have to look it up in some book that tells about this part of the country,' said Dick. 'I expect it was called that because of some queer happenings or other, hundreds of years ago, when people believed in witches and things like that.'

They followed no road or path, but rode where they pleased. There were great stretches of wiry grass, masses of heather springing up afresh, and, blazing its gold everywhere on this lovely April day, was the gorse.

Anne sniffed continually as they rode past the gorse bushes. Dick looked at her.

'You sound like Sniffer!' he said. 'Have you got a cold?'

Anne laughed. 'No, of course not. But I do so love the smell of the gorse. What does it smell of? Vanilla? Hot coconut? It's a lovely *warm* smell!'

'Look! What's that moving over there?' said Julian, suddenly reining in his horse. They all strained their eyes to see.

'Why, it's caravans!' said Julian, at last. 'Of course! They were setting out today, weren't they? Well, they must find it very rough going, that's all I can say. There's no real road anywhere, as far as I can see.'

'Where can they be going?' wondered Anne. 'What's over in that direction?'

'They'll come to the coast if they keep on the way they are going,' said Julian, considering. 'Let's ride over and have a look at them, shall we?'

'Yes. Good idea!' said Dick. So they turned their horses' heads to the right, and rode towards the far-away caravans. These made quite a splash of colour as they went along. There were four of them – two red ones, a blue one and a yellow one. They went very slowly indeed, each pulled by a small, wiry horse.

'They all look like skewbalds, brown and white,' said Dick. 'It's funny that so many gypsies have skewbald horses. I wonder why it is?'

They heard shouting as they came near the caravans, and saw one man pointing them out to another. It was Sniffer's father!

'Look, that's the fellow who woke us up in the stable last night,' said Julian to Dick. 'Sniffer's father! What a nasty bit of work he is! Why doesn't he get a hair-cut?'

'Good morning!' called Dick, as they rode up to the caravans on their horses. 'Nice day!'

There was no answer. The gypsies driving their caravans and those walking alongside, looked sourly at the four riders.

'Where are you going?' asked Henry. 'To the coast?'

'It's naught to do with you,' said one of the gypsies, an old man with curly grey hair.

'Surly folk, aren't they?' said Dick to Julian. 'I suppose they think we're spying on them, or something. I wonder how they manage about food on this moor, no shops or anything. I suppose they take it all with them.'

'I'll ask them,' said Henry, not at all put off by the surly looks. She rode right up to Sniffer's father.

'How do you manage about food, and water?' she asked.

'We got food there,' said Sniffer's father, jerking his head back towards one of the caravans. 'As for water, we know where the springs are.'

'Are you camping on the moor for a long time?' asked Henry, thinking that a gypsy's life might be a fine one, for a time! Fancy living out here on this lovely moor with gorse blazing gold all around, and primroses by the thousand in the sheltered corners!

'That's naught to do with *you*!' shouted the old man with curly grey hair. 'You clear off and let us alone!'

'Come on, Henry,' said Julian, swinging round to go off. 'They don't like us asking them questions. They think it's prying, not interest. Maybe they have lots of things to hide, and don't want us poking around – one or two chickens from a farm, a duck or so from some pond. They live from hand to mouth, these folk.'

Some dark-eyed children peered from the vans as they went by. One or two were running outside, but they sheered off like frightened rabbits when Henry cantered towards them.

'Oh well, they simply don't *want* to be friendly,' she said, and went to join the other three. 'What a strange life they lead, in their houses on wheels! Never staying anywhere for long, always on the move. Get up, there, Sultan. Go after the others!'

Her horse obediently followed the other three, taking care not to step into any rabbit-holes! What fun it was to be out here in the sunshine, jogging up and down on a horse's back, without a care in the world! Henry was very happy.

The other three were enjoying their day, but they were not quite so happy. They kept wondering about George. They missed Timmy too. He should be trotting beside them, enjoying the day as well!

They lost sight of the caravans after a time. Julian kept track of the way they went, half-afraid of being lost. He had a compass with him, and checked their direction continually. 'It would never do to have to spend a night out here!' he said. 'Nobody would ever find us!'

They had a magnificent lunch about half-past twelve. Really, Mrs Johnson had surpassed herself! Egg and sardine sandwiches, tomato and lettuce, ham – there seemed no end to them! Great slices of cherry cake were added too, and a large, juicy pear each.

'I like this kind of cherry cake,' said Dick, looking at his enormous slice. 'The cherries have all gone to the bottom. They make a very nice last mouthful!'

'Any drinks?' said Henry, and was handed a bottle of ginger-beer. She drank it thirstily.

'Why does ginger-beer taste so nice on a picnic?' she said. '*Much* nicer than drinking it sitting down in a shop, even if it's got ice in it!'

'There's a spring or something near by,' said Julian. 'I can hear it bubbling.'

They all listened. Yes, there was a little bubbling, tinkling noise. Anne got up to trace it. She found it in a few minutes and called the others. There was a round pool, cool and blue, lying two or three feet down, and into it, from one side, fell a crystal clear spring of water, tinkling as it fell.

'One of the springs that the gypsies use, when they travel this deserted moor, I expect,' said Julian. He cupped his hands under the falling water and got his palms full. He carried the water to his mouth and sipped it.

'Delicious! Cool as an ice-box,' he said. 'Taste it, Anne.'

They rode a little farther, but the moor seemed the same everywhere, heather, wiry grass, grose, a clear spring falling into a pool or tiny stream here and there, and a few trees, mostly silver birch.

Larks sang all the time, soaring high in the air, almost too far up to see.

'Their song falls down like raindrops,' said Anne, holding out her hands as if to catch them. Henry laughed. She liked this family, and was very glad they had asked her to come out with them. She thought George was silly to have stayed at the stables.

'I think we ought to go home,' said Julian at last, looking at his watch. 'We're a good way away. Let me see now. We want to make more or less for the setting sun. Come on!'

He led the way, his horse picking its own path over the heather. The others followed. Dick stopped after a while.

'Are you sure we're quite right, Ju? I don't somehow feel that we are. The moor is different here, rather sandy and not so much gorse.'

Julian stopped his horse and looked round and about. 'Yes, it does look a bit different,' he said. 'But yet we seem to be going in the right direction. Let's go a bit more to the west. If only there was something on the horizon to guide us. But this moor hasn't a thing that stands out anywhere!'

They went on again, and then Henry gave an exclamation. 'I say! What's this? Do come here.'

The two boys and Anne swerved over to Henry. She was now off her horse, and was bending over, scraping away at the heather.

'Look, it seems like rails, or something,' said Henry. 'Very old and rusty. But they can't be, surely?'

Everyone was now down on their knees, scraping sand and heather away. Julian sat back and considered.

'Yes, it's rails. Old ones, as you say. But what in the world were rails laid down here for?'

'I can't think,' said Henry. 'I only caught sight of them by chance, they're so overgrown. I couldn't believe my eyes!'

'They must lead from somewhere *to* somewhere!'

said Dick. 'Perhaps there was a quarry, or something on the moor and they ran little engines with trucks there, to fetch the sand, and take it back to town to sell.'

'That's about it,' said Julian. 'It's very sandy here, as we noticed. Good, fine sand. Maybe there *is* a quarry on the moor. Well, *that* way, behind us goes right out on the moor, so *this* way must lead back to some town or village, probably Milling Green or somewhere like that.'

'Yes. You're right,' said Dick. 'In which case, if we follow the lines along, we'll get back to civilization sooner or later!'

'Well, seeing that we seem to be more or less lost, that would be quite a good idea!' said Henry. She mounted her horse again and rode along the lines.

'They're fairly easy to see!' she called. 'If you ride between them, that is, because they go so straight.'

The lines ran steadily over the moor, sometimes very overgrown, and in about half an hour's time Henry gave a cry and pointed forward. 'Houses! I thought we'd soon come to some place!'

'It *is* Milling Green!' said Julian, as the rails came to a sudden end, and they rode out into a small cart-road.

'Well, we haven't far to go now, to get to the

stables,' said Henry, pleased. 'I say, wouldn't it be fun to follow those lines all across the moor and see where they really lead to?'

'Yes. We might do that one day,' said Julian. 'Gosh, it's getting late. I wonder how old George has been getting on today!'

They walked quickly along to the stables, thinking of George. Would she have retired to bed? Would she still be cross, or worse still, hurt and grieved? It was anybody's guess!

7 George, Sniffer and Liz

George had had quite an interesting day. First she had gone down to help Captain Johnson do Clip's leg again and bandage it up. The little skewbald stood very patiently, and George felt a sudden liking for the ugly little creature.

'Thanks, George,' said Captain Johnson, who, to her relief, had said nothing about her not having gone riding with the others. 'Now would you like to come and put jumps up for the youngsters? They're longing to do some more jumping.'

George found that it was quite amusing to teach the younger ones how to jump. They were so very proud of themselves when they went over even a foot-high jump on their little ponies.

After that Sniffer arrived, accompanied by a peculiar little mongrel called Liz. Liz was a bit of a spaniel, a bit of a poodle, and odd bits of something else – and looked rather like a small, walking hearthrug of black curly fur.

Timmy was amazed to see this walking mat, and sat and watched Liz sniffing here and there for some time, before he came to the conclusion that it really *was* some kind of dog. He gave a sharp little bark to see what this comical creature would do when she heard it.

Liz took no notice at all. She had unearthed a small bone, which smelt extremely interesting. Timmy considered that all bones within the radius of at least a mile, belonged to him and him alone. So he ran over to Liz at once and gave a small, warning growl.

Liz immediately dropped the bone humbly at his feet, then sat up on her hind-legs and begged. Timmy eyed her in astonishment. Then Liz stood up on her hindlegs and walked daintily all round Timmy and back again.

Timmy was astounded. He had never seen a dog do that before. *Could* this hearthrug affair be a dog after all?

Liz saw that Timmy was really impressed, and went on with yet another trick she had learnt during the time she had been with the circus.

She turned head-over-heels, yapping all the time. Timmy retreated a few steps into the bushes. This was going *too* far! What was this animal doing? Trying to stand on its head?

Liz went on turning head-over-heels very rapidly and ended up almost on Timmy's front paws. He had now backed into the bush as far as he could.

Liz remained on her back, paws in air, tongue hanging out, panting. She gave a very small, beseeching whine.

Timmy bent his head down and sniffed at her paws. Behind him his tail began to move a little, yes, it had a wag in it! He sniffed again. Liz leapt on to her four feet and pranced all round Timmy, yapping as if to say 'Come on and play! Do come!'

And then suddenly Timmy fell upon the absurd little creature and pretended to worry it. Liz gave a delighted volley of yaps and rolled over and over. They had a marvellous game, and when it was all over, Timmy sank down panting for breath, in a sunny corner of the yard, and Liz settled herself between his front paws, as if she had known him all her life!

When George came out of the stable with Sniffer, she could hardly believe her eyes. 'What's that Timmy's got between his paws?' she said. 'It's surely not a *dog*!'

'It's Liz,' said Sniffer. 'She can get round any dog there is, Master George! Liz! You're a monkey, aren't you! Walk, then, walk!'

Liz left Timmy and ran over to Sniffer, walking daintily on her hind legs. George laughed. 'What a funny little creature, like a bit cut out of a furry hearthrug!'

'She's clever,' said Sniffer and patted Liz. 'Well, Master George, when can I have Clip, do you think? My father has gone off with the other caravans and he's left me with ours. So it doesn't matter whether it's today or tomorrow, or even the next day.'

'Well, it won't be today, that's certain,' said George, pleased that Sniffer called her *Master George* not Miss. 'It might perhaps be tomorrow.

Haven't you got a hanky, Sniffer? I never on my life heard anyone sniff as often as you do.'

Sniffer rubbed his sleeve across his nose. 'I never had no hanky,' he said. 'But I've got my sleeve, see?'

'I think you're quite disgusting,' said George. 'I'm going to give you one of my own hankies, and you're to use it. You're *not* to keep sniffing like that.'

'Didn't know I did,' said Sniffer, half sulkily. 'What's it matter, anyway?'

But George had gone indoors and up the stairs. She chose a large hanky, in red and white stripes. That would do nicely for Sniffer! She took it down to him. He looked at it in surprise.

'That's a scarf for my neck!' he said.

'No, it isn't. It's a hanky for your nose,' said George. 'Haven't you a pocket to put it in? That's right. Now, use it instead of sniffing, for goodness' sake!'

'Where are the others?' asked Sniffer, putting the hanky carefully into his pocket, almost as if it were made of glass.

'Gone riding,' said George, shortly.

'They said they would come and see my caravan,' said Sniffer. 'They said so!'

'Well, they won't be able to today,' said George. 'They'll be back too late, I expect. I'll come and see it, though. There's nobody in it, is there?'

George was not keen on meeting Sniffer's father or any other of his relations! He shook his head. 'No, it's empty. My father's gone, I told you, and my aunt and my grandma too.'

'What do you *do* on the moor?' asked George, as she followed Sniffer across the field and up the hill to where the caravans had stood. Now only one was left – Sniffer's.

'Play around,' said Sniffer, and gave an enormous sniff. George gave him a shove in the back.

'Sniffer! What did I give you the hanky for? *Don't* do that! It gets on my nerves!'

Sniffer used his sleeve at once, but fortunately George didn't notice. She had now come to the caravan and was staring at it. She thought of Sniffer's answer to her question a minute or two back.

'You said you just played around on the moor. But what does your *father* do, and your uncle and grandad and all the rest of the men? There's nothing to do there at all, as far as I can see, and no farmhouse to beg eggs or milk or anything from.'

Sniffer shut up like a clam. He was just about to

sniff and thought better of it. He stared at George, his mouth set in an obstinate line.

George looked at him impatiently. 'Captain Johnson said you and your caravans went there every three months,' she said. 'What for? There must be *some* reason?'

'Well,' said Sniffer, looking away from her, 'we make pegs, and baskets, and . . .'

'I know that! All gypsies make things to sell,' said George. 'But you don't need to go into the middle of a deserted moor to make them. You can do them just as well in a village, or sitting in a field near a farmhouse. *Why* go to such a lonely place as the moor?'

Sniffer said nothing, but bent over a queer little arrangement of sticks set on the path beside his caravan. George saw them and bent over them too, her question forgotten.

'Oh! Is that a patrin? A gypsy message! What does it mean?'

There were two sticks, one long and one short, neatly arranged in the shape of a cross. A little farther up on the path were a few single, straight sticks, all pointing in the same direction.

'Yes,' said Sniffer, very glad to have the subject changed. 'It's our way of telling things to those who may come after us. See the sticks in the shape of the cross? That's a patrin that says we've been along this way and we're going in the direction that the long stick points.'

'I see,' said George. 'How simple! But what about these four straight sticks, all pointing the same way too. What do *they* mean?'

'They mean that the travellers went in caravans,' said Sniffer, giving a sudden sniff. 'See, four sticks, four caravans, going that way!'

'I *see*,' said George, making up her mind that she herself would evolve quite a few 'patrins' for use at school when they went for walks. 'Are there any more patrins Sniffer?'

'Plenty,' said the boy. 'Look, when I leave here, I shall put a patrin like this!' he picked a large leaf from a nearby tree, and then a small one. He placed them side by side, and weighted them down with small stones.

'What in the world does that mean?' said George.

'Well, it's a patrin, a message, to say that me and my little dog have gone in the caravan too,' said Sniffer, picking up the leaves. 'Suppose my father came back to find me, and he saw those leaves there, he'd know I'd gone on with my dog.

It's simple. Big leaf for me, little leaf for my dog!'

'Yes. I like it,' said George, pleased. 'Now let's look at the caravan.'

It was an old-fashioned kind of caravan, not very big, and with high wheels. The door and the steps down were in front. The shafts rested on the ground waiting for Clip to come back. The caravan was black, with red designs on it here and there.

George went up the steps. 'I've been inside a few caravans,' she said. 'But never one quite like this.'

She peeped in curiously. It certainly wasn't very clean, but it wasn't as dirty as she expected either.

'It's not smelly, is it?' said Sniffer, quite anxiously. 'I tidied it up today, seeing as how I thought you were all visiting me. That's our bed at the back. We all sleep on it.'

George stared at the big bunk-like bed stretched at the end of the caravan, covered with a bright quilt. She imagined the whole family sleeping there, close together. Well at least they would be warm in the winter.

'Don't you get hot in the summer, sleeping in this small caravan?' asked George.

'Oh no, only my grandma sleeps here then,' said Sniffer, swallowing a sniff in a hurry, before George could hear it. 'Me and the others sleep under the caravan. Then if it rains it don't matter.'

'Well, thanks for showing me so many things,' said George, looking round at the cupboards, the little locker-seats, and the over-big chest of drawers. 'How you all get in here is a miracle.'

She didn't go in. Even though Sniffer had tidied up, there was still a distinctly peculiar smell hanging about!

'Come and see us tomorrow, Sniffer,' she said, going down the steps. 'Clip may be all right by then. And Sniffer, don't you forget you've got a hanky now!'

'I won't forget,' said Sniffer proudly. 'I'll keep it as clean as can be, Master George!'

8 Sniffer makes a promise

George was feeling very lonely by the time the evening came. How had the others got on without her? Had they missed her at all? Perhaps they hadn't even *thought* of her!

'Anyway, they didn't have *you*, Timmy!' said George. 'You wouldn't go off and leave me, would you?'

Timmy pressed against her, glad to see that she was happier again. He wondered where the others were, and where they had gone to all day.

There was suddenly a clattering of hooves in the stableyard and George flew to the door. Yes, they were back! How should she behave? She felt cross and relieved and rather humble and glad all at once! She stood there, not knowing whether to frown or to smile.

The others made up her mind for her. 'Hallo, George!' shouted Dick. 'We did miss you!'

'How's your head?' called Anne. 'I hope it's better!'

'Hallo!' called Henry. 'You ought to have come. We've had a super day!'

'Come and help us stable the horses, George,' shouted Julian. 'Tell us what you've been doing!'

Timmy had sped over to them, barking in delight. George found her legs running towards them too, a welcoming smile on her face.

'Hallo!' she called. 'Let me help! Did you really miss me? I missed you too.'

The boys were very relieved to see that George was herself again. Nothing more was said about her headache! She busied herself unsaddling the horses and listening to their story of the day. Then she told them about Sniffer and his patrins, and how she had given him a brand-new handkerchief.

'But I'm sure he thinks he's got to keep it spotlessly clean!' she said. 'He never used it once when I was with him. There's the supper-bell, we'll only *just* be in time! Are you hungry?'

'You bet we are!' said Dick. 'Though after Mrs Johnson's sandwiches I never thought I'd be able to eat any supper at all. How's Clip?'

'Never mind now. I'll tell you everything at supper,' said George. 'Do you want any help, Henry?'

Henry was surprised to hear George call her Henry instead of Henrietta. 'No thanks – er – George,' she said. 'I can manage.'

It was a very jolly supper-time that evening. The youngsters were set at a table by themselves, so the older ones talked to their hearts' content.

Captain Johnson was very interested to hear about the old railway they had found. 'I never knew there was anything like that on the moors,' he said. 'Though, of course, we've only been here about fifteen years, so we don't know a great deal of the local history. You want to go and ask old Ben the blacksmith about that. He's lived here all his life, and a long life it is, for he's over eighty!'

'Well, we've got to take some of the horses to be shod tomorrow, haven't we?' said Henry, eagerly. 'We could ask him then! Why, he might even have helped to make the rails!'

'We saw the caravans, George, when we had got pretty far out on the moor,' said Julian. 'Goodness knows where they were heading for, towards the coast, I should think. What's the coast like beyond the moor, Captain Johnson?'

'Wild,' said the Captain. 'Great, unclimbable cliffs, and reefs or rocks stretching out to sea. Only the birds live there. There's no bathing, not boating, no beach.'

'Well, it beats me where those caravans are going,' said Dick. 'It's a mystery. They go every three months, don't they?'

'About that,' said Captain Johnson. 'I've no idea what the attraction of the moor is for the gypsies. It just beats me! Usually they won't go anywhere where there are not a few farms, or at least a small village where they can sell their goods.'

'I'd like to go after them and see where they are and what they're doing,' said Julian, eating his third hard-boiled egg.

'All right. Let's,' said George.

'But how? We don't know where they've gone,' said Henry.

'Well, Sniffer's going to join them tomorrow, or as soon as Clip is all right for walking,' said George. 'And he's got to follow the patrins left on the way by the others. He says that he looks at the places where fires have been made on the way, and beside them somewhere he will see the patrins, the sticks that point in the direction he must follow.'

'He's sure to destroy them,' said Dick. '*We* couldn't follow them!'

'We'll ask him to leave his *own* patrins,' said George. 'I think he will. He's not a bad little boy, really. I could ask him to leave *plenty* of patrins, so that we could easily find the way.'

'Well, it might be fun to see if we could read the right road to go, just as easily as the gypsies do,' said Julian. 'We could make it a day's ride. It would be interesting!'

Henry gave a most enormous yawn, and that made Anne yawn too, though hers was a very polite one.

'Henry!' said Mrs Johnson.

'Sorry,' said Henry. 'It just came, almost like a sneeze does. I don't know why, but I feel almost asleep.'

'Go to bed then,' said Mrs Johnson. 'You've had such a day of air and sunshine! You all look very brown too. The April sun has been as hot as June today.'

The five of them, and Timmy, went out for a last look at the horses, and to do one or two small jobs. Henry yawned again, and that set everyone else off, even George.

'Me for the straw!' said Julian, with a laugh. 'Oh, the thought of that warm, comfy straw bed is too good for words! You girls are welcome to the beds!'

'I hope Sniffer's Pa doesn't come in the middle of the night again,' said Dick.

'I shall tie up the latch,' said Julian. 'Well, let's go and say goodnight to Mrs Johnson.'

It wasn't long before the three girls were in bed and the two boys cuddled down in the straw of the stable. Clip was there still, but he no longer fidgeted. He lay down quietly, and did not once move his bad leg. It was getting much better. He would certainly be able to go after the others the next day!

Julian and Dick fell asleep at once. No one came creeping in at the stable door that night. Nothing disturbed them until the morning, when a cock got into the stable through a window, sat on a rafter just above them, and crowed loudly enough to wake both boys with a jump.

'What's that!' said Dick. 'That awful screeching in my ear! Was it you, Ju?'

The cock crowed again and the boys laughed. 'Blow him!' said Julian, settling down again. 'I could do with another couple of hours' sleep!'

That morning Sniffer came slipping in at the gate again. He never came boldly in, he slid through the hedge, or crept in at the gate, or appeared round a corner. He saw George and went over to her.

'Master George,' he called, much to Julian's amusement. 'Is Clip better?'

'Yes!' called back George. 'Captain Johnson says you can take him today. But wait a bit, Sniffer, I want to ask you something before you go.'

Sniffer was pleased. He liked this girl who had presented him with such a magnificent handkerchief. He took it carefully out of his pocket, hoping to please her.

'See,' he said. 'How clean it is! I have kept it very carefully.' He sniffed loudly.

'You're a fathead,' said George, exasperated. 'I gave it to you to *use*, not to keep clean in your pocket. It's to stop your *sniffing*. Honestly, you're a bit of a mutt, Sniffer. I shall take that hanky away if you don't use it!'

Sniffer looked alarmed. He shook it out carefully and then lightly touched his nose with it. He then folded it up conscientiously in the right creases and put it back into his pocket again.

'Now, NO sniffing!' commanded George, trying not to laugh. 'Listen, Sniffer, you know those patrins you showed me yesterday?'

'Yes, Master George,' said Sniffer.

'Well, will the other gypsies who have gone in front, leave you patrins to follow, so that you will know the way?' said George.

Sniffer nodded. 'Yes, but not many, because I have been that way twice before. They will only leave them in places where I might go wrong.'

'I see,' said George. 'Now Sniffer, we want to have a sort of game. We want to see which of us can follow patrins, and we want you to lay patrins for us quite often, on your way to your family today. Will you?'

'Oh yes, I will,' said Sniffer, quite proud to have a favour asked of him. 'I will lay the ones I showed you, the cross, the long sticks, and the big and little leaves.'

'Yes, do,' said George. 'That will mean that you have passed in a certain direction and you are a boy and a dog. That's right, isn't it?'

'Yes,' said Sniffer, nodding his head. 'You have remembered!'

'Right. And we're going to have a kind of game, trying to pretend we are travelling gypsies following others who have passed,' said George. 'You must not show yourselves when you come up to our caravans,' said Sniffer, looking suddenly alarmed. 'I should get into trouble for laying patrins for you.'

'All right. We'll be careful,' said George. 'Now let's go and get Clip.'

They fetched the patient little skewbald who came out gladly. He no longer limped, and his rest seemed to have done him good. He went off at a good pace with Sniffer. The last George heard of them was a very loud sniff indeed!

'Sniffer!' she shouted, warningly. He put his hand in his pocket and pulled out the hanky. He waved it gaily in the air, a sudden grin lighting up his face.

George went to find the others. 'Sniffer has taken Clip,' she said. 'What about going down to the blacksmith, and taking those horses that want shoeing?'

'Good idea,' said Julian. 'We can ask him all about Mystery Moor then, and the strange little railway line, or whatever it is! Come on.'

They took the horses that needed shoeing. There were six of them, so they each rode one, and Julian led the sixth. Timmy ran happily along beside them. He loved the horses, and they regarded him as a real friend, bending their long noses down to sniff at him, whenever he came near.

They went slowly down the long lane to the blacksmith's. 'There it is!' said George. 'A proper old smithy with a lovely fire! And there's the smith!'

Old Ben was a mighty figure of a man, even though he was over eighty. He didn't shoe many horses now, but sat in the sun, watching all that was going on. He had a great mane of white hair, and eyes that were as black as the coal he had so many times heated to a fiery flame.

'Good morning, young masters and Miss,' he said and Julian grinned. That would please George and Henry!

'We've got some questions to ask you,' said George, dismounting.

'Ask away!' said the old man. 'If it's about this place, there's nothing much old Ben can't tell you! Give Jim your horses. Now, ask away!'

9 The blacksmith tells a tale

'Well,' began Julian, 'we went riding on Mystery Moor yesterday, and for one thing we'd like to know if there is any reason for the curious name. *Was* there ever a mystery on that moor?'

'Oh, there be plenty of mysteries away there,' said Old Ben. 'People lost and never come back again, noises that no one could find the reason of . . .'

'What kind of noises?' said Anne, curiously.

'Ah now, when I were a boy, I spent nights up on that moor,' said old Ben, solemnly, 'and the noises that went on there! Screeches and howls and the like, and moans and the sweep of big wings . . .'

'Well, all that might have been owls and foxes and things like that,' said Dick. 'I've heard a barn-owl give a screech just over my head which made me nearly jump out of my skin. If I hadn't known it was an owl I'd have run for miles!'

Ben grinned and his face ran into a score of creases and wrinkles.

'Why is it called *Mystery* Moor?' persisted Julian. 'Is it a very old name?'

'When my Grandad was a boy it were called *Misty* Moor,' said the old blacksmith, remembering. 'See, *Misty*, not *Mystery*. And that were because of the sea-fogs that came stealing in from the coast, and lay heavy on the moor, so that no man could see his hand in front of his face. Yes, I've been lost in one of them mists, and right scared I was too. It swirled round me like a live thing, and touched me all over with its cold damp fingers.'

'How horrid!' said Anne with a shiver. 'What did you do?'

'Well, first I ran for my life,' said Ben, getting out his pipe and looking into the empty bowl. 'I ran over heather and into gorse. I fell a dozen times, and all the time the mist was feeling me with its damp fingers, trying to get me, that's what the old folk used to say of that mist, it was always trying to get you!'

'Still, it was only a mist,' said George, feeling that the old man was exaggerating. 'Does it still come over the moor?'

'Oh ay,' said Ben, ramming some tobacco into his pipe. 'Autumn's the time, but it comes sudden-like at any moment of the year. I've knowed it come at the end of a fine summer's day, creeping in stealthy-like, and my, if you don't happen to see it soon enough, it gets you!'

'What do you mean, it *gets* you?' said George.

'Well, it may last for days,' said old Ben. 'And if you're lost on them moors, you're lost proper, and you never come back. Ah, smile if you like, young sir, but I *knows!*' He went off into memories of long ago, looking down at his pipe. 'Let's see now, there was old Mrs Banks, who went bilberry-picking with her basket on a summer's afternoon, and no one ever heard of her again, after the mist came down. And there was young Victor who played truant and went off to the moors, and the mist got him too.'

'I can see we'd better watch out for the mist if we go riding there,' said Dick. 'This is the first I've heard of it.'

'Yes. You keep your eyes skinned,' said old Ben. 'Look away to the coast-side and watch there, that's where it comes from. But there baint many mists nowadays, I don't know for why. No, now I think on it, there haven't been a mist, not a proper wicked one, for nigh on three years.'

'What I'd like to know is why was the name changed to *Mystery* Moor,' said Henry. 'I can understand its being called Misty Moor, but now everyone calls it *Mystery*, not Misty.'

'Well now, that must have been about seventy years ago, when I were a bit of a boy,' said Ben, lighting his pipe and puffing hard. He was enjoying himself. He didn't often get such an interested audience as this, five of them, including a dog who sat and listened too!

'That was when the Bartle Family built the little railway over the moor,' he began, and stopped at the exclamations of his five listeners.

'Ah! We wanted to know about *that!*'

'Oh! You know about the railway then!'

'Do go on!'

The blacksmith seemed to get some trouble with his pipe and pulled at it for an exasperatingly long time. George wished she was a horse and could stamp her foot impatiently!

'Well, the Bartle Family was a big one,' said Ben at last. 'All boys, but for one ailing little girl. Big strong fellows they were, I remember them well. I was scared of them, they were so free with their fists. Well, one of them, Dan, found a mighty good stretch of sand out there on the moor . . .'

'Oh yes, we *thought* there might have been a sand-quarry,' said Anne. Ben frowned at the interruption.

'And as there were nine or ten good strong Bartles, they reckoned to make a fine do of it,' said Ben. 'They got wagons and they went to and from the quarry they dug, and they sold their sand for miles around, good, sharp sand it were . . .'

'We saw some,' said Henry. 'But what about the rails?'

'Don't hurry him,' said Dick, with a frown.

'They made a mort of money,' said Ben, remembering. 'And they set to work and built a little railway to carry an injin and trucks to the quarry and back, to save labour. My, my, that were a nine days' wonder, that railway! Us youngsters used to follow the little injin, puffing along, and it were the longing of us all to drive it. But we never did. Them Bartles kept a big stick, each one of them, and they whipped the hide off any boy that got too near them. Fierce they were, and quarrelsome.'

'Why did the railway fall into ruin?' asked Julian. 'The rails are all overgrown with heather and grass now. You can hardly see them.'

'Well, now we come to that there Mystery you keep on about,' said Ben, taking an extra big puff at his pipe. 'Them Bartles fell foul of the gypsies up on the moor . . .'

'Oh, were there gypsies on the moor *then*?' said Dick. 'There are some now!'

'Oh ay, there's always been gypsies on the moor, long as I can remember,' said the blacksmith. 'Well, it's said them gypsies quarrelled with the Bartles, and it wasn't hard to do that, most people did! And the gypsies pulled up bits of the line, here and there, and the little injin toppled over and pulled the trucks with it.'

The children could quite well imagine the little engine puffing along, coming to the damaged rails and falling over. What a to-do there must have been up on the moor then!

'The Bartles weren't ones to put up with a thing like that,' said Ben, 'so they set about to drive all the gypsies off the moor, and they swore that if so much as one caravan went there, they'd set fire to it and chase the gypsies over to the coast and into the sea!'

'They *must* have been a fierce family,' said Anne.

'You're right, there,' said Ben. 'All nine or ten of them were big upstanding men, with great shaggy eyebrows that almost hid their eyes, and loud voices. Nobody dared to cross them. If they did, they'd have the whole family on their door-step with sticks. They ruled this place, they did, and my, they were hated! Us children ran off as soon as we saw one coming round a corner.'

'What about the gypsies? Did the Bartles manage to drive them off the moor?' asked George, impatiently.

'Now you let me go my own pace,' said Ben, pointing at her with his pipe. 'You want a Bartle after you, young sir, that's what you want!' He thought she was a boy, of course. He did something to his pipe and made them all wait a little. Julian winked at the others. He liked this old fellow with his long, long memories.

'Now, you can't cross the gypsies for long,' said Ben, at last. 'That's a fact, you can't. And one day all them Bartles disappeared and never came back home. No, not one of them. All that was left of the family was little lame Agnes, their sister.'

Everyone exclaimed in surprise and old Ben looked round with satisfaction. Ah, he could tell a story, he could!

'But whatever happened?' said Henry.

'Well, no one rightly knows,' said Ben. 'It happened in a week when the mist came swirling over the moors and blotted everything out. Nobody went up there except the Bartles, and they were safe because all they had to do was to follow their railway lines there and back. They went up to the quarry each day the mist was there, and worked the same as usual. Nothing stopped they Bartles from working!'

He paused and looked round at his listeners. He dropped his voice low, and all five of the children felt little shivers up their backs.

'One night somebody in the village saw twenty or more gypsy caravans slinking through the village at dead of night,' said Ben. 'Up on the moor they went in the thick mist. Mebbe they followed the railway; nobody knows. And next morning, up to the quarry went the Bartles as usual, swallowed up in the mist.'

He paused again. 'And they never came back,' he said. 'No, not one of them. Never heard of again!'

'But what *happened*?' said George.

'Search-parties were sent out when the mist cleared,' said old Ben. 'But never one of the Bartles did they find, alive or dead. Never a one! And they didn't find any gypsy caravans either. They'd all come creeping back the next night, and passed through the village like shadows. I reckon them gypsies set upon the Bartles in the mist that day, fought them and defeated them, and took them and threw them over the cliffs into the roaring sea!'

'How horrible!' said Anne, feeling sick.

'Don't worrit yourself!' said the blacksmith. 'It all happened a mort of time ago, and there wasn't many that mourned them Bartles, I can tell you. Funny thing was, their weakly little sister, Agnes, she lived to be a hale old woman of ninety-six, and only died a few years ago! And to think them strong fierce brothers of hers went all together like that!'

'It's a most interesting story, Ben,' said Julian. 'So Misty Moor became *Mystery* Moor then, did it? And nobody ever *really* found out what happened, so the mystery was never solved. Didn't anyone work the railway after that, or get the sand?'

'No, not a soul,' said Ben. 'We was all scared, you see, and young Agnes, she said the railway and the trucks and injin could rot, for all she cared. I never dared to go near them after that. It was a long time before anyone but the gypsies set foot on Misty Moor again. Now it's all forgotten, the tale of the Bartles, but them gypsies still remember, I've no doubt! They've got long memories, they have.'

'Do you know why they come to Mystery Moor every so often?' asked Dick.

'No. They come and they go,' said Ben. 'They've their own queer ways. They don't belong anywhere, them folk. What they do on the moor is their own business, and I wouldn't want to poke *my* nose into it. I'd remember them old Bartles, and keep away!'

A voice came from inside the smithy, where Jim, the blacksmith's grandson, had been shoeing the horses. 'Grandad! You stop jabbering away there, and let the children come and talk to *me*! I've shod nearly all the horses.'

Ben laughed. 'You go along,' he said to the children. 'I know you like to be in there and see the sparks fly, and the shoes made. I've wasted your time, I have, telling you long-ago things. You go along into the smithy. And just you remember two things – watch out for that mist, and keep away from the gypsies on the moor!'

10 Sniffer's patrins

It was fun in the smithy, working the bellows, seeing the fire glow, and watching the red-hot shoes being shaped. Jim was quick and clever, and it was a pleasure to watch him.

'You been hearing Grandad's old stories?' he said. 'It's all he's got to do now, sit there and remember, though when he wants to he can make a horse-shoe as well as I can! There, that's the last one. Stand still, Sultan. That's right!'

The five children were soon on their way back again. It was a lovely morning, and the banks and ditches they passed were bright gold with thousands of celandines.

'All beautifully polished!' said Anne, picking two or three for her button-hole. It *did* look as if someone had polished the inside of each petal, for they gleamed like enamel.

'What a queer tale the old man told,' said Julian. 'He told it well!'

'Yes. He made me feel I don't want to go up on the moor again!' said Anne.

'Don't be feeble!' said George. 'It all happened ages ago. Jolly interesting too. I wonder if the gypsies who are there now know the story. Maybe their great – grandparents were the ones who set on the Bartles that misty day!'

'Well, Sniffer's father looked sly enough to carry out a plan like that,' said Henry. 'What about us having a shot at following the way they went, and seeing if we can make out the patrins that Sniffer told George he would leave?'

'Good idea,' said Julian. 'We'll go this afternoon. I say, what's the time? I should think it must be half-past dinner-time!'

They looked at their watches. 'Yes, we're late, but we always are when we get back from the blacksmith,' said George. 'Never mind, I bet Mrs Johnson will have an extra special meal for us!'

She had! There was an enormous plate of stew for everyone, complete with carrots, onions, parsnips and turnips, and a date pudding to follow. Good old Mrs Johnson!

'You three girls must wash up for me afterwards,' she said. 'I've such a lot to do today.'

'Why can't the boys help?' said George at once.

'*I'll* do all the washing-up,' said Anne with a sudden grin. 'You four *boys* can go out to the stables!'

Dick gave her a good-natured shove. 'You know we'll help, even if we're not good at it. I'll dry. I hate those bits and pieces that float about in the washing-bowl.'

'Will it be all right if we go up on the moors this afternoon?' asked George.

'Yes, quite all right. But if you want to take your tea, you'll have to pack it yourselves,' said Mrs Johnson. 'I'm taking the small children out for a ride, and there's one on the leading-rein still, as you know.'

They were ready to set off at three o'clock, their tea packed and everything. The horses were caught in the field and got ready too. They set off happily.

'Now we'll see if we are as clever as we think we are, at reading gypsy patrins!' said George. 'Timmy, don't chase *every* rabbit you see, or you'll be left behind!'

They cantered up on to the moor, passing the place where the caravans had stood. They knew the direction they had taken, and here and there they saw wheel-marks. It was fairly easy to follow their trail, because five caravans made quite a path to follow.

'Here's where they camped first,' said Julian, riding up to a blackened spot that showed where a fire had been lit. 'We ought to find a message left somewhere here.'

They searched for one. George found it. 'It's here, behind this tree!' she called. 'Out of the wind.'

They dismounted and came round George. On the ground was the patrin, the shape of a cross, the long stick pointing forwards, in the direction they were going. Other single sticks lay there, to show that a caravan had gone that way, and beside them were the large and the small leaves, weighted with tiny stones.

'What did those leaves show now? Oh yes, Sniffer and his dog!' said Dick. 'Well, we're on the right way, though we'd know that anyhow, by the fire!'

They mounted again and went on. It proved quite easy to find and follow the patrins. Only once did they find any difficulty and that was when they came to a place, marked by two trees, where there was no apparent sign in the heather of any caravan marks.

They set off . . . and almost at once found signs of the passing of caravans.

'The heather's so jolly thick here that it's taken the caravans as if it were a feather-bed, springing up when they had gone, and giving no sign of where they had passed,' said Julian. He dismounted and had a good look round. No, there was no sign.

'We'll go on a little way,' he said. 'We may come to a camping place, then we'll know.'

But they came to no old camping place, and stopped at last in bewilderment. 'We've lost the trail,' said Dick. 'We're not such good gypsies after all!'

'Let's go back to those two trees,' said George. 'We can still just see them. If it's so easy to lose the way there, there *might* be a patrin, although there are no camp-marks. After all, a patrin is left to show the way, in case the ones following take the wrong route.'

So back they rode to the two trees, and there, sure enough, was Sniffer's patrin! Henry found it set carefully between the trees, so that nothing could disturb it.

'Here's the cross, and the single sticks, and the leaves!' she said. 'But look, the long stick of the cross points to the east and we went off to the north. No wonder we found no signs of the caravans!'

They set off to the east this time, across the thick, springy heather, and almost at once found signs of the passing of caravans, twigs broken off the bushes, a wheel rut on a soft piece of ground.

'We're right now,' said Julian, pleased. 'I was beginning to think it was all too easy for words! But it isn't!

They rode for two hours, and then decided to have tea. They sat down in a little glade of silver birches, with an unexpected copse of pale primroses behind. Timmy had to make up his mind which to choose, a rabbit-chase, or titbits from the children's tea!

He chose both, racing after an imaginary rabbit, and then coming back for a sandwich!

'You know, it's a lot better for us when Mrs Johnson makes sandwiches of tomato or lettuce or something like that,' said Henry. 'We do get them all then, but when we have meat or sardine or egg sandwiches Timmy gets as much as we do!'

'Well, surely you don't mind that, Henrietta,' said George at once. 'You make Timmy sound very greedy. After all, you don't need to give him any of *your* sandwiches!'

'Now, Georgina!' murmured Dick, in her ear.

'Sorry, Georgina,' said Henry, with a grin. 'I just can't *help* giving him a sandwich or two when he comes and sits down and looks at me so longingly.'

'Woof,' said Timmy, and at once sat down in front of Henry, his tongue out, and his eyes fixed unblinkingly on her.

'He sort of *hypnotises* me,' complained Henry. 'Make him go away, George, I shan't be able to keep a single sandwich or bit of cake for myself. Go and stare at someone else, Timmy, for goodness' sake!'

Julian looked at his watch. 'I don't think we ought to spend *too* long over tea,' he said. 'I know we've got summertime now, and the evenings are nice and light, but we haven't reached the gypsy camp yet, and after that we've got to go all the way back. What about starting off again?'

'Right,' said everyone and remounted their horses. They set off through the heather. Soon they found it unexpectedly easy to follow the caravan route, because the soil became sandy, and there were many bare patches on which the marks of the wheels could plainly be seen.

'Goodness, if we go to the east much more, we'll come to the sea!' said Dick.

'No, it's still some miles away,' said Julian. 'Hallo, there's a little hill or something in the distance. First time we've seen anything but complete flatness!'

The wheel-marks led steadily towards the little

hill, which, as they came near, seemed to grow considerably bigger. 'I bet the caravans are there,' said George. 'That hill would give a nice bit of shelter from the wind that came from the sea. I believe I can see one!'

George was right. The caravans were there. They showed up well against the hill, in their bright colours.

'They've even got up a washing-line as usual!' said Anne. 'Clothes flapping in the wind!'

'Let's go and ask if Clip is all right,' said Julian. 'It will be a very good excuse for going right up to the camp.'

So they cantered straight up to the little group of five caravans. Four or five men appeared as soon as they heard the sound of hooves. They looked silent and rather forbidding. Sniffer ran out and shouted.

'Hallo! Clip's fine! Quite all right again!'

His father gave him a push and said something sharp to him. He disappeared under the nearest caravan.

Julian rode up to Sniffer's father. 'Did I hear Sniffer say that Clip was quite all right?' he asked. 'Where is he?'

'Over there,' said the man, with a nod of his head. 'No need for you to see him. He's mended fine.'

'All right, all right! I'm not going to take him away from you!' said Julian. 'This is a nice sheltered place you've got, isn't it? How long are you staying?'

'What's that to do with you?' said an old gypsy, unpleasantly.

'Nothing,' said Julian, surprised. 'Just a polite question, that's all!'

'How do you get water?' called George. 'Is there a good spring here?'

There was no reply at all. The four or five men had now been joined by others, and there were three mangy-looking dogs growling round. Timmy was beginning to growl back.

'You'd better go before our dogs get at you,' said Sniffer's father, sourly.

'Where's Liz?' said George, remembering Sniffer's dog, but before she got an answer the three dogs suddenly made an attack on Timmy! They pounced on him and he had hard work to keep them off. He was far bigger than they were, but they were nippy little things.

'Call off those dogs!' yelled Julian, seeing that George was dismounting to go to Timmy's help.

'Hallo! Clip's fine!'

She would get bitten. 'Do you hear me? Call off those dogs.'

Sniffer's father whistled. The three dogs reluctantly left Timmy and went over to the men, their tails down. George had reached Tim and had now got her hand on his collar to stop him from chasing the other three dogs.

'Mount your horse, whistle Timmy, and we'll go,' shouted Julian, not at all liking the silent, sour-looking gypsies. George did as she was told. Timmy ran beside her, and they all cantered away from the unpleasant camp.

The men stood watching them in complete silence. 'What's up with them?' said Dick puzzled. 'Anyone would think they were planning another Bartle affair!'

'Don't!' said Anne. 'They're planning *some*thing, all alone out here, far away from anywhere! I shan't go near them again.'

'They thought we were prying and spying,' said Dick. 'That's all. Poor old Sniffer. What a life he has!'

'We couldn't even tell him that we found his patrins useful,' said George. 'Oh well, there's probably nothing in it, not even an adventure!'

Was she right or wrong? Julian looked at Dick and Dick looked back, his eyebrows raised. They didn't know. Oh well, time would tell!

11 A nice little plan

The five of them told Captain and Mrs Johnson about their afternoon's experience, as they were having supper.

'Patrins!' said Mrs Johnson. 'So Sniffer told you about those? But I really don't think you should visit the gypsy camp. Those particular gypsies are a surly, bad-tempered lot.'

'Did you ever hear the tale of the Big Bartles?' said Henry, getting ready to relate it, and add little bits of her own, here and there!

'No. But it can wait, I'm sure,' said Mrs Johnson, knowing Henry's habit of leaving her food quite uneaten once she began on some marvellous tale. 'Is it one of your tales? You can tell it after supper.'

'It's *not* Henry's tale,' said George, annoyed that Henry should get all the limelight again, and take the blacksmith's tale for her own. 'It's one old Ben told us. Ju, *you* tell it!'

'Nobody is to tell it *now*,' said Captain Johnson. 'You came in late for supper, we waited for you, and the least you can do is to get on with your eating.'

The five juniors at the other table were disappointed. They had hoped to hear another of Henry's marvellous stories. But Captain Johnson was hungry and tired.

'Old Ben is a great age, as you said,' began Henry, after a few mouthfuls. 'He –'

'Not another word, please, Henrietta,' said the Captain, curtly. Henry went red and George grinned, kicking at Dick under the table. Unfortunately she kicked Henry instead, and the girl glared at her for a whole minute.

'Oh dear!' thought Anne. 'Just as we'd had such a lovely day! I suppose we're all tired and scratchy.'

'*Why* did you kick me?' began Henry in a cross voice, as soon as she and George left the table with the others.

'Shut up, you two,' said Julian. 'She probably meant to kick me or Dick, not you.'

Henry shut up. She didn't like Julian to tick her off. George looked mutinous and went off with Timmy.

Dick yawned. 'What jobs are there to do, if any?' he said. 'Don't say there's washing-up again. I feel I might break a few things.'

Mrs Johnson heard him and laughed. 'No, there's no washing-up. The woman has come in to do it tonight. Have a look at the horses – and see that Jenny the mare is not with Flash, you know she doesn't like her for some reason, and *will* kick out at her. She must always be kept in another field.'

'That's all right, Mrs Johnson,' said William, suddenly appearing, stolid and competent as ever. 'I've seen to that. I've seen to everything, really.'

'You're better than any stable-boy, William,' said Mrs Johnson, smiling at him. 'I wish you'd take a permanent job here!'

'I wish you meant that,' said William, earnestly. There was nothing he would have liked better! He went off looking pleased.

'I think you'd better all go to bed then, as William appears to have done everything necessary,' said Mrs Johnson. 'Any plans for tomorrow?'

'Not yet,' said Julian, trying to stop a yawn. 'So if you want anything done, we'll do it.'

'We'll see what tomorrow brings,' said Mrs Johnson and said good night. The boys said good night to the three girls and went off to the stable.

'Gosh, we've forgotten to undress and wash and everything,' said Julian, half-asleep. 'What's the matter with us at this place? I can't seem to keep my eyes open after half-past eight!'

The next day certainly brought a few things. It brought a letter for Henry that filled her with disgust. It brought two letters for Mrs Johnson that made her start fussing and worrying. It brought a telegram for Captain Johnson that sent him down to the station at once.

Henrietta's letter was from two of her great-aunts. They announced that as they would be near the stables that day and the following, they would like to fetch her and take her out with them.

'Blow!' said Henrietta, ungratefully. 'Great-Aunts Hannah and Lucy *would* choose this very week to come along and see me! Just when Julian and Dick are here, and everything is such fun. Can't I phone and say I'm too busy, Mrs Johnson?'

'Certainly not,' said Mrs Johnson, shocked. 'That would be very rude, Henry, and you know it. You're having the whole of the Easter holidays here, and yet you think you can't spare two days. As a matter of fact I shall be glad if your aunts *do* take you off my hands for a couple of days.'

'Why?' asked Henry, astonished. 'Have I been a nuisance?'

'Oh no, but I've had two letters this morning telling me that four children are coming unexpectedly,' said Mrs Johnson. 'They were not supposed to come till three of the others left this week-end, but there you are! These things happen. *Where* I am to put them I really don't know!'

'Oh dear!' said Anne. 'Do you think Dick and Julian ought to go home, Mrs Johnson? You didn't plan for them, you know, they just came.'

'Yes. I know,' said Mrs Johnson. 'But we're more or less used to that, and I do like having bigger boys, I must say, they're such a help. Now let me see. What *can* we do?'

Captain Johnson came in, looking hurried. 'I've just had a telegram, dear,' he said. 'I've got to go down to the station. Those two new horses have arrived. Two days before I wanted them – what a nuisance!'

'This is one of those *days*!' said Mrs Johnson, desperately. 'Good gracious, how many shall we be in the house? And however many horses shall we have? No, I can't count this morning. I'm all muddle-headed!'

Anne felt that it was a pity that she and George and the boys couldn't immediately pack and go home. After all, poor Mrs Johnson had thought that she and George *would* have gone home three or four days ago, and instead of that they had stayed on and the boys had arrived as well!

Anne hurried to find Julian. He would know what to do. She found him with Dick, carrying straw for the stables.

'Julian! Listen! I want to talk to you,' said Anne. Julian let the load of straw slip to the ground, and turned to Anne.

'What's up?' he said. '*Don't* tell me it's a row between George and Henry again, because I shan't listen!'

'No. Nothing like that,' said Anne. 'It's Mrs Johnson. She's got four children coming unexpectedly, before the others go. She's in a great state about it, and I wondered what we could do to help. You see, she didn't expect any of *us* four to be here this week.'

'No. That's true,' said Julian, sitting down on his straw. 'Let's think hard.'

'It's easy!' said Dick. 'We'll simply take our tents, some food, and go and camp out on the moor by some spring. *What* could be nicer?'

'Oh *yes*!' said Anne, her eyes shining. 'Oh Dick,

that's a *marvellous* idea! Mrs Johnson will get rid of us all and Timmy too, then, and we would have a lovely time all by ourselves!'

'Killing quite a lot of birds with one stone!' said Julian. 'We've got a couple of tents in our kit, Anne. Very small ones, but they'll do. And we can borrow rubber sheets to put on the heather, though it's as dry as a bone, as far as I can see!'

'I'll go and tell George!' said Anne, joyfully. 'Let's go today, Julian, and be out of the way before the new children come. Captain Johnson's got two new horses coming too. He'll be very glad to have a few of us out of the way!'

She flew off to tell George. George was busy polishing some harness, a job she liked very much. She listened to Anne's excited tale. Henry was there too, looking gloomy. She looked gloomier still at the end.

'It's too bad,' she said, when Anne had finished. 'I could have come with you if it hadn't been for these great-aunts of mine. *Why* did they have to come just at this very moment? Don't you think it's maddening?'

Neither Anne nor George thought it was maddening. They were secretly very pleased indeed to think that they could once more go off entirely on their own, with Timmy, as they had so often done before. But they would have *had* to ask Henry if her aunts hadn't written at this very lucky moment!

George didn't like to show how delighted she was to think of going off camping on the moor. She and Anne did a little comforting of poor Henry and then went off to make arrangements with Mrs Johnson.

'Well, that's a very bright idea of Dick's!' she said in delight. 'It solves a whole lot of problems. And I know you don't mind. You're thrilled at the chance, aren't you! It's really very helpful. I only wish poor Henry could go too, but she *must* go out with her old great-aunts. They adore her!'

'Of course she must,' said George, solemnly. She and Anne exchanged a look. Poor Henry. But really, it would be very nice to be without her for a little while.

Everyone began to be suddenly very busy. Dick and Julian undid their packs to find out exactly what was in them. Mrs Johnson looked out rubber sheets and old rugs. She was a wonder at producing things like that!

William wanted to go with them and help to carry the things, but nobody wanted his help.

They just wanted to be off and away by themselves, just the Five and nobody else! Timmy caught the excitement too and his tail thumped and wagged the whole morning.

'You'll be pretty well loaded,' said Mrs Johnson, doubtfully. 'It's a good thing that fine weather is forecast, or you'd have to take macs as well. Still, I imagine you won't go very far on the moors, will you? You can easily get back to the stable if you have forgotten anything, or want more food.'

They were ready at last, and went to find Henry to say good-bye. She stared at them mournfully. She had changed into a smart little coat and dress. She looked completely different and very gloomy.

'What part of the moor are you going to?' she asked eagerly. 'Up the railway?'

'Yes. We thought we would,' said Julian. 'Just to see where it goes to. And it's a nice straight way to follow. We can't lose our way if we keep near the railway!'

'Have a good time, Henry,' said George, with a grin. 'Do they call you Henrietta?'

'Yes,' said poor Henry, putting on a pair of gloves. 'Well, good-bye. For goodness' sake don't stay away too long. Thank goodness you're all such a hungry lot. You'll simply *have* to come back and get more food in a couple of days!'

They grinned and left her, Timmy at their heels. They made their way to the moor, intending to cut out the part of the railway that ran to Milling Green, and join it some way before that.

'Now we're off,' said George, contentedly. 'Without that chatterbox of a Henry.'

'She's *really* not too bad,' said Dick. 'All the same, it's fine to be on our own, just the Famous Five together!'

12 The little railway

It was a very hot day. The five had had their lunch before they started, as Mrs Johnson said it would be easier to carry that inside than outside!

Even Timmy carried something. George said that he ought to do his share, and had neatly fastened a bag of his pet biscuits on his back.

'There now!' she said. 'You've got your load too. No, don't try and sniff the biscuits all the time, Timmy. You can't walk with your head screwing round like that. You ought to be used to the smell of biscuits by this time!'

They set off to the railway line, or where they hoped it would be. It took a little time to discover it running under the heather. Julian was glad. He didn't want to walk right into Milling Green to find the beginning of it and then walk all the way up again!

Anne found it by tripping over it! 'Oh!' she said, 'here it is! I caught my foot in a bit of rusty line. Look, you can hardly see it!'

'Good,' said Julian, and stepped in between the narrow pair of old, rusty lines. In some places they had rusted away, and there were gaps. In other places the heather had grown completely over the lines, and unless the children had known that they must keep straight forward, they would have lost them completely. As it was they sometimes missed them and once had to do quite a bit of scrabbling about in the heather to see if they could feel them.

It was very hot. Their packs began to feel distinctly heavy. Timmy's biscuits began to slide round his body and eventually hung below his tummy. He didn't like that, and George suddenly spied him sitting down trying to prise open the bag with his teeth!

She put down her own pack and adjusted Timmy's. 'If only you didn't keep chasing rabbits, and making your pack swing about, it wouldn't slip,' she said. 'There now, it's all right again, Tim. Walk to heel and it won't slip any more.'

They went on and on up the railway lines. Sometimes the rails took a curve round an unexpected rock. Soon the soil began to look sandy, and the heather did not grow so thickly. It was easier to see the lines, though in some places the sand had sifted over them and hidden them.

'I really *must* have a rest!' said Anne, sitting down in some heather. 'I feel I want to pant and hang my tongue out like Timmy!'

'I wonder how far these lines go,' said Dick. 'It's so very sandy now underfoot that I feel we must be getting near the quarry!'

They lay back in the heather and felt very sleepy. Julian yawned and sat up.

'This really won't do!' he said. 'If we fall asleep

we'll never want to start off with our heavy packs again. Stir yourselves, lazy-bones!'

They all got up again. Timmy's biscuits had slithered round to his tummy once more, and George had to put them right again. Timmy stood quietly, panting, his tongue hanging out. He thought the biscuits were a great nuisance. It would be much easier to eat them!

The sand got deeper and soon there were big sandy patches with no heather or grass at all. The wind blew the sand up in the air, and the five found that they had to shut their eyes against it.

'I say! The lines end here!' said Julian, stopping suddenly. 'Look, they're broken, wrenched out of place, the engine couldn't go any farther.'

'They may appear again a bit farther on,' said Dick, and went to look. But he couldn't find any, and came back to look at the lines again.

'It's funny,' he said. 'We aren't at any quarry yet, are we! I quite thought that the line would run right to the quarry, the trucks would fill up there, and the engine would pull them back to Milling Green. *Where* is the quarry? Why do the lines stop so suddenly here?'

'Yes. The quarry *should* be near here, shouldn't it?' said Julian. 'Well, there simply must be more lines somewhere! Ones that go to the quarry. Let's look for the quarry first, though. We ought to see that easily enough!'

But it wasn't really very easy to find because it was behind a great mass of thick tall gorse-bushes. Dick rounded them and stopped. Behind the enormous spread of bushes was a great pit, a

The others came to look.

sandy pit, quarried and hollowed for its beautiful sand.

'Here it is!' called Dick. 'Come and look! My word, there's been some quarrying here for sand. They must have taken tons and tons out of it!'

The others came to look. It certainly was an enormous pit, deep and wide. They put their packs beside it and leapt down. Their feet sank into the fine sand.

'The sides are pitted with holes,' said Dick. 'I bet hundreds of sand-martins nest here in May!'

'There are even some caves,' said George, in surprise. 'Sand-caves! Well, we can easily shelter here if we have rain. Some of these caves seem to go quite a long way back.'

'Yes. But I'd be a bit afraid of the sand falling in and burying me, if I crawled in,' said Anne. 'It's quite loose, look!' She scraped some down with her hand.

'I've found the lines!' called Julian. 'Here, look. The sand has almost covered them. I trod on a rail and it was so rotten it broke beneath my foot!'

The others went to see, Timmy too. He was quite delighted with this place. The rabbit-holes in it! What fun he was going to have!

'Let's follow these lines,' said Julian. So they kicked away the sand from the rails and followed them slowly out of the quarry and towards the ends of the other broken lines.

About ten yards from these the lines they were following were wrenched apart. Some were flung into near by heather, and could be seen there, bent and rusty.

The children stared at them. 'I guess the gypsies did that, when the Bartles were here years ago,' said Dick. 'The day they attacked them perhaps. I say look, what*ever's* that great lump over there, with gorse growing over it?'

They went to see. Timmy saw the lump and couldn't make it out. He growled warningly at it.

Julian took up a broken piece of rail and forced back the gorse bush that had grown over and around the great lump, almost hiding it.

'See what it is?' he said, startled.

They all stared. 'Why, it's the engine! The little "injin" old Ben the blacksmith told us about!' said Dick. 'It must have run right off the broken lines and over-turned here, and through the years these great gorse-bushes grew up and hid it. Poor old engine!'

Julian forced the gorse back a little more. 'What a funny old-fashioned affair!' he said. 'Look at the funnel, and the fat little boiler. And see, there's the small cab. It can't have had much power, only just enough to puff along with a few trucks!'

'What happened to the trucks?' wondered Anne.

'Well, they would be easy enough to set upright again and put on the rails, and hand-pushed to Milling Green,' said Dick. 'But this engine couldn't be lifted, except by some kind of machinery. Not even a dozen men could lift it and set it on the rails!'

'The gypsies must have set on the Bartles in the mist, having first broken up the lines so that the engine would run off and overturn,' said Julian. 'They may even have used the broken rails to attack them with. Anyway, they won the battle, because not one of the Bartles ever returned.'

'Some of the villagers must have gone to see what became of them and have got the trucks back on the lines and pushed them to Milling Green,' said George, trying to reconstruct the long-ago happenings in her mind. 'But they couldn't do anything about the engine.'

'That's about it,' said Julian. 'My word, what a shock for the Bartles when they saw the gypsies creeping out at them from the mist, like shadows!'

'I hope we don't dream about this tonight,' said Anne.

They went back to the quarry. 'This wouldn't be a bad place to camp in,' said Dick. 'The sand is so dry and so soft. We could make lovely beds for ourselves. We wouldn't need the tents up, either, because the sides of the quarry shelter us beautifully from the wind.'

'Yes. Let's camp here,' said Anne, pleased. 'There are quite a lot of nice holes to store our things in.'

'What about water?' asked George. 'We want to be fairly near it, don't we? Timmy, find some water! Drink, Timmy, drink! Aren't you thirsty? Your tongue looks as if it is, the way you are hanging it out like a flag!'

Timmy put his head on one side as George talked to him. Water? Drink? He knew what both those words meant! He ran off, sniffing the air. George watched him.

He disappeared round a bush and was away for about half a minute. When he came back George gave a pleased shout.

'He's found some water! Look – his mouth is all wet! Timmy, where is it?'

Timmy wagged his tail vigorously, glad that George was pleased with him. He ran round the bush again and the others followed.

He led them to a little green patch and stopped. A spring bubbled up like a small fountain, dancing a little in the sunshine. The water fell from it into a little channel it had made for itself in the sand, ran away for a short distance, and then disappeared underground again.

'Thank you, Tim,' said George. 'Julian, is the water all right to drink here?'

'Well I can see some that *is*!' said Julian, pointing to the right. 'The Bartles must have put a pipe in that bank, look, and caught another spring there, a much bigger one. It's as clear as can be. That will do fine for us!'

'Good,' said Anne, pleased. 'It's hardly any way from the quarry. It's as cold as ice, too – feel!'

They felt, and then they drank from their palms. How cold and pure! The moor must be full of these little bubbling springs, welling up from underground. That explained the brilliant green patches here and there.

'Now let's sit down and have some tea,' said Anne, unpacking the bag she had carried. 'It's too hot to feel really hungry.'

'Oh no, it isn't,' said Dick. 'Speak for yourself, Anne!'

They sat in the sunny quarry, the sand warm to their legs. 'Far away from everybody!' said Anne, pleased. 'Nobody near us for miles!'

But she wasn't quite right. There was somebody much nearer than she thought!

13 A noise in the night

It was Timmy who first knew there was somebody not far off. He pricked up his ears and listened. George saw him.

'What is it, Tim?' she said. 'Nobody is coming here, surely?'

Timmy gave a tiny growl, as if he were not quite sure of himself. Then he leapt up, his tail wagging, and tore out of the quarry!

'Where's he gone to?' said George astonished. 'Gosh, here he is, back again!'

So he was, and with him was a funny little hearth rug of a dog – yes, Liz! She was not quite sure of her welcome and crawled up to the children on her tummy, looking more like a hearthrug than ever!

Timmy leapt round her in delight. She might have been his very best friend, he was so delighted! George patted the funny little dog and Julian looked thoughtful.

'I hope this doesn't mean that we are anywhere near the gypsy camp,' he said. 'It's quite likely that the lines might end somewhere near them. I've rather lost my sense of direction.'

'Oh goodness, I do HOPE we're not near their camp!' said Anne, in dismay. 'Those old-time gypsies must have camped pretty near to the Bartles' quarry before they attacked them, so perhaps the present camp is near too.'

'Well, what's it matter if it is?' said Dick. 'Who's afraid of them? *I'm* not!'

They all sat still, thinking hard, Liz licking Anne's hand. And in the silence they heard an all-too-familiar sound.

Sniff! Sniff!

'Sniffer!' called George. 'Come on out, wherever you are hiding. I can hear you!'

A pair of legs stuck out from a great clump of heather at the edge of the quarry, and then the whole of Sniffer's wiry little body slithered out and down into the sand. He sat there, grinning at them, half-afraid to come any nearer in case they were cross with him.

'What are *you* doing here?' said Dick. 'Not spying on us, I hope?'

'No,' said Sniffer. 'Our camp isn't very far

away. Liz heard you, I think, and ran off. I followed her.'

'Oh blow. We hoped we weren't near anyone else,' said George. 'Does anyone at your camp know we're here.'

'Not yet,' said Sniffer. 'But they'll find out. They always do. I won't tell, though, if you don't want me to.'

Dick tossed him a biscuit. 'Well, keep your mouth shut if you can,' he said. 'We're not interfering with anyone and we don't want anyone interfering with us. See?'

Sniffer nodded. He suddenly put his hand in his pocket and pulled out the red and white hanky that George had given him. It was still clean and beautifully folded.

'Not dirty yet!' he said to George.

'Well, it ought to be,' said George. 'It's for your sniffs. No *don't* use your coat-sleeve.'

Sniffer simply could *not* understand why he should use a beautiful clean hanky when he had a dirty coat-sleeve. He put the hanky carefully back into his pocket.

Liz ran to him and fawned on him. Sniffer fondled the peculiar little creature, and then Timmy went over and played with them both. The four finished their tea, threw Sniffer one last biscuit, and got up to put their things away safely. Now that Sniffer was about, and the gypsy camp near, they didn't feel it was terribly safe to leave anything unguarded or unhidden.

'Scoot off, now Sniffer,' said Julian. 'And no spying on us, mind! Timmy will know immediately you arrive anywhere near, and come hunting for you. If you want to see us, give a whistle when you get near. No creeping or slipping into the quarry. Understand?'

'Yes,' said Sniffer, standing up. He took the hanky from his pocket again, waved it at George, and disappeared with Liz at his heels.

'I'm just going to see exactly how near to the gypsy camp we are,' Julian said. He walked to the entrance of the quarry and up on to the moor. He looked in the direction that Sniffer had gone. Yes, there was the hill in the shelter of which the gypsies had their caravans. It wasn't more than a quarter of a mile away. Blow! Still, it was far enough for the gypsies not to discover them, unless by chance.

'Or unless Sniffer gives the game away,' thought Julian. 'Well, we'll spend the night here, anyway, and we can move off somewhere else tomorrow if we feel like it.'

They felt rather energetic that evening and played a ball game in the quarry, in which Timmy joined wholeheartedly. But as he always got the ball before anyone else did they had to tie him up in order to get a game themselves. Timmy was very cross. He turned his back on them and sulked.

'He looks like you now, George,' said Dick, grinning, and got the ball bang on the side of his head from an angry George!

Nobody wanted much supper. Julian took a little aluminium jug to the spring and filled it once for everyone. It really was lovely water from that bubbling spring!

'I wonder how Henry's getting on,' said Anne. 'Spoilt to bits by her great-aunts, I expect. Didn't she look odd in proper clothes, gloves and all!'

'Yes, she ought to have been a boy,' said Dick. 'Like you, George,' he added hastily. 'Both of you are real sports, plucky as anything.'

'How do you know Henry's plucky?' said George, scornfully. 'Only by her silly tales! I bet they're all made-up and exaggerated.'

Julian changed the subject. 'Shall we want rugs tonight, do you think?' he said.

'Rather! It may be warm now, and the sand is hot with the sun, but it won't be quite so nice when it's gone down,' said Anne. 'Anyway we can always creep into one of those cosy little caves if we feel chilly. They're as warm as toast. I went into one, so I know.'

They settled down quite early to sleep. The boys took one side of the quarry, the girls the other. Tim, as usual, was on George's feet, much to Anne's discomfort.

'He's on mine too,' she complained to George. 'He's *so long*, he stretches over my feet as well. Move him, George.'

So George moved him, but as soon as Anne was asleep he stretched out again and lay on both girls' legs. He slept with one ear open.

He heard a scurrying hedgehog. He heard all the rabbits out for a night-time game. He heard the frogs in a far-off pool croaking in the night. His sharp ear even heard the tinkle of the little spring outside the pit.

Nobody moved in the quarry. There was a small moon but it gave very little light. The stars that studded the sky seemed to give more light than the moon.

Timmy's one open ear suddenly pricked itself right up. Then the other ear stood up too. Timmy

was still asleep but his ears were both listening very hard!

A low, humming sound came slowly over the night. It came nearer and nearer. Timmy awoke properly and sat up, listening, his eyes wide open now.

The sound was now very loud indeed. Dick awoke and listened. What *was* that noise? An aeroplane? It must be jolly low! Surely it wasn't about to land on the moor in the dark!

He woke Julian and they both got up and went out of the quarry. 'It's an aeroplane all right,' said Dick, in a low voice. 'What's it doing? It doesn't seem to be going to land. It's gone round in a low circle two or three times.'

'Is it in trouble, do you think?' asked Julian. 'Here it comes again.'

'Look, what's that light over there?' suddenly said Dick, pointing to the east. 'See, that sort of glow. It's not very far from the gypsies' camp.'

'I don't know,' said Julian, puzzled. 'It's not a fire, is it? We can't see any flames and it doesn't seem to flicker like a fire would.'

'I think it may be some sort of guide to that plane,' said Dick. 'It seems to be circling round and about over the glow. Let's watch it.'

They watched it. Yes, it did seem to be circling round the glow, whatever it was, and then, quite suddenly it rose in the air, circled round once more and made off to the east.

'There it goes,' said Dick, straining his eyes. 'I can't tell what kind it is, except that it's very small.'

'What can it have been doing?' said Julian, puzzled. 'I thought the glow might have been to guide it in landing, though where it could land here in safety I simply don't know. But it didn't land at all, it just circled and made off.'

'Where would it have come from?' said Dick. 'From the coast, I suppose, from over the sea, do you think?'

'I simply don't know,' said Julian. 'It beats me! And why should the gypsies have anything to do with it? Gypsies and planes don't seem to mix, somehow.'

'Well, we don't know that they do have anything to do with the plane, except that we saw that glow,' said Dick. 'And that's going now, look.'

Even as they watched, the bright glow died completely away. Now the moor lay in darkness again.

'Funny,' said Julian, scratching his head. 'I can't make it out. It's true that the gypsies may be up to something, the way they come out here secretly, apparently for no purpose at all, and also they don't want us snooping round, that's clear.'

'I think we'd better try and find out what that glow is,' said Dick. 'We could have a bit of a snoop tomorrow. Or perhaps Sniffer could tell us.'

'He might,' said Julian. 'We'll try him. Come on, let's get back into the quarry. It's cold out here!'

The quarry struck quite warm to them as they went down into it. The girls were sound asleep still. Timmy, who had been with them, did not wake them. He had been as puzzled as Julian and Dick over the low-flying plane, but he had not barked at all. Julian had been glad about that, Timmy's bark might have carried right over to the gypsy camp and warned it that someone was camping near.

They got back under their rug, keeping close to one another for warmth. But they soon lost their shivers, and Dick threw off his share of the rug. In a few minutes they were asleep.

Timmy awoke first and stretched himself out in the warm morning sunshine. Anne sat up with a little scream. 'Oh Timmy, *don't*! You nearly squashed me to bits. Do that to George if you must stretch yourself all over somebody!'

The boys awoke then, and went to the spring to splash their faces and bring back a jugful of water to drink. Anne got the breakfast, and over it the boys told the girls of the aeroplane in the night.

'How queer!' said Anne. 'And that glow too. It *must* have been a guide of some sort to the plane. Let's go and see where it was. It must have been a fire of *some* kind!'

'Right,' said Dick. 'I vote we go this morning, but we'll take Tim with us in case we meet those gypsies!'

14 The gypsies are not pleased

Julian and Dick went to stand where they had stood the night before, trying to see exactly in what direction the glow had been.

'I *think* it was beyond the gypsies' camp, to the left,' said Julian. 'What do you think, Dick?'

'Yes. That's about it,' said Dick. 'Shall we go now?' He raised his voice. 'We're going, George and Anne. Are you coming? We can leave our stuff here, tucked away in the caves because we shan't be very long.'

George called back. 'Julian, I think Timmy's got a thorn in his foot or something. He's limping. Anne and I think we'll stay here with him and try to get it out. You go, but for goodness' sake don't get into trouble with the gypsies!'

'We shan't,' said Julian. 'We've as much right on this moor as they have and they know it. All right, we'll leave you two here then with Timmy. Sure you don't want any help with his paw?'

'Oh no,' said George. 'I can manage, thank you.'

The two boys went off, leaving Anne and George fussing over Timmy's paw. He had leapt into a gorse bush after a rabbit and a thorn had gone right into his left fore-paw. Then it had broken off, leaving the point in poor Timmy's pad. No wonder he limped! George was going to have quite a time trying to ease out the bit of thorn.

Julian and Dick set off over the moor. It was a day like summer, far too warm for April. There was not a single cloud to be seen in the sky, which was as blue as forget-me-nots. The boys felt too hot in their pullovers and longed to take them off. But that would mean carrying them, which would be an awful nuisance.

The gypsy camp was not really far away. They soon came near to the curious hill that stood up from the flatness of the moor. The caravans still stood in its shelter, and the boys saw that a little group of men were sitting together, talking earnestly.

'I bet they're having a jaw about that aeroplane last night,' said Dick. 'And I bet it was they who set that light or fire, or whatever it was, to guide it. I wonder why it didn't land?'

They kept in the shelter of big gorse bushes, as they skirted the camp. They were not particularly anxious to be seen. The dogs, sitting round the group of men, apparently did not see or hear them, which was lucky.

The boys made their way towards the place where they thought they had seen the glow, some way to the left of the camp, and beyond it.

'Doesn't seem to be anything out of the ordinary anywhere,' said Julian, stopping and looking round. 'I was expecting to see a big burnt patch, or something.'

'Wait – what's in that dip over there?' said Dick, pointing to where the ground seemed to dip downwards. 'It looks like another old quarry, rather like the one we're camping in, but smaller, much smaller. I bet that's where the fire was!'

They made their way to the quarry. It was much more overgrown than theirs was, and was evidently one that had been worked at an earlier time. It dipped down to quite a pit in the middle and set there was something unusual. What was it?

The boys scrambled down into the pit-like quarry and made their way to the middle. They stared at the big thing that was set there, pointing to the sky.

'It's a lamp, a powerful lamp of some kind,' said Dick. 'Like those we see making a flare-path at an aerodrome, guiding planes in to land. Fancy seeing one here!'

'How did the gypsies get it?' wondered Dick, puzzled. 'And why signal to a plane that doesn't land? It looked as if it wanted to, circling round low like that.'

'Maybe the gypsies signalled that it wasn't safe to land for some reason,' said Julian. 'Or perhaps they were going to give something to the pilot and it wasn't ready.'

'Well, it's a puzzle,' said Dick. 'I can't *imagine* what's going on. Something is, that's certain. Let's snoop round a bit.'

They found nothing else, except a trail that led to the lamp and back. Just as they were examining it, a shout came to their ears. They swung round – and saw the figure of a gypsy at the edge of the pit.

'What are you doing here?' he shouted, in a harsh voice. He was joined by a few others, and they all looked threateningly at Julian and Dick as they climbed out of the pit.

Julian decided to be honest. 'We're camping out on the moor for a night or two,' he said, 'and we heard a plane last night, circling low. We also saw a glow that appeared to be guiding it, and we came along to see what it was. Did *you* hear the plane?'

'Mebbe we did and mebbe we didn't,' said the nearest gypsy, who was Sniffer's father. 'What of it? Planes fly over this moor any day!'

'We found that powerful lamp,' said Dick, pointing back at it. 'Do you know anything about *that*?'

'Nothing,' said the gypsy, scowling. 'What lamp?'

'Well, as far as I can see there's no charge for looking at it,' said Julian. 'Go and have a squint, if you don't know anything about it! But I can't believe that you didn't see the light it gave last night! It's a jolly good place to hid it, I must say.'

'We don't know anything about any lamp,' said another gypsy, the old one with grey hair. 'This is our usual camping-place. We don't interfere with anything or anybody – unless they interfere with us. Then we make them sorry for it.'

The boys at once thought of the long-ago mystery of the disappearance of the Bartles. They felt quite uncomfortable.

'Well, we're going now, so don't worry,' said Julian. 'We're only camping for a night or two, as I said. We won't come near here again, if you object to us.'

He saw Sniffer creeping up behind the men, with Liz, who for some reason of her own, was walking sedately on her hind-legs. Sniffer pulled at his father's arm.

'They're all right,' he said. 'You know our Clip got his leg made better at the stables. They're all right!'

All he got was a savage cuff that sent him to the ground, where he rolled over and over. Liz dropped down on all fours and went to lick him.

'Here, I say!' said Julian, shocked. 'Leave that kid alone! You've no right to hit him like that!'

Sniffer set up such a yelling that some of the women left the caravans not far off and came running to see what was up. One of them began to shout at Sniffer's father and he shouted back. Soon there was quite a row going on between the men and the angry women, one of whom had picked up poor Sniffer and was dabbing his head with a wet cloth.

'Come on, it's a good time to go,' said Julian to Dick. 'What an unfriendly lot they are, except poor Sniffer, and he was doing his best for us, poor kid.'

The two boys went off quickly, glad to be away from the men and their dogs. They were puzzled about everything. The men said they knew nothing about the lamp, but they *must* know something about it. Nobody but a gypsy could have lighted it last night.

They went back to the girls and told them what had happened. 'Let's go back to the stables,' said Anne. 'There's something queer going on. We'll be in the middle of an adventure before we know where we are!'

'We'll stay one more night,' said Julian. 'I want to see if that plane comes again. Those gypsies don't know where we're camping and though Sniffer knows, I'm pretty sure he won't tell. It was plucky of him to try and stick up for us to his father.'

'All right. We'll stay,' said George. 'I'm not particularly anxious for Timmy to have that long walk home today. I *think* I've got most of that thorn out of his pad, but he still won't put his foot to the ground.'

'He's jolly clever at running about on three legs,' said Dick, watching Timmy tearing round the quarry, sniffing as usual for rabbits.

'The amount of quarrying that Timmy has done in this pit already is colossal!' said Julian, staring round at the places where Timmy had tried to get in at some rabbit-hole and scrabbled out big heaps of sand. 'He would have been a great help to the Bartles when they dug out sand! Poor old Tim – your bad foot has stopped you scraping for rabbits, hasn't it?'

Timmy ran over on three legs. He enjoyed all the fussing he got when anything happened to him. He meant to make the most of his bad foot!

They had a very lazy day indeed. It really was too hot to do anything much. They went to the little spring and sat with their feet in the rivulet it made – it was deliciously cool! They went and had a look at the old engine again, lying on its side, half-buried.

Dick scraped away a lot of the sand that had seeped into the cab. Soon they were all helping. They uncovered the old handles and levers and tried to move them. But they couldn't, of course.

'Let's go round to the other side of the gorse bush and see if we can see the funnel again,' said Dick, at last. 'Blow these thorns. I'm getting pricked all over. Timmy's very sensible, sitting there, not attempting to examine this old Puffing Billy!'

They had to cut away some of the gorse before they could examine the funnel properly. Then they exclaimed in wonder.

'Look! It's very like the long funnel that Puffing Billy had, you know, one of the first engines ever made!'

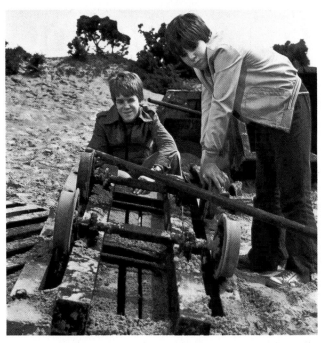

Poor old engine, lying here for years, quite forgotten.

'It's filled with sand,' said Dick, and tried to scrape it out. It was fairly loose, and soon he was able to peer down the funnel quite a long way.

'Funny to think of smoke puffing out of this queer old funnel,' said Dick. 'Poor old engine, lying here for years, quite forgotten. I'd have thought *someone* would rescue it!'

'Well, you know what the blacksmith told us,' said George. 'The Bartle sister that was left wouldn't have anything more to do with the railway or the engine or the quarry. And certainly nobody could move this great thing on their own.'

'I shouldn't be surprised if we're the only people in the world who know where the old engine is,' said Anne. 'It's so overgrown that nobody could see it except by accident!'

'I feel jolly hungry, all of a sudden,' said Dick, stopping his work of getting sand off the engine. 'What about something to eat?'

'We've got enough to last for a day or two more,' said Anne. 'Then we'll have to get something else – or go back to the stables.'

'I *must* spend one more night here,' said Julian. 'I want to see if that plane returns again.'

'Right. We'll all watch this time,' said George. 'It will be fun. Come on, let's go and get something to eat. Don't you think that's a good idea, Timmy?'

Timmy certainly did. He limped off at top speed on three legs, though really his right fore-paw no longer hurt him. Timmy, you're a fraud!

15 A startling night

No gypsies came near them that day, not even Sniffer. The evening was as lovely as the day had been, and almost as warm.

'It's extraordinary!' said Dick, looking up into the sky. 'What weather for April! The bluebells will be rushing out soon if the sun goes on being as hot as this!'

They lay on the sand in the quarry and watched the evening star shine in the sky. It looked very big and bright and round.

Timmy scrabbled round in the sand. 'His paw is much better,' said George. 'Though I notice that he still sometimes holds it up.'

'Only when he wants you to say "Poor Timmy, does it hurt?"' said Dick. 'He's a baby, likes to be fussed!'

They talked for a while and then Anne yawned. 'It's early, I know – but I believe I'm going to sleep.'

There was soon a trek to the spring, and everyone sluiced themselves in the cool water. There was only one towel between them, but that did very well. Then they settled down in their sandy beds. The sand was beautifully warm and they did not bother about putting down the rubber sheets. There could not possibly be any dampness in that quarry after it had been baked so much by the hot sun!

'I hope we wake when the plane comes, if it does come,' said Julian to Dick, as they lay without any covering in their soft, sandy bed. 'My goodness, isn't it hot? No wonder Timmy's panting over there!'

They went to sleep at last, but Dick awoke suddenly, feeling much too hot. Phew! What a night! He lay looking up at the brilliant stars, and then shut his eyes again. But it was no use, he couldn't go to sleep.

He sat up cautiously, so as not to awake Julian. I think I'll just go and have a squint to see if that big lamp is lighted again, down in that pit by the gypsy camp, he thought.

He went to the edge of the quarry and climbed up. He looked towards the gypsy camp and gave a sudden exclamation. Yes! he thought. It's glowing again! I can't see the lamp, of course, but its light is so jolly powerful that I can easily see the glow it makes. It must be very bright, looked down on from the sky. I wonder if the plane is due to come, now that the lamp is lighted?

He listened, and yes, he could distinctly hear a low humming noise from the east. It must be the plane coming again? Would it land this time, and if so, who was in it?

He ran to wake Julian and the girls. Timmy was alert at once, wagging his tail excitedly. He was always ready for anything, even in the middle of the night! Anne and George got up too, very thrilled.

'Is the lamp really alight again? And I can hear the plane too now! Oh, I say! This is exciting! George, Timmy won't bark and give us away, will he?'

'No. I've told him to be quiet,' said George. 'He won't make a sound. Listen, the plane is coming nearer!'

The noise was now loud enough for them to search the starry sky for the plane. Julian gave Dick a nudge. 'Look, you can just see it, straight over where the gypsy camp is!'

Dick managed to pick it out. 'It's very small,' he said. 'Smaller even than I thought it was last night. Look, it's coming down!'

But it wasn't. It merely swept low, and then went round in a circle, as it had done the night before. It rose a little again and then came in low once more, almost over the boys' heads.

Then something extraordinary happened. Something fell not far from Julian, something that bounced and then came to rest! It made a thud as it fell, and all four jumped. Timmy gave a startled whine.

Thud! Something else fell. Thud, thud, thud! Anne gave a squeal. 'Are they trying to bomb us or something? Julian, what are they doing?'

Thud! Thud! Julian ducked at the last two thuds, they sounded so near. He took hold of Anne and pulled her down into the quarry, calling to Dick and George.

'Get down here, quickly! Force yourselves into the caves somewhere! We shall get hit!'

They ran across the quarry as the plane swooped round in a circle once more and then again began dropping the things that went 'thud! thud!' Some even fell into the quarry this time. Timmy got the shock of his life when one bounced in front of his nose and rolled away. He yelped and tore after George.

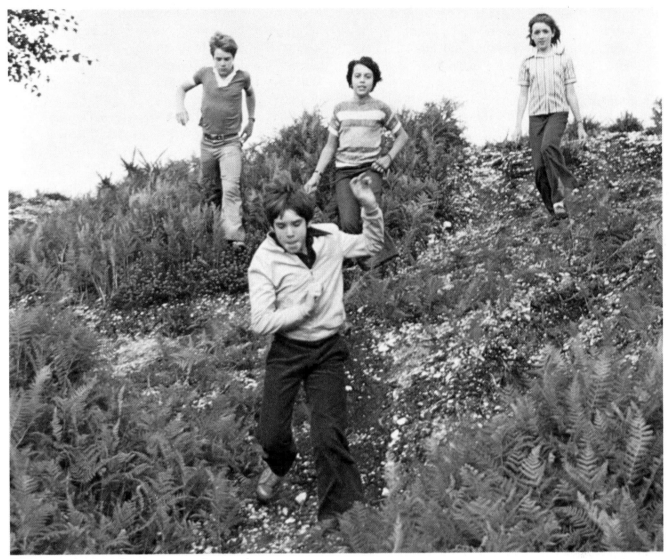

In great excitement they ran to get the parcels.

Soon they were all safely squeezed into the little caves that lined the sides of the quarry. The plane swept round once more, up and then round, and the thud-thudding began again. The four could hear that some of the thuds were actually in the quarry again and they were thankful they were well sheltered.

'Well, nothing is exploding,' said Dick, thankfully. 'But what on earth is the plane dropping? And why? This is a most peculiar adventure to have.'

'It's probably a dream,' said Julian, and laughed. 'No, not even a dream could be so mad. Here we are, snuggling into sandy caves in a quarry on Mystery Moor, while a plane drops something all round us in the middle of the night! Quite mad.'

'I believe the plane's going away now,' said Dick. 'It's circled round but hasn't dropped any-

thing. Now it's climbing, it's going away! The engine doesn't sound nearly so loud. Goodness, when we were standing out there at the edge of the quarry, I almost thought the plane would take my head off, it was so low!'

'I thought that too,' said Anne, very glad that there was to be no more swooping down and dropping dozens of unknown things. 'Is it safe to go out?'

'Oh yes,' said Julian, scrambling out of the sand. 'Come on. We shall easily hear if the plane comes back again. I want to see what it has dropped!'

In great excitement they ran to get the parcels. The stars gave so much light on that clear night that the four did not even need a torch.

Julian picked up something first. It was a firm, flattish parcel, done up well, sewn into canvas covering. He examined it.

107

'No name. Nothing,' he said. 'This is most exciting. Let's have three guesses what's inside.'

'Bacon for breakfast, I hope!' said Anne at once.

'Idiot,' said Julian, getting out a knife to slit the string threads that sewed up the canvas. 'I guess it's smuggled goods of some sort. That's what that plane was doing, I should think, flying over from France, and dropping smuggled goods in a pre-arranged place, and I suppose the gypsies pick them up, and take them away, well hidden in their caravans, to deliver them somewhere. Very clever!'

'Oh Julian, it *that* the explanation?' said Anne. 'What would be in the parcels then, cigarettes?'

'No,' said Julian. 'The parcels wouldn't be so heavy if they only contained cigarettes. There, I've slit the threads at last!'

The others crowded round to see. George took her torch out of her pocket so that they could see really well. She flashed it on.

Julian ripped off the canvas covering. Next came some strong brown paper. He ripped that off too. Then came strong cardboard, tied round with string. That was undone as well, and the cardboard fell to the ground.

'Now, what have we got?' said Julian, excited. 'Thin sheets of paper, dozens and dozens of them packed together. Shine your torch nearer, George.'

There was a silence as all the four craned over Julian's hands.

'Whew! I say! Gosh, do you see what they are?' said Julian, in awe. 'American money, dollar notes. But look what they are, *one hundred*-dollar notes! And my word there are scores and scores of them in this one packet.'

The four stared in amazement as Julian riffled through the packet of notes. However much would they be worth?

'Julian, how much is a hundred-dollar note worth in our money?' asked George.

'About forty pounds, I think,' said Julian. 'Yes, just about that. Gosh, and there are scores in this one packet, and we know they dropped *dozens* of the packets too. Whatever is it all about?'

'Well, there must be thousands and thousands of dollars lying around us, here in the quarry and outside it,' said George. 'I *say*! Surely this *isn't* a dream?'

'Well, I must say it's a very *extravagant* kind of dream, if so,' said Dick. 'A dream worth thousands of pounds isn't very usual. Ju, hadn't we better get busy picking up these parcels?'

'Yes. We certainly had,' said Julian. 'I'm beginning to see it all now. The smugglers come over in a plane from France, say, having previously arranged to drop these packets in a lonely spot on this moor. The gypsies are in the plot to the extent that they light the guiding lamp and pick up the parcels.'

'I see, and then they quietly pack them into their caravans, slip off the moor, and deliver them to somebody else, who pays them well for their trouble,' said Dick. 'Very smart!'

'That's about it,' said Julian. 'But I can't for the life of me see why *dollar* notes have to be smuggled here. They can be brought freely enough into the country – why *smuggle* them?'

'Stolen ones, perhaps?' said George. 'Oh well, its quite beyond *me*. What a thing to do! No wonder the gypsies didn't want us around.'

'Better buck up and collect all these parcels and clear off back to the stables with them,' said Julian, picking up one near him. 'The gypsies will be after them, there's no doubt about that! We must be gone before they come.'

The four of them went about looking for the parcels. They found about sixty of them, and they made quite a heavy load.

'We'll put them somewhere safe, I think,' said Julian. 'What about stuffing them into one of the sand-caves? I don't very well see how we can carry them like this.'

'We could put them in the rugs and tie up the ends and carry them like that,' said George. 'It would be mad to leave them hidden somewhere in this quarry. It's the first place the gypsies would search.'

'All right. We'll follow your idea,' said Julian. 'I think we've about collected all the packets there are. Get the rugs.'

George's idea proved to be a good one. Half the parcels were rolled into one rug, and tied up, and half into the other.

'Good thing the rugs are nice and big,' said Dick tying his up strongly. 'Now I can just about manage mine nicely on my back. You all right, Ju?'

'Yes, come along, you girls,' said Julian. 'Follow behind us. We'll go down the railway line. Leave everything else here. We can easily get it another time. We *must* leave before the gypsies come.'

Timmy began to bark suddenly. 'That must mean the gypsies are coming,' said Dick. 'Come on, quick! Yes, I can hear their voices – for goodness' sake, HURRY!'

16 The terrible mist

Yes, the gypsies were certainly coming! Their dogs were with them, barking. The four children hurried out of the quarry with Timmy at their heels, quite silent.

'Those fellows may not know we were camping in the quarry,' panted Dick. 'They may just be coming to find the parcels, and while they are hunting around, we may be able to get a good start. Buck up!'

They set off to where the lines ended, near where the old engine lay half-buried. The gypsy dogs heard them and set up a yelping and howling. The gypsies stopped to see what had excited them.

They spied shadows moving in the distance, the four children slipping away from the quarry. One of the men shouted loudly.

'Hey, you – stop! Who are you? Stop, I say!'

But the five didn't stop. They were now stumbling between the railway lines, glad of George's torch, and Anne's. The boys could not have held one, for it was all they could do to hang on to the heavy-laden rugs.

'Quick, oh quick!' whispered Anne, but it was impossible to go very quickly.

'They must be catching us up,' said Julian, suddenly. 'Look round and see, George.'

George looked round. 'No, I can't see anyone,' she said. 'Julian, everywhere looks peculiar. What's happening? Julian, stop. Something queer is happening!'

Julian stopped and looked round. His eyes had been fixed on his feet, trying to see where he was going without stumbling. Anne had shone her torch down for him but it was still difficult to get along properly. Julian gazed all round, wondering what George meant.

Then he gave a gasp. 'Gosh! How queer! There's a mist come up, look. It's even blotted out the stars. No wonder it seems so jolly dark all of a sudden.'

'A mist!' said Anne, scared. 'Not that *awful* mist

that sometimes covers the moor! Oh Julian, is it?'

Julian and Dick watched the swirling mist in astonishment. 'It's come from the sea,' Julian said. 'Can't you smell the salt in it? It's come just as suddenly as we've been told it comes, and look, it's getting thicker every minute!'

'What a good thing we're on the railway lines!' said George. 'What shall we do? Go on?'

Julian stood and thought. 'The gypsies won't come after us in this mist,' he said. 'I've a good mind to hide this money somewhere, and then walk back to get the police. If we keep on the lines we can't go wrong. But we must be sure not to leave them, or we'll be completely lost!'

'Yes, let's do that,' said Dick, who was heartily sick already of lugging along his heavy load. 'But where do you propose to hid them, Ju? Not in the quarry! We'd have to walk through this awful mist to do that, and we'd get lost at once.'

'No. I've thought of a fine place,' said Julian, and he lowered his voice. 'Remember that old engine, fallen on its side? Well, what about stuffing these packets all the way down that great long funnel, and then stopping the top of it up with sand? I bet you anything you like that nobody would find the packets there.'

'Grand idea!' said Dick. 'The gypsies will be sure we've gone off carrying the money, and they'll not hunt about for it long, once they find the dropped packets are all gone. We'll be half-way home by the time they try to catch us, if they dare to brave this mist.'

Anne and George thought Julian's idea was first-rate, a stroke of genius. 'I'd never, never have thought of the engine funnel!' said Anne.

'Now, there's no need for you two girls and Timmy to walk all the way to the engine with us,' said Julian. 'You sit down here on the lines, and wait for us to come back. We shan't be long. We'll walk straight up the railway, find the engine, pack the money into the funnel, and walk back.'

'Right,' said George squatting down. 'Bring the rugs back with you, though. It's cold now!'

Julian and Dick went off together, with Anne's torch. George kept hers. Timmy pressed close against her, astonished at the thick mist that had so suddenly swirled up and around them.

'That's right. Keep close to us and keep us warm, Tim,' said George. 'It's jolly cold now. This mist is damp!'

Julian stumbled along, keeping a look-out for the gypsies. He could see nothing of them, but then, if they had been only two feet away he could not have seen anything of them in the mist! It seemed to get thicker and thicker.

I know what old Ben meant now, when he said that it had damp fingers, thought Julian, feeling little touches like fingers on his face, hands and legs as the mist wreathed itself round him.

Dick nudged him. 'Here we are,' he said. 'The lines are broken here. The engine should be just over there, a yard or two away.'

They stepped cautiously away from the lines. The big gorse-bush could not be seen, but it could be felt! Julian felt thorns pricking his legs, and knew he was beside it.

'Shine your torch here, Dick,' he whispered. 'That's right. There's the cab of the engine, see? Now let's circle the bush, and we'll come to the funnel.'

'Here it is,' said Dick, in a few moments. 'Look! Now then, let's do a bit of work, shoving these packets down. Gosh, what a lot of them there are! I hope the funnel will take them all.'

They spent ten minutes ramming the packets into the wide funnel. Down they went to the bottom! More and more followed and then, at last, the final one was shoved in and rammed down.

'That's the lot,' said Dick, relieved. 'Now we'll pack some sand in. Gosh, isn't this bush full of prickles! It's really spiteful!'

'The packets *almost* fill the funnel,' said Julian. 'Hardly any room for sand. Still, we can put in enough to hide the money all right. There, that's done. Now pull this gorse-branch over the top of the funnel. My word, I never knew a bush so set with spines! I'm scratched to bits!'

'Can you hear anything of the gypsies?' asked Dick, in a low voice, as they prepared to go back to the lines.

They listened. 'Not a thing,' said Julian. 'It's my belief they're scared of this mist, and are lying low till it clears.'

'They may be in the quarry,' said Dick. 'Waiting there in safety. Well, long may they be there! They won't get the money now!'

'Come on,' said Julian, and walked round the bush. 'It's just about here that we step out to get to the lines. Take my arm. We mustn't get separated. Did you ever see such a mist in your life? It's the thickest fog I ever knew. We can't even see our feet in the light of the torch now.'

They took a few steps and then felt about for the rails. They couldn't feel even one. 'A bit farther, I think,' said Julian. 'No, this way.'

But they still couldn't find the railway lines. Where *were* the wretched things? A small feeling of panic came into Julian's mind. Which way should they step now, to find the rails? How had they gone wrong?

Now both boys were on hands and knees, feeling for the broken rails. 'I've got one,' said Dick. 'No, blow, it isn't. It's a bit of wood, or something. For goodness' sake, keep close to me, Ju.'

After ten minutes' search, the two boys sat back on their heels, the little torch between them.

'Somehow we've just missed those two or three correct steps from the gorse-bush to the rails,' said Julian. 'Now we're done! I don't see anything for it but to wait till the mist clears.'

'But what about the two girls?' said Dick, anxiously. 'Let's try a bit longer. Look, the mist is clearing a little there. Let's go forward and hope we'll stumble over the lines soon. If the mist does clear, we shall soon be able to ger our bearings.'

So they went forward hopefully, seeing the mist

clear a little in front of them, so that the torch made a longer beam for them to see by. Now and again, when their feet knocked against something hard, they felt for the rails. But they could not find even one!

'Let's shout,' said Julian, at last. So they shouted loudly. 'George! Anne! Can you hear us?'

They stood and listened. No answer.

'GEORGE!' yelled Dick. 'TIMMY!'

They thought they heard a far-off bark. 'That was Timmy!' said Julian. 'Over there!'

They stumbled along and then shouted again. But this time there was no bark at all. Not a sound came out of that dreadful mist, which had now closed tightly round them again.

'We'll be walking in it all night long,' said Julian, desperately. 'Why did we leave the girls? Suppose this frightful fog doesn't clear by tomorrow? Sometimes it lasts for days.'

'What a horrible idea,' said Dick, lightly, sounding much more cheerful than he felt. 'I don't think we need worry about the girls, Ju. Timmy's with them and he can easily take them back to the stables across the moor, in the mist. Dogs don't mind fogs.'

Julian felt most relieved. He hadn't thought of that. 'Oh yes, I'd forgotten old Tim,' he said. 'Well, seeing that the girls will probably be all right with Timmy to guide them, let's sit down somewhere and have a rest. I'm tired out!'

'Here's a good thick bush,' said Dick. 'Let's get into the middle of it if we can, and keep the damp out of us. Thank goodness it's not a gorse-bush!'

'I wish I knew if the girls had had the sense not to wait for us any longer, but to try to find their way back down the lines,' said Julian. 'I wonder where they are now?'

Anne and George were no longer where Julian and Dick had left them! They had waited and waited, and then had become very anxious indeed.

'Something's happened,' said George. 'I think we ought to go and get help, Anne. We can easily follow the railway down to where we have to break off for the stable. Timmy will know, anyway. Don't you think we ought to go back and get help?'

'Yes, I do,' said Anne, getting up. 'Come on, George. Gosh, this mist is worse than ever! We'll have to be careful we don't lose the lines! Even Timmy might find it hard to smell his way in this fog!'

They got up. Anne followed George and Timmy

They thought they heard a far-off bark.

followed behind, looking puzzled. He couldn't understand this night-time wandering about at all!

Anne and George kept closely to the railway lines, walking slowly along, shining the light of the torch downwards, and following carefully.

After a time George stopped, puzzled. 'This line's broken here,' she said. 'There's no more of it. That's funny, I don't remember it being as badly broken as this. The lines simply stop. I can't see any more.'

'Oh *George*!' said Anne, peering down. 'Do you know what we've done. We've come all the way *up* the lines again – instead of going down them, homewards! How *could* we have been so mad? Look, this is where they break off, so the old engine must be somewhere near, and the quarry!'

'Blow!' said George, quite in despair. 'What asses we are. It shows how we can lose our sense of direction in a mist like this.'

'I can't see or hear anything of the boys,' said Anne, fearfully. 'George, let's go to the quarry and wait there till daylight comes. I'm cold and tired. We can squeeze into one of those warm sand-caves.'

'All right,' said George, very much down in the dumps. 'Come along, and for goodness' sake don't let's lose our way to the quarry!'

111

17 Prisoners together

The two girls and Timmy made their way carefully, hoping to come across the lines that led to the quarry. They were lucky. They went across the gap in the lines where once long ago the gypsies had wrenched out the rails, and came to where they began again, and led to the edge of the quarry.

'Here they are!' said George, thankfully. 'Now we're all right. We've only just got to follow these and we'll be in the quarry. I hope it will be warmer than here. Brrrr! This mist is terribly cold and clammy.'

'It came up so *suddenly*,' said Anne, shining her torch downwards. 'I couldn't believe my eyes when I looked round and saw it creeping up on us. I . . .'

She stopped suddenly. Timmy had given a low growl. 'What's up, Tim?' whispered George. He stood quite still, his hackles up and his tail motionless. He looked steadfastly into the mist.

'Oh dear. What can be the matter now?' whispered Anne. 'I can't hear a thing, can you?'

They listened. No, there was nothing to hear at all. They went on into the quarry, thinking that Timmy might have heard a rabbit or hedgehog, and growled at it as he sometimes did.

Timmy heard a sound and ran to the side, lost in the mist at once. He suddenly yelped loudly, then there was a heavy thud, and no more sound from Timmy!

'Timmy! What's happened! Timmy, come here!' shouted George, at the top of her voice. But no Timmy came. The girls heard the sound of something heavy being dragged away, and George ran after the sound.

'Timmy! Oh, Timmy, what's happened!' she cried. 'Where are you? Are you hurt?'

The mist swirled round, and she tried to beat against it with her fists, angry that she could not see. 'Tim! Tim!'

Then a pair of hands took her arms from behind and a voice said, 'Now you come with me! You were warned not to snoop about on the moor!'

George struggled violently, less concerned for herself than for Timmy.

'Where's my dog?' she cried. 'What have you done to him?'

'I knocked him on the head,' said the voice, which sounded very like Sniffer's father. 'He's all right, but he won't feel himself for a bit! You can have him back if you're sensible.'

George wasn't sensible. She kicked and fought and wriggled and struggled. It was no use. She was held in a grip like iron. She heard Anne scream once and knew that she had been caught too.

When George was too tired to struggle any more, she was led firmly out of the quarry with Anne.

'Where's my dog?' she sobbed. 'What have you done with him?'

'He's all right,' said the man behind her. 'But if you make any more fuss I'll give him another blow on the head. *Now* will you be quiet?'

George was quiet at once. She was taken with Anne across the moor for what seemed like miles, but was really only the fairly short distance between the quarry and the gypsies' camp.

'Are you bringing my dog?' asked George, unable to contain her fears about Timmy.

'Yes. Somebody's got him,' said her captor. 'You shall have him back safe and sound, if you do what you're told!'

George had to be content with that. What a night! The boys gone, Timmy hurt, she and Anne captured, and this horrible, wreathing mist all the time!

The mist cleared a little as they came near to the gypsy camp. The hill behind seemed to keep it off. George and Anne saw the light of a fire, and of a few lanterns here and there. More men were gathered together, waiting. Anne thought she could see Sniffer and Liz in the background but she couldn't be sure.

'If only I could get hold of Sniffer,' she thought. 'He would soon find out if Timmy is really hurt. Oh Sniffer, do come nearer if it's you!'

Their captors took them to the little fire, and made both girls sit down. One of the men there exclaimed in surprise.

'But these are not those two boys! This is a boy and a girl, not as tall as the others were!'

'We're two girls,' said Anne, thinking that the men might treat George less roughly if they knew she was not a boy. 'I'm a girl and so is she.'

She got a scowl from George, but took no notice. This was not the time to pretend anything. These men were ruthless, and very angry. They thought their plans had gone wrong, all because of two boys. Perhaps when they found they had got two girls, they would let them go.

The men began to question them. 'Where are the boys then?'

'We've no idea! Lost in the mist,' said Anne. 'We all went out to go back home, and got separated, so George, I mean Georgina, and I went back to the quarry.'

'Did you hear the plane?'

'Of course!'

'Did you see or hear it dropping anything?'

'We didn't *see* anything drop, we heard it,' said Anne. George stared at her furiously. Why was Anne giving all this away? Perhaps she thought that Timmy would be given back to them if they proved helpful? George immediately changed her mind about feeling cross with Anne. If only Timmy were all right!

'Did you pick up what the plane dropped?' The man rapped out the question so sharply that Anne jumped. What should she say?

'Oh yes,' she heard herself saying. 'We picked up a few queer parcels. What was in them, do you know?'

'Never you mind,' said the man. 'What did you do with the parcels?'

George stared at Anne, wondering what she was going to say. Surely, surely she wouldn't give *that* secret away?

'I didn't do anything with them,' said Anne, in an innocent voice. 'The boys said they would hide them. So they went off into the mist with them, but they didn't come back. So George and I went to the quarry again. That's when you caught us.'

The men talked among themselves in low voices. Then Sniffer's father turned to the girls again.

'Where did the boys hide these packets?'

'How do I know?' said Anne. 'I didn't go with them. I didn't see what they did with them.'

'Do you think they will still have got them with them?' asked the man.

'Why don't you go and *find* the boys and ask them?' said Anne. 'I haven't seen or heard of the boys since they left us and went into the mist. I don't know *what* became of them or the parcels!'

'They're probably lost somewhere on the moors,' said the old, grey-haired gypsy. 'With the packets! We'll look for the boys tomorrow. They won't get home in this! We'll fetch them back here.'

'They wouldn't come,' said George. 'As soon as they saw you, they'd run. You'd never catch them. Anyway, they'd get back home as soon as the mist cleared.'

'Take these girls away,' said the old gypsy, sounding tired of them. 'Put them in the far cave, and tie them up.'

'Where's my dog?' shouted George, suddenly. 'You bring me my dog!'

'You haven't been very helpful,' said the old gypsy. 'We'll question you again tomorrow, and if you are *more* helpful, you shall have your dog.'

Two men took the girls away from the fire and over to the hill. A large opening led into the queer hill. One of the men had a lantern and led the way, the other man walking behind.

A passage led straight into the hill. There was sand underfoot, and it seemed to Anne as if even the walls were made of sand. How strange!

The hill was honeycombed with passages. They criss-crossed and forked like burrows in a rabbit-warren. Anne wondered however the men could find their way!

They came at last to a cave that must have been right in the heart of the hill, a cave with a sandy floor, and a post that was driven deeply into the ground.

Ropes were fastened firmly to it. The two girls looked at them in dismay. Surely they were not going to be tied up like prisoners!

But they were! The ropes were fastened firmly round their waists and knotted at the back. The knots were gypsy knots, firm, tight and complicated. It would take the girls hours to unpick those, even supposing they could manage to reach right round to their backs!

'There you are,' said the men, grinning at the two angry girls. 'Maybe in the morning you will remember where those packets were put?'

'You go and get my dog,' ordered George. But they only laughed loudly and went out of the cave.

It was stuffy and hot in there. George was worried to death about Timmy, but Anne was almost too tired to think.

She fell asleep, sitting up uncomfortably with the ropes round her waist, and the knots digging into her back. George sat brooding. Timmy – where was he? Was he badly hurt? George was very miserable indeed.

She didn't go to sleep. She sat there, worrying, wide awake. She made an attempt to get at the knots behind her, but it was no use, she couldn't.

Suddenly she thought she heard a noise. Was that someone creeping up the passage to the cave? She felt frightened. Oh, if only Timmy were here!

Sniff! Sniff!

'Gracious goodness, it must be Sniffer!' thought George, and at that moment she almost loved the dirty little gypsy boy!

'Sniffer!' she called quietly, and put on her torch. Sniffer's head appeared and then his body. He was crawling quietly up the passage on all fours.

He came right into the cave, and stared at her and the sleeping Anne. 'I've sometimes been tied up here too,' he said.

'Sniffer, how is Timmy?' asked George, anxiously. 'Tell me, quickly!'

'He's all right,' said Sniffer. 'He's just got a bad cut on his head. I bathed it for him. *He's* tied up too, and he's mad about it!'

'Sniffer, listen, go and get Timmy and bring him to me,' said George, breathlessly. 'And bring me a knife too, to cut these ropes. Will you? Can you?'

'Oooh, I dunno,' said Sniffer, looking frightened. 'My father would half kill me!'

'Sniffer, is there anything you want, anything you've *always* wanted?' said George. 'I'll give it to you if you do this for me. I promise you!'

'I want a bike,' said Sniffer, surprisingly. 'And I want to live in a house, and ride my bike to school.'

'I'll see that you have what you want, Sniffer,' said George, wildly. 'Only, do, do go and get Timmy, and a knife! You got here without being seen, you can surely get back again safely with Timmy. Think of that bike!'

Sniffer thought of it. Then he nodded and disappeared down the passage as silently as he had come.

George waited and waited. Would he bring dear old Timmy to her, or would he be caught?

18 George's trick

George sat in the darkness of the cave, hearing Anne's peaceful breathing nearby, waiting for Sniffer to come back. She was longing to see Timmy again. Was the cut on his head *very* bad?

A thought came in to her mind. She would send Timmy back to the stables with a note! He was very clever, he knew what to do when he had a note tied to his collar. Then help would come very quickly indeed. Timmy would know his way all right out of this hill, once he had been in it!

Ah, here was Sniffer coming back again. Was Timmy with him? She heard Sniffer's sniff-sniff-sniff, but no sound of Timmy. Her heart sank.

Sniffer appeared cautiously in the cave.

'I didn't dare to take Timmy,' he said. 'My father has him tied up too near to him, and I'd have waked him. But I've brought you a knife, look.'

'Thank you, Sniffer,' said George, taking the knife and putting it into her pocket. 'Listen, there's something important I'm going to do and you've got to help.'

'I'm scared,' said Sniffer. 'I'm real scared.'

'Think of that bicycle,' said George. 'A red one, perhaps, with silver handles?'

Sniffer thought of it. 'All right,' he said. 'What are you going to do?'

'I'm going to write a note,' said George, feeling in her pocket for her note-book and pencil. 'And I want you to tie it on to Timmy's collar, under his chin, and set him free somehow. Will you do that? He'll run off back to the stables with the note, and then Anne and I will be rescued, and you will get the most beautiful bicycle in the world!'

'And a house to live in,' said Sniffer, at once. 'So's I can ride my bike to school?'

'All right,' said George, hoping that somehow he could have that too. 'Now, wait a minute.'

She scribbled the note, but she had hardly written more than a few words, when a sound came up the passage. Someone was coughing.

'It's my father!' said Sniffer, in fright. 'Listen, if you cut your ropes and escape, can you find your way out from here? It's very twisty and turny.'

'I don't know. I don't think I can!' whispered George, in a panic.

'I'll leave patrins for you!' said Sniffer. 'Look out for them! Now I'm going to slip into the cave next door, and wait till my father's finished talking to you. Then I'll go back to Timmy.'

He slipped out just in time. The lantern shone

into George's cave and Sniffer's father stood there.

'Have you seen Sniffer?' he asked. 'I missed him when I woke just now. If I catch him in here I'll whip him till he squeals.'

'Sniffer? He's not here,' said George, trying to sound surprised. 'Look round the cave and see!'

The man caught sight of the note-book and pencil in George's hand. 'What's that you're writing?' he said suspiciously and took it from her.

'So you're writing for help, are you!' he said. 'And how do you think you're going to get help, I'd like to know? Who's going to take this note home for you? Sniffer?'

'No,' said George, truthfully.

The man frowned as he looked again at the note. 'Look here,' he said, 'you can write another note, to those two boys. And I'll tell you what to say.'

'No,' said George.

'Oh yes, you will,' said the man. 'I'm not going to hurt those boys. I'm just going to get back those packets from wherever they are hidden. Do you want your dog back safely?'

'Yes,' said George, with a gulp.

'Well, if you don't write this note you won't see him again,' said the man. 'Now then, take your pencil and write in that note-book of yours.'

George took up her pencil. 'This is what you must write,' said the man, frowning as he thought hard.

'Wait a minute,' said George. 'How are you going to get this note to the boys? You don't know where they are! You won't be able to find them if this mist still goes on.'

The man scratched his head and thought.

'The only way to get the note to them is to tie it on my dog's collar and send him to find them,' said George. 'If you bring him here to me I can make him understand. He always does what I tell him.'

'You mean he'll take the note to whoever you tell him to take it?' said the man, his eyes gleaming. 'Well, write it then. Say this:

"We are prisoners. Follow Timmy and he will bring you to us and you can save us."

Then sign your name, whatever it is.'

'It's Georgina,' said George, firmly. 'You go and get my dog while I write the note.'

The man turned and went. George looked after him, her eyes bright. *He* thought he was making her play a trick on Julian and Dick, to bring them

here so that they could be threatened and questioned about the packets, and where they were hidden!

'But *I'm* going to play a trick on him,' thought George. 'I'm going to tell Timmy to take the note to *Henry*, and she'll be suspicious and get Captain Johnson to follow Tim back here, and that will give the gypsies an *awful* shock! I expect the Captain will be sensible enough to get the police as well. Aha, *I'm* playing a trick too!'

In ten minutes' time Sniffer's father returned with Timmy. It was a rather subdued Timmy, with a very bad cut on his head, which really needed stitching. He pattered soberly across to George, and she flung her arms round his neck and cried into his thick hair.

'Does your head hurt you?' she said. 'I'll take you to the vet when I get back, Tim.'

'You can get back as soon as we've got those two boys here and they've told us where those packets are hidden,' said the man.

Timmy was licking George as if he would never stop, and his tail waved to and fro, to and fro. He couldn't understand what was happening at all! Why was George here? Never mind, he was with her again. He settled down on the floor with a thump and put his head on her knee.

'Write the note,' said the man, 'and tie it on to his collar, on the top, so that it can easily be seen.'

'I've written it,' said George. The gypsy held out a dirty hand for it and read it.

'We are prisoners. Follow Timmy and he will bring you to us and you can save us.

GEORGINA.'

'Is that really your name, Georgina?' asked the man. George nodded. It was one of the few times she ever owned to a girl's name!

She tied the note firmly to Timmy's collar, on the top of his neck. It was quite plainly to be seen. Then she gave him a hug and spoke urgently to him.

'Go to Henry, Tim, go to HENRY. Do you understand, Timmy dear, take this note to HENRY.' She tapped the paper on his collar as he listened to her. Then she gave him a push. 'Go along. Don't stay here any longer. Go and find HENRY.'

'Hadn't you better tell him the other boy's name too?' said the man.

'Oh no, I don't want to *muddle* Timmy,' said George hastily. 'Henry, Henry, HENRY!'

'Woof,' said Timmy, and George knew that he understood. She gave him another push.

'Go, then,' she said. 'Hurry!'

Timmy gave her rather a reproachful look as if to say, 'You haven't let me stay with you very long!' Then he padded off down the passage, the note showing clearly on his collar.

'I'll bring the boys up here as soon as they come with the dog,' said the man, and he turned on his heel, and went out. George wondered if Sniffer was still about and she called him. But there was no answer. He must have slipped away down the back to his caravan.

Anne woke up then, and wondered where she was. George switched on her torch again and explained all that had happened.

'You should have wakened me,' said Anne. 'Oh blow these ropes. They're *so* uncomfortable.'

'I've got a knife now,' said George. 'Sniffer gave it to me. Shall I cut our ropes?'

'Oh yes!' said Anne, in delight. 'But don't let's try and escape yet. It's still night-time and if that mist is about, we'll only get lost. We can pretend we're still tied up if anyone comes.'

George cut her own ropes with Sniffer's exceedingly blunt knife. Then she cut Anne's. Oh, what a relief to lie down properly, and not to have to sit up all the time and feel the knots at the back!

'Now do remember, if we hear anyone coming, we must tie the ropes loosely round us,' she said. 'We will stay here till we know it's day, and perhaps we can find out if the mist is still about, or if it's gone. If it's gone, we'll go.'

They fell asleep on the sandy floor, both glad to lie down flat. Nobody came to disturb them, and they slept on and on, tired out.

Where were the boys? Still under the bush, half-sleeping, half-waking, for they were cold and uncomfortable. They hoped the girls were now safely at home. They must have gone right down the railway, and made their way back to the stables, thought Julian, every time he awoke. I do hope they are safe, and Timmy too. Thank goodness he is with them.

But Timmy wasn't with them, of course. He was padding across the misty moor all by himself, puzzled, and with a badly-aching head. Why had George sent him to Henry? He didn't like Henry. He didn't think that George did, either. And yet she had sent him to find her. Very strange!

Still, George had given him his orders, and he loved her and always obeyed her. He padded over the heather and grass. He didn't bother about keeping to the railway line. He knew the way back without even thinking about it!

It was still night, though soon the dawn would come. But the mist was so thick that even the dawn would not be able to break through it. The sun would have to remain hidden behind the thick swathes of mist.

Timmy came to the stables. He paused to remember which was Henry's bedroom. Ah yes, it was upstairs, next to the room that Anne and George had had.

Timmy leapt in to the kitchen through a window left open for the cat. He padded upstairs and came to Henry's room. He pushed at the door and it opened.

In he went and put his paws on her bed. 'Woof,' he said in her ear. 'Woof! Woof! Woof!'

19 Good old Tim!

Henry had been fast asleep and snoring. She awoke with a tremendous jump when she felt Timmy's paw on her arm and heard his sharp little bark.

'Oooh! What is it?' she said, sitting up straight in bed and fumbling for her torch. She was quite panic-stricken. She switched on the torch with trembling fingers and then saw Timmy, his big brown eyes looking at her beseechingly.

'Why, Timmy!' said Henry, in amazement. '*Timmy!* Whatever are you doing here? Have the others come back? No, they couldn't have, not in the middle of the night! Why have *you* come then, Timmy?'

'Woof,' said Timmy, trying to make her understand that he was bringing a message. Henry put out her hand to pat his head, and suddenly caught sight of the paper tied to his collar at the back.

'What's this on your collar?' she said, and reached out for it. 'Why, it's paper. Tied on, too. It must be a message!'

She untied the piece of paper and unrolled it. She read it.

'We are prisoners. Follow Timmy and he will bring you to us and you can save us.

GEORGINA.'

Henry was astounded. She looked at Timmy and he looked back, wagging his tail. He pawed at her arm impatiently. Henry read the note again. Then she pinched herself to make sure she was not dreaming.

'Oooh, no, I'm awake all right,' she said. 'Timmy, is this note true? *Are* they prisoners? And who does "we" mean? George and Anne, or the whole four? Oh, Timmy, I *do* wish you could speak!'

Timmy wished the same! He pawed energetically at Henry. She suddenly saw the cut on his head and was horrified.

'You're hurt, Timmy! Oh, you poor, poor thing. Who did that to you? You ought to have that wound seen to!'

Timmy certainly had a very outsize headache,

but he couldn't bother to think about that. He gave a little whine and ran to the door and back.

'Yes, I know you want me to follow you, but I've got to *think*,' said Henry. 'If Captain Johnson was here I'd go and fetch him. But he's away for the night, Timmy. And I'm sure Mrs Johnson would have the fright of her life if I fetched her. I simply don't know what to do.'

'Woof,' said Timmy, scornfully.

'It's all very well to say "Woof" like that,' said Henry, 'but I'm not as brave as you are. I *pretend* I am, Timmy, but I'm not really. I'm afraid of following you! I'm afraid of going to find the others. I might be caught too. And there's a terrible mist, Timmy, you know.'

Henry slid out of bed, and Timmy looked suddenly hopeful. Was this silly girl going to make up her mind at last?

'Timmy, there's no grown-up here tonight except Mrs Johnson, and I really *can't* wake her,' said Henry. 'She's had such a very hard, busy day. I'm going to dress, and then get William. He's only eleven, I know, but he's very sensible, and he's a boy. He'll know what to do. I only *pretend* to be a boy.'

She dressed quickly in her riding things and then set off to William's room. He slept by himself across the landing. Henry walked in and switched on her torch.

William awoke at once. 'Who's there?' he demanded, sitting up at once. 'What do you want?'

'It's me. Henry,' said Henry. 'William, a most extraordinary thing has happened. Timmy has arrived in my room with a note on his collar. Read it!'

William took the note and read it. He was most astonished. 'Look,' he said. 'George has signed herself *Georgina*. She wouldn't do that unless things were very urgent. She never, never lets herself be called anything but George. We'll have to follow Tim and go, at once, too!'

'But I can't walk miles in a mist over the moor,' said Henry, in a panic.

'We don't need to. We'll saddle our horses and go on those,' said William, beginning to dress, and sounding very sensible indeed. 'Timmy will lead the way. You go and get the horses out. *Do* buck up, Henry. The others may be in danger. You're acting like a Henrietta!'

That made Henry cross. She went out of the room at once and down into the yard. What a pity

Captain Johnson happened to be away just that night. He would have decided everything at once.

Courage came to her when she got the horses. They were surprised but quite willing to go for a night-time ride, even in this thick mist! William came up in a very short time with Timmy behind him. Timmy was delighted to have William with him. He liked him, but he was not very fond of Henry.

He ran forward, just in front of the horses, and they followed behind. Both Henry and William had excellent torches, and kept them shining downwards, so that they should not miss Timmy. He did go out of sight once or twice, but came back immediately, when he heard the horses stopping.

Over the moor they rode. They didn't follow the railway, of course. Timmy didn't need to. He knew the way perfectly!

Once he stopped and sniffed the air. What had he smelt? Henry and William had no idea, but Timmy was puzzled by what he had smelt on the misty air.

Surely he had smelt the smell of the two boys, Julian and Dick? It had come on the air for a moment or two, and Timmy was half-inclined to follow it and see if the smell was right. Then he remembered George and Anne and went on through the swirling mist.

The boys were actually not very far away when Timmy smelt them. They were still in the middle of the bush, trying to keep warm, and sleep. If only they had known that Timmy was near, with Henry and William! But they didn't.

Timmy led the way. Soon they came to the quarry, but did not see it because of the mist. They went round it, led by Timmy, and rode towards the gypsy camp. Timmy slowed down, and they took warning.

'He's getting near wherever he wants to take us,' whispered William. 'Had we better dismount and tie the horses up, do you think? Their hooves may give a warning that we are near.'

'Yes. Yes, William,' said Henry, thinking that the boy was really very sensible. They dismounted quietly and tied the horses to a nearby birch tree.

They were quite near the hill in front of which was the gypsy camp. The mist was not so thick here, and the two suddenly caught sight of a dark, shadowy caravan, outlined against a campfire, left burning nearby. 'We'll have to be very quiet,' whispered William. 'Timmy's brought us to the gypsy camp on the moor. I had an idea that he would. The others must be held prisoner somewhere near – be as quiet as you can.'

Timmy watched them dismount. He hung his head, panting, his tail down. His head was hurting him very much, and he felt decidedly queer and giddy. But he must get to George, he must!

He led the way to the opening in the hill. William and Henry were most astonished. They followed Timmy through the maze of passages, wondering how he knew the way so surely. But Timmy didn't falter. He only needed to go somewhere once, and after that he never forgot the way!

He was going very slowly now, and his legs felt queer and shaky. He wanted to lie down and put his aching head on his paws. But no, he must find George. He must find George.

George and Anne were lying in the little cave, asleep. They were uncomfortable, and the cave was hot, so they were restless, waking up every few minutes. But both were asleep when Timmy walked slowly into the cave, and flopped down beside George.

George awoke when she heard William and Henry come into the cave. She thought it might be Sniffer's father coming back, and she hastily put the ropes round her waist so that she would look as if she were still tied up. Then she heard Timmy panting, and switched on her torch eagerly.

It showed her Timmy, and Henry and William! Henry was full of amazement when she saw George and Anne with ropes round their waists. She gaped at them.

Oh Timmy darling, you fetched help!' said George, putting her arms round his neck. 'Oh Henry, I'm so glad you've come. But didn't you bring Captain Johnson too?'

'No. He's away,' said Henry. 'But William's here. We rode, and Timmy guided us. Whatever's happened, George?'

Anne awoke just then, and couldn't believe her eyes when she saw the visitors! There was a hasty discussion, and then William spoke firmly.

'If you want to escape, you'd better come now, while the gypsy camp is asleep. Timmy can guide us out of this rabbit-warren of a hill. We'd never be able to find our way out alone. Come on!'

'Come on, Tim,' said George, shaking him gently. But poor old Timmy was feeling very peculiar. He couldn't see things properly. George's voice sounded blurred to him. His head felt as heavy as lead, and somehow his legs wouldn't carry him. The blow on his head was taking real effect now, and the hurried journey over the moor and back was making it worse.

'He's ill!' said George, in a panic. 'He can't get up! Oh Timmy, what's the matter?'

'It's that cut on his head,' said William. 'It's pretty bad, and he's worn out with coming to fetch us and running all the way back again. He can't possibly guide us back, George. We'll have to do the best we can by ourselves.'

'Oh, poor, poor Timmy!' said Anne, horrified at seeing the dog stretched out quite limp, on the floor of the cave. 'George, can you carry him?'

'I think so,' said George, and she lugged him up in her arms. 'He's awfully heavy, but I think I can just manage him. Perhaps the fresh air will revive him when we get outside.'

'But George, we don't know our way out of here,' said Anne, fearfully. 'If Timmy can't lead us, we're lost! We'd end up by wandering miles and miles inside this hill and never getting out!'

'Well, we'll simply *have* to make a shot at it,' said William. 'Come on, I'll lead the way. We really MUST go!'

He went out of the cave and down a passage; the others followed, George carrying the limp Timmy. But very soon William came to a fork and stopped.

'Oh dear – do we go to the left or the right?' he wondered.

Nobody kew. George shone her torch here and there, trying to remember. The beam of light picked up something on the ground near by.

It was two sticks, one short and one long, in the shape of a cross! George gave an exclamation.

'Look – a patrin! Left by Sniffer to show us the way out. We have to take the passage that the long stick points to! Oh, I hope that Sniffer has left patrins at every corner and every fork!'

They took the right-hand way and went on, their torches making long beams in the darkness, and at every place where they might go wrong, they saw a patrin, a message left by Sniffer to show them the right way to go.

'Another cross, we go *this* way,' said Anne.

'Here's a patrin again, we take *this* fork!' said George. And so it went on until they came safely to the entrance of the hill. How thankful they were to see the mist. At least it meant that they were in the open air!

'Now to get to the horses,' said William. 'They will each have to carry two of us at once, I'm afraid.'

'*But George, we don't know our way out of here.*'

And then, just as they were making their way to where they had left the horses, the gypsies' dogs began to bark the place down!

'They've heard us!' said William, desperately. 'Buck up! We'll be stopped if we don't get off at once!'

Then a voice shouted loudly. 'I can see you over there, with your torches! Stop at once! Do you hear me? STOP!'

20 Excite- ment in the morning

The dawn was coming now. The mist was no longer full of darkness, but was white, and thinning rapidly. The four children hurried to the horses, which were stamping impatiently by the trees. George couldn't go very fast because of Timmy. He really was very heavy.

Suddenly he began to struggle. The fresh, cool air had revived him and he wanted to be set down. George put him down thankfully, and he began to bark defiantly at the gypsies who were now coming out of their caravans, their dogs with them.

The four children mounted hurriedly and the horses were surprised at the double weight. William swung his horse's head round and set off with George sitting behind him. Henry took Anne. Timmy, feeling much better, ran after them, his legs no longer feeling so shaky.

The gypsies ran too, shaking their fists and shouting. Sniffer's father was amazed beyond measure. Why, there were the two girls he had tied up – and that dog he had sent off to trick the other two boys on the moor.

Then who were these on horse-back, and how had they found their way to the hill? How had the prisoners been able to find their way *out* of the hill, too? That was a real puzzle to Sniffer's father.

The gypsies tore after the horses, but the dogs contented themselves with excited barks. Not one of them dared to go after Timmy. They were afraid of him.

The horses went off as fast as they dared in the mist, Timmy running in front. He seemed very much better, though George was afraid it was only the excitement that now kept him going. She glanced back at the gypsies. They would never catch up now, thank goodness!

Somewhere behind the mist the sun was shining. Soon it would disperse the strange fog that had come up so suddenly from the sea. She glanced down at her watch. Good gracious, could it really be almost six o'clock in the morning? It was tomorrow now!

She wondered what had happened to Julian and Dick.

She thought of Sniffer gratefully, and all those patrins he had left in the hill. They would never have got out but for those. She thought of Henry and William, and gave William a sudden tight hug round the waist for coming out in the middle of the night and rescuing them!

'Where are Julian and Dick, do you suppose?' she said to William. 'Do you think they are still lost on the moor? Ought we to shout, and look for them?'

'No,' called back William over his shoulder. 'We're going straight back to the stables. They can look after themselves!'

Dick and Julian had certainly tried to look after themselves, that cold, misty night, but not very successfully. By the time that their torch showed them that it was a quarter to five by their watches, they had had enough of the bush they were in. If only they had known it, Henry and William, with Timmy, were just then riding over the moor, not a great distance from where they were!

They got out of the bush, damp and stiff. They stretched themselves and looked into the dark night, still full of mist.

'Let's walk,' said Julian. 'I can't bear keeping still in this mist. I've got my compass. If we walk due west we should surely come to the edge of the moor, not far from Milling Green.'

They set off, stumbling in the now dim light of the torch, whose battery was getting low. 'It will give out soon,' groaned Dick, giving it a shake. 'Blow the thing! It hardly gives us any light now, and we simply must keep looking at the compass.'

Julian tripped against something hard and almost fell. He snatched the torch from Dick. 'Quick, let me have it!'

He shone it on what had tripped him and gave a delighted exclamation. 'Look, it's a rail! We're on the railway line again. What a bit of luck!'

'I should *think* so!' said Dick, relieved. 'This torch is just about finished. Now, for *goodness'* sake don't let's lose this railway line. Stop at once if you can't feel it with your foot.'

'To think we were so jolly near the line after all, and didn't know it!' groaned Julian. 'We could have been back at the stables ages ago. I do hope the girls got back safely and didn't alarm anyone about us. They'd know we would come back as soon as it was daylight, anyhow, if we could follow the lines!'

They stumbled in at the stables' entrance about six o'clock, tired out. Nobody was yet up, it seemed. They found the garden door open, left ajar by William and Henry, and went up to the girls' room, hoping to find them in bed.

But the beds were empty of course. They went to Henry's room, to ask her if she had heard anything of the girls, but her bed, though slept in, was empty too!

They went across the landing to William's room. '*He's* gone as well!' said Dick, in great astonishment. 'Where are they all?'

'Let's wake Captain Johnson,' said Julian, who had no idea that the Captain was away for the night. So they awakened a very startled Mrs Johnson, and almost scared the life out of her, for she thought they were far away, camping on the moor!

She was even more startled when she heard their tale and realised that George and Anne were missing. 'Where *are* the girls, then?' she said, flinging on a dressing-grown. 'This is serious, Julian. They might be completely lost on the moor, or those gypsies might have got them! I must telephone my husband, and the police too. Oh dear, oh dear, why did I ever let you go camping out?'

She was in the middle of telephoning, with Julian and Dick beside her, looking very anxious indeed, when the sound of horses' hooves came in the yard below.

'Now goodness me! Who's that?' said Mrs Johnson. 'Horses! Who's riding them at this time of the morning!'

They all went to the window and looked down into the yard. Dick gave a yell that almost made Mrs Johnson fall out of the window!

'Anne! George! Look, there they are, and Timmy too. And gosh, there's Henry, and William! What *is* all this!'

Anne heard the yell and looked up. Tired as she was, she gave a cheerful wave and a grin. George gave a shout.

'Oh Julian! Oh Dick, you're back then? We did hope you would be. After you left us we went back up the lines the wrong way and arrived at the quarry again!'

'And the gypsies took us prisoner!' yelled Anne.

'But – but – how do Henry and William come into this?' said poor Mrs Johnson, thinking she must really still be asleep. 'And what's the matter with Timmy?'

Timmy had suddenly flopped on the ground. The excitement was over, they were home, now he could put his poor aching head on his paws and sleep!

George was off her horse immediately. 'Timmy! Darling Timmy! *Brave* Timmy! Help me, William. I'll take him upstairs to my room and see to that cut.'

By this time all the other children were awake and there was such a pandemonium going on that Mrs Johnson couldn't make herself heard.

Children in dressing-gowns and without, children shouting and yelling, children pouring into the yard and asking questions; William trying to quiet the two horses which were getting very excited at all this sudden clamour; and all the cocks round about crowing their heads off! *What* an excitement!

The sun suddenly shone out brilliantly, and the last wisps of mist disappeared. 'Hurrah! That mist has gone!' shouted George. 'The sun's out. Cheer up, Timmy. We'll all be all right now!'

Timmy was half-carried, half-dragged up the stairs by William and George. George and Mrs Johnson examined his cut head carefully, and bathed it.

'It really should have been stitched up,' said Mrs Johnson, 'but it seems to be healing already. How wicked to hit a dog like that!'

Soon there was the sound of horse's hooves again in the yard, and Captain Johnson arrived, looking very anxious. At almost the same moment a car slid in at the gates, a police car, with two policemen who had been sent to inquire about the missing girls! Mrs Johnson had forgotten to telephone again to say they had arrived.

'Oh dear, I'm so sorry to have bothered you,' said Mrs Johnson to the police sergeant. 'The girls have just arrived back, but I still don't know what has really happened. Still, they're safe, so please don't bother any more.'

'Wait!' said Julian, who was in the room, too. 'I think we *shall* need the police! Something very peculiar has been happening up on the moor.'

'Really, sir? What's that?' said the sergeant, taking out a note-book.

'We were camping there,' said Julian. 'And a plane came over, very low, guided by a lamp set in a sandpit by the gypsies.'

'A lamp set by the *gypsies*!' said the sergeant, surprised. 'But why should they need to guide a plane? I suppose it landed?'

'Now we know. This explains a lot . . .'

'No. It didn't,' said Julian. 'It came again the next night, and did exactly the same thing, swooping low and circling. But this time it dropped packages, sir!'

'Oh, it did, did it?' said the sergeant, more interested. 'For the gypsies to pick up, by any chance?'

'Yes, sir,' said Julian. 'But the plane's aim wasn't very good, and the packets fell all round *us* and almost hit us. We ran for shelter, because we didn't know if there were any explosives or not!'

'Did you pick up any of the packages?' asked the sergeant. Julian nodded.

'Yes, we did, and I opened one.'

'What was in it?'

'Paper money, dollars!' said Julian. 'In one packet alone there were scores of notes and each note was for a hundred dollars, about forty pounds a time! Thousands of pounds-worth thrown all around us!'

The sergeant looked at his companion. 'Ha! Now we know! This explains a lot that has been puzzling us, doesn't it, Wilkins?'

Wilkins, the other policeman, nodded grimly. 'It certainly does. So that's what happens! That's how the gang get the dollars over here, from that printing-press in Northern France. Just a nice little run in a plane!'

'But why do they throw the packets down for the *gypsies* to collect?' asked Julian. 'Is it so that they can give them to someone else? Why don't they bring them openly into the country? Surely anyone can bring *dollars* here?'

'Not *forged* ones, my lad,' said the sergeant. 'These will all be forged, you mark my words. The gang have got a headquarters near London, and as soon as those packets are handed over to them by one of the gypsies, they will set to work passing them off as real ones, paying hotel bills with them, buying all kinds of goods and paying for them in notes that aren't worth a penny!'

'Whew!' said Julian. 'I never thought of them being forged!'

122

'Oh yes. We've known of this gang for some time, but all we knew was that they had a printing-press to print the notes in Northern France, and that somehow the rest of the gang here, near London, received them and passed them off as real ones,' said the sergeant. 'But we didn't know how they were brought here, nor who took them to the gang near London.'

'But now we know all right!' said Wilkins. 'My word, this is a pretty scoop, Sergeant. Good kids these, finding out what we've been months trying to discover!'

'Where are these packages?' said the sergeant. 'Did you hide them? Did the gypsies get them?'

'No, we hid them,' said Julian. 'But I guess the gypsies will be hunting all over the place for them today, so we'd better get on the moors quick, Sergeant.'

'Where did you hide them?' said the sergeant. 'In a safe place, I hope!'

'Oh very!' said Julian. 'I'll call my brother, Sergeant. He'll come with us. Hey, Dick! Come on in here, and you'll hear a very interesting bit of news!'

21 The end of the mystery

Mrs Johnson was amazed to hear that the police wanted Julian and Dick to go out on the moors again.

'But they're tired out!' she said. 'They need something to eat. Can't it wait?'

'I'm afraid not,' said the sergeant. 'You needn't worry, Mrs Johnson. These boys are tough!'

'Well actually I don't think that the gypsies can *possibly* find the packets,' said Julian. 'So it wouldn't matter if we had a bite to eat. I'm ravenous!'

'All right,' said the big policeman, putting away his note-book. 'Have a snack and we'll go afterwards.'

Well, of course, George, Anne and Henry all wanted to go too, as soon as they heard about the proposed jaunt over the moors!

'What! Leave us out of *that*!' said George, indignantly. 'What a hope! Anne wants to come too.'

'So does Henry,' said Anne, looking at George, 'even though she didn't help to find the packages of notes.'

'Of *course* Henry must come,' said George at once, and Henry beamed. George had been very struck indeed with Henry's courage in coming with William to rescue her and Anne, and very pleased that she hadn't boasted about it! But

Henry knew that William was the one mostly to praise, and she had been unexpectedly modest about the whole affair.

It was quite a large party that set off after everyone had made a very good breakfast. Mrs Johnson had set to work cooking huge platefuls of bacon and egg, exclaiming every now and again

It was quite a large party that set off.

123

when she thought of all that had happened up on the moors.

'Those gypsies! And fancy that plane coming like that – dropping money all over the place! And the gypsies tying up Anne and George in that hill. I never heard anything like it in my life!'

Captain Johnson went with the party too. He could hardly believe the extraordinary tale that the four had to tell, five, with old Timmy! Timmy now had a beautiful patch on his head, and was feeling extremely important. Wait till Liz saw that!

Ten people set out, including Timmy, for William had been included in the party too. He tried to guess where Julian had hidden the notes, but he couldn't, of course. Julian firmly refused to tell anyone. He wanted it to be a real surprise.

They came to the quarry at last, having walked all the way up the old railway line. Julian stood on the edge of the quarry and pointed out the gypsy camp.

'Look, they're leaving,' he said. 'I bet they were afraid we'd spread the news of their behaviour, after the girls escaped.'

Sure enough, the caravans were moving slowly away.

'Wilkins, as soon as you get back, give word to have every gypsy watched if he leaves the caravans,' said the sergeant. 'One of them is sure to have arranged a meeting-place to give the gang the packets dropped from the plane, and if we watch those caravans, and every gypsy in them, we'll soon be able to put our hands on the gang that spends the forged notes.'

'I bet it's Sniffer's father,' said Dick. 'He's the ring-leader, anyway.'

They watched the caravans move away one by one. Anne wondered about Sniffer. So did George. What had she promised him last night, if he would help them? A bicycle, and to live in a house so that he could ride it to school! Well, it wasn't likely she would ever see the dirty little boy again, but if she did she would certainly have to keep her word!

'Now, where's this wonderful hiding-place?' asked the sergeant, as Julian turned from watching the caravans. He had tried to make out Sniffer and Liz, but the vans were too far away.

'Follow me!' said Julian, with a sudden grin and led the way back up the lines to where they broke off. The gorse-bush was there, and the old engine lay on its side as before, almost hidden.

'Whatever's that?' said the sergeant, surprised.

'It's the old Puffing Billy that used to pull the trucks of sand from the quarry,' said Dick. 'Apparently there was a quarrel long ago between the owners of the quarry and the gypsies, and the gypsies pulled up the lines and the engine ran off and fell over. There it's been ever since, as far as I can see!'

Julian went round to the funnel-end, and bent back the prickly gorse-branch that hid it. The sergeant looked on in surprise. Dick scraped the sand out of the top of the funnel and then pulled out one of the packages. He had been afraid they would not be there.

'Here you are!' he said, and tossed the packet to the sergeant. 'There are plenty more. I'll come to the one we opened in a minute – yes – here it is.'

The sergeant and Wilkins were amazed to see the packages hauled up from such a peculiar hiding-place. No wonder the gypsies hadn't found them. Nobody would ever have looked down the funnel of the old engine, even if they had spotted it, half-buried as it was.

The sergeant looked at the hundred-dollar notes in the opened parcel and whistled. 'My word, this is it! We've seen these before, beautiful forgeries they are! If the gang had got rid of *this* lot, a great many people would have suffered. The money is worth nothing! How many packets did you say there were?'

'Dozens!' said Dick, and pulled more of them out of the funnel. 'Gosh, I can't reach the ones at the bottom.'

'Never mind,' said the sergeant. 'Put some sand in to hide them and I'll send a man to poke the rest out with a stick. The gypsies have gone and they are the only people likely to hunt for them. This is a wonderful scoop! You kids have certainly put us on to something.'

'I'm glad,' said Julian. 'I say, we'd better collect all the things we left here yesterday, hadn't we? We went off in rather a hurry, you see, Sergeant, and left our things in the quarry.'

He and George went into the quarry to collect the things they had left there. Timmy went with them. He suddenly growled, and George stopped, her hand on his collar.

'What's up, Tim? Ju, there must be somebody here! Is it one of the gypsies, do you think?'

Then Timmy stopped growling and wagged his tail. He dragged away from George's hand and ran over to one of the little caves in the sandy walls. He looked most peculiar with the patch on his head.

Out of the cave came Liz! As soon as she saw Timmy she began to turn head-over-heels as fast as she could. Timmy stared in wonder – what a dog! How could she turn somersaults like that?

'Sniffer!' called George. 'Come on out. I know you're there!'

A pale, worried face looked out of the cave. Then Sniffer's thin, wiry little body followed, and soon he was standing in the quarry, looking scared.

'I got away from them,' he said, nodding his head towards where the gypsy camp had been. He went up to George, and gave a sniff.

'You said I could have a bike,' he said.

'I know,' said George. 'You *shall* have one, Sniffer. If you hadn't left us patrins in that hill, we'd never have escaped!'

'And you said I could live in a house and ride my bike to school,' said Sniffer urgently. 'I can't go back to my father, he'd half-kill me now. He saw those patrins I left in the hill and he chased me all over the moor for miles. But he didn't catch me. I hid.'

'We'll do the best we can for you,' promised Julian, sorry for this little waif. Sniffer sniffed.

'Where's that hanky?' demanded George. He pulled it out of his pocket, still clean and folded. He beamed at her.

'You're quite hopeless,' said George. 'Listen, if you want to go to school, you'll *have* to stop that awful sniff and use your hanky. See?'

Sniffer nodded, but put the hanky carefully back into his pocket. Then the sergeant came into the quarry and Sniffer fled at the sight of him!

'Funny little thing,' said Julian. 'Well, I should imagine that his father will be sent to prison for his share in this affair, so Sniffer will be able to get his wish and leave the caravan life to live in a house. We might be able to get him into a good home.'

'And I shall keep my word, and take some money out of my savings-bank and buy him a bicycle,' said George. 'He deserves it! Oh, do look at Liz – simply *adoring* Timmy and his patch. Don't look so important, Tim – it's only a patch on your cut!'

'Sniffer!' called Julian. 'Come back. You needn't be afraid of this policeman. He is a friend of ours. He'll help us to choose a bicycle for you.'

The sergeant looked extremely surprised at this remark, but at any rate it brought Sniffer back at once!

'Well, we'll go back now,' said the sergeant.

It was quite an adventure.

'We've got what we want, and Wilkins has already started back to get somebody on to watching the gypsies. Once we find out who they have to report to about this forged money we shall feel happy.'

'I hope Wilkins went along down the railway,' said Julian. 'It's so easy to get lost on this moor.'

'Yes. He had the sense to do that, after hearing how *you* got lost!' said the sergeant. 'It's wonderful up here, isn't it? So peaceful and quiet and calm.'

'Yes, you'd never think that mysteries could happen up here, would you?' said Dick. 'Old ones, and new ones! Well, I'm glad we happened to be mixed up in the newest one. It was quite an adventure!'

They all went back to the stables, to find that it was now almost dinner-time and that everyone had a very large appetite to match the very large dinner that Mrs Johnson had got ready. The girls went upstairs to wash. George went into Henry's room.

'Henry,' she said. 'thanks most awfully. You're as good as a boy any day!'

'Thanks, George,' said Henry, surprised. 'You're *better* than a boy!'

Dick was passing the door and heard all this. He laughed, and stuck his head in at the door.

'I say, do let me share in these compliments!' he said. 'Just tell me I'm as good as a girl, will you?'

But all he got was a well-aimed hair-brush and a shoe, and he fled away, laughing.

Anne gazed out of her bedroom window over the moor. It looked so peaceful and serene under the April sun. No mystery about it now!

'All the same, it's a good name for you,' said Anne. 'You're full of mystery and adventure, and your last adventure waited for *us* to come and share it. I really think I'd call this adventure "Five Go To Mystery Moor".'

It's a good name, Anne. We'll call it that too!

Five go off in a caravan

1 The beginning of the holidays

'I do love the beginning of the summer hols,' said Julian. 'They always seem to stretch out ahead for ages and ages.'

'They go so nice and slowly at first,' said Anne, his little sister. 'Then they start to gallop.'

The others laughed. They knew exactly what Anne meant. 'Woof,' said a deep voice, as if someone else thoroughly agreed too.

'Timmy thinks you're right, Anne,' said George, and patted the big dog laying panting beside them. Dick patted him, too, and Timmy licked them both.

The four children were lying a sunny garden in the first week of the holidays. Usually they went to their cousin Georgina's home for holidays, at Kirrin – but this time, for a change, they were all at the home of Julian, Dick and Anne.

Julian was the oldest, a tall, sturdy boy with a strong and pleasant face. Dick and Georgina came next. Georgina looked more like a curly-headed boy than a girl, and she insisted on being called George. Even the teachers at school called her George. Anne was the youngest, though, much to her delight, she was really growing taller now.

'Daddy said this morning that if we didn't want to stay here all the hols we could choose what we wanted to do,' said Anne. 'I vote for staying here.'

'We could go off somewhere just for two weeks, perhaps,' said Dick. 'For a change.'

'Shall we go to Kirrin, and stay with George's mother and father for a bit?' said Julian, thinking that perhaps George would like this.

'No,' said George at once. 'I went home at half-term, and Mother said Father was just beginning one of his experiments in something or other – and you know what *that* means. If we go there we'd have to walk about on tiptoe, and talk in whispers, and keep out of his way the whole time.'

'That's the worst of having a scientist for a father,' said Dick, lying down on his back and shutting his eyes. 'Well, your mother couldn't cope with us and with your father, too, in the middle of one of his experiments at the same time. Sparks would fly.'

'I like Uncle Quentin, but I'm afraid of him when he's in one of his tempers,' said Anne. 'He shouts so.'

'It's decided that we won't go to Kirrin, then,' said Julian, yawning. 'Not these hols, anyhow. You can always go and see Mother for a week or so, George, when you want to. What shall we do, then? Stay here all the time?'

They were now all lying down on their backs in the sun, their eyes shut. What a hot afternoon! Timmy sat up by George, his pink tongue hanging out, panting loudly.

'Don't, Timmy,' said Anne. 'You sound as if you have been running for miles, and you make me feel hotter then ever.'

Timmy put a friendly paw on Anne's middle and she squealed. 'Oh, Timmy – your paw's heavy. Take it off.'

'You know, I think if we were allowed to go off by ourselves somewhere, it would be rather fun,' said George, biting a blade of grass and squinting up into the deep blue sky. 'The biggest fun we've ever had was when we were alone on Kirrin Island, for instance. Couldn't we go off somewhere all by ourselves?'

'But where?' said Dick. 'And how? I mean we aren't old enough to take a car – though I bet I could drive one. It wouldn't be much fun going on bicycles, because Anne can't ride as fast as we can.'

'And somebody always gets a puncture,' said Julian.

It would be jolly good fun to go off on horses,' said George. 'Only we haven't got even one.'

'Yes, we have – there's old Dobby down in the field,' said Dick. 'He is ours. He used to draw the pony-cart, but we don't use it any more now he's turned out to grass.'

'Well, one horse wouldn't take four of us, silly,' said George. 'Dobby's no good.'

There was a silence, and everyone thought lazily about holidays. Timmy snapped at a fly, and his teeth came together with a loud click.

'Wish I could catch flies like that,' said Dick, flapping away a blue-bottle. 'Come and catch this one, Timmy, old thing.'

'What about a walking tour?' said Julian after a pause. There was a chorus of groans.

'What! In this weather! You're mad!'

'We shouldn't be allowed to.'

'All right, all right,' said Julian. 'Think of a better idea, then.'

'I'd like to go somewhere where we could bathe,' said Anne. 'In a lake, for instance, if we can't go to the sea.'

'Sounds nice,' said Dick. 'My goodness, I'm sleepy. Let's hurry up and settle this matter, or I shall be snoring hard.'

But it wasn't easy to settle. Nobody wanted to go off to an hotel, or to rooms. Grown-ups would want to go with them and look after them. And nobody wanted to go walking or cycling in the hot August weather.

'Looks as if we'll have to stay at home all the hols, then,' said Julian. 'Well – I'm going to have a snooze.'

In two minutes they were all asleep on the grass except Timmy. If his family fell asleep like this, Timmy considered himself on guard. The big dog gave his mistress George a soft lick and sat up firmly beside her, his ears cocked, and his eyes bright. He panted hard, but nobody heard him. They were all snoozing deliciously in the sun, getting browner and browner.

The garden sloped up a hillside. From where he sat Timmy could see quite a long way, both up and down the road that ran by the house. It was a wide road, but not a very busy one, for it was a country district.

Timmy heard a dog barking in the distance, and his ears twitched in that direction. He heard people walking down the road and his ears twitched again. He missed nothing, not even the robin that flew down to get a caterpillar on a bush not far off. He growled softly in his throat at the robin – just to tell it that he was on guard, so beware.

Then something came down the wide road, something that made Timmy shake with excitement, and sniff at the strange smells that came floating up to the garden. A big procession came winding up the road, with a rumble and clatter of wheels – a slow procession, headed by a very strange thing.

Timmy had no idea what it was that headed the procession. Actually it was a big elephant, and Timmy smelt its smell, strange and strong, and didn't like it. He smelt the scent of the monkeys in their travelling cage, too, and he heard the barking of the performing dogs in their van.

He answered them defiantly: 'WOOF, WOOF, WOOF.'

The loud barking awoke all four children at once. 'Shut up, Timmy,' said George crossly. 'What a row to make when we're all having a nap.'

'WOOF,' said Timmy obstinately, and pawed at his mistress to make her sit up and take notice. George sat up. She saw the procession at once and gave a yell.

'Hey, you others. There's a circus procession going by. Look.'

They all sat up, wide awake now. They stared down at the caravans going slowly along, and listened to an animal howling, and the dogs barking.

'Look at that elephant, pulling the caravan along,' said Anne. 'He must be jolly strong.'

'Let's go down to the gate of the drive and watch,' said Dick. So they all got up and ran down the garden, then round the house and into the drive that led to the road. The procession was just passing the gates.

It was a gay sight. The caravans were painted in brilliant colours, and looked spick and span from the outside. Little flowery curtains hung at the windows. At the front of each caravan sat the man or woman who owned it, driving the horse that pulled it. Only the front caravan was pulled by an elephant.

'Golly – doesn't it look exciting?' said George. 'I wish I belonged to a circus that went wandering all over the place all the year. That's just the sort of life I'd like.'

They all got up and ran down the garden.

'Fat lot of good you'd be in the circus,' said Dick rudely. 'You can't even turn a cart-wheel.'

'What's a cart-wheel?' said Anne.

'What that boy's doing over there,' said Dick. 'Look.'

He pointed to a boy who was turning cart-wheels very quickly, going over and over on his hands and feet, turning himself like a wheel. It looked so easy, but it wasn't, as Dick very well knew.

'Oh, is he turning a cart-wheel?' said Anne admiringly. 'I wish I could do that.'

The boy came up to them and grinned. He had two terrier dogs with him. Timmy growled and George put her hand on his collar.

'Don't come too near,' she called. 'Timmy isn't quite sure about you.'

'We won't hurt him!' said the boy, and grinned again. He had an ugly, freckled face, with a shock of untidy hair. 'I won't let my dogs eat your Timmy.'

'As if they could!' began George scornfully, and then laughed. The terriers kept close to the boy's heels. He clicked and both dogs rose at once on their hind legs and walked sedately behind him with funny little steps.

'Oh – are they performing dogs?' said Anne. 'Are they yours?'

'These two are,' said the boy. 'This is Barker and this is Growler. I've had them from pups – clever as paint they are!'

'Woof,' said Timmy, apparently disgusted at seeing dogs walk in such a peculiar way. It had never occurred to him that a dog could get up on his hind legs.

'Where are you giving your next show?' asked George eagerly. 'We'd like to see it.'

'We're off for a rest,' said the boy. 'Up in the hills, where there's a blue lake at the bottom. We're allowed to camp there with our animals – it's wild and lonely and we don't disturb nobody. We just camp there with our caravans.'

'It sounds fine,' said Dick. 'Which is your caravan?'

'This one, just coming' said the boy, and he pointed to a brightly painted van, whose sides were blue and yellow, and whose wheels were red. 'I live in it with my Uncle Dan. He's the chief clown of the circus. There he is, sitting on the front, driving the horse.'

The children stared at the chief clown, and thought that they had never seen anyone less like a clown. He was dressed in dirty grey flannel trousers and a dirty red shirt open at an equally dirty neck.

He didn't look as if he could make a single joke, or do anything in the least funny. In fact, he looked really bad-tempered, the children thought, and he scowled so fiercely as he chewed on an old pipe that Anne felt quite scared. He didn't look at the children at all, but called in a sharp voice to the boy:

'Nobby! You come on along of us. Get in the caravan and make me a cup of tea.'

The boy Nobby winked at the children and ran to the caravan. It was plain that Uncle Dan kept him in order all right! He poked his head out of the little window in the side of the caravan nearest to the children.

'Sorry I can't ask you to tea too!' he called. 'And the dog. Barker and Growler wouldn't half like to know him!'

The caravan passed on, taking the scowling clown with it, and the grinning Nobby. The children watched the others going by, too; it was quite a big circus. There was a cage of monkeys, a chimpanzee sitting in a corner of a dark cage, asleep, a string of beautiful horses, sleek and shinning, a great wagon carrying benches and forms and tents, caravans for the circus folk to live in, and a host of interesting people to see, sitting on the steps of their vans or walking together outside to stretch their legs.

At last the procession was gone and the children went slowly back to their sunny corner in the garden. They sat down – and then George announced something that made them sit up straight.

'*I* know what we'll do these hols! We'll hire a caravan and go off in it by ourselves. Do let's! Oh, do let's!'

2 George's great idea

The others stared at George's excited face. She had gone quite red. Dick thumped on the ground.

'A jolly good idea! Why didn't we think of it before?'

'Oh, *yes*! A caravan to ourselves! It sounds too good to be true!' said Anne, and her eyes shone.

'Well, I must say it would be something we've never done before,' said Julian, wondering if it was really possible. 'I say – wouldn't it be gorgeous if we could go off into the hills – where that lake is that the boy spoke about? We could bathe there – and we could perhaps get to know the circus folk. I've always wanted to know about circuses.'

'Oh, *Julian*! That's a better idea still!' said George, rubbing her hands together in delight. 'I liked that boy Nobby, didn't you?'

'Yes,' said everyone.

'But I didn't like his uncle,' said Dick. 'He looked a nasty bit of work. I bet he makes Nobby toe the mark and do what he's told.'

'Julian, do you think we'd be allowed to go caravanning by ourselves?' asked Anne earnestly. 'It does seem to me to be the most marvellous idea we've ever had.'

'Well – we can ask and see,' said Julian. 'I'm old enough to look after you all.'

'Pooh!' said George. 'I don't want any looking after, thank you. And anyway, if we want looking after, Timmy can do that. I bet the grown-ups will be glad to be rid of us for a week or two. They always think the summer hols are too long.'

'We'll take Dobby with us to pull the caravan!' said Anne suddenly, looking down at the field where Dobby stood, patiently flicking away the flies with his long tail. 'Dobby would love that! I always think he must be lonely, living in that field all by himself, just being borrowed by people occasionally.'

'Of course – Dobby could come,' said Dick. 'That would be fine Where could we get the caravan from? Are they easy to hire?'

'Don't know,' said Julian. 'I knew a chap at school – you remember him, Dick, that big fellow called Perry – he used to go caravanning every hols with his people. They used to hire caravans, I know. I might find out from him where he got them from.'

'Daddy will know,' said Anne. 'Or Mummy. Grown-ups always know things like that. I'd like a nice large caravan – red and blue – with a little chimney, and windows each side, and a door at the back, and steps to go up into the caravan, and . . .'

The others interrupted with their own ideas, and soon they were all talking excitedly about it – so loudly that they didn't see someone walking up and standing near by, laughing at the excitement.

'Woof,' said Timmy politely. He was the only one who had ears and eyes for anything else at the moment. The children looked up.

'Oh, hallo, Mother!' said Julian. 'You've just come at the right moment. We want to tell you about an idea we've got.'

His mother sat down, smiling. 'You seem very excited about something,' she said. 'What is it?'

'Well, it's like this, Mummy,' said Anne, before anyone else could get a word in, 'we've made up our minds that we'd like to go off in a caravan for a holiday by ourselves! Oh, Mummy – it would be such fun!'

'By yourselves?' said her mother doubtfully. 'Well, I don't know about that.'

'Julian can look after us,' said Anne.

'So can Timmy,' put in George at once, and Timmy thumped the ground with his tail. Of course he could look after them! Hadn't he done it for years, and shared all their adventures? Thump, thump, thump!

130

'I'll have to talk it over with Daddy,' said Mother. 'Now don't look so disappointed – I can't decide a thing like this all by myself in a hurry. But it may fit in quite well because I know Daddy has to go up north for a little while, and he would like me to go with him. So he might think a little caravanning quite a good idea. I'll talk to him tonight.'

'We could have Dobby to pull the caravan, Mummy,' said Anne, her eyes bright. 'Couldn't we? He'd love to come. He has such a dull life now.'

'We'll see, we'll see,' said her mother, getting up. 'Now you'd better all come in and wash. It's nearly tea-time. Your hair is terrible, Anne. What *have* you been doing?'

Everyone rushed indoors to wash, feeling distinctly cheerful. Mother hadn't said NO. She had even thought it might fit in quite well. Golly, to go off in a caravan all alone – doing their own cooking and washing – having Dobby for company, and Timmy as well, of course. How simply gorgeous.

The children's father did not come home until late that evening, which was a nuisance, for nobody felt that they could wait for very long to know whether they might or might not go. Everyone but Julian was in bed when he came home, and even when he, too, came to bed he had nothing to report.

He stuck his head into the girls' bedroom. 'Daddy's tired and he's having a late supper, and Mother won't bother him till he's feeling better. So we shan't know till morning, worse luck!'

The girls groaned. How could they possibly go to sleep with thoughts of caravans floating deliciously in their heads – not knowing whether or not they would be allowed to go!

'Blow!' said George. 'I shan't go to sleep for ages. Get off my feet, Timmy. Honestly, it's too hot to have you anywhere near me this weather.'

In the morning good news awaited the four children. They sat down at the breakfast-table, all very punctual for once, and Julian looked expectantly at his mother. She smiled at him and nodded.

'Yes, we've talked it over,' she said. 'And Daddy says he doesn't see why you shouldn't have a caravan holiday. He thinks it would be good for you to go off and rough it a bit. But you will have to have two caravans, not one. We couldn't have all four of you, and Timmy too, living in one caravan.'

'Oh – but Dobby couldn't pull *two* caravans, Mummy,' said Anne.

'We can borrow another horse,' said Julian. 'Can't we, Mother? Thanks awfully, Daddy, for saying we can go. It's jolly sporting of you.'

'Absolutely super,' said Dick.

'Wizard!' said George, her fingers scratching Timmy's head excitedly. 'When can we go? Tomorrow?'

'Of course not!' said Julian. 'We've got to get the caravans – and borrow a horse – and pack – and all sorts of things.'

'You can go next week, when I take your mother up north with me,' said his father. 'That will suit us very well. We can give Cook a holiday, too, then. You will have to send us a card every single day to tell us how you are and where you are.'

'It does sound thrilling,' said Anne. 'I really don't feel as if I can eat any breakfast, Mummy.'

'Well, if that's the effect the idea of caravanning has on you, I don't think you'd better go,' said her mother. Anne hastily began to eat her shredded wheat, and her appetite soon came back. It was too good to be true – to have *two* caravans – and *two* horses – and sleep in bunks perhaps – and cook meals outside in the open air – and . . .

'You will be in complete charge, you understand, Julian,' said the boy's father. 'You are old enough now to be really responsible. The others must realise that you are in charge and they must do as you say.'

'Yes, sir,' said Julian, feeling proud. 'I'll see to things all right.'

'And Timmy will be in charge, too,' said George. 'He's just as responsible as Julian.'

'Woof,' said Timmy, hearing his name, and thumping the floor with his tail.

'You're a darling, Timmy,' said Anne. 'I'll always do what *you* say, as well as what Julian says!'

'Idiot!' said Dick. He patted Timmy's head. 'I bet we wouldn't be allowed to go without you, Timothy. You are a jolly good guard for anyone.'

'You certainly wouldn't be allowed to go without Timmy,' said his mother. 'We know you'll be safe with him.'

It was all most exciting. The children went off to talk things over by themselves when breakfast was finished.

'I vote we go caravanning up into the hills that boy spoke of, where the lake lies at the bottom – and camp there,' said Julian. 'We'd have company then – jolly exciting company, too. We wouldn't live *too* near the circus camp – they might not like stangers butting in – but we'll live near enough to see the elephant going for his daily walk, and the dogs being exercised . . .'

'And we'll make friends with Nobby, won't we?' said Anne eagerly. 'I liked him. We won't go near his uncle, though. I think it's queer that such a bad-tempered looking man should be the chief clown in a circus.'

'I wonder when and where Mother will get the caravans!' said Julian. 'Gosh, won't it be fun when we see them for the first time!'

'Let's go and tell Dobby!' said Anne. 'He is sure to be excited, too!'

'Baby! He won't understand a word you tell him!' said George. But off she went with Anne just the same, and soon Dobby was hearing all about the wonderful holiday plan. Hrrrrumph! So long as it included him, too, he was happy!

3 The caravans arrive

At last the great day came when the two caravans were due to arrive. The children stood at the end of the drive for hours, watching for them.

Mother had managed to borrow them from an old friend of hers. The children had promised faithfully to look after them well, and not to damage anything. Now they stood at the end of the drive, watching eagerly for the caravans to arrive.

'They are being drawn by cars today,' said Julian. 'But they are fitted up to be horse-drawn, too. I wonder what they are like – and what colour they are?'

'Will they be like gypsy caravans, on high wheels, do you think?' asked Anne. Julian shook his head.

'No, they're modern, Mother says. Streamlined and all that. Not too big either, because a horse can't draw too heavy a van.'

'They're coming, they're coming! I can see them!' suddenly yelled George, making them all jump. 'Look, isn't that them, far down the road?'

They all looked hard into the distance. No one had such good eyes as George, and all they could see was a blotch, a moving speck far away on the road. But George's eyes saw two caravans, one behind the other.

'George is right,' said Julian, straining his eyes. 'It's our caravans. They're each drawn by a small car.'

'One's red and the other's green,' said Anne. 'Bags I the red one. Oh, hurry up, caravans!'

At last they were near enough to see properly. The children ran to meet them. They certainly were very nice ones, quite modern and 'streamlined', as Julian had said, well built and comfortable.

'They almost reach the ground!' said Anne. 'And look at the wheels, set so neatly into the side of the vans. I do like the red one, bags I the red one.'

Each van had a little chimney, long, narrow windows down the two sides, and tiny ones in front by the driver's seat. There was a broad door at the back and two steps down. Pretty curtains fluttered at the open windows.

'Red curtains for the green caravan, and green ones for the red caravan!' said Anne. 'Oh, I want to go inside!'

But she couldn't because the doors were locked. So she had to be content to run with the others up the drive after the two caravans, shouting loudly:

'Mummy! They're here, the caravans are here.'

Her mother came running down the steps to see. Soon the doors were unlocked and the children went inside the caravans. Delighted shouts came from both vans.

'Bunks along one side – is that where we sleep? How gorgeous!'

'Look at this little sink – we can really wash up. And golly, water comes out of these taps!'

'There's a proper stove to cook on – but I vote we cook out of doors on a camp fire. I say, look at the bright frying-pans – and all the cups and saucers hanging up!'

'It's like a proper little house inside. Doesn't it seem nice and *big*? Mother, isn't it beautifully planned? Don't you wish you were coming with us?'

'Hey, you girls! Do you see where the water comes from? Out of that tank on the roof. It must collect rainwater. And look at this gadget for heating water. Isn't it all super?'

The children spent hours examining their caravans and finding out all the secrets. They certainly were very well fitted, spotlessly clean, and very roomy. George felt as if she couldn't wait to start out. She really must get Dobby and set out at once!

'No, you must wait, silly,' said Julian. 'You know we've to get the other horse. He's not coming till tomorrow.'

The other horse was a sturdy little black fellow called Trotter. He belonged to the milkman, who often lent him out. He was a sensible little horse, and the children knew him very well and liked him. They all learnt riding at school, and knew how to groom and look after a horse, so there would be no difficulty over their managing Dobby and Trotter.

Mother was thrilled over the caravans, too, and looked very longingly at them. 'If I wasn't going with Daddy I should be most tempted to come with you,' she said. 'Don't look so startled, Anne dear – I'm not really coming!'

'We're jolly lucky to get such decent caravans,' said Julian. 'We'd better pack our things today, hadn't we, Mother? – and start off tomorrow, now we've got the caravans.'

'You won't need to pack,' said his mother. 'All you have to do is to pop your things straight into the cupboards and drawers – you will only want clothes and books and a few games to play in case it's rainy.'

'We don't need any clothes except our night things, do we?' said George, who would have lived in a jersey and jeans all day and every day if she had been allowed to.

'You must take plenty of jerseys, another pair of jeans each, in case you get wet, your rain-coats, bathing-things, towels, a change of shoes, night things, and some cool shirts or blouses,' said Mother. Everyone groaned.

'What a frightful lot of things!' said Dick. 'There'll never be room for all those.'

'Oh yes there will,' said Mother. 'You will be sorry if you take too few clothes, get soaked through, have nothing to change into, and catch fearful colds that will stop you from enjoying a lovely holiday like this.'

'Come on, let's get the things,' said Dick. 'Once Mother starts off about catching cold there's no knowing what else she'll make us take – is there, Mother?'

'You're a cheeky boy,' said his mother, smiling. 'Yes, go and collect your things. I'll help you to put them into the cupboards and drawers. Isn't it marvellous how everything folds so neatly into the walls of the caravans – there seems to be room for everything, and you don't notice the cupboards.'

'I shall keep everything very clean,' said Anne. 'You know how I like *playing* at keeping house, don't you, Mother? – well, it will be real this time. I shall have two caravans to keep clean, all by myself.'

'All by yourself!' said her mother. 'Well, surely the boys will help you – and certainly George must.'

'Pooh, the boys!' said Anne. 'They won't know how to wash and dry a cup properly – and George never bothers about things like that. If I don't make the bunks and wash the crockery, they would never be made or washed, I know that!'

'Well, it's a good thing that one of you is sensible!' said her mother. 'You'll find that everyone will share in the work, Anne. Now off you go and get your things. Bring all the rain-coats, to start with.'

It was fun taking things down to the caravans and packing them all in. There were shelves for a few books and games, so Julian brought down snap cards, ludo, lexicon, happy families and dominoes, as well as four or five books for each of them. He also brought down some maps of the district, because he meant to plan out where they were to go, and the best roads to follow.

Daddy had given him a useful little book in which were the names of farms that would give permission to caravanners to camp in fields for the night. 'You must always choose a field where there is a stream, if possible,' said his father, 'because Dobby and Trotter will want water.'

'Remember to boil every drop of water you drink,' said the children's mother. 'That's very important. Get as much milk from the farms as they will let you have. And remember that there is plenty of ginger-beer in the locker under the second caravan.'

'It's all so thrilling,' said Anne, peering down to look at the locker into which Julian had put the bottles of ginger-beer. 'I can't believe we're really going tomorrow.'

But it was true. Dobby and Trotter were to be taken to the caravans the next day and harnessed. How exciting for them, too, Anne thought.

Timmy couldn't quite understand all the excitement, but he shared in it, of course, and kept his tail on the wag all day long. He examined the caravans thoroughly from end to end, found a rug he liked the smell of, and lay down on it. 'This is *my* corner,' he seemed to say. 'If you go off in these peculiar houses on wheels, this is my own little corner.'

'We'll have the red caravan, George,' said Anne. 'The boys can have the green one. They don't care what colour they have – but I love red. I say, won't it be sport to sleep in those bunks? They look jolly comfortable.'

At last tomorrow came – and the milkman brought the sturdy little black horse, Trotter, up the drive. Julian fetched Dobby from the field. The horses nuzzled one another and Dobby said 'Hrrrumph' in a very civil horsey voice.

'They're going to like each other,' said Anne. 'Look at them nuzzling. Trotter, you're going to draw *my* caravan.'

The two horses stood patiently while they were harnessed. Dobby jerked his head once or twice as if he was impatient to be off and stamped a little.

'Oh, Dobby, I feel like that, too!' said Anne. 'Don't you, Dick, don't you, Julian?'

'I do rather,' said Dick with a grin. 'Get up there, Dobby – that's right. Who's going to drive, Julian – take it in turns, shall we?'

'I'm going to drive *our* caravan,' said George. 'Anne wouldn't be any good at it, though I'll let her have a turn at it sometimes. Driving is a man's job.'

'Well, you're only a girl!' said Anne indignantly. 'You're not a man, nor even a boy!'

George put on one of her scowls. She always wanted to be a boy, and even thought of herself as one. She didn't like to be reminded that she was only a girl. But not even George could scowl for long that exciting morning! She soon began to caper round and about again, laughing and calling out with the others:

'We're ready! Surely we're ready!'

'Yes. Do let's go! JULIAN! He's gone indoors, the idiot, just when we want to start.'

'He's gone to get the cakes that Cook has baked this morning for us. We've heaps of food in the larder. I feel hungry already.'

'Here's Julian. Do come on, Julian. We'll drive off without you. Good-bye, Mother! We'll send you a card every single day, we faithfully promise.'

Julian got up on the front of the green caravan. He clicked to Dobby. 'Get on, Dobby! We're off! Good-bye, Mother!'

Dick sat beside him, grinning with pure happiness. The caravans moved off down the drive. George pulled at Trotter's reins and the little horse followed the caravan in front. Anne, sitting beside George, waved wildly.

'Good-bye, Mother! We're off at last on another adventure. Hurrah! Three cheers! Hurrah!'

4 Away they go!

The caravans went slowly down the wide road. Julian was so happy that he sang at the top of his voice, and the others joined in the choruses. Timmy barked excitedly. He was sitting on one side of George and as Anne was on the other George was decidedly squashed. But little things like that did not bother her at all.

Dobby plodded on slowly, enjoying the sunshine and the little breeze that raised the hairs on his mane. Trotter followed at a short distance. He was very much interested in Timmy, and always turned his head when the dog barked or got down for a run. It was fun to have two horses and a dog to travel with.

It had been decided that they should make their way towards the hills where they hoped to find the circus. Julian had traced the place in his map. He was sure it must be right because of the lake that lay in the valley at the foot of the hills.

'See?' he said to the others, pointing. 'There it is – Lake Merran. I bet we'll find the circus camp somewhere near it. It would be a very good place for all their animals – no one to interfere with the camp, plenty of water for both animals and men, and probably good farms to supply them with food.'

'We'll have to find a good farm ourselves tonight,' said Dick. 'And ask permission to camp. Lucky we've got that little book telling us where to go and ask.'

Anne thought with delight of the coming evening, when they would stop and camp, cook a meal, drowse over a camp fire, and go to sleep in the little bunks. She didn't know which was nicer – ambling along down country lanes with the caravans – or preparing to settle in for the night. She was sure it was going to be the nicest holiday they had ever had.

'Don't you think so?' she asked George as they sat together on the driving-seat, with Timmy, for once, trotting beside the caravan, and leaving them a little more room than usual. 'You know, most of our hols have been packed with adventures – awfully exciting, I know – but I'd like an *ordinary* holiday now, wouldn't you? – not *too* exciting.'

'Oh, I like adventures,' said George, shaking the reins and making Trotter do a little trot. 'I wouldn't a bit mind having another one. But we shan't this time, Anne. No such luck!'

They stopped for a meal at half-past twelve, all of them feeling very hungry. Dobby and Trotter moved towards a ditch in which long, juicy grass grew, and munched away happily.

The children lay on a sunny bank and ate and drank. Anne looked at George. 'You've got more freckles these hols, George, than you ever had in your life before.'

'That doesn't worry *me!*' said George, who never cared in the least how she looked, and was even angry with her hair for being too curly, and making her look too much like a girl. 'Pass the sandwiches, Anne – the tomato ones – golly, if we always feel as hungry as this we'll have to buy eggs

and bacon and butter and milk at every farm we pass!'

They set off again. Dick took his turn at driving Dobby, and Julian walked to stretch his legs. George still wanted to drive, but Anne felt too sleepy to sit beside her with safety.

'If I shut my eyes and sleep I shall fall off the seat,' she said. 'I'd better go into the caravan and sleep there.'

So in she went, all by herself. It was cool and dim inside the caravan, for the curtains had been pulled across the window to keep the inside cool. Anne climbed on to one of the bunks and lay down. She shut her eyes. The caravan rumbled slowly on, and the little girl fell asleep.

Julian peeped in at her and grinned. Timmy came and looked, too, but Julian wouldn't let him go in and wake Anne by licking her.

'You come and walk with me, Tim,' he said. 'You're getting fat. Exercise will do you good.'

'He's *not* getting fat!' called George, indignantly. 'He's a very nice shape. Don't you listen to him, Timothy.'

'Woof,' said Timmy, and trotted along at Julian's heels.

The two caravans covered quite a good distance that day, even though they went slowly. Julian did not miss the way once. He was very good indeed at map-reading. Anne was disappointed that they could not see the hills they were making for, at the end of the day.

'Goodness, they're miles and miles away!' said Julian. 'We shan't arrive for at least four or five days, silly! Now, look out for a farm, kids. There should be one near here, where we can ask permission to camp for the night.'

'There's one, surely,' said George, after a few minutes. She pointed to where a red-roofed building with moss-covered barns, stood glowing in the evening sun. Hens clucked about it, and a dog or two watched them from a gateway.

'Yes, that's the one,' said Julian, examining his map. 'Longman's Farm. There should be a stream near it. There it is, look – in that field. Now, if we could get permission to camp just here, it would be lovely.'

Julian went to the farm to see the farmer, and Anne went with him to ask for eggs. The farmer was not there, but the farmer's wife, who liked the look of the tall, well-spoken Julian very much, gave them permission at once to spend the night in the field by the stream.

'I know you won't leave a lot of litter, or go chasing the farm animals,' she said. 'Or leave the gates open like some ill-bred campers do. And what's that you want, Missy – some new-laid eggs? Yes, of course you can have some – and you can pick the ripe plums off that tree, too, to go with your supper!'

There was bacon in the larder of the caravans, and Anne said she would fry that and an egg each for everyone. She was very proud of being able to cook them. She had taken a few lessons from Cook in the last few days, and was very anxious to show the others what she had learnt.

Julian said it was too hot to cook in the caravan, and he built her a fine fire in the field. Dick set the two horses free and they wandered off to the stream, where they stood knee-high in the cool water, enjoying it immensely. Trotter muzzled against Dobby, and then tried to nuzzle down to Timmy, too, when the big dog came to drink beside him.

'Doesn't the bacon smell lovely?' called Anne to George, who was busy getting plates and mugs out of the red caravan. 'Let's have ginger-beer to drink, George. I'm jolly thirsty. Watch me crack these eggs on the edge of this cup, everybody, so that I can get out the yolk and white and fry them.'

Crack! The egg broke against the edge of the cup – but its contents unfortunately fell outside the cup instead of inside. Anne went red when everyone roared with laughter.

Timmy came and licked up the mess. He was very useful for that sort of thing. 'You'd make a good dust-bin, Timmy,' said Anne. 'Here's a bit of bacon-rind, too. Catch!'

Anne fried the bacon and eggs really well. The others were most admiring, even George, and they all cleared their plates well, wiping the last bit of fat off with bread, so that they would be easy to wash.

'Do you think Timmy would like me to fry him a few dog-biscuits, instead of having them cold?' said Anne, suddenly. 'Fried things are so nice. I'm sure Timmy would like fried biscuits better than ordinary ones.'

'Well, he wouldn't,' said George. 'They would just make him sick.'

'How do you know?' said Anne. 'You can't possibly tell.'

'I always know what Timmy would really like and what he wouldn't,' said George. 'And he wouldn't like his biscuits fried. Pass the plums, Dick. They look super.'

They lingered over the little camp-fire for a long time, and then Julian said it was time for bed.

'You'd make a good dust-bin, Timmy,' said Anne.

Nobody minded, because they all wanted to try sleeping on the comfortable-looking bunks.

'Shall I wash at the stream or in the little sink where I washed the plates?' said Anne. 'I don't know which would be nicer.'

'There's more water to spare in the stream,' said Julian. 'Hurry up, won't you, because I want to lock your caravan door so that you'll be safe.'

'Lock our door!' said George, indignantly. 'You jolly well won't! Nobody's going to lock *me* in! I might think I'd like to take a walk in the moonlight or something.'

'Yes, but a tramp or somebody might . . .' began Julian. George interrupted him scornfully.

'What about Timmy? You know jolly well he'd never let anyone come *near* our caravans, let alone into them! I won't be locked in, Julian. I couldn't bear it. Timmy's better than any locked door.'

'Well, I suppose he is,' said Julian. 'All right, don't look so furious, George. Walk half the night in moonlight if you want to – though there won't be any moon tonight, I'm sure. Golly, I'm sleepy!'

They climbed into the two caravans, after washing in the stream. They all undressed, and got into the inviting bunks. There was a sheet, one blanket and a rug – but all the children threw off both blanket and rug and kept only a sheet over them that hot night.

At first Anne tried sleeping in the lower bunk, beneath George – but Timmy would keep on trying to clamber up to get to George. He wanted to lie on her feet as usual. Anne got cross.

'George! You'd better change places with me. Timmy keeps jumping on me and walking all over me trying to get up to your bunk. I'll never get to sleep.'

So George changed places, and after that Timmy made no more noise, but lay contentedly at the end of George's bunk on the rolled-up blanket, while Anne lay in the bunk above, trying not to go to sleep because it was such a lovely feeling to be inside a caravan that stood by a stream in a field.

Owls hooted to one another, and Timmy growled softly. The voice of the stream, contented and babbling, could be quite clearly heard now that everything was so quiet. Anne felt her eyes closing. Oh dear – she would simply *have* to go to sleep.

But something suddenly awoke her with a jump, and Timmy barked so loudly that both Anne and George almost fell out of their bunks in fright. Something bumped violently against the caravan, and shook it from end to end! Was somebody trying to get in?

Timmy leapt to the floor and ran to the door, which George had left open a little because of the heat. Then the voices of Dick and Julian were heard.

'What's up? Are you girls all right? We're coming!' And over the wet grass raced the two boys in their dressing-gowns. Julian ran straight into something hard and warm and solid. He yelled.

Dick switched on his torch and began to laugh helplessly. 'You ran straight into Dobby. Look at him staring at you! He must have lumbered all round our caravans making the bumps we heard. It's all right, girls. It's only Dobby.'

So back they all went again to sleep, and this time they slept till the morning, not even stirring when Trotter, too, came to nuzzle round the caravan and snort softly in the night.

5 The way to Merran Lake

The next three of four days were absolutely perfect, the children thought. Blue skies, blazing sun, wayside streams to paddle or bathe in, and two houses on wheels that went rumbling for miles down roads and lanes quite new to them – what could be lovelier for four children all on their own?

Timmy seemed to enjoy everything thoroughly, too, and had made firm friends with Trotter, the little back horse. Trotter was always looking for Timmy to run beside him, and he whinnied to Timmy whenever he wanted him. The two horses were friends, too, and when they were set free at night they made for the steam together, and stood in the water side by side, nuzzling one another happily.

'I like this holiday better than any we've ever had,' said Anne, busily cooking something in a pan. 'It's exciting without being adventurous. And although Julian thinks he's in charge of us, *I* am really! You'd never get your bunks made, or your meals cooked, or the caravans kept clean if it wasn't for me!'

'Don't boast!' said George, feeling rather guilty because she let Anne do so much.

'I'm not boasting!' said Anne, indignantly. 'I'm just telling the truth. Why, you've never even made your own bunk once, George. Not that I mind doing it. I love having two houses on wheels to look after.'

'You're a very good little housekeeper,' said Julian. 'We couldn't possibly do without you!'

Anne blushed with pride. She took the pan off the camp-fire and put the contents on to four plates. 'Come along!' she called, in a voice just like her mother's. 'Have your meal while it's hot.'

'I'd rather have mine when it's cold, thank you,' said George. 'It doesn't seem to have got a bit cooler, even though it's evening-time.'

They had been on the road four days now, and Anne had given up looking for the hills where they hoped to find the circus folk camping. In fact she secretly hoped they wouldn't find them, because she was so much enjoying the daily wanderings over the lovely countryside.

Timmy came to lick the plates. The children always let him do that now because it made them so much easier to wash. Anne and George took the things down to a little brown brook to rinse, and Julian took out his map.

He and Dick pored over it. 'We're just about here,' said Julian, pointing. 'And if so, it looks as if tomorrow we ought to come to those hills above the lake. Then we should see the circus.'

'Good!' said Dick. 'I hope Nobby will be there. He would love to show us round, I'm sure. He would show us a good place to camp, too, perhaps.'

'Oh, we can find that ourselves,' said Julian, who now rather prided himself on picking excellent camping-sites. 'Anyway, I don't want to be *too* near the circus. It might be a bit smelly. I'd rather be up in the hills some way above it. We'll get a place with a lovely view.'

'Right,' said Dick, and Julian folded up the map. The two girls came back with the clean crockery, and Anne put it neatly back on the shelves in the red caravan. Trotter came to look for Timmy, who was lying panting under George's caravan.

Timmy wouldn't budge, so Trotter tried to get

under the caravan too. But he couldn't possibly, of course, for he was much too big. So he lay down on the shady side, as near to Timmy as he could get.

'Trotter's really a comic horse,' said Dick. 'He'd be quite good in a circus, I should think! Did you see him chasing Timmy yesterday – just as if they were playing "He"?'

The word 'circus' reminded them of Nobby and his circus, and they began to talk eagerly of all the animals there.

'I liked the look of the elephant,' said George. 'I wonder what his name is. And wouldn't I like to hold a monkey!'

'I bet that chimpanzee's clever,' said Dick. 'I wonder what Timmy will think of him. I hope he'll get on all right with all the animals, especially the other dogs.'

'I hope we don't see much of Nobby's uncle,' said Anne. 'He looked as if he'd like to box anybody's ears if they so much as answered him back.'

'Well, he won't box *mine*,' said Julian. 'We'll keep out of his way. He doesn't look a very pleasant chap, I must say. Perhaps he won't be there.'

'Timmy, come out from under the caravan!' called George. 'It's quite cool and shady where we are. Come on!'

He came, panting. Trotter immediately got up and came with him. The little horse lay down beside Timmy and nuzzled him. Timmy gave his nose a lick and then turned away, looking bored.

'Isn't Trotter funny?' said Anne. 'Timmy, what *will* you think of all the circus animals, I wonder! I do hope we see the circus tomorrow. Shall we get as far as the hills, Julian? Though really I shan't mind a bit if we don't; it's so nice being on our own like this.'

They all looked out for the hills the next day as the caravans rumbled slowly down the lanes, pulled by Trotter and Dobby. And, in the afternoon, they saw them, blue in the distance.

'There they are!' said Julian. 'Those must be the Merran Hills – and Merran Lake must lie at the foot. I say, I hope the two horses are strong enough to pull the caravans a good way up. There should be an absolutely marvellous view over the lake if we get up high enough.'

The hills came nearer and nearer. They were high ones, and looked lovely in the evening light. Julian looked at his watch.

'We shan't have time to climb them and find a camping site there tonight, I'm afraid,' he said. 'We'd better camp a little way on this evening, and then make our way up into the hills tomorrow morning.'

'All right,' said Dick. 'Anything you say, Captain! There should be a farm about two miles on, according to the book. We'll camp there.'

They came to the farm, which was set by a wide stream that ran swiftly along. Julian went as usual to ask permission to camp, and Dick went with him, leaving the two girls to prepare a meal.

Julian easily got permission, and the farmer's daughter, a plump jolly girl, sold the boys eggs, bacon, milk, and butter, besides a little crock of yellow cream. She also offered them raspberries from the garden if they liked to pick them and have them with the cream.

'Oh, I say, thanks awfully,' said Julian. 'Could you tell me if there's a circus camping in those hills? Somewhere by the lake.'

'Yes, it went by about a week ago,' said the girl. 'It goes camping there every year, for a rest. I always watch the caravans go by – quite a treat in a quiet place like this! One year they had lions, and at night I could hear them roaring away. That fair frizzled my spine!'

The boys said good-bye and went off, chuckling to think of the farm-girl's spine being 'fair frizzled' by the roars of the distant lions.

'Well, it looks as if we'll pass the circus camp tomorrow all right,' said Julian. 'I shall enjoy camping up in the hills, won't you, Dick? It will be cooler up there, I expect – usually there's a breeze on the hills.'

'I hope we shan't get our spines fair frizzled by the noise of the circus animals at night,' grinned Dick. 'I feel fair frizzled up by the sun today, I must say!'

The next morning the caravans set off again on what the children hoped would be the last lap of their journey. They would find a lovely camping-place and stay there till they had to go home.

Julian had remembered to send a post-card each day to his parents, telling them where he was, and that everything was fine. He had found out from the farm-girl the right address for that district, and he planned to arrange with the nearest post office to take in any letters for them that came. They had not been able to receive any post, of course, when they were wandering about in their caravans.

Dobby and Trotter walked sedately down the narrow country lane that led towards the hills. Suddenly George caught sight of something flashing blue between the trees.

'Look! There's the lake! Merran Lake!' she shouted. 'Make Dobby go more quickly, Ju. I'm longing to come out into the open and see the lake.'

Soon the lane ended in a broad cart-track that led over a heathery common. The common sloped right down to the edge of an enormous blue lake that lay glittering in the August sunshine.

'I say! Isn't it magnificent?' said Dick, stopping Dobby with a pull. 'Come on, let's get down and go to the edge, Julian. Come on, girls!'

'It's lovely!' said Anne, jumping down from the driving-seat of the red caravan. 'Oh, do let's bathe straight away!'

'Yes, let's,' said Julian, and they all dived into their caravans, stripped off jeans and blouses and pulled on bathing-things. Then, without even a towel to dry themselves on, they tore down to the lake-side, eager to plunge into its blue coolness.

It was very warm at the edge of the water, but further in, where it was deep, the lake was deliciously cold. All the children could swim strongly, and they splashed and yelled in delight. The bottom of the lake was sandy, so the water was as clear as crystal.

When they were tired they all came out and lay on the warm sandy bank of the lake. They dried at once in the sun. Then as soon as they felt too hot in they went again, squealing with joy at the cold water.

'What gorgeous fun to come down here every day and bathe!' said Dick. 'Get away, Timmy, when I'm swimming on my back. Timmy's enjoying the bathe as much as we are, George.'

'Yes, and old Trotter wants to come in, too,' shouted Julian. 'Look at him – he's brought the red caravan right down to the edge of the lake. He'll be in the water with it if we don't stop him!'

They decided to have a picnic by the lake, and to set the horses free to have a bathe if they wanted one. But all they wanted was to drink and to stand knee-high in the water, swishing their tails to keep away the flies that worried them all day long.

'Where's the circus camp?' said George suddenly as they sat munching ham and tomato sandwiches. 'I can't see it.'

The children looked all round the edge of the lake, which stretched as far as they could see. At last George's sharp eyes saw a small spire of smoke rising in the air about a mile or so round the lake.

'The camp must be in that hollow at the foot of the hills over there,' she said. 'I expect the road leads round to it. We'll go that way, shall we, and then go up into the hills behind?'

'Yes,' agreed Julian. 'We shall have plenty of time to have a word with Nobby, and to find a good camping-place before night comes – and to find a farm, too, that will let us have food. Won't Nobby be surprised to see us?'

They cleared up, put the horses into their harness again and set off for the circus camp. Now for a bit of excitement!

6 The circus camp and Nobby

It did not take the caravans very long to come in sight of the circus camp. As George had said, it was in a comfortable hollow, set at the foot of the hills – a quiet spot, well away from any dwelling-places, where the circus animals could enjoy a certain amount of freedom and be exercised in peace.

The caravans were set round in a wide circle. Tents had been put up here and there. The big elephant was tied by a thick rope to a stout tree. Dogs ran about everywhere, and a string of shining horses was being paraded round a large field nearby.

'There they all are!' said Anne, excitedly, standing up on the driving-seat to see better. 'Golly, the chimpanzee is loose, isn't he? No, he isn't – someone has got him on a rope. Is it Nobby with him?'

'Yes, it is. I say, fancy walking about with a live chimp like that!' said Julian.

The children looked at everything with the greatest interest as their caravans came nearer to the circus camp. Few people seemed to be about that hot afternoon. Nobby was there with the chimpanzee, and one or two women were stirring pots over small fires – but that seemed to be all.

The circus dogs set up a great barking as the red and green caravans drew nearer. One or two men came out of the tents and looked up the track that led to the camp. They pointed to the children's caravans and seemed astonished.

Nobby, with the chimpanzee held firmly by the paw, came out of the camp in curiosity to meet the strange caravans. Julian hailed him.

'Hi, Nobby! You didn't think you'd see *us* here, did you?'

Nobby was amazed to hear his name called. At first he did not remember the children at all. Then he gave a yell.

'Jumping Jiminy, it's you kids I saw away back on the road! What are *you* doing here?'

Timmy growled ominously and George called to Nobby. 'He's never seen a chimpanzee before. Do you think they'll be friends?'

'Don't know,' said Nobby doubtfully. 'Old Pongo likes the circus dogs all right. Anyway, don't you let your dog fly at Pongo, or he'll be eaten alive! A chimp is very strong, you know.'

'Could I make friends with Pongo, do you think?' asked George. 'If he would shake hands with me, or something, Timmy would know I was friends with him and he'd be all right. Would Pongo make friends with me?'

''Course he will!' said Nobby. 'He's the sweetest-tempered chimp alive – ain't you, Pongo? Now, shake hands with the lady.'

Anne didn't feel at all inclined to go near the chimpanzee, but George was quite fearless. She walked up to the big animal and held out her hand. The chimpanzee took it at once, raised it to his mouth and pretended to nibble it, making friendly noises all the time.

George laughed. 'He's nice, isn't he?' she said. 'Timmy, this is Pongo, a friend. Nice Pongo, good Pongo!'

She patted Pongo on the shoulder to show Timmy that she liked the chimpanzee, and Pongo at once patted her on the shoulder, too, grinning amiably. He then patted her on the head and pulled one of her curls.

Timmy wagged his tail a little. He looked very doubtful indeed. What was this strange creature that his mistress appeared to like so much. He took a step towards Pongo.

'Come on, Timmy, say how do you do to Pongo,' said George. 'Like this.' And she shook hands with the chimpanzee again. This time he wouldn't let her hand go, but went on shaking it up and down as if he was pumping water with a pump-handle.

'He won't let go,' said George.

'Don't be naughty, Pongo,' said Nobby in a stern voice. Pongo at once dropped George's hand and covered his face with a hairy paw as if he was ashamed. But the children saw that he was peeping through his fingers with wicked eyes that twinkled with fun.

'He's a real monkey!' said George, laughing.

'You're wrong – he's an ape!' said Nobby. 'Ah, here comes Timmy to make friends. Jumping Jiminy, they're shaking paws!'

So they were. Timmy, having once made up his mind that Pongo was to be a friend, remembered his manners and held out his right paw as he had been taught. Pongo seized it and shook it vigorously. Then he walked round to the back of Timmy and shook hands with his tail. Timmy didn't know what to make of it all.

The children yelled with laughter, and Timmy sat down firmly on his tail. Then he stood up again, his tail wagging, for Barker and Growler had come rushing up. Timmy remembered them, and they remembered him.

'Well, *they're* making friends all right,' said Nobby, pleased. 'Now they'll introduce Timmy to all the other dogs, and there'll be no trouble. Hey, look out for Pongo, there!'

The chimpanzee had stolen round to the back of Julian and was slipping his hand into the boy's pocket. Nobby went to him and slapped the chimpanzee's paw hard.

'Naughty! Bad boy! Pickpocket!'

The children laughed again when the chimpanzee covered his face with his paws, pretending to be ashamed.

'You'll have to watch out when Pongo's about,' said Nobby. 'He loves to take things out of people's pockets. I say – do tell me – are those your caravans? Aren't they posh?'

'They've been lent to us,' said Dick. 'As a matter of fact, it was seeing your circus go by, with all its gay caravans, that made us think of borrowing caravans, too, and coming away for a holiday.'

'And as you'd told us where you were going we thought we'd follow you and find you out, and get you to show us round the camp,' said Julian. 'Hope you don't mind.'

'I'm proud,' said Nobby, going a bright red. ''Tisn't often folks want to make friends with a circus fellow like me – not gentlefolk like you, I mean. I'll be proud to show you round – and you can make friends with every blessed monkey, dog and horse on the place!'

'Oh, thanks!' said all four at once.

'Jolly decent of you,' said Dick. 'Gosh, look at that chimp – he's trying to shake hands with Timmy's tail again. I bet he's funny in the circus ring, isn't he, Nobby?'

'He's a scream,' said Nobby. 'Brings the house down. You should see him act with my Uncle Dan. He's the chief clown, you know. Pongo is just as big a clown as my uncle is – it's a fair scream to see them act the fool together.'

'I wish we *could* see them,' said Anne. 'Acting in the ring, I mean. Will your uncle mind you showing us all the animals and everything?'

'Why should he?' said Nobby. 'Shan't ask him! But you'll mind and act polite to him, won't you? He's worse than a tiger when he's in a temper. They call him Tiger Dan because of his rages.'

Anne didn't like the sound of that at all – Tiger Dan! It sounded very fierce and savage.

'I hope he isn't about anywhere now,' she said nervously, looking round.

'No. He's gone off somewhere,' said Nobby. 'He's a lonesome sort of chap – got no friends much in the circus, except Lou, the acrobat. That's Lou over there.'

Lou was a long-limbed, loose-jointed fellow with an ugly face, and a crop of black shining hair that curled tightly. He sat on the steps of a caravan, smoking a pipe and reading a paper. The children thought that he and Tiger Dan would make a good pair – bad-tempered, scowling and unfriendly.

They all made up their minds that they would have as little as possible to do with Lou the acrobat and Tiger Dan the clown.

'Is he a very good acrobat?' said Anne in a low voice, though Lou was much too far away to hear her.

'Fine. First class,' said Nobby with admiration in his voice. 'He can climb anything anywhere – he could go up that tree there like a monkey – and I've seen him climb a drainpipe straight up the side of a tall building just like a cat. He's a marvel. You should see him on the tight-rope, too. He can dance on it!'

The children gazed at Lou with awe. He felt their glances, looked up and scowled. 'Well,' though Julian, 'he may be the finest acrobat that ever lived – but he's a jolly nasty-looking fellow. There's not much to choose between him and Tiger Dan!'

Lou got up, uncurling his long body like a cat. He moved easily and softly. He loped to Nobby, still with the ugly scowl on his face.

'Who are these kids?' he said. 'What are they doing messing about here?'

'We're not messing about,' said Julian politely. 'We came to see Nobby. We've seen him before.'

'Them your caravans?' he asked, jerking his head towards them.

Lou looked at Julian as if he was something that smelt nasty. 'Them your caravans?' he asked, jerking his head towards them.

'Yes,' said Julian.

'Posh, aren't you?' said Lou sneeringly.

'Not particularly,' said Julian, still polite.

'Any grown-ups with you?' asked Lou.

'No. I'm in charge,' said Julian, 'and we've got a dog that flies at people he doesn't like.'

Timmy clearly didn't like Lou. He stood near him, growling in his throat. Lou kicked out at him.

George caught hold of Timmy's collar just in time. 'Down, Tim, down!' she cried. Then she turned on Lou, her eyes blazing.

'Don't you dare kick my dog!' she shouted. 'He'll have you down on the ground if you do. You keep out of his way, or he'll go for you now.'

Lou spat on the ground in contempt and turned to go. 'You clear out,' he said. 'We don't want no kids messing about here. And I ain't afraid of no dog. I got ways of dealing with bad dogs.'

'What do you mean by that?' yelled George, still in a furious temper. But Lou did not bother to reply. He went up the steps of his caravan and slammed the door shut. Timmy barked angrily and tugged at his collar, which George was still holding firmly.

'Now you've torn it!' said Nobby dismally. 'If Lou catches you about anywhere he'll hoof you out. And you be careful of that dog of yours, or he'll disappear.'

George was angry and alarmed. 'Disappear! What do you mean? If you think Timmy would let anyone steal him, you're wrong.'

'All right, all right. I'm only telling you. Don't fly at me like that!' said Nobby. 'Jumping Jiminy, look at that chimp. He's gone inside one of your caravans!'

The sudden storm was forgotten as everyone rushed to the green caravan. Pongo was inside, helping himself liberally from a tin of sweets. As soon as he saw the children he groaned and covered his face with his paws – but he sucked hard at the sweets all the time.

'Pongo! Bad boy! Come here!' scolded Nobby. 'Shall I whip you?'

'Oh, no, don't,' begged Anne. 'He's a scamp, but I do like him. We've plenty of sweets to spare. You have some, too, Nobby.'

'Well, thank you,' said Nobby, and helped himself. He grinned round at everyone. 'Nice to have friends like you,' he said. 'Ain't it, Pongo?'

7 A tea-party – and a visit in the night

Nobody particularly wanted to see round the camp just then, as Lou had been so unpleasant. So instead they showed the admiring Nobby over the two caravans. He had never seen such beauties.

'Jumping Jiminy, they're like palaces!' he said. 'Do you mean to say them taps turn on and water comes out? Can I turn on a tap? I've never turned a tap in my life!'

He turned the taps on and off a dozen times, exclaiming in wonder to see the water come gushing out. He thumped the bunks to see how soft they were. He admired the gay soft rugs and shining crockery. He was, in fact, a very nice guest to have, and the children liked him more and more. They liked Barker and Growler, too, who were both well-behaved, obedient, merry dogs.

Pongo, of course, wanted to turn the taps on and off, too, and he threw all the coverings off the two bunks to see what was underneath. He also took the kettle off the stove, put the spout to his thick lips and drank all the water out of it very noisily indeed.

'You're forgetting your manners, Pongo!' said Nobby in horror, and snatched the kettle away from him. Anne squealed with laughter. She loved the chimpanzee, and he seemed to have taken a great fancy to Anne, too. He followed her about and stroked her hair and made funny affectionate noises.

'Would you like to stay and have tea here with us?' asked Julian, looking at his watch. 'It's about time.'

'Coo – I don't have tea as a rule,' said Nobby. 'Yes, I'd like to. Sure you don't mind me staying, though? I ain't got your manners, I know, and I'm a bit dirty, and not your sort at all. But you're real kind.'

'We'd love to have you stay,' said Anne in delight. 'I'll cut some bread and butter and make some sandwiches. Do you like potted meat sandwiches, Nobby?'

'Don't I just!' said Nobby. 'And Pongo does,

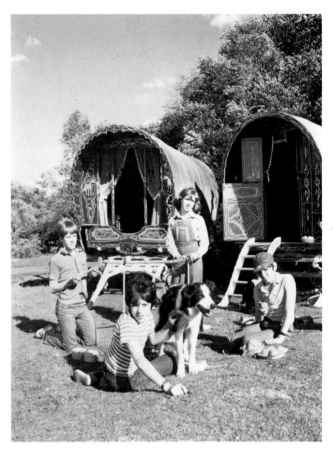

'Would you like to stay and have tea here with us?' asked Julian.

too. Don't you let him get near them or he'll finish up the lot.'

It was a pleasant and amusing little tea-party. They all sat out on the heather, on the shady side of the caravan. Barker and Growler sat with Timmy. Pongo sat beside Anne, taking bits of sandwich from her most politely. Nobby enjoyed his tea immensely, eating more sandwiches than anyone and talking all the time with his mouth full.

He made the four children yell with laughter. He imitated his Uncle Dan doing some of his clown tricks. He turned cart-wheels all round the caravan while he was waiting for Anne to cut more sandwiches. He stood solemnly on his head and ate a sandwich like that, much to Timmy's amazement. Timmy walked round and round him, and sniffed at his face as if to say: 'Strange! No legs! Something's gone wrong.'

At last nobody could eat any more. Nobby stood up to go, suddenly wondering if he had stayed too long.

'I was enjoying myself so much I forgot the time,' he said awkwardly. 'Bet I've stayed too long and you've been too polite to tell me to get out.

143

Coo, that wasn't half a good tea! Thanks, Miss, awfully, for all them delicious sandwiches. 'Fraid my manners aren't like yours, kids, but thanks for a very good time.'

'You've got very good manners indeed,' said Anne, warmly. 'You've been a splendid guest. Come again, won't you?'

'Well, thanks, I will,' said Nobby, forgetting his sudden awkwardness, and beaming round. 'Where's Pongo? Look at that chimp! He's got one of your hankies, and he's blowing his nose!'

Anne squealed in delight. 'He can keep it!' she said. 'It's only an old one.'

'Will you be here camping for long?' asked Nobby.

'Well, not just exactly *here*,' said Julian. 'We thought of going up higher into the hills. It will be cooler there. But we might camp here just for tonight. We meant to go up higher this evening, but we might as well stay here and go tomorrow morning now. Perhaps we could see round the camp tomorrow morning.'

'Not if Lou's there you can't,' said Nobby. 'Once he's told people to clear out he means it. But it will be all right if he's not. I'll come and tell you.'

'All right,' said Julian. 'I'm not afraid of Lou – but we don't want to get *you* into any trouble, Nobby. If Lou's there tomorrow morning, we'll go on up into the hills, and you can always signal to us if he's out of the camp, and we can come down any time. And mind you come up and see us when you want to.'

'And bring Pongo,' said Anne.

'You bet!' said Nobby. 'Well – so long!'

He went off with Barker and Growler at his heels and with Pongo held firmly by the paw. Pongo didn't want to go at all. He kept pulling back like a naughty child.

'I do like Nobby and Pongo,' said Anne. 'I wonder what Mummy would say if she knew we'd made friends with a chimpanzee. She'd have a fit.'

Julian suddenly looked rather doubtful. He was wondering if he had done right to follow the circus and let Anne and the others make friends with such queer folk and even queerer animals. But Nobby was so nice. He was sure his mother would like Nobby. And they could easily keep away from Tiger Dan and Lou the acrobat.

'Have we got enough to eat for supper tonight and breakfast tomorrow?' he asked Anne. 'Because there doesn't seem to be a farm near enough to go to just here. But Nobby says there's one up on the

hill up there – the circus folk get their supplies from it, too – what they don't get from the nearest town. Apparently somebody goes in each day to shop.'

'I'll just see what we've got in the larder, Julian,' said Anne, getting up. She knew perfectly well what there was in the larder – but it made her feel grown-up and important to go and look. It was nice to feel like that when she so often felt small and young, and the others were big and knew so much.

She called back to them: 'I've got eggs and tomatoes and potted meat, and plenty of bread, and a cake we bought today, and a pound of butter.'

'That's all right then,' said Julian. 'We won't bother about going to the farm tonight.'

When darkness fell that night, there were clouds across the sky for the first time. Not a star showed and there was no moon. It was pitch-black, and Julian, looking out of the window of his caravan, before clambering into his bunk, could not even see a shimmer of water from the lake.

He got into his bunk and pulled the covers up. In the other caravan George and Anne were asleep. Timmy was, as usual, on George's feet. She had pushed him off them once or twice, but now that she was asleep he was undisturbed, and lay heavily across her ankles, his head on his paws.

Suddenly his ears cocked up. He raised his head cautiously. Then he growled softly in his throat. He had heard something. He sat there stiffly, listening. He could hear footsteps from two different directions. Then he heard voices – cautious voices, low and muffled.

Timmy growled again, more loudly. George awoke and reached for his collar. 'What's the matter?' she whispered. Timmy listened and so did she. They both heard the voices.

George slipped quietly out of the bunk and went to the half-open door of the caravan. She could not see anything outside at all because it was so dark. 'Don't make a noise, Tim,' she whispered.

Timmy understood. He did not growl again, but George could feel the hairs rising all along the back of his neck.

The voices seemed to come from not very far away. Two men must be talking together, George thought. Then she heard a match struck, and in its light she saw two men lighting their cigarettes from the same match. She recognised them at once – they were Nobby's Uncle Dan and Lou the acrobat.

What were they doing there? Had they got a meeting-place there – or had they come to steal something from the caravans? George wished she could tell Julian and Dick – but she did not like to go out of her caravan in case the men heard her.

At first she could not hear anything the men said. They were discussing something very earnestly. Then one raised his voice.

'Okay, then – that's settled.' Then came the sound of footsteps again, this time towards George's caravan. The men walked straight into the side of it, exclaimed in surprise and pain, and began to feel about to find out what they had walked into.

'It's those posh caravans!' George heard Lou exclaim. 'Still here! I told those kids to clear out!'

'What kids?' asked Tiger Dan, in surprise. Evidently he had come back in the dark and did not know they had arrived.

'Some kids Nobby knows,' said Lou in an angry voice. He rapped loudly on the walls of the caravan, and Anne woke up with a jump. George, just inside the caravan with Timmy, jumped in fright, too. Timmy barked in rage.

Julian and Dick woke up. Julian flashed on his torch and went to his door. The light picked out the two men standing by George's caravan.

'What are you doing here at this time of night?' said Julian. 'Making a row like that! Clear off!'

This was quite the wrong thing to have said to Dan and Lou, both bad-tempered men who felt that the whole of the camping-ground around belonged to them and the circus.

'Who do you think you're talking to?' shouted Dan angrily. 'You're the ones to clear off! Do you hear?'

'Didn't I tell you to clear out this afternoon?' yelled Lou, losing his temper, too. 'You do as you're told, you young rogue, or I'll set the dogs on you and have you chased for miles.'

Anne began to cry. George trembled with rage. Timmy growled. Julian spoke calmly but determinedly.

'We're going in the morning, as we meant. But if you're suggesting we should go now, you can think again. This is as much our camping-ground as yours. Now get off, and don't come disturbing us again.'

'I'll give you a leathering, you young cockerel!' cried Lou, and began to unfasten the leather belt from round his waist.

George let go her hold of Timmy's collar. 'Go for them, Timmy,' she said. 'But don't bite. Just worry them!'

'You're the ones to clear off! Do you hear?'

Timmy sprang down to the ground with a joyful bark. He flung himself at the two men. He knew what George wanted him to do, and although he longed to snap at the two rogues with his sharp teeth, he didn't. He pretended to, though, and growled so fiercely that they were scared out of their wits.

Lou hit out at Timmy, threatening to kill him. But Timmy cared for no threats of that kind. He got hold of Lou's right trouser-leg, pulled, and ripped it open from knee to ankle.

'Come on – the dog's mad!' cried Dan. 'He'll have us by the throat if we don't go. Call him off, you kids. We're going. But mind you clear out in the morning, or we'll see you do! We'll pay you out one day.'

Seeing that the men really meant to go, George whistled to Timmy. 'Come here, Tim. Stand on guard till they're really gone. Fly at them if they come back.'

But the men soon disappeared – and nothing would have made either of them come back and face Timmy again that night!

8 Up in the hills

The four children were upset and puzzled by the behaviour of the two men. George told how Timmy had wakened her by growling and how she had heard the men talking together in low voices.

'I don't really think they had come to steal anything,' she said. 'I think they were just meeting near here for a secret talk. They didn't know the caravans were here and walked straight into ours.'

'They're bad-tempered brutes,' said Julian. 'And I don't care what you say, George, I'm going to lock your caravan door tonight. I know you've got Timmy – but I'm not running any risk of these men coming back, Timmy or no Timmy.'

Anne was so scared that George consented to let Julian lock the red caravan door. Timmy was locked in with them. The boys went back to their own caravan, and Julian locked his door, too, from the inside. He wanted to be on the safe side.

'I'll be glad to get away from here up into the hills,' he said. 'I shan't feel safe as long as we are quite so near the camp. We'll be all right up in the hills.'

'We'll go first thing after breakfast,' said Dick, settling down to his bunk again. 'Gosh, it's a good thing the girls had Timmy tonight. Those fellows looked as if they meant to go for you properly, Ju.'

'Yes. I shouldn't have had much chance against the two of them either,' said Julian. 'They are both hefty, strong fellows.'

The next morning all the four awoke early.

Nobody felt inclined to lie and snooze – all of them were anxious to get off before Lou and Dan appeared again.

'You get the breakfast, Anne and George, and Dick and I will catch the horses and put them in the caravan shafts,' said Julian. 'Then we shall be ready to go off immediately after breakfast.'

They had breakfast and cleared up. They got up on the driving-seats and were just about to drive away when Lou and Dan came down the track towards them.

'Oh, you're going, are you?' said Dan, with an ugly grin on his face. 'That's right. Nice to see kids so obedient. Where you going?'

'Up into the hills,' said Julian. 'Not that it's anything to do with you where we go.'

'Why don't you go round the foot of the hills, instead of over the top?' said Lou. 'Silly way to go – up there, with the caravans dragging them horses back all the way.'

Julian was just about to say that he didn't intend to go right up to the top of the hills and over to the other side, when he stopped himself. No – just as well not to let these fellows know that he meant to camp up there, or they might come and worry them all again.

He clicked to Dobby. 'We're going the way we want to go,' he said to Lou in a curt voice. 'And that's up the hill. Get out of the way, please.'

As Dobby was walking straight at them, the men had to jump to one side. They scowled at the four children. Then they all heard the sound of running footsteps and along came Nobby, with Barker and Growler at his heels as usual.

'Hey, what you going so early for?' he yelled. 'Let me come part of the way with you.'

'No, you don't,' said his uncle, and gave the

surprised boy an unexpected cuff. 'I've told these kids to clear out, and they're going. I won't have no meddling strangers round this camp. And don't you kid yourself they want to make friends with you, see? You go and get out those dogs and exercise them, or I'll give you another box on the ears that'll make you see all the stars in the sky.'

Nobby stared at him, angry and afraid. He knew his uncle too well to defy him. He turned on his heel sullenly and went off back to the camp. The caravans overtook him on the way. Julian called to him in a low voice:

'Cheer up, Nobby. We'll be waiting for you up in the hills – don't tell Lou and your uncle about it. Let them think we've gone right away. Bring Pongo up some time!'

Nobby grinned. 'Right you are!' he said. 'I can bring the dogs up to exercise them, too – but not today. I dursent today. And as soon as them two are safely out for the day I'll bring you down to the camp and show you round, see? That all right?'

'Fine,' said Julian, and drove on. Neither Lou nor Dan had heard a word, or even guessed that this conversation was going on, for Nobby had been careful to walk on all the time and not even turn his face towards the children.

The road wound upwards into the hills. At first it was not very steep, but wound to and fro across the side of the hill. Half-way up, the caravans crossed a stone bridge under which a very swift stream flowed.

'That stream's in a hurry!' said George, watching it bubble and gurgle downwards. 'Look – is that where it starts from – just there in the hillside?'

She pointed someway up the hill, and it seemed as if the stream really did suddenly start just where she pointed.

'But it can't suddenly start there – not such a big fast stream as this!' said Julian, stopping Dobby on the other side of the bridge. 'Let's go and see, I'm thirsty, and if there's a spring there, it will be very cold and clear – lovely to drink from. Come on, we'll go and see.'

But there was no spring. The stream did not 'begin' just there, but flowed out of a hole in the hillside, as big and as fast as it was just under the stone bridge. The children bent down and peered into the water-filled hole.

'It comes out from inside the hill,' said Anne, surprised. 'Fancy it running around in the hill itself. It must be glad to find a way out!'

They didn't like to drink it as it was not the clear, fresh spring they had hoped to find. But, wandering a little farther on, they came to a real spring that gushed out from beneath a stone, cold and crystal clear. They drank from this and voted that it was the nicest drink they had ever had in their lives. Dick followed the spring-water downwards and saw that it joined the little rushing stream.

'I suppose it flows into the lake,' he said. 'Come on. Let's get on and find a farm, Julian. I'm sure I heard the crowing of a cock just then, so one can't be far away.'

They went round a bend of the hill and saw the farm, a rambling collection of old buildings sprawling down the hillside. Hens ran about, clucking. Sheep grazed above the farm, and cows chewed the cud in fields nearby. A man was working not far off, and Julian hailed him. 'Good morning! Are you the farmer?'

'No. Farmer's over yonder,' said the man, pointing to a barn near the farm house. 'Be careful of the dogs.'

The two caravans went on towards the farm. The farmer heard them coming and came out with his dogs. When he saw that there were only children driving the two caravans he looked surprised.

Julian had a polite, well-mannered way with him that all the grown-ups liked. Soon he was deep in a talk with the man, with most satisfactory results. The farmer was willing to supply them with any farm produce they wanted, and they could have as much milk as they liked at any time. His wife, he was sure, would cook them anything they asked her to, and bake them cakes, too.

'Perhaps I could arrange payment with her?' said Julian. 'I'd like to pay for everything as I buy it.'

'That's right, son,' said the farmer. 'Always pay your way as you go along, and you won't come to any harm. You go and see my old woman. She likes children and she'll make you right welcome. Where are you going to camp?'

'I'd like to camp somewhere with a fine view over the lake,' said Julian. 'We can't see it from just here. Maybe a bit farther on we'll get just the view I want.'

'Yes, you go on about half a mile,' said the farmer. 'The track goes that far – and when you come to a clump of fine birch trees you'll see a sheltered hollow, set right in the hillside, with a wonderful fine view over the lake. You can pull your caravans in there, son, and you'll be sheltered from the winds.'

'Thanks awfully,' said all the children together, thinking what a nice man this old farmer was. How different from Lou and Dan, with their threats and rages!

'We'll go and see your wife first, sir,' said Julian. 'Then we'll go on and pull into the hollow you suggest. We'll be seeing you again some time, I expect.'

They went to see the farmer's wife, a fat, round-cheeked old woman, whose little curranty eyes twinkled with good humour. She made them very welcome, gave them hot buns from the oven and told them to help themselves to the little purple plums on the tree outside the old farm house.

Julian arranged to pay on the spot for anything they bought each day. The prices the farmer's wife asked seemed very low indeed, but she would not hear of taking any more money for her goods.

'It'll be a pleasure to see your bonny faces at my door!' she said. 'That'll be part of my payment, see? I can tell you're well-brought-up children by your nice manners and ways. You'll not be doing any damage or foolishness on the farm, I know.'

The children came away laden with all kinds of food, from eggs and ham to scones and ginger cakes. She pushed a bottle of raspberry syrup into Anne's hand when the little girl said good-bye. But when Julian turned back to pay her for it she was quite annoyed.

'If I want to make a present to somebody, I'll do it!' she said. 'Go on with you . . . paying for this and paying for that. I'll have a little something extra for you each time, and don't you dare to ask to pay for it, or I'll be after you with my rolling pin!'

'Isn't she awfully nice?' said Anne as they made their way back to the caravans. 'Even Timmy offered to shake hands with her without you telling him to, George – and he hardly ever does that to anyone, does he?'

They packed the things away into the larder, got up into the driving-seats, clicked to Dobby and Trotter and set off up the track again.

Just over half a mile away was a clump of birch trees. 'We'll find that sheltered hollow near them,' said Julian.

'Yes, look – there it is – set back into the hill, a really cosy place! Just right for camping in – and oh, what a magnificent view!'

It certainly was. They could see right down the steep hillside to the lake. It lay spread out, flat and smooth, like an enchanted mirror. From where they were they could now see right to the opposite banks of the lake – and it was indeed a big stretch of water.

'Isn't it blue?' said Anne, staring. 'Bluer even than the sky. Oh, won't it be lovely to see this marvellous view every single day we're here?'

Julian backed the caravans into the hollow. Heather grew there, like a springy purple carpet. Harebells, pale as an evening sky, grew in clumps in crevices of the hill behind. It was a lovely spot for camping in.

George's sharp ears caught the sound of water and she went to look for it. She called back to the others. 'What do you think? There's another spring here, coming out of the hill. Drinking and washing water laid on! Aren't we lucky?'

'We certainly are,' said Julian. 'It's a lovely place – and nobody will disturb us here!'

But he spoke too soon!

9 An unpleasant meeting

It really was fun settling into that cosy hollow. The two caravans were backed in side by side. The horses were taken out and led to a big field where the farmer's horses were kept when they had done their day's work. Trotter and Dobby seemed very pleased with the green, sloping field. It had a spring of its own that ran into a stone trough and out of it, keeping it always filled with fresh cold water. Both horses went to take a long drink.

'Well, that settles the two horses all right,' said Julian. 'We'll tell the farmer he can borrow them if he wants to – he'll be harvesting soon and may like to have Dobby and Trotter for a few days. They will enjoy hobnobbing with other horses again.'

At the front of the hollow was a rocky ledge, hung with heathery tufts. 'This is the front seat for Lake View!' said Anne. 'Oh, it's warm from the sun! How lovely!'

'I vote we have all our meals on this ledge,' said

George, sitting down too. 'It's comfortable and roomy – and flat enough to take our cups and plates without spilling anything – and honestly the view from here is too gorgeous for words. Can anyone see anything of the circus from up here?'

'There's a spire or two of smoke over yonder,' said Dick, pointing. 'I should think that's where the camp is. And look – there's a boat pushing out on the lake – doesn't it look tiny?'

'Perhaps Nobby is in it,' said Anne. 'Haven't we brought any field-glasses, Julian? I thought we had.'

'Yes – we have,' said Julian, remembering. 'I'll get them.' He went to the green caravan, rummaged about in the drawers, and came out with his field-glasses swinging on the end of their straps.

'Here we are!' he said, and set them to his eyes. 'Yes – I can see the boat clearly now – and it *is* Nobby in it – but who's with him? Golly, it's Pongo!'

Everyone had to look through the glasses to see Nobby and Pongo in the boat. 'You know, we could always get Nobby to signal to us somehow from his boat when he wanted to tell us that Lou and his uncle were away,' said Dick. 'Then we should know it was safe, and we could pop down to the camp and see round it.'

'Yes. Good idea,' said George. 'Give me the glasses, Dick. Timmy wants to have a turn at seeing, too.'

'He can't see through glasses like these, idiot,' said Dick, handing them to George. But Timmy most solemnly glued his eyes to the glasses, and appeared to be looking through them very earnestly indeed.

'Woof,' he remarked, when he took his eyes away at last.

'He says he's seen Nobby and Pongo, too,' said George, and the others laughed. Anne half-believed that he had. Timmy was such an extraordinary dog, she thought, as she patted his smooth head.

It was a terribly hot day. Too hot to do anything – even to walk down to the lake and bathe! The children were glad they were up in the hills, for at least there was a little breeze that fanned them now and again. They did not expect to see Nobby again that day, but they hoped he would come up the next day. If not they would go down and bathe in the lake and hope to see him somewhere about there.

Soon the rocky ledge got too hot to sit on. The children retreated to the clump of birch trees, which at least cast some shade. They took books with them, and Timmy came along, too, panting as if he had run for miles. He kept going off to the little spring to drink. Anne filled a big bowl with the cold water, and stood it in a breezy place near by, with a cup to dip into it. They were thirsty all day long, and it was pleasant to dip a cup into the bowl of spring-water and drink.

The lake was unbelievably blue that day, and lay as still as a mirror. Nobby's boat was no longer in the water. He and Pongo had gone. There was not a single movement to be seen down by the lake.

'Shall we go down to the lake this evening, when it's cooler, and bathe there?' said Julian, at tea-time. 'We haven't had much exercise today, and it would do us good to walk down and have a swim. We won't take Timmy in case we happen to come across Lou or Dan. He'd certainly fly at them today. We can always keep an eye open for those two and avoid them ourselves – but Timmy would go for them as soon as he spotted them. We might be in the water and unable to stop him.'

'Anyway, he'll guard the caravans for us,' said Anne. 'Well, I'll just take these cups and plates and rinse them in the stream. Nobody wants any more to eat, do they?'

'Too hot,' said Dick, rolling over on to his back. 'I wish we were by the lake at this moment – I'd go straight into the water now!'

At half-past six it was cooler, and the four children set off down the hill. Timmy was angry and hurt at being left behind.

'You're to be on guard, Timmy,' said George firmly. 'See? Don't let anyone come near our caravans. On guard, Timmy!'

'Woof,' said Timmy dismally, and put his tail down. On guard! Didn't George know that the caravans wouldn't walk off by themselves, and that he wanted a good splash in the lake?

Still, he stayed behind, standing on the rocky ledge to see the last of the children, his ears cocked to hear their voices and his tail still down in disgust. Then he went and lay down beneath George's caravan, and waited patiently for his friends to return.

The children went down the hill with their bathing-things, taking short cuts, and leaping like goats over the steep bits. It had seemed quite a long way up when they had gone so slowly in the caravans with Dobby and Trotter – but it wasn't nearly so far when they could go on their own legs, and take rabbit-paths and short cuts whenever they liked.

There was one steep bit that forced them back on to the track. They went along it to where the track turned a sharp corner round a cliff-like bend – and to their surprise and dismay they walked almost straight into Lou and Tiger Dan!

'Take no notice,' said Julian, in a low voice. 'Keep together and walk straight on. Pretend that Timmy is somewhere just behind us.'

'Tim, Tim!' called George, at once.

Lou and Dan seemed just as surprised to see the children as they had been to see the two men. They stopped and looked hard at them, but Julian hurried the others on.

'Hey, wait a minute!' called Dan. 'I thought you had gone off – over the hill-top!'

'Sorry we can't stop!' called back Julian. 'We're in rather a hurry!'

Lou looked round for Timmy. He wasn't going to lose his temper and start shouting in case that mad dog came at him again. He spoke to the children loudly, forcing himself to appear good-tempered.

'Where are your caravans? Are you camping up here anywhere?'

But the children still walked on, and the men had to go after them to make them hear.

'Hey! What's the matter? We shan't hurt you! We only want to know if you're camping here. It's better down below, you know.'

'Keep on walking,' muttered Julian. 'Don't tell them anything. Why do they tell us it's better to camp down below when they were so anxious for us to clear out yesterday? They're mad!'

'Timmy, Timmy!' called George, again, hoping that the men would stop following them if they heard her calling for her dog.

It did stop them. They gave up going after the children, and didn't shout any more. They turned angrily and went on up the track.

'Well, we've thrown them off all right,' said Dick, with relief. 'Don't look so scared, Anne. I wonder what they want up in the hills? They don't look the sort that would go walking for pleasure.'

'Dick – we're not going to have another adventure, are we?' said Anne suddenly, looking very woebegone. 'I don't want one. I just want a nice ordinary, peaceful holiday.'

''Course we're not going to have an adventure!'

said Dick, scornfully. 'Just because we meet two bad-tempered fellows from a circus camp you think we're in for an adventure, Anne! Well, *I* jolly well wish we were! Every hols we've been together so far we've had adventures – and you must admit that you love talking about them and remembering them.'

'Yes, I do. But I don't like it much when I'm in the *middle* of one,' said Anne. 'I don't think I'm a very adventurous person, really.'

'No, you're not,' said Julian, pulling Anne over a very steep bit. 'But you're a very nice little person, Anne, so don't worry about it. And, anyway, you wouldn't like to be left out of any of our adventures, would you?'

'Oh *no*,' said Anne. 'I couldn't bear it. Oh, look – we're at the bottom of the hill – and there's the lake, looking icy-cold!'

It wasn't long before they were all in the water – and suddenly there was Nobby too, waving and yelling. 'I'm coming in! Lou and my uncle have gone off somewhere. Hurray!'

Barker and Growler were with Nobby, but not Pongo the chimpanzee. Nobby was soon in the water, swimming like a dog, and splashing George as soon as he got up to her.

It wasn't long before they were all in the water . . .

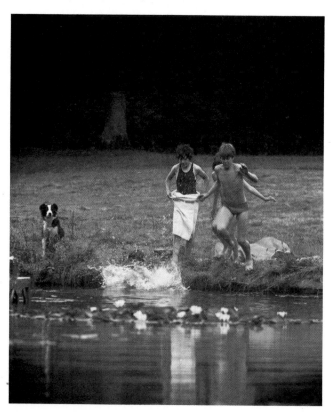

'We met Lou and your uncle as we came down,' called George. 'Shut up, Nobby, and let me talk to you. I said, we met Lou and your uncle just now – going up into the hills.'

'Up into the hills?' said Nobby, astonished. 'Whatever for? They don't go and fetch things from the farm. The women do that, early each morning.'

'Well, we met those two,' said Dick, swimming up. 'They seemed jolly surprised to see us. I hope they aren't going to bother us any more.'

'I've had a bad day,' said Nobby, and he showed black bruises on his arms. 'My uncle hit me like anything for making friends with you. He says I'm not to go talking to strangers no more.'

'Why ever not?' said Dick. 'What a surly, selfish fellow he is! Well, you don't seem to be taking much notice of him now!'

''Course not!' said Nobby. 'He's safe up in the hills, isn't he? I'll have to be careful he doesn't see me with you, that's all. Nobody else at the camp will split on me – they all hate Lou and Tiger Dan.'

'We saw you out in your boat with Pongo,' said Julian, swimming up to join in the conversation. 'We thought that if ever you wanted to signal to us you could easily do it by going out in your boat, and waving a handkerchief or something. We've got field-glasses, and we can easily see you. We could come along down if you signalled. We'd know it would be safe.'

'Right,' said Nobby. 'Come on, let's have a race. Bet you I'm on the shore first!'

He wasn't, of course, because he didn't swim properly. Even Anne could race him. Soon they were all drying themselves vigorously.

'Golly, I'm hungry!' said Julian. 'Come on up the hill with us, Nobby, and share our supper!'

10 A curious change of mind

Nobby felt very much tempted to go and have a meal up in the hills with the children. But he was afraid of meeting Lou and his uncle coming back from their walk.

'We can easily look out for them and warn you if we see or hear them,' said Dick, 'and you can flop under a bush and hide till they go past. You may be sure we'll be on the look-out for them ourselves, because *we* don't want to meet them either!'

'Well, I'll come,' said Nobby. 'I'll take Barker and Growler too. They'll like to see Timmy.'

So all five of them, with the two dogs, set off up the hill. They climbed up short cuts at first, but they were soon panting, and decided to take the track, which, although longer, was easier to follow.

They all kept a sharp look-out for the two men, but they could see no sign of them. 'We shall be at our caravans soon,' said Julian. Then he heard Timmy barking in the distance. 'Hallo! What's old Tim barking for? I wonder if those fellows have been up to our caravans?'

'Good thing we left Timmy on guard if so,' said Dick. 'We might have missed something if not.'

Then he went red, remembering that it was Nobby's uncle he had been talking of. Nobby might feel upset and offended to hear someone speaking as if he thought Tiger Dan would commit a little robbery.

But Nobby wasn't at all offended. 'Don't you worry about what you say of my uncle,' he said, cheerfully. 'He's a bad lot. I know that. Anyway, he's not really my uncle, you know. When my father and mother died, they left a little money for me – and it turned out that they had asked Tiger Dan to look after me. So he took the money, called himself my uncle, and I've had to be with him ever since.'

'Was he in the same circus, then?' asked Julian.

'Oh yes. He and my father were both clowns,' said Nobby. 'Always have been clowns in my family. But wait till I'm old enough, and I'll do a bunk – clear off and join another circus, where they'll let me look after the horses. I'm mad on horses. But the fellow at our circus won't often let me go near them. Jealous because I can handle them, I suppose!'

The children gazed at Nobby in wonder. He seemed an extraordinary boy to them – one who walked about with a tame chimpanzee, exercised hordes of performing dogs, lived with the chief clown in the circus, could turn the most marvellous cart-wheels, and whose only ambition was to work with horses! What a boy! Dick half-envied him.

'Haven't you ever been to school?' he asked Nobby.

The boy shook his head. 'Never! I can't write. And I can only read a bit. Most circus folk are like that, so nobody minds. Jumping Jiminy, I bet *you're* all clever, though! I bet even little Anne can read a book!'

'I've been able to read for *years*,' said Anne. 'And I'm up to fractions now in numbers.'

'Coo! What's fractions?' said Nobby, impressed.

'Well – quarters and halves and seven-eighths, and things like that,' said Anne. 'But I'd rather be able to turn a cart-wheel like you can, Nobby, than know how to do fractions.'

'Whatever *is* Timmy barking for?' said George as they came near the clump of birch trees. Then she stopped suddenly, for she had seen two figures lying down in the grass below the trees. Lou – and Tiger Dan!

It was too late for Nobby to hide. The men saw him at once. They got up and waited for the children to come near. George felt thankful that Timmy was within whistling distance. He would come at the first call or whistle, she knew.

Julian looked at the men. To his surprise they appeared to be quite amiable. A faint scowl came over Tiger Dan's face when he caught sight of Nobby, but it passed at once.

'Good evening,' said Julian curtly, and would have passed on without another word, but Lou stepped up to him.

'We see you're camping up by here,' said Lou, and smiled, showing yellow teeth. 'Ain't you going over the hill?'

'I don't need to discuss my affairs with either you or your friend,' said Julian, sounding extremely grown-up. 'You told us to clear out from down below, and we have. What we do now is nothing to do with you.'

'Ho yes, it is,' said Tiger Dan, sounding as if he was being polite with great difficulty. 'We come up here tonight to plan a place for some of our animals, see? And we don't want you to be in no danger.'

'We shan't be,' said Julian, scornfully. 'And there is plenty of room on these hills for you and your animals and for us, too. You won't scare us off, so don't think it. We shall stay here as long as we want to – and if we want help there's the farmer and his men quite near by – to say nothing of our dog.'

'Did you leave that there dog on guard?' asked Lou, as he heard Timmy barking again. 'He ought to be destroyed, that dog of yours. He's dangerous.'

'He's only dangerous to rogues and scamps,' said George, joining in at once. 'You keep away from our caravans when Timmy's on guard. He'll maul you if you go near.'

Lou began to lose his temper. 'Well, are you going or ain't you?' he said. 'We've told you we want this here bit of the hill. You can come down and camp by the lake again if you want to.'

'Yes – you come,' said Tiger Dan to the children's growing astonishment. 'You come, see? You can bathe in the lake every day, then – and Nobby here can show you round the camp, and you can make friends with all the animals, see?'

Now it was Nobby's turn to looked amazed.

'Jumping Jiminy! Didn't you beat me black and blue for making friends with these kids?' he demanded. 'What's the game, now? You've never

'. . . *we don't want you to be in no danger.*'

152

had animals up in the hills before. You've . . .'

'Shut up,' said Tiger Dan in such a fierce voice that all the children were shocked. Lou nudged Dan, and he made an effort to appear pleasant again.

'We didn't want Nobby to make friends with posh folk like you,' he began again. 'But it seems as if you want to pal up with him – so it's okay with us. You come on down and camp by the lake, and Nobby'll show you everything in the circus. Can't say fairer than that.'

'You've got other reasons for making all these suggestions,' said Julian, scornfully. 'I'm sorry – but our plans are made, and I am not going to discuss them with you.'

'Come on,' said Dick. 'Let's go and find Timmy. He's barking his head off because he can hear us, and it won't be long before he comes flying along here. Then we shall find it difficult to keep him off these two fellows.'

The four children began to move off. Nobby looked doubtfully at his uncle. He didn't know whether to go with them or not. Lou nudged Dan again.

'You go, too, if you want to,' said Tiger Dan, trying to grin amiably at the surprised Nobby. 'Keep your fine friends, see! Much good may they do you!' The grin vanished into a scowl, and Nobby skipped smartly out of reach of his uncle's hand. He was puzzled and wondered what was behind his uncle's change of mind.

He tore after the children. Timmy came to meet them, barking his head off, waving his plumy tail wildly in joy.

'Good dog, good dog!' said George, patting him. 'You keep on guard beautifully. You knew I would have whistled for you if I'd wanted you, didn't you, Timmy? Good dog!'

'I'll get you some supper,' said Anne to everyone. 'We're all famishing. We can talk while we eat. George, come and help. Julian, can you get some ginger-beer? And, Dick, do fill up the water-bowl for me.'

The boys winked at one another. They always thought that Anne was very funny when she took command like this, and gave her orders. But everyone went obediently to work.

Nobby went to help Anne. Together they boiled ten eggs hard in the little saucepan. Then Anne made tomato sandwiches with potted meat and got out the cake the farmer's wife had given them. She remembered the raspberry syrup, too – how lovely!

Soon they were all sitting on the rocky ledge, which was still warm, watching the sun go down into the lake. It was a most beautiful evening, with the lake as blue as a cornflower and the sky flecked with rosy clouds. They held their hard-boiled eggs in one hand had a piece of bread and butter in the other, munching happily. There was a dish of salt for everyone to dip their eggs into.

'I don't know why, but the meals we have on picnics always taste so much nicer than the ones we have indoors,' said George. 'For instance, even if we had hard-boiled eggs and bread and butter indoors, they wouldn't taste as nice as these.'

'Can everyone eat two eggs?' asked Anne. 'I did two each. And there's plenty of cake – and more sandwiches and some plums we picked this morning.'

'Best meal I've ever had in my life,' said Nobby, and picked up his second egg. 'Best company I've ever been in, too!'

'Thank you,' said Anne, and everyone looked pleased. Nobby might not have their good manners, but he always seemed to say just the right thing.

'It's a good thing your uncle didn't make you go back with him and Lou,' said Dick. 'Funny business – changing his mind like that!'

They began to talk about it. Julian was very puzzled indeed, and had even begun to wonder if he hadn't better find another camping site and go over the hill.

The others raised their voices scornfully.

'JULIAN! We're not cowards. We'll jolly well stay here!'

'What, leave now – why should we? We're in nobody's way, whatever those men say!'

'*I'm* not moving *my* caravan, whatever *anyone* says!' That was George, of course.

'No, don't you go,' said Nobby. 'Don't you take no notice of Lou and my uncle. They can't do nothing to you at all. They're just trying to make trouble for you. You stay and let me show you over the camp, see?'

'It isn't that I *want* to give in to those fellows' ideas,' said Julian. 'It's just that – well, I'm in charge of us all – and I *don't* like the look of Lou and Tiger Dan – and, well . . .'

'Oh, have another egg and forget about it,' said Dick. 'We're going to stay here in this hollow, however much Dan and Lou want us out of it. And, what's more, I'd like to find out why they're so keen to push us off. It seems jolly queer to me.'

The sun went down in a blaze of orange and

red, and the lake shimmered with its fiery reflection. Nobby got up regretfully, and Barker and Growler, who had been hobnobbing with Timmy, got up, too.

'I'll have to go,' said Nobby. 'Still got some jobs to do down there. What about you coming down tomorrow to see the animals? You'll like Old Lady, the elephant. She's a pet. And Pongo will be pleased to see you again.'

11 Fun at the circus camp

Next morning, while Anne cleared up the breakfast things with George, and Dick went off to the farm to buy whatever the farmer's wife had ready for him, Julian took the field-glasses and sat on the ledge to watch for Nobby to go out on the lake in his boat.

Dick sauntered along, whistling. The farmer's wife was delighted to see him, and showed him two big baskets full of delicious food.

'Slices of ham I've cured myself,' she said, lifting up the white cloth that covered one of the baskets. 'And a pot of brawn I've made. Keep it in a cool place. And some fresh lettuces and radishes I pulled myself this morning early. And some more tomatoes.'

'How gorgeous!' said Dick, eyeing the food in delight. 'Just the kind of things we love! Thanks awfully, Mrs Mackie. What's in the other basket?'

'Eggs, butter, milk, and a tin of shortbread I've baked,' said Mrs Mackie. 'You should do all right till tomorrow, the four of you! And in that paper there is a bone for the dog.'

'How much do I owe you?' asked Dick. He paid his bill and took up the baskets. Mrs Mackie slipped a bag into his pocket.

'Just a few home-made sweets,' she said. That was her little present. Dick grinned at her.

'Well, I won't offer to pay you for them because I'm afraid of that rolling-pin of yours,' he said. 'But thank you very, very much.'

He went off delighted. He thought of Anne's pleasure when she came to unpack the baskets.

'Your uncle may have changed his mind again by tomorrow, and not want us near the camp,' said Dick.

'Well – I'll signal to you,' said Nobby. 'I'll go out in the boat, see? And wave a hanky. Then you'll know it's all right. Well – so long! I'll be seeing you.'

How she would love to put the things in the little larder – and pop the butter in a dish set in a bowl of cold water – and set the eggs in the little rack!

When he got back Julian called to him: 'Nobby's out in his boat. Come and look. He's waving something that can't possibly be a hanky. It must be the sheet off his bed!'

'Nobby doesn't sleep in sheets,' said Anne. 'He didn't know what they were when he saw them in our bunks. Perhaps it's a table-cloth.'

'Anyway, it's something big, to tell us that it's absolutely all right to come down to the camp,' said Julian. 'Are we ready?'

'Not quite,' said Anne, unpacking the baskets Dick had brought. 'I must put away these things – and do you want to take a picnic lunch with you? Beacause if so I must prepare it. Oh – look at all these gorgeous things!'

They all came back to look. 'Mrs Mackie is a darling,' said Anne. 'Honestly, these things are super – look at this gorgeous ham. It smells heavenly.'

'Here's her little present – home-made sweets,' said Dick, remembering them and taking them out of his pocket. 'Have one?'

Anne had everything ready in half an hour. They had decided to take a picnic lunch with them for themselves and for Nobby as well. They took their bathing-things and towels, too.

'Are we going to take Timmy or not?' said George. 'I want to. But as these two men seem rather interested in our caravans, perhaps we had better leave him on guard again. We don't want to come back and find the caravans damaged or half the things stolen.'

'I should think not!' said Dick. 'They're not our things, nor our caravans. They belong to somebody else and we've got to take extra good care of them. I think we ought to leave Timmy on guard, don't you, Ju?'

'Yes, I do,' said Julian at once. 'These caravans are too valuable to leave at the mercy of any passing tramp – though I suppose we could lock them up. Anyway – we'll leave Timmy on guard today – poor old Timmy, it's a shame, isn't it?'

Timmy didn't answer. He looked gloomy and miserable. What! They were all going off without him again? He knew what 'on guard' meant – he was to stay here with these houses on wheels till the children chose to come back. He badly wanted to see Pongo again. He stood with his ears and tail drooping, the picture of misery.

But there was no help for it. The children felt that they couldn't leave the caravans unguarded while they were still so uncertain about Lou and Tiger Dan. So they all patted poor Timmy and fondled him, and then said good-bye. He sat down on the rocky ledge with his back to them and wouldn't even watch them go.

'He's sulking,' said George. 'Poor Timothy!'

It didn't take them very long to get down to the camp, and they found Nobby, Pongo, Barker and Growler waiting for them. Nobby was grinning from ear to ear.

'You saw my signal all right?' he said. 'Uncle hasn't changed his mind – in fact, he seems quite to have taken to you, and says I'm to show you all round and let you see anything you want to. That was his shirt I waved. I thought if I waved something enormous you'd know things were absolutely safe.'

'Where shall we put the bathing-things and the picnic baskets while we see round the camp?' asked Anne. 'Somewhere cool, if possible.'

'Put them in my caravan,' said Nobby, and led them to a caravan painted blue and yellow, with red wheels. The children remembered having seen it when the procession passed by their house a week or two before.

They peeped inside. It wasn't nearly so nice as theirs. It was much smaller, for one thing, and very untidy. It looked dirty, too, and had a nasty smell. Anne didn't like it very much.

'Not so good as yours!' said Nobby. 'I wish I had a caravan like yours. I'd feel like a prince. Now what do you want to see first? The elephant? Come on, then.'

They went to the tree to which Old Lady the elephant was tied. She curled her trunk round Nobby and looked at the children out of small, intelligent eyes.

'Well, Old Lady!' said Nobby. 'Want a bathe?'

The elephant trumpeted and made the children jump. 'I'll take you later on,' promised Nobby. 'Now then – hup, hup, hup!'

At these words the elephant curled her trunk tightly round Nobby's waist and lifted him bodily into the air, placing him gently on her big head!

Anne gasped.

'Oh! Did he hurt you, Nobby?'

''Course not!' said Nobby. 'Old Lady wouldn't hurt anyone, would you, big one?'

A small man came up. He had bright eyes that shone as if they had been polished, and a very wide grin. 'Good morning,' he said. 'How do you like my Old Lady? Like to see her play cricket?'

'Oh, yes!' said everyone, and the small man produced a cricket bat and held it out to Old Lady. She took it in her trunk and waved it about. Nobby slipped deftly off her head to the ground.

'I'll play with her, Larry,' he said, and took the ball from the small man. He threw it to Old Lady and she hit it smartly with the bat. It sailed over their heads!

Julian fetched the ball. He threw it at the elephant, and again the great creature hit the ball with a bang. Soon all the children were playing with Old Lady and enjoying the game very much.

Some small camp children came up to watch. But they were as scared as rabbits as soon as Julian or George spoke to them and scuttled off to their caravans at once. They were dirty and ragged, but most of them had beautiful eyes and thick curly hair, though it wanted brushing and washing.

Nobby went to fetch Pongo, who was dancing to and fro in his cage, making anguished sounds, thinking he was forgotten. He was simply delighted to see the children again, and put his arm right round Anne at once. Then he pulled George's hair and hid his face behind his paws, peeping out mischievously.

'He's a caution, aren't you, Pongo?' said Nobby. 'Now you keep with me, Pongo, or I'll put you back into your cage, see?'

They went to see the dogs and let them all out. They were mostly terrier dogs, or mongrels, smart, well-kept little things who jumped up eagerly at Nobby, and made a great fuss of him. It was clear that they loved him and trusted him.

'Like to see them play football?' asked Nobby. 'Here, Barker – fetch the ball. Go on, quick!'

Barker darted off to Nobby's caravan. The door was shut, but the clever little dog stood on his hind legs and jerked the handle with his nose. The door opened and in went Barker. He came out dribbling a football with his nose. Down the steps it went and into the camp field. All the dogs leapt on it with howls of delight.

'Yap-yap-yap! Yap-yap!' They dribbled that football to and fro, while Nobby stood with his legs open to make a goal for them.

It was Barker's job and Growler's to score the goals, and the task of the other dogs to stop them. So it was a most amusing game to watch. Once, when Barker scored a goal by hurling himself on the ball and sending it rolling fast between Nobby's arched legs, Pongo leapt into the fray, picked up the ball and ran off with it.

'Foul, foul!' yelled Nobby and all the dogs rushed after the mischievous chimpanzee. He leapt on to the top of a caravan and began to bounce the ball there, grinning down at the furious dogs.

'Oh, this is such fun!' said Anne, wiping the tears of laughter from her eyes. 'Oh, dear! I've got such a pain in my side from laughing.'

Nobby had to climb up to the roof of the caravan to get the ball. Pongo jumped down the other side, but left the ball balanced neatly on the chimney. He was really a most mischievous champanzee.

Then they went to see the beautiful horses. All of them had shining satiny coats. They were being trotted round a big field by a slim, tall young fellow called Rossy, and they obeyed his slightest word.

'Can I ride Black Queen, Rossy?' asked Nobby eagerly. 'Do let me!'

'Okay,' said Rossy, his black hair shining like the horses' coats. Then Nobby amazed the watching children, for he leapt on to a great black horse, stood up on her back and trotted all round the field like that!

'He'll fall!' cried Anne. But he didn't, of course. Then he suddenly swung himself down on to his hands and rode Black Queen standing upside down.

'Good, good!' cried Rossy. 'You are good with horses, young one! Now ride Fury!'

Fury was a small, fiery-looking horse, whose gleaming eyes showed a temper. Nobby ran to her and leapt on her bare-backed. She rose up, snorting, and tried to throw him off. But he wouldn't be thrown off. No matter what she did, Nobby clung on like a limpet to a rock.

At last Fury tired of it and began to canter round the field. Then she galloped – and suddenly she stopped absolutely dead, meaning to fling Nobby over her head!

But the boy was waiting for that trick and threw himself backwards at once. 'Good, good!' cried Rossy. 'She will soon eat out of your hand, Nobby! Good boy.'

'Nobby, Nobby, you're terribly clever!' yelled Anne. 'Oh, I wish I could do the things you do! I wish I could.'

Nobby slid off Fury's back, looking pleased. It was nice to show off a little to his 'posh' friends. Then he looked round and about. 'I say – where's that chimp? Up to some mischief, I'll be bound! Let's go and find him.'

12 A lovely day–with a horrid end

They soon saw Pongo. He was coming round one of the caravans, looking exceedingly pleased with himself. He went to Anne and held out his paw to her, making little affectionate noises.

Anne took what he held. She looked at it. 'It's a hard-boiled egg! Oh, Nobby, he's been at the picnic baskets!'

So he had! Two of the eggs were gone, and some of the tomatoes! Nobby smacked the chimpanzee and took him back to his cage. He was very sad and made a noise as if he was crying, hiding his face in his paws. Anne was upset.

'Is he really crying? Oh, do forgive him, Nobby. He didn't mean to be naughty.'

'He's not crying. He's only pretending,' said Nobby. 'And he did mean to be naughty. I know him!'

The morning soon went in visiting the circus animals. It was dinner-time before they had had time to see the monkeys. 'We'll see them afterwards,' said Nobby. 'Let's have a meal now. Come on. We'll go and have it by the lake.'

The children hadn't seen Lou or Tiger Dan at all, much to their joy. 'Where are they?' asked Julian. 'Gone out for the day?'

'Yes, thank goodness,' said Nobby. 'Gone out on one of their mysterious jaunts. You know, when we're on the road, going from place to place, my uncle sometimes disappears at night. I wake up – and he's not there.'

'Where does he go?' asked George.

'I wouldn't dare to ask,' said Nobby. 'Anyway, he and Lou are out of the way today. I don't expect they'll be back till night.'

They had their meal by the lake. It glittered at their feet, calm and blue, and looked very inviting.

'What about a swim?' asked Dick when they had eaten as much as they could. Julian looked at his watch.

'Can't swim directly after a good meal,' he said. 'You know that, Dick. We'll have to wait a bit.'

'Right,' said Dick and lay down. 'I'll have a snooze – or shall we go and see the monkeys?'

They all had a short nap and then got up to go and see the monkeys. When they got back to the camp they found it alive with people, all excited and yelling.

'What's up?' said Nobby. 'Jumping Jiminy, the monkeys are all loose!'

So they were. Wherever they looked the children saw a small brown monkey, chattering to itself, on the roof of a caravan or tent!

A brown-faced woman with sharp eyes came up to Nobby. She caught him by the shoulder and shook him. 'See what that chimp of yours has done?' she said. 'You put him in his cage and couldn't have locked it properly. He got out and let all the monkeys loose. Drat that chimp – I'll take a broomstick to him if ever I catch him!'

'Where's Lucilla then?' asked Nobby, dragging himself away from the cross woman. 'Can't she get them in?'

'Lucilla's gone to the town,' scolded the woman. 'And fine and pleased she'll be to hear this when she comes back!'

'Aw, let the monkeys be!' said Nobby. 'They won't come to any harm. They'll wait for Lucilla all right!'

'Who's Lucilla?' asked Anne, thinking that life in a circus camp was very exciting.

'She owns the monkeys,' said Nobby. 'Hi, look – there's Lucilla coming back! Now we'll be all right!'

A little wizened old woman was hurrying towards the camp. She really looked rather like a monkey herself, Anne thought. Her eyes were bright and sharp, and her tiny hands clutched a red shawl round her. They looked like brown paws.

'Your monkeys are out!' yelled the camp children. 'LUCILLA! Your monkeys are out.'

Lucilla heard and, raising her voice, she scolded everyone in sight fully and shrilly. Then she stood still and held out her arms. She spoke some soft words in a language the children didn't know – magic words, Anne said afterwards.

One by one the wandering monkeys came scampering over to her, flinging themselves down from the caravan roofs, making little chattering sounds of love and welcome. They leapt on to Lucilla's shoulders and into her arms, cuddling against her like tiny brown children. Not one monkey was left out – all went to Lucilla as if drawn by some enchantment.

She walked slowly towards their cage, murmuring her soft words as she went. Everyone watched in silence.

'She's a queer one,' said the brown-faced woman to Nobby. 'She don't love nobody but her monkeys – and there's nobody loves her but them. You mind out she doesn't go for that chimp of yours, letting out her precious monkeys!'

'I'll take him and Old Lady down to bathe,' said Nobby, hastily. 'By the time we're back, Lucilla will have forgotten.'

They fetched Old Lady and discovered where naughty Pongo was hiding under a caravan. As quickly as possible they went back to the lake, Old Lady stepping out well, looking forward to her bathe.

'I suppose things like that are always happening in a circus camp,' said Anne. 'It's not a bit like real life.'

'Isn't it?' said Nobby, surprised. 'It's real life all right to *me*!'

It was cool in the lake and they all enjoyed themselves very much, swimming and splashing. Pongo wouldn't go in very far, but splashed everyone who came within reach, laughing and cackling loudly. He gave Old Lady a shock by leaping up on to her back, and pulling one of her big ears.

She dipped her trunk into the lake, sucked up a lot of water, turned her trunk over her back, and squirted the water all over the startled chimpanzee! The children yelled with laughter, and roared again to see Pongo falling in fright off Old Lady's back. Splash! He went right in and got himself wet from head to foot – a thing he hated doing.

'Serves you right, you scamp!' shouted Nobby. 'Hey, Old Lady, stop it! Don't squirt at me!'

The elephant, pleased with her little joke, didn't want to stop it. So the children had to keep well away from her, for her aim was very good.

'I've never had such a lovely time in my life!' said Anne, as she dried herself. 'I shall dream all night of monkeys and elephants, horses, dogs and chimpanzees!'

Nobby turned about twenty cart-wheels by the edge of the lake from sheer good spirits – and Pongo at once did the same. He was even better at it than Nobby. Anne tried and fell down flop immediately.

They went back to the camp. 'Sorry I can't offer you any tea,' said Nobby, 'but we never seem to have tea, you know – we circus folk, I mean. Anyway, I'm not hungry after that enormous lunch. Are you?'

Nobody was. They shared out Mrs Mackie's home-made toffees, and gave one to Pongo. It stuck his teeth together, and he looked so comically alarmed when he found that he couldn't open his mouth that the children roared at him.

He sat down, swayed from side to side, and began to groan dismally. But the toffee soon melted away, and he found that he could open his mouth after all. He sucked the rest of the sweet

noisily, but wouldn't have another.

They wandered round the camp, looking at the different caravans. Nobody took much notice of them now. They were just Nobby's 'posh' friends – that was all. Some of the smaller children peeped out and stuck out their little red tongues – but at Nobby's roar they vanished.

'Got no manners at all!' said Nobby. 'But they're all right really.'

They came to where big wagons stood, stored with all kinds of circus things. 'We don't bother to unpack these when we're resting in camp like this,' said Nobby. 'Don't need them here. One of my jobs is to help to unpack this stuff when we're camping to give a show. Have to get out all them benches and set them up in the big top – that' the circus tent, you know. We're pretty busy then, I can tell you!'

'What's in *this* cart?' asked Anne, coming to a small wagon with a tightly-fitting hood of tarpaulin.

'Don't know,' said Nobby. 'That cart belongs to my uncle. He won't never let me unpack it. I don't know what he keeps there. I've wondered if it was things belonging to my Dad and Mum. I told you they were dead. Anyway, I thought I'd peep and see one day; but Uncle Dan caught me and half-killed me!'

'But if they belonged to your parents, they ought to be yours!' said George.

'Funny this is, sometimes that cart's crammed full,' said Nobby. 'And sometimes it isn't. Maybe Lou puts some of his things there too.'

'Well, nobody could get anything else in there at the moment!' said Julian. 'It's full to bursting!'

They lost interest in the little wagon and wandered round to see the 'props' as Nobby called them. Anne pictured these as clothes-props, but they turned out to be gilt chairs and tables, the shining poles used for the tight-rope, gaily-painted stools for the performing dogs to sit on, and circus 'props' of that kind.

'*Prop*erties, Anne,' said Julian 'Circus *prop*erties. Props for short. Look here, isn't it about time we went back? My watch has stopped. Whatever time is it?'

'Golly, it's quite late!' said Dick, looking at his watch. 'Seven o' clock. No wonder I feel jolly hungry. Time we went back. Coming with us, Nobby? You can have supper up there, if you like. I bet you could find your way back in the dark.'

'I'll take Pongo with me, and Barker and

Growler,' said Nobby, delighted at the invitation. 'If *I* lose the way back, *they* won't!.

So they all set off up the hill, tired with their long and exciting day. Anne began to plan what she would give the little company for supper. Ham, certainly – and tomatoes – and some of that raspberry syrup diluted with icy-cold spring-water.

They all heard Timmy barking excitedly as soon as they came near the caravans. He barked without ceasing, loudly and determinedly.

'He sounds cross,' said Dick. 'Poor old Tim! He must think we've quite deserted him.'

They came to the caravans and Timmy flung himself on George as if he hadn't seen her for a year. He pawed her and licked her, then pawed her again.

Barker and Growler were pleased to see him too, and as for Pongo, he was delighted. He shook hands with Timmy's tail several times, and was disappointed that Timmy took no notice of him.

'Hallo! What's Barker gnawing at?' suddenly said Dick. 'Raw meat! How did it come here? Do you suppose the farmer has been by and given Timmy some? Well, why didn't he eat it, then?'

They all looked at Barker, who was gnawing some meat on the ground. Growler ran to it too. But Timmy would not go near it. Nor would Pongo. Timmy put his tail down and Pongo hid his furry face behind his paws.

'Funny,' said the children, puzzled at the queer behaviour of the two animals. Then suddenly they understood – for poor Barker suddenly gave a terrible whine, shivered from head to foot, and rolled over on his side.

'Jiminy – it's poisoned!' yelled Nobby, and kicked Growler away from the meat. He picked Barker up, and to the children's utter dismay they saw that Nobby was crying.

'He's done for,' said the boy, in a choking voice. 'Poor old Barker.'

Carrying Barker in his arms, with Growler and Pongo behind him, poor Nobby stumbled down the hill. No one liked to follow him. Poisoned meat! What a terrible thing!

13 Julian thinks of a plan

George was trembling. Her legs felt as if they wouldn't hold her up, and she sank down on the ledge. She put her arms round Timmy.

'Oh, Timmy! That meat was meant for you! Oh, thank goodness, thank goodness you were clever enough not to touch it! Timmy, you might have been poisoned!'

Timmy licked his mistress soberly. The others stood round, staring, not knowing what to think. Poor Barker! Would he die? Suppose it had been old Timmy? They had left him all alone, and he might have eaten the meat and died.

'I'll never, never leave you up here alone again!' said George.

'Who threw him the poisoned meat, do you think?' said Anne, in a small voice.

'Who do you suppose?' said George, in a hard, scornful voice. 'Lou and Tiger Dan!'

'They want to get us away from here, that's plain,' said Dick. 'But again – why?'

'What can there be about this place that makes the men want to get rid of us all?' wondered Julian. 'They're real rogues. Poor Nobby. He must have an awful life with them. And now they've gone and poisoned his dog.'

Nobody felt like eating very much that evening. Anne got out the bread and the butter and a pot of jam. George wouldn't eat anything. What a horrid end to a lovely day!

They all went to bed early, and nobody objected when Julian said he was going to lock both caravans. 'Not that I think either Lou or Dan will be up here tonight,' he said. 'But you never know!'

Whether they came or not the children didn't know, for although Timmy began to bark loudly in the middle of the night, and scraped frantically at the shut door of George's caravan, there was nothing to be seen or heard when Julian opened his door and flashed on his torch.

Timmy didn't bark any more. He lay quite quietly sleeping with one ear cocked. Julian lay in bed and thought hard. Probably Lou and Dan had come creeping up in the dark, hoping that Timmy had taken the meat and been poisoned. But when they heard him bark, they knew he was all right, and they must have gone away again. What plan would they make next?

'There's something behind all this,' Julian thought, again and again. 'But what can it be? Why do they want us out of this particular spot?'

He couldn't imagine. He fell asleep at last with a vague plan in his mind. He would tell it to the others tomorrow. Perhaps if he could make Lou and Dan think they had all gone off for the day – with Timmy – but really, he, Julian, would be left behind, in hiding – maybe he could find out something, if Lou and Dan came along . . .

Julian fell asleep in the middle of thinking out his plan. Like the others, he dreamt of elephants squirting him with water, of Pongo chasing the monkeys, of the dogs playing football with excited yaps – and then into the dream came lumps of poisoned meat! Horrid.

Anne woke with a jump, having dreamt that someone had put poison into the hard-boiled eggs they were going to eat. She lay trembling in her bunk, and called to George in a small voice.

'George! I've been having an awful dream!'

George woke up, and Timmy stirred and stretched himself. George switched on her torch.

'I've been having beastly dreams, too,' she said. 'I dreamt that those men were after Timmy. I'll leave my torch on for a bit and we'll talk. I expect that with all the excitement we've had today, and the horrid end to it this evening, we're just in the mood for horrid dreams! Still – they are only dreams.'

'Woof,' said Timmy, and scratched himself.

'Don't,' said George. 'You shake the whole caravan when you do that, Timmy. Stop it.'

Timmy stopped. He sighed and lay down heavily. He put his head on his paws and looked sleepily at George, as if to say, 'Put that torch out. I want to go to sleep.'

The next morning was not so warm, and the sky was cloudy. Nobody felt very cheerful, because they kept thinking of Nobby and poor Barker. They ate their breakfast almost in silence, and then Anne and George began to stack the plates, ready to take them to the spring to rinse.

'I'll go to the farm this morning,' said Julian. 'You sit on the ledge and take the field-glasses, Dick. We'll see if Nobby goes out in his boat and waves. I've an idea that he won't want us down in the camp this morning. If he suspects his Uncle

Dan and Lou of putting down the meat that poisoned Barker, he'll probably have had a frightful row with them.'

He went off to the farm with two empty baskets. Mrs Mackie was ready for him, and he bought a further supply of delicious-looking food. Her present this time was a round ginger cake, warm from the oven!

'Do the circus folk come up here often to buy food?' asked Julian, as he paid Mrs Mackie.

'They come sometimes,' said Mrs Mackie. 'I don't mind the women or the children – dirty though they are, and not above taking one of my chickens now and again – but it's the men I can't abide. There were two here last year, messing about in the hills, that my husband had to send off quick.'

Julian pricked up his ears. 'Two men? What were they like?'

'Ugly fellows,' said Mrs Mackie. 'And one had the yellowest teeth I ever saw. Bad-tempered chaps, both of them. They came up here at night, and we were afraid our chickens would go. They swore they weren't after our chickens – but what else would they be up here at night for?'

'I can't imagine,' said Julian. He was sure that the two men Mrs Mackie spoke of were Lou and Tiger Dan. Why did they wander about in the hills at night?

He went off with the food. When he got near the camping-place, Dick called to him excitedly.

'Hey, Julian! Come and look through the glasses. Nobby's out in his boat with Pongo, and I simply can't make out what it is they're both waving.'

Julian took the glasses and looked through them. Far down the hill, on the surface of the lake, floated Nobby's little boat. In it was Nobby, and with him was Pongo. Both of them were waving something bright red.

'Can't see what they're waving – but that doesn't matter,' said Julian. 'The thing is – what they're waving is red, not white. Red for danger. He's warning us.'

'Golly – I didn't think of that. What an idiot I am!' said Dick. 'Yes – red for danger. What's up, I wonder?'

'Well, it's clear we'd better not go down to the camp today,' said Julian. 'And it's also clear that whatever danger there is, is pretty bad – because both he *and* Pongo are waving red cloths – doubly dangerous!'

'Julian, you're jolly sharp,' said George, who was listening. 'You're the only one of us who tumbled to all that. Double-danger. What can it be?'

'Perhaps it means danger down at the camp, and danger here too,' said Julian, thoughtfully. 'I hope poor old Nobby is all right. Tiger Dan is so jolly beastly to him. I bet he's had a beating or two since last night.'

'It's a shame!' said Dick.

'Don't tell Anne we think there is double-danger about,' said Julian, seeing Anne coming back from the spring. 'She'll be scared. She was hoping we wouldn't have an adventure these hols – and now we seem to be plunged into the middle of one. Golly, I really think we ought to leave these hills and go on somewhere else.'

But he only said this half-heartedly, because he was burning to solve the curious mystery behind Lou's behaviour and Dan's. The others pounced on him at once.

'We can't leave! Don't be a coward, Ju!'

'I *won't* leave. Nor will Timmy.'

'Shut up,' said Julian. 'Here comes Anne.'

They said no more. Julian watched Nobby for a little while longer. Then the boy and the chimpanzee drew in to the shore and disappeared.

When they were all sitting together on the ledge, Julian proposed the plan he had been thinking out the night before.

'I'd like to find out what there is about this place that attracts Lou and Dan,' he said. 'There is *something* not far from here that makes the men want to get rid of us. Now suppose we four and Timmy go off down the hill and pass the camp, and yell out to Nobby that we're *all – all* of us – going to the town for the day – and you three do go, but I slip back up the hill – maybe Lou and Dan will come up here, and if I'm in hiding I shall see what they're up to!'

'You mean, we'll all four pretend to go to town – but really only three of us go, and you get back and hide,' said Dick. 'I see. It's a good idea.'

'And you'll hide somewhere and watch for the men to come,' said George. 'Well, for goodness sake don't let them see you, Julian. You won't have Timmy, you know! Those men could make mincemeat of you if they wanted to.'

'Oh, they'd want to all right. I know that,' said Julian grimly. 'But you can be sure I'll be jolly well hidden.'

'I don't see why we can't have a good look round and see if we can't find the cave or whatever it is the men want to come to,' said Dick. 'If they can find it, we can, too!'

'We don't know that it *is* a cave,' said Julian. 'We haven't any idea at all what attracts the men up here. Mrs Mackie said they were up here last year, too, and the farmer had to drive them away. They thought the men were after the chickens – but I don't think so. There's *some*thing in these hills that makes the men want to get us away.'

'Let's have a good look round,' said George, feeling suddenly thrilled. 'I've gone all adventurous again!'

'Oh dear!' said Anne. But she couldn't help feeling rather thrilled, too. They all got up and Timmy followed, wagging his tail. He was pleased that his friends hadn't gone off and left him on guard by himself that morning.

'We'll all go different ways,' said Julian. 'Up, down and sideways. I'll go up.'

They separated and went off, George and Timmy together, of course. They hunted in the hillside for possible caves, or even for some kind of hiding-place. Timmy put his head down every rabbit-hole and felt very busy indeed.

After about half an hour the others heard Julian yelling. They ran back to the caravans, sure that he had found something exciting.

But he hadn't. He had simply got tired of hunting and decided to give it up. He shook his head when they rushed up to him, shouting to know what he had found.

'Nothing,' he said. 'I'm fed up with looking. There's not a cave anywhere here. I'm sure of that! Anyone else found anything?'

'Not a thing,' said everyone in disappointment. 'What shall we do now?'

'Put our plan into action,' said Julian, promptly. 'Let the men themselves show us what they're after. Off we go down the hills, and we'll yell out to Nobby that we're off for the day – and we'll hope that Lou and Tiger Dan will hear us!'

14 A very good hiding-place

They went down the hill with Timmy. Julian gave Dick some instructions. 'Have a meal in the town,' he said. 'Keep away for the day, so as to give the men a chance to come up the hill. Go to the post office and see if there are any letters for us – and buy some tins of fruit. They'll make a nice change.'

'Right, Captain!' said Dick. 'And just you be careful, old boy. These men will stick at nothing – bad-tempered brutes they are.'

'Look after the girls,' said Julian. 'Don't let George do anything mad!'

Dick grinned. 'Who can stop George doing what she wants to? Not me!'

They were now at the bottom of the hill. The circus camp lay nearby. The children could hear the barking of the dogs and the shrill trumpeting of Old Lady.

They looked about for Nobby. He was nowhere to be seen. Blow! It wouldn't be any good setting off to the town and laying such a good plan if they couldn't tell Nobby they were going!

Nobody dared to go into the camp. Julian thought of the two red cloths that Nobby and Pongo had waved. Double-danger! It would be wise not to go into the camp that morning. He stood still, undecided what to do.

Then he opened his mouth and yelled:

'Nobby! NOBBY!'

No answer and no Nobby. The elephant man heard him shouting and came up. 'Do you want Nobby? I'll fetch him.'

'Thanks,' said Julian.

The little man went off, whistling. Soon Nobby appeared from behind a caravan, looking rather scared. He didn't come near Julian, but stood a good way away, looking pale and troubled.

'Nobby! We're going into the town for the day,' yelled Julian at the top of his voice. 'We're . . .'

Tiger Dan suddenly appeared behind Nobby and grabbed his arm fiercely. Nobby put up a hand to protect his face, as if he expected a blow. Julian yelled again:

'We're going into the town, Nobby! We shan't be back till evening. Can you hear me? WE'RE GOING TO THE TOWN!'

The whole camp must have heard Julian. But he was quite determined that, whoever else didn't hear, Tiger Dan certainly should.

Nobby tried to shake off his uncle's hand, and opened his mouth to yell back something. But Dan roughly put his hand across Nobby's mouth and hauled him away, shaking him as a dog shakes a rat.

'HOW'S BARKER?' yelled Julian. But Nobby had disappeared, dragged into his uncle's caravan by Dan. The little elephant man heard, however.

'Barker's bad,' he said. 'Not dead yet. But nearly. Never saw a dog so sick in my life. Nobby's fair upset!'

The children walked off with Timmy. George had had to hold his collar all the time, for once he saw Dan he growled without stopping, and tried to get away from George.

'Thank goodness Barker isn't dead,' said Anne. 'I do hope he'll get better.'

'Not much chance,' said Julian. 'That meat must have been chockful of poison. Poor old Nobby. How awful to be under the thumb of a fellow like Tiger Dan.'

'I just simply can't *imagine* him as a clown – Tiger Dan, I mean,' said Anne. 'Clowns are always so merry and gay and jolly.'

'Well, that's just acting,' said Dick. 'A clown needn't be the same out of the ring as he has to be when he's in it. If you look at photographs of clowns when they're just being ordinary men, they've got quite sad faces.'

'Well, Tiger Dan hasn't got a sad face. He's got a nasty, ugly, savage, cruel, fierce one,' said Anne, looking quite fierce herself.

That made the others laugh. Dick turned round to see if anyone was watching them walking toward the bus-stop, where the buses turned to go to the town.

'Lou the acrobat is watching us,' he said. 'Good! Can he see the bus-stop from where he is, Ju?'

Julian turned round. 'Yes, he can. He'll watch to see us all get into the bus – so I'd better climb in, too, and I'll get out at the first stop, double back, and get into the hills by some path he won't be able to see.'

'Right,' said Dick, enjoying the thought of playing a trick on Lou. 'Come on. There's the bus. We'll have to run for it.'

They all got into the bus. Lou was still watching, a small figure very far away. Dick felt inclined to wave cheekily to him, but didn't.

The bus set off. They took three tickets for the town and one for the nearest stop. Timmy had a ticket, too, which he wore proudly in his collar. He loved going in a bus.

Julian got out at the first stop. 'Well, see you this evening!' he said. 'Send Timmy on ahead to the caravans when you come back – just in case the men are anywhere about. I may not be able to warn you.'

'Right,' said Dick. 'Good-bye – and good luck!'

Julian waved and set off back down the road he had come. He saw a little lane leading off up into the hills and decided to take it. It led him not very far from Mrs Mackie's farm, so he soon knew where he was. He went back to the caravans, and quickly made himself some sandwiches and cut some cake to take to his hiding-place. He might have a long wiat!

'Now – where shall I hide?' thought the boy. 'I want somewhere that will give me a view of the track so that I can see when the men come up it. And yet it must be somewhere that gives me a good view of their doings, too. What would be the best place?'

A tree? No, there wasn't one that was near enough or thick enough. Behind a bush? No, the men might easily come round it and see him. What about the middle of a thick gorse bush? That might be a good idea.

But Julian gave that up very quickly, for he found the bush far too prickly to force his way into the middle. He scratched his arms and legs terribly.

'Blow!' he said. 'I really must make up my mind, or the men may be here before I'm in hiding!'

And then he suddenly had a real brainwave, and he crowed in delight. Of course! The very place!

'I'll climb up on to the roof of one of the caravans!' thought Julian. 'Nobody will see me there – and certainly nobody would guess I was there! That really is fine idea. I shall have a fine view of the track and a first-rate view of the men and where they go!'

It wasn't very easy to climb up on to the high roof. He had to get a rope, loop it at the end, and try to lasso the chimney in order to climb up.

He managed to lasso the chimney, and the rope hung down over the side of the caravan, ready for him to swarm up. He threw his packet of food up on to the roof and then climbed up himself. He pulled up the rope and coiled it beside him.

Then he lay down flat. He was certain that nobody could see him from below. Of course, if the men went higher up the hill and looked down on the caravans, he could easily be spotted – but he would have to chance that.

He lay there quite still, watching the lake, and keeping eyes and ears open for anyone coming up the hillside. He was glad that it was not a very hot sunny day, or he would have been cooked up on the roof. He wished he had thought of filling a bottle with water in case he was thirsty.

He saw spirals of smoke rising from where the circus camp lay, far below. He saw a couple of boats on the lake, a good way round the water – people fishing, he supposed. He watched a couple of rabbits come out and play on the hillside just below.

The sun came out from behind the clouds for about ten minutes and Julian began to feel uncomfortably hot. Then it went in again and he felt better.

He suddenly heard somebody whistling and stiffened himself in expectation – but it was only someone belonging to the farm, going down the hill some distance away. The whistle had carried clearly in the still air.

Then he got bored. The rabbits went in, and not even a butterfly sailed by. He could see no birds except a yellow-hammer that sat on the topmost spray of a bush and sang: 'Little-bit-of-bread-and-no-cheese', over and over again in a most maddening manner.

Then it gave a cry of alarm and flew off. It had heard something that frightened it.

Julian heard something, too, and glued his eyes to the track that led up the hill. His heart began to beat. He could see two men. Were they Lou and Dan?

He did not dare to raise his head to see them when they came nearer, in case they spotted him. But he knew their voices when they came near enough!

Yes – it was Lou and Tiger Dan all right. There was no mistaking those two harsh, coarse voices.

The men came right into the hollow, and Julian heard them talking.

'Yes, there's nobody here. Those kids have really gone off for the day at least – and taken that wretched dog with them!'

'I saw them get on the bus, dog and all, I told you,' growled Lou. 'There'll be nobody here for the day. We can get what we want to.'

'Let's go and get it, then,' said Dan.

Julian waited to see where they would go to. But they didn't go out of the hollow. They stayed there, apparently beside the caravans. Julian did not dare to look over the edge of the roof to see what they were up to. He was glad he had fastened all the windows and locked the doors.

Then there began some curious scuffling sounds, and the men panted. The caravan on which Julian was lying began to shake a little.

'What *are* they doing?' thought Julian in bewilderment. In intense curiosity he slid quietly to the edge of the caravan roof and cautiously peeped over, though he had firmly made up his mind not to do this on any account.

He looked down on the ground. There was nobody there at all. Perhaps the men were the other side. He slid carefully across and peeped over the opposite side of the caravan, which was still shaking a little, as if the men were bumping against it.

There was nobody the other side either! How very extraordinary! 'Golly! They must be underneath the caravan!' thought Julian, going back to the middle of the roof. 'Underneath! What in the wide world for?'

It was quite impossible to see underneath the caravan from where he was, so he had to lie quietly and wonder about the men's doings. They grunted and groaned, and seemed to be scraping and scrabbling about, but nothing happened. Then Julian heard them scrambling out from underneath, angry and disappointed.

'Give us a cigarette,' said Lou in a disagreeable voice. 'I'm fed up with this. Have to shift this van. Those tiresome brats! What did they want to choose this spot for?'

Julian heard a match struck and smelt cigarette smoke. Then he got a shock. The caravan he was on began to move! Heavens! Were the men going to push it over the ledge and send it rolling down the hillside?

15 Several things happen

Julian was suddenly very scared. He wondered if he had better slide off the roof and run. He wouldn't have much chance if the caravan went hurtling down the hill! But he didn't move. He clung to the chimney with both hands, whilst the men shoved hard against the caravan.

It ran a few feet to the rocky ledge, and then stopped. Julian felt his forehead getting very damp, and he saw that his hands were trembling. He felt ashamed of being so scared, but he couldn't help it.

'Hey! Don't send it down the hill!' said Lou in alarm, and Julian's heart felt lighter. So they didn't mean to destroy the caravan in that way!

They had just moved it to get at something underneath. But what could it be? Julian racked his brains to try and think what the floor of the hollow had been like when Dobby and Trotter pulled their caravans into it. As far as he could remember it was just an ordinary heathery hollow.

The men were now scrabbling away again by the back steps of the caravan. Julian was absolutely eaten up with curiosity, but he did not dare even to move. He could find out the secret when the men had gone. Meanwhile he really must be patient or he would spoil everything.

There was some muttered talking, but Julian couldn't catch a word. Then, quite suddenly, there was complete and utter silence. Not a word. Not a bump against the caravan. Not a pant or even a grunt. Nothing at all.

Julian lay still. Maybe the men were still there. He wasn't going to give himself away. He lay for quite a long time, waiting and wondering. But he heard nothing.

Then he saw a robin fly to a nearby bramble spray. It flicked its wings and looked about for crumbs. It was a robin that came around when the children were having a meal – but it was not as tame as most robins, and would not fly down until the children had left the hollow.

Then a rabbit popped out of a hole on the hill-side and capered about, running suddenly up to the hollow.

'Well,' thought Julian, 'it's plain the men aren't here now, or the birds and animals wouldn't be about like this. There's another rabbit. Those men have gone somewhere – though goodness knows where. I can peep over now and have a look, quite safely, I should think.'

He slid himself round and peered over the roof at the back end of the caravan. He looked down at the ground. There was absolutely nothing to be seen to tell him what the men had been doing, or where they had gone! The heather grew luxuri-antly there as it did everywhere else. There was nothing to show what the men had been making such a disturbance about.

'This is really very queer,' thought Julian, beginning to wonder if he had been dreaming. 'The men are certainly gone – vanished into thin air, apparently! Dare I get down and explore a bit? No, I daren't. The men may appear at any moment, and it's quite on the cards they'll lose their temper if they find me here, and chuck both me and the caravans down the hill! It's pretty steep just here, too.'

He lay there, thinking. He suddenly felt very hungry and thirsty. Thank goodness he had been sensible enough to take food up to the roof! He could at least have a meal while he was waiting for the men to come back – if they ever did!

He began to eat his sandwiches. They tasted very good indeed. He finished them all and began on the cake. That was good, too. He had brought a few plums up as well, and was very glad of them because he was thirsty. He flicked the plum stones from the roof before he thought what he was doing.

'Dash! Why did I do that? If the men notice them they may remember they weren't there before. Still, they've most of them gone into the heather!'

The sun came out a little and Julian felt hot. He wished the men would come again and go down the hill. He was tired of lying flat on the hard roof. Also he was terribly sleepy. He yawned silently and shut his eyes.

How long he slept he had no idea – but he was suddenly awakened by feeling the caravan being moved again! He clutched the chimney in alarm,

listening to the low voices of the two men.

They were pulling the caravan back into place again. Soon it was in the same position as before. Then Julian heard a match struck and smelt smoke again.

The men went and sat on the rocky ledge and took out food they had brought. Julian did not dare to peep at them, though he felt sure they had their backs to him. The men ate, and talked in low voices, and then, to Julian's dismay, they lay down and went to sleep! He knew that they were asleep because he could hear them snoring.

'Am I going to stay on this awful roof all day long?' he thought. 'I'm getting so cramped, lying flat like this. I want to sit up!'

'R-r-r-r-r!' snored Lou and Dan. Julian felt that surely it would be all right to sit up now that the men were obviously asleep. So he sat up cauti-ously, stretching himself with pleasure.

He looked down on the two men, who were lying on their backs with their mouths open. Beside them were two neat sacks, strong and thick. Julian wondered what was inside them. They cer-tainly had not had them when they came up the track.

The boy gazed down the hillside, frowning, try-ing to probe the mystery of where the men had been, and what they were doing up here – and suddenly he jumped violently. He stared as if he could not believe his eyes.

A squat and ugly face was peering out from a bramble bush there. There was almost no nose, and an enormous mouth. Who could it be? Was it someone spying on Lou and Dan? But what a face! It didn't seem human.

A hand came up to rub the face – and Julian saw that it was hairy. With a start he knew who the face belonged to – Pongo the chimpanzee! No wonder he had thought it such an ugly, inhuman face. It was all right on a chimp, of course – quite a nice face – but not on a man.

Pongo stared at Julian solemnly, and Julian stared back, his mind in a whirl. What was Pongo doing there? Was Nobby with him? If so, Nobby was in danger, for at any moment the men might wake up. He couldn't think what to do. If he called out to warn Nobby, he would wake the men.

Pongo was pleased to see Julian, and did not seem to think the roof of a caravan a curious place to be in at all. After all, *he* often went up on the roofs of caravans. He nodded and blinked at the boy, and then scratched his head for a long time.

Then beside him appeared Nobby's face – a tear-stained face, bruised and swollen. He suddenly saw Julian looking over the roof of the caravan, and his mouth fell open in surprise. He seemed about to call out, and Julian shook his head frantically to stop him, pointing downwards to try to warn Nobby that somebody was there.

But Nobby didn't understand. He grinned and, to Julian's horror, began to climb up the hillside to the rocky ledge! The men were sleeping there, and Julian saw with dismay that Nobby would probably heave himself up right on top of them.

'Look out!' he said, in a low, urgent voice. 'Look out, you fathead!'

But it was too late. Nobby heaved himself up on to the ledge, and, to his utmost horror, found himself sprawling on top of Tiger Dan! He gave a yell and tried to slide away – but Dan, rousing suddenly, shot out a hand and gripped him.

Lou woke up, too. The men glared at poor Nobby, and the boy began to tremble, and to beg for mercy.

'I didn't know you were here, I swear it! Let me go, let me go! I only came up to look for my knife that I lost yesterday!'

Dan shook him savagely. 'How long have you been here? You been spying?'

'No, no! I've only just come! I've been at the camp all morning – you ask Larry and Rossy. I been helping them!'

'You been spying on us, that's what you've been doing!' said Lou, in a cold, hard voice that filled the listening Julian with dread. 'You've had plenty of beatings this week, but seemingly they ain't enough. Well, up here, there's nobody to hear your yells, see? So we'll show you what a real beating is! And if you can walk down to the camp after it, I'll be surprised.'

Nobby was terrified. He begged for mercy, he promised to do anything the men asked him, and tried to jerk his poor swollen face away from Dan's hard hands.

Julian couldn't bear it. He didn't want to give away the fact that it was he who had been spying, nor did he want to fight the men at all, for he was pretty certain he would get the worst of it. But nobody could lie in silence, watching two men treat a young boy in such a way. He made up his mind to leap off the roof right on to the men, and to rescue poor Nobby if he could.

Nobby gave an anguished yell as Lou gave him a flick with his leather belt – but before Julian could jump down to help him, somebody else bounded up! Somebody who bared his teeth and made ugly animal noises of rage, somebody whose arms were far stronger than either Lou's or Dan's – somebody who loved poor Nobby, and wasn't going to let him be beaten any more!

It was Pongo. The chimpanzee had been watching the scene with his sharp little eyes. He had still hidden himself in the bush, for he was afraid of Lou and Dan – but now, hearing Nobby's cries, he leapt out of the brambles and flung himself on the astonished men.

He bit Lou's arm hard. Then he bit Dan's leg. The men yelled loudly, much more loudly than poor Nobby had. Lou lashed out with his leather belt, and it caught Pongo on the shoulder. The chimpanzee made a shrill chattering noise, and leapt on Lou with his arms open, clasping the man to him, trying to bite his throat.

Tiger Dan rushed down the hill at top speed, terrified of the angry chimpanzee. Lou yelled to Nobby:

'Call him off! He'll kill me!'

'Pongo!' shouted Nobby. 'Stop it! Pongo! Come here.'

Pongo gave Nobby a look of the greatest surprise. 'What!' he seemed to say, 'you won't let me punish this bad man who beat you? Well, well – whatever you say must be right!'

And the chimpanzee, giving Lou one last vicious nip, let the man go. Lou followed Dan down the hill at top speed, and Julian heard him crashing through the bushes as if a hundred chimpanzees were after him.

Nobby sat down, trembling. Pongo, not quite sure if his beloved friend was angry with him or not, crept up to him, putting a paw on the boy's knee. Nobby put his arm round the anxious animal, and Pongo chattered with joy.

Julian slid down from the roof of the caravan and went to Nobby. He, too, sat down beside him. He put his arm round the trembling boy and gave him a hug.

'I was just coming to give you a hand, when Pongo shot up the hill,' he said.

'Were you really?' said Nobby, his face lighting up. 'You're a real friend, you are. Good as Pongo, here.'

And Julian felt quite proud to be ranked in bravery with the chimpanzee!

16 A surprising discovery

'Listen – somebody's coming!' said Nobby, and Pongo gave an ugly growl. The sound of voices could be heard coming up the hill. Then a dog barked.

'It's all right. It's Timmy – and the others,' said Julian, unspeakably glad to welcome them back. He stood up and yelled.

'All right! Come along!'

George, Timmy, Dick and Anne came running up the track. 'Hallo!' shouted Dick. 'We thought it would be safe, because we saw Lou and Dan in the distance, running along at the bottom of the hill. I say – there's Pongo!'

Pongo shook hands with Dick, and then went to the back of Timmy, to shake hands with his tail. But Timmy was ready for him, and backing round, he held out his paw to Pongo instead. It was very funny to see the two animals solemnly shaking hands with one another.

'Hallo, Nobby!' said Dick. 'Goodness – what have you been doing to yourself! You look as if you've been in the wars.'

'Well, I have, rather,' said Nobby, with a feeble grin. He was very much shaken, and did not get up. Pongo ran to Anne and tried to put his arms round her.

'Oh, Pongo – you squeeze too hard,' said Anne. 'Julian, did anything happen? Did the men come? Have you any news?'

'Plenty,' said Julian. 'But what I want first is a jolly good drink. I've had none all day. Ginger-beer, I think.'

'We're all thirsty. I'll get five bottles – no, six, because I expect Pongo would like some.'

Pongo loved ginger-beer. He sat down with the children on the rocky ledge, and took his glass from Anne just like a child. Timmy was a little jealous, but as he didn't like ginger-beer he couldn't make a fuss.

Julian began to tell the others about his day, and how he had hidden on the caravan roof. He described how the men had come – and had gone under the caravan – and then moved it. They all listened with wide eyes. What a story!

Then Nobby told his part. 'I butted in and almost gave the game away,' he said, when Julian had got as far as the men falling asleep and snoring. 'But, you see, I had to come and warn you. Lou and Dan swear they'll poison Timmy somehow, even if they have to dope him, put him into a sack and take him down to the camp to do it. Or they might knock him on the head.'

'Let them try!' said George, in her fiercest voice, and put her arm round Timmy. Pongo at once put his arm round Timmy too.

'And they said they'd damage your caravans too – maybe put a fire underneath and burn them up,' went on Nobby.

The four children stared at him in horror. 'But they wouldn't do a thing like that, surely?' said Julian, at last. 'They'd get into trouble with the police if they did.'

'Well, I'm just telling you what they said,' Nobby went on. 'You don't know Lou and Tiger Dan like I do. They'll stick at nothing to get their way – or to get anybody *out* of their way. They tried to poison Timmy, didn't they? And poor old Barker got it instead.'

'Is – is Barker – all right?' asked Anne.

'No,' said Nobby. 'He's dying, I think. I've given him to Lucilla to dose. She's a marvel with sick animals. I've put Growler with the other dogs. He's safe with them.'

He stared round at the other children, his mouth trembling, sniffing as if he had a bad cold.

'I dursent go back,' he said, in a low voice, 'I dursent. They'll half kill me.'

'You're not going back, so that's settled,' said Julian, in a brisk voice. 'You're staying here with us. We shall love to have you. It was jolly decent of you to come up and warn us – and bad luck to have got caught like that. You're our friend now – and we'll stick together.'

Nobby couldn't say a word, but his face shone. He rubbed a dirty hand across his eyes, then grinned his old grin. He nodded his head, not trusting himself to speak, and the children all thought how nice he was. Poor old Nobby.

They finished their ginger-beer and then Julian got up. 'And now,' he said, 'we will do a little exploring and find out where those men went, shall we?'

'Oh, yes!' cried George, who had sat still quite long enough. 'We *must* find out! Do we have to get under the caravan, Julian?'

''Fraid so,' said Julian. 'You sit there quietly, Nobby, and keep guard in case Lou or Dan come back.'

He didn't think for a moment that they would, but he could see that Nobby needed to sit quietly for a while. Nobby, however, had different ideas. He was going to share this adventure!

'Timmy's guard enough, and so is Pongo,' he said. 'They'll hear anyone coming half a mile away. I'm in on this!'

And he was. He went scrabbling underneath the low-swung base of the caravan with the others, eager to find out anything he could.

But it was impossible to explore down in the heather, with the caravan base just over their heads. They had no room at all. Like Dan and Lou they soon felt that they would have to move the van.

It took all five of them, with Pongo giving a shove, too, to move the caravan a few feet away. Then down they dropped to the thick carpet of heather again.

The tufts came up easily by the roots, because the men had already pulled them up once that day and then replanted them. The children dragged up a patch of heather about five feet square, and then gave an exclamation.

'Look! Boards under the heather!'

'Laid neatly across and across. What for?'

'Pull them up!'

The boys pulled up the planks one by one and piled them on one side. Then they saw that the boards had closed up the entrance of a deep hole. 'I'll get my torch,' said Julian. He fetched it and flashed it on.

The light showed them a dark hole, going down into the hillside, with footholds sticking out of one side. They all sat and gazed down in excitement.

'To think we went and put our caravan *exactly* over the entrance of the men's hiding-place!' said Dick. 'No wonder they were wild! No wonder they changed their minds and told us we could go down to the lake and camp there instead of here!'

'Gosh!' said Julian, staring into the hole. 'So that's where the men went! Where does it lead to? They were down there a mighty long time. They were clever enough to replace the planks and drag some of the heather over them, too, to hide them when they went down.'

Pongo suddenly took it into his head to go down the hole. Down he went, feeling for the footholds with his hairy feet, grinning up at the others. He

disappeared at the bottom. Julian's torch could not pick him out at all.

'Hey, Pongo! Don't lose yourself down there!' called Nobby, anxiously. But Pongo had gone.

'Blow him!' said Nobby. 'He'll never find his way back, if he goes wandering about underground. I'll have to go after him. Can I have your torch, Julian?'

'I'll come too,' said Julian. 'George, get me your torch as well, will you?'

'It's broken,' said George. 'I dropped it last night. And nobody else has got one.'

'What an awful nuisance!' said Julian. 'I want us to go and explore down there – but we can't with only one torch. Well, I'll just go down with Nobby and get Pongo – have a quick look round and come back. I may see something worth seeing!'

Nobby went down first, and Julian followed, the others all kneeling round the hole, watching them enviously. They disappeared.

'Pongo!' yelled Nobby. 'Pongo! Come here, you idiot!'

Pongo had not gone very far. He didn't like the dark down there very much, and he came to Nobby as soon as he saw the light of the torch. The boys found themselves in a narrow passage at the bottom of the hole, which widened as they went further into the hill.

'Must be caves somewhere,' said Julian, flashing his torch round. 'We know that a lot of springs run out of this hill. I dare say that through the cen-

168

turies the water has eaten away the softer stuff and made caves and tunnels everywhere in the hill. And somewhere in a cave Lou and Dan store away things they don't want anyone to know about. Stolen goods, probably.'

The passage ended in a small cave that seemed to have no other opening out if it at all. There was nothing in it. Julian flashed his torch up and down the walls.

He saw footholds up one part, and traced them to a hole in the roof, which must have been made, years before, by running water. 'That's the way we go!' he said. 'Come on.'

'Wait!' said Nobby. 'Isn't your torch getting rather faint?'

'Goodness – yes!' said Julian in alarm, and shook his torch violently to make the light brighter. But the battery had almost worn out, and no better light came. Instead the light grew even fainter, until it was just a pin-prick in the torch.

'Come on – we'd better get back at once,' said Julian, feeling a bit scared. 'I don't want to wan-

der about here in the pitch dark. Not my idea of fun at all.'

Nobby took firm hold of Pongo's hairy paw and equally firm hold of Julian's jersey. He didn't mean to lose either of them! The light in the torch went out completely. Now they must find their way back in black darkness.

Julian felt round for the beginning of the passage that led back to the hole. He found it and made his way up it, feeling the sides with his hands. It wasn't a pleasant experience at all, and Julian was thankful that he and Nobby had only gone a little way into the hill. It would have been like a nightmare if they had gone well in, and then found themselves unable to see the way back.

They saw a faint light shining further on and guessed it was the daylight shining down the entrance-hole. They stumbled thankfully towards it. They looked up and saw the anxious faces of the other three peering down at them, unable to see them.

'We're back!' called Julian, beginning to climb

'If you're going on an adventure, I'm coming, too.'

up. 'My torch went out, and we daren't go very far. We've got Pongo, though.'

The others helped to pull them out at the top of the hole. Julian told them about the hole in the roof of the little cave.

'That's where the men went,' he said. 'And tomorrow, when we've all bought torches, and matches and candles, that's where we're going, too! We'll go down to the town and buy what we want, and come back and do a Really Good Exploration!'

17 Another visit from Lou and Dan

Nobody disturbed the children that night, and Timmy did not bark once. Nobby slept on a pile of rugs in the boys' caravan, and Pongo cuddled up to him. The chimpanzee seemed delighted at staying with the caravanners. Timmy was rather jealous that another animal should be with them, and wouldn't take any notice of Pongo at all.

The next morning, after breakfast, the children discussed who was to go down to the town. 'Not Nobby and Pongo, because they wouldn't be allowed in the bus together,' said Julian. 'They had better stay behind.'

'Not by ourselves?' said Nobby, looking alarmed. 'Suppose Lou and Uncle Dan come up? Even if I've got Pongo I'd be scared.'

'Well, I'll stay here, too,' said Dick. 'We don't all need to go to buy torches. Don't forget to post that letter to Daddy and Mother, Julian.'

They had written a long letter to their parents, telling them of the exciting happenings. Julian put it into his pocket. 'I'll post it all right,' he said. 'Well, I suppose we might as well go now. Come on, girls. Keep a look-out, Dick, in case those rogues come back.'

George, Timmy, Anne and Julian went down the hill together, Timmy running on in front, his tail wagging nineteen to the dozen. Pongo climbed up to the roof of the red caravan to watch them go. Nobby and Dick sat down in the warm sun on the ledge, their heads resting on springy clumps of heather.

'It's nice up here,' said Nobby. 'Much nicer than down below. I wonder what everyone is thinking about Pongo and me. I bet Mr Gorgio, the head of the circus, is wild that the chimpanzee's gone. I bet he'll send up to fetch us.'

Nobby was right. Two people were sent up to get him – Lou and Tiger Dan. They came creeping up through the bracken and heather, keeping a sharp eye for Timmy or Pongo.

Pongo sensed them long before they could be seen and warned Nobby. Nobby went very pale. He was terrified of the two scoundrels.

'Get into one of the caravans,' said Dick in a low voice. 'Go on. I'll deal with those fellows – if it *is* them. Pongo will help me if necessary.'

Nobby scuttled into the green caravan and shut the door. Dick sat where he was. Pongo squatted on the roof of the caravan, watching.

Lou and Dan suddenly appeared. They saw Dick, but did not see Pongo. They looked all round for the others.

'What do you want?' said Dick.

'Nobby and Pongo,' said Lou with a scowl. 'Where are they?'

'There're going to stay on with us,' said Dick.

'Oh, no, they're not!' said Tiger Dan. 'Nobby's in my charge, see? I'm his uncle.'

'Funny sort of uncle,' remarked Dick. 'How's that dog you poisoned, by the way?'

Tiger Dan went purple in the face. He looked as if he would willingly have thrown Dick down the hill.

'You be careful what you say to me!' he said, beginning to shout.

'We're going to have an adventure after all,' said Anne, in rather a small voice.

''Fraid so,' said Julian. 'But you can stay at the farm with Mrs Mackie for the day, Anne dear. Don't you come with us.'

'If you're going on an adventure, I'm coming, too,' said Anne. 'So there! I wouldn't *dream* of not coming.'

'All right,' said Julian. 'We'll all go together. Golly, things are getting exciting!'

Nobby, hidden in the caravan, trembled when he heard his uncle's angry yell. Pongo kept quite still, his face set and ugly.

'Well, you may as well say good-bye and go,' said Dick in a calm voice to Dan. 'I've told you that Nobby and Pongo are staying with us for the present.'

'Where *is* Nobby?' demanded Tiger Dan, looking as if he would burst with rage at any moment. 'Wait till I get my hands on him. Wait . . .'

He began to walk towards the caravans – but Pongo was not having any of that! He leapt straight off the roof on to the horrified man, and flung him to the ground. He made such a terrible snarling noise that Dan was terrified.

'Call him off!' he yelled. 'Lou, come and help.'

'Pongo won't obey *me*,' said Dick, still sitting down looking quite undisturbed. 'You'd better go before he bites big pieces out of you.'

Dan staggered to the rock ledge, looking as if he would box Dick's ears. But the boy did not move, and somehow Dan did not dare to touch him. Pongo let him go and stood glowering at him, his great hairy arms hanging down his sides, ready to fly at either of the men if they came near.

Tiger Dan picked up a stone – and as quick as lightning Pongo flung himself on him again and sent the man rolling down the hill. Lou fled in terror. Dan got up and fled, too, yelling furiously as he went. Pongo chased them in delight. He, too, picked up stones and flung them with a very accurate aim, so that Dick kept hearing yells of pain.

Pongo came back, looking extremely pleased with himself. He went to the green caravan, as Dick shouted to Nobby:

'All right, Nobby. They've gone. Pongo and I won the battle!'

Nobby came out. Pongo put his arm round him at once and chattered nonsense in his ear. Nobby looked rather ashamed of himself.

'Bit of a coward, aren't I?' he said. 'Leaving you out here all alone.'

'I enjoyed it,' said Dick truthfully. 'And I'm sure Pongo did!'

'You don't know what dangerous fellows Lou and Dan are,' said Nobby, looking down the hillside to make sure the men were really gone. 'I tell you they'd stick at nothing. They'd burn your caravans, hurl them down the hill, poison your dog, and do what harm they could to you, too. You don't know them like I do!'

'Well, as a matter of fact, we've had some pretty exciting adventures with men just as tough as Dan and Lou,' said Dick. 'We always seem to be falling into the middle of some adventure or other. Now, last hols we went to a place called Smuggler's Top – and, my word, the adventures we had there! You wouldn't believe them!'

'You tell me and Pongo,' said Nobby, sitting down beside Dick. 'We've plenty of time before the others come back.'

So Dick began to tell the tale of all the other thrilling adventures that the five of them had had, and the time flew. Both boys were surprised when they heard Timmy barking down the track, and knew that the others were back.

George came tearing up with Timmy at her heels. 'Are you all right? Did anything happen while we were away? Do you know, we saw Lou and Tiger Dan getting on the bus when we got off it! They were carrying bags as if they meant to go away and stay somewhere.'

Nobby brightened up at once. 'Did you really? Good! They came up here, you know, and Pongo chased them down the hill. They must have gone back to the camp, collected their bags, and gone to catch the bus. Hurrah!'

'We've got fine torches,' said Julian, and showed Dick his. 'Powerful ones. Here's one for you, Dick – and one for you, Nobby.'

'Oooh – thanks,' said Nobby. Then he went red. 'I haven't got enough money to pay you for such a grand torch,' he said awkwardly.

'It's a present for you,' said Anne at once, 'a present for a friend of ours, Nobby!'

'Coo! Thanks awfully,' said Nobby, looking quite overcome. 'I've never had a present before. You're decent kids, you are.'

Pongo held out his hand to Anne and made a chattering noise as if to say: 'What about one for me, too?'

'Oh – we didn't bring one for Pongo!' said Anne. 'Why ever didn't we?'

'Good thing you didn't, said Nobby. 'He would have put it on and off all day long and wasted the battery in no time!'

'I'll give him my old torch,' said George. 'It's broken, but he won't mind that!'

Pongo was delighted with it. He kept pressing down the knob that should make the light flash – and when there was no light he looked all about on the ground as if the light must have dropped out! The children roared at him. He liked them to laugh at him. He did a little dance all round them to show how pleased he was.

'Look here – wouldn't it be a jolly good time to explore underground now that we know Lou and Dan are safely out of the way?' asked Julian suddenly. 'If they've got bags with them, surely that means they're going to spend the night somewhere and won't be back till tomorrow at least. We'd be quite safe to go down and explore.'

'Yes, we would,' said George eagerly. 'I'm longing to get down there and Make Discoveries!'

'Well, let's have something to eat first,' said Dick. 'It's long past our dinner-time. It must be about half-past one. Yes, it is!'

'George and I will get you a meal,' said Anne. 'We called at the farm on our way up and got a lovely lot of food. Come on, George.'

George got up unwillingly. Timmy followed her, sniffing expectantly. Soon the two girls were busy getting a fine meal ready, and they all sat on the rocky ledge to eat it.

'Mrs Mackie gave us this enormous bar of chocolate for a present today,' said Anne, showing a great slab to Dick and Nobby. 'Isn't it lovely? No, Pongo, it's not for you. Eat your sandwiches properly, and don't grab.'

'I vote we take some food down into the hill with us,' said Julian. 'We may be quite a long time down there, and we shan't want to come back at tea-time.'

'Oooh – a picnic inside the hill!' said Anne. 'That would be thrilling. I'll soon pack up some food in the kit-bag. I won't bother to make sandwiches. We'll take a new loaf, butter, ham and a cake, and cut what we want. What about something to drink?'

'Oh, we can last out till we get back,' said Julian. 'Just take something to eat to keep us going till we have finished exploring.'

George and Nobby cleared up and rinsed the plates. Anne wrapped up some food in greased paper, and packed it carefully into the kitbag for Julian to carry. She popped the big bar of chocolate into the bag, too. It would be nice to eat at odd moments.

At last they were all ready. Timmy wagged his tail. He knew they were going somewhere.

The five of them pushed the caravan back a few feet to expose the hole. They had all tugged the van back into place the night before, in case Lou and Dan came to go down the hole again. No one could get down it if the caravan was over it.

The boards had been laid roughly across the hole and the boys took them off, tossing them to one side. As soon as Pongo saw the hole he drew back, frightened.

'He's remembered the darkness down there,' said George. 'He doesn't like it. Come on, Pongo. You'll be all right. We've all got torches!'

But nothing would persuade Pongo to go down that hole again. He cried like a baby when Nobby tried to make him.

'It's no good,' said Julian. 'You'll have to stop up here with him.'

'What – and miss all the excitement?' cried Nobby indignantly. 'I jolly well won't. We can tie old Pongo up to a wheel of the van so that he won't wander off. Lou and Dan are away somewhere, and no one else is likely to tackle a big chimp like Pongo. We'll tie him up.'

So Pongo was tied firmly to one of the caravan wheels. 'You stay there like a good chimp till we come back,' said Nobby, putting a pail of water beside him in case he should want a drink. 'We'll be back soon!'

Pongo was sad to see them go – but nothing would have made him go down that hole again! So he sat watching the children disappear one by one. Timmy jumped down, too, and then they were all gone. Gone on another adventure. What would happen now?

18 Inside the hill

The children had all put on extra jerseys, by Julian's orders, for he knew it would be cold inside the dark hill. Nobby had been lent an old one of Dick's. They were glad of them as soon as they were walking down the dark passage that led to the first cave, for the air was very chilly.

They came to the small cave and Julian flashed his torch to show them where the footholds went up the wall to a hole in the roof.

'It's exciting,' said George, thrilled. 'I like this sort of thing. Where does that hole in the roof lead to, I wonder? I'll go first, Ju.'

'No, you won't,' said Julian firmly. 'I go first. You don't know what might be at the top!'

Up he went, his torch held in his mouth, for he needed both hands to climb. The footholds were strong nails driven into the rock of the cave-wall, and were fairly easy to climb.

He got to the hole in the roof and popped his head through. He gave a cry of astonishment.

'I say! There's a most ENORMOUS cavern here – bigger than six dance-halls – and the walls are all glittering with something – phosphorescence, I should think.'

He scrambled out of the hole and stood on the floor of the immense cave. Its walls twinkled in their queer light, and Julian shut off his torch. There was almost enough phosphorescent light in the cavern to see by!

One by one the others came up and stared in wonder. 'It's like Aladdin's cave!' said Anne. 'Isn't that a queer light shining from the walls – and from the roof, too, Julian?'

Dick and George had rather a difficulty in getting Timmy up to the cavern, but they managed it at last. Timmy put his tail down at once when he saw the curious light gleaming everywhere. But it went up again when George patted him.

'What an enormous place!' said Dick. 'Do you suppose this is where the men hide their stuff, whatever it is?'

Julian flashed his torch on again and swung it round and about, picking out the dark, rocky corners. 'Can't see anything hidden,' he said. 'But we'd better explore the cave properly before we go on.'

So the five children explored every nook and cranny of the gleaming cave, but could find nothing at all. Julian gave a sudden exclamation and picked something up from the floor.

'A cigarette end!' he said 'That shows that Lou and Dan have been here. Come on, let's see if there's a way out of this great cave.'

Right at the far end, half-way up the gleaming wall, was a large hole, rather like a tunnel. Julian climbed up to it and called to the others. 'This is the way they went. There's a dead match just at the entrance to the tunnel or whatever this is.'

It was a curious tunnel, no higher than their shoulders in some places, and it wound about as it went further into the hill. Julian thought that at one time water must have run through it. But it was quite dry now. The floor of the tunnel was worn very smooth, as if a stream had hollowed it out through many, many years.

'I hope the stream won't take it into its head to begin running suddenly again!' said George. 'We should get jolly wet!'

The tunnel went on for some way, and Anne was beginning to feel it must go on for ever. Then the wall at one side widened out and made a big rocky shelf. Julian, who was first, flashed his torch into the hollow.

'I say!' he shouted. 'Here's where those fellows keep their stores! There's a whole pile of things here!'

The others crowded up as closely as they could, each of them flashing their torch brightly. On the wide, rocky shelf lay boxes and packages, sacks and cases. The children stared at them. 'What's in them?' said Nobby, full of intense curiosity. 'Let's see!'

He put down his torch and undid a sack. He slid in his hand – and brought it out holding a piece of shining gold plate!

'Coo!' said Nobby. 'So that's what the police were after last year when they came and searched the camp! And it was hidden safely here. Coo, look at all these things. Jumping Jiminy, they must have robbed the Queen herself!'

The sack was full of exquisite pieces of gold plate – cups, dishes, small trays. The children set them all out on the ledge. How they gleamed in the light of their torches!

'They're thieves in a very big way.' said Julian. 'No doubt about that. Let's look in this box.'

The box was not locked, and the lid opened easily. Inside was a piece of china, a vase so fragile that it looked as if it might break at a breath!

'Well, I don't know anything about china,' said Julian, 'but I suppose this is a very precious piece, worth thousands of pounds. A collector of china would probably give a very large sum for it. What rogues Lou and Dan are!'

'Look here!' suddenly said George, and she pulled leather boxes out of a bag. 'Jewellery!'

She opened the boxes. The children exclaimed in awe. Diamonds flashed brilliantly, rubies glowed, emeralds shone green. Necklaces, bracelets, rings, brooches – beautiful things gleamed in the light of the five torches.

There was a tiara in one box that seemed to be made only of big diamonds. Anne picked it out of its box gently. Then she put it on her hair.

'I'm a princess! It's my crown!' she said.

'You look lovely,' said Nobby, admiringly. 'You look as grand as Delphine the Bareback Rider when she goes into the ring on her horse, with jewels shining all over her!'

Anne put on necklaces and bracelets and sat there on the ledge like a little princess, shining brightly in the magnificent jewels. Then she took them off and put them carefully back into their satin-lined boxes.

'Well – what a haul those two rogues have made!' said Julian, pulling out some gleaming silver plate from another package. 'They must be very fine burglars!'

'I know how they work,' said Dick. 'Lou's a wonderful acrobat, isn't he? I bet he does all the climbing about up walls and over roofs and into windows – and Tiger Dan stands below and catches everything he throws down.'

'You're about right,' said Nobby, handling a beautiful silver cup. 'Lou could climb anywhere – up ivy, up pipes – even up the bare wall of a house, I shouldn't wonder! And jump! He can jump like a cat. He and Tiger Dan have been in this business for a long time, I expect. That's where Uncle Dan went at night, of course, when we were on tour, and I woke up and found him gone out of the caravan!'

'And I expect he stores the stolen goods in that wagon of his you showed us,' said Julian, remembering. 'You told us how angry he was with you once when you went and rummaged about in it. He probably stored it there, and then he and Lou came up here each year and hid the stuff underground – waiting till the police had given up the search for the stolen things – and then they come and get it and sell it somewhere safe.'

'A jolly clever plan,' said Dick. 'What a fine chance they've got – wandering about from place to place like that hearing of famous jewels or plate – slipping out at night – and Lou climbing up to bedrooms like a cat. I wonder how they found this place – it's a most wonderful hidey-hole!'

'Yes. Nobody would ever dream of it!' said George.

'And then we go and put our caravan bang on the top of the entrance – just when they want to put something in and take something out!' said Julian. 'I *must* have annoyed them.'

'What are we going to do about it?' said Dick.

'Tell the police, of course,' said Julian, promptly. 'What do you suppose? My word, I'd like to see the face of the policeman who first sees this little haul.'

They put everything back carefully. Julian shone his torch up the tunnel. 'Shall we explore a bit further, or not?' he said. 'It still goes on. Look!'

'Better get back,' said Nobby. 'Now we've found this we'd better do something about it.'

'Oh, let's just see where the tunnel goes to,' said George. 'It won't take a minute!'

'All right,' said Julian, who wanted to go up the

tunnel as much as she did. He led the way, his torch shining brightly.

The tunnel came out into another cave, not nearly as big as the one they had left behind. At one end something gleamed like silver, and seemed to move. There was a curious sound there, too.

'What is it?' said Anne, alarmed. They stood and listened.

'Water!' said Julian, suddenly. 'Of course! Can't you hear it flowing along? It's an underground stream, flowing through the hill to find an opening where it can rush out.'

'Like that stream we saw before we came to our caravan camping-place,' said George. 'It rushed out of the hill. Do you remember? This may be the very one!'

'I expect it is!' said Dick. They went over to it and watched it. It rushed along in its own hollowed out channel, close to the side of the cave-wall.

'Maybe at one time it ran across this cave and down the tunnel we came up by,' said Julian. 'Yes, look – there's a big kind of groove in the floor of the cave here – the stream must have run there once. Then for some reason it went a different way.'

'Let's get back,' said Nobby. 'I want to know if Pongo's all right. I don't somehow feel very comfortable about him. And I'm jolly cold, too. Let's go back to the sunshine and have something to eat.

I don't want a picnic down here, after all.'

'All right,' said Julian, and they made their way back through the tunnel. They passed the rock shelf on which lay the treasure, and came at last to the enormous gleaming cavern. They went across it to the hole that led down into the small cave. Down they went, Julian and George trying to manage Timmy between them. But it was very awkward, for he was a big dog.

Then along the passage to the entrance-hole. They all felt quite pleased at the idea of going up into the sunshine again.

'Can't see any daylight shining down the hole,' said Julian puzzled. 'It would be near here.'

He came up against a blank wall, and was surprised. Where was the hole? Had they missed their way? Then he flashed his torch above him and saw the hole there – but there was no daylight shining in!

'I say!' said Julian, in horror. 'I say! What do you think's happened?'

'What?' asked everyone, in panic.

'The hole is closed!' said Julian. 'We can't get out! Somebody's been along and put those planks across – and I bet they've put the caravan over them, too. We can't get out!'

Everyone stared up at the closed entrance in dismay. They were prisoners.

'Whatever are we to do?' said George. 'Julian – what *are* we going to do?'

Everyone stared at the closed entrance in dismay.

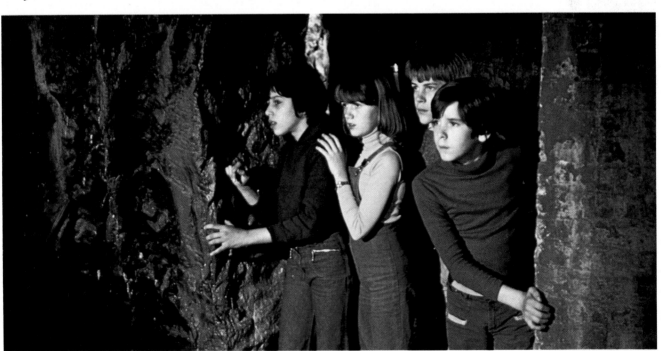

19 Prisoners underground

Julian didn't answer. He was angry with himself for not thinking that this might happen! Although Lou and Dan had been seen getting on the bus with bags, they might easily not have been spending the night away – the bags might contain things they wanted to sell – stolen goods of some kind.

'They came back quickly – and came up the hill, I suppose, to have another try at getting Nobby and Pongo back,' said Julian, out loud. 'What an idiot I am to leave things to chance like that. Well – I'll have a try at shifting these planks. I should be able to, with luck.'

He did his best, and did shift them to a certain extent – but, as he feared, the caravan had been run back over the hole, and even if he managed to shift some of the planks it was impossible to make a way out.

'Perhaps Pongo can help,' he said suddenly. He shouted loudly: 'Pongo! Pongo! Come and help!'

Everyone stood still, hoping that they would hear Pongo chattering somewhere near, or scraping at the planks above. But there was no sign or sound of Pongo.

Everyone called, but it was no use. Pongo didn't come. What had happened to him? Poor Nobby felt very worried.

'I wish I knew what has happened,' he kept saying. 'I feel as if something horrid has happened to poor old Pongo. Where can he be?'

Pongo was not very far away. He was lying on his side, his head bleeding. He was quite unconscious, and could not hear the frantic calls of the children at all. Poor Pongo!

What Julian had feared had actually happened. Lou and Dan had come back up the hill, bringing money with them to tempt Nobby and Pongo back. When they had got near to the hollow, they had stood still and called loudly.

'Nobby! Nobby! We've come to make friends, not to hurt you! We've got money for you. Be a sensible boy and come back to the camp. Mr Gorgio is asking for you.'

When there had been no reply at all, the men had gone nearer. Then they had seen Pongo and had stopped. The chimpanzee could not get at them because he was tied up. He sat there snarling.

'Where have those kids gone?' asked Lou. Then he saw that the caravan had been moved back a little, and he at once guessed.

'They've found the way underground! The interfering little brutes! See, they've moved one of the caravans off the hole. What do we do *now*!'

'This first,' said Tiger Dan, in a brutal voice, and he picked up an enormous stone. He threw it with all his force at poor Pongo, who tried to leap out of the way. But the rope prevented him, and the stone hit him full on the head.

He gave a loud scream and fell down at once, lying quite still.

'You've gone and killed him,' said Lou.

'So much the better!' said Tiger Dan. 'Now let's go and see if the entrance-hole is open. Those kids want their necks wringing!'

They went to the hollow and saw at once that the hole had been discovered, opened, and that the children must have gone down it.

'They're down there now,' said Tiger Dan, almost choking with rage. 'Shall we go down and deal with them – and get our stuff and clear off? We meant to clear off tomorrow, anyway. We might as well get the stuff out now.'

'What – in the daylight – with any of the farm men about to see us?' said Lou with a sneer. 'Clever, aren't you?'

'Well, have you got a better idea?' asked Tiger Dan.

'Why not follow our plan?' said Lou. 'Go down when it's dark and collect the stuff. We can bring our wagon up as we planned to do tonight. We don't need to bother about forcing the children to go now – they're underground – and we can make them prisoners till we're ready to clear off!'

'I see,' said Dan, and he grinned suddenly, showing his ugly teeth. 'Yes – we'll close up the hole and run the caravan back over it – and come up tonight in the dark with the wagon – go down – collect everything – and shut the hole again with the children in it. We'll send a card to Gorgio when we're safe and tell him to go up and set the kids free.'

'Why bother to do that?' said Lou, in a cruel voice. 'Let 'em starve underground, the interfering little beasts. Serve 'em right.'

'Can't do that,' said Dan. 'Have the police after

us worse than ever. We'll have to chuck some food down the hole, to keep them going till they're set free. No good starving them, Lou. There'd be an awful outcry if we do anything like that.'

The two men carefully put back the boards over the top of the hole and replaced the heather tufts. Then they ran the caravan back over the place. They looked at Pongo. The chimpanzee was still lying on his side, and the men could see what a nasty wound he had on his head.

'He ain't dead,' said Lou, and gave him a kick. 'He'll come round all right. Better leave him here. He might come to himself if we carried him back to camp, and fight us. He can't do us any harm tonight, tied up like that.'

They went away down the track. Not ten minutes afterwards the children came to the hole and found it blocked up! If only they hadn't stopped to explore that tunnel a bit further, they would have been able to get out and set Timmy on the two men.

But it was too late now. The hole was well and truly closed. No one could get out. No one could find poor Pongo and bathe his head. They were real prisoners.

They didn't like it at all. Anne began to cry, though she tried not to let the others see her. Nobby saw that she was upset, and put his arm round her.

'Don't cry, little Anne,' he said. 'We'll be all right.'

'It's no good staying here,' said Julian, at last. 'We might as well go somewhere more comfortable, and sit down and talk and eat. I'm hungry.'

They all went back down the passage, up through the hole in the roof, and into the enormous cavern. They found a sandy corner and sat down. Julian handed Anne the kit-bag and she undid it to get the food inside.

'Better only have one torch going,' said Julian. 'We don't know how long we'll be here. We don't want to be left in the dark!'

Everybody immediately switched off their torches. The idea of being lost in the dark inside the hill wasn't at all nice! Anne handed out slices of bread and butter, and the children put thin slices of Mrs Mackie's delicious ham on them.

They felt distinctly better when they had all eaten a good meal. 'That was jolly good,' said Dick. 'No, we won't eat the chocolate, Anne. We may want it later on. Golly, I'm thirsty!'

'So am I,' said Nobby. 'My tongue's hanging out like old Timmy's. Let's go and get a drink.'

'Well, there was a stream in that other cave beyond the tunnel, wasn't there?' said Nobby. 'We can drink from that. It'll be all right.'

'Well, I hope it will,' said Julian. 'We were told not to drink water that wasn't boiled while we were caravanning – but we didn't know this sort of thing was going to happen! We'll go through the tunnel and get some water to drink from the stream.'

They made their way through the long, winding tunnel, and passed the shelf of stolen goods. Then on they went and came out into the cave through which the stream rushed so quickly. They dipped in their hands and drank thirstily. The water tasted lovely – so clear and cold.

Timmy drank too. He was puzzled at this adventure, but so long as he was with George he was happy. If his mistress suddenly took it into her head to live underground like a worm, that was all right – so long as Timmy was with her!

'I wonder if this stream *does* go to that hole in the hillside, and pours out there?' said Julian, suddenly. 'If it does, and we could follow it, we might be able to squeeze out.'

'We'd get terribly wet, said George, 'but that wouldn't matter. Let's see if we can follow the water.'

They went to where the stream disappeared into a tunnel rather like the dry one they had come along. Julian shone his torch into it.

'We could wade along, I think,' he said. 'It is very fast but not very deep. I know – I'll go along it myself and see where it goes, and come back and tell you.'

'No,' said George, at once. 'If you go, we all go. You might get separated from us. That would be awful.'

'All right,' said Julian. 'I thought there was no sense in us all getting wet, that's all. Come on, we'll try now.'

One by one they waded into the stream. The current tugged at their legs, for the water ran very fast. But it was only just above their knees there. They waded along by the light of their torches, wondering where the tunnel would lead to.

Timmy half-waded, half-swam. He didn't like this water-business very much. It seemed silly to him. He pushed ahead of Julian and then a little farther down, jumped up to a ledge that ran beside the water.

'Good idea, Tim,' said Julian, and he got up on

to it too. He had to crouch down rather as he walked because his head touched the roof of the tunnel if he didn't – but at least his legs were out of the icy-cold water! All the others did the same, and as long as the ledge ran along beside the stream they all walked along it.

But at times it disappeared and then they had to wade in the water again, which now suddenly got deeper. 'Gracious! It's almost to my waist,' said Anne. 'I hope it doesn't get any deeper. I'm holding my clothes up as high as I can, but they'll get soaked soon.'

Fortunately the water got no deeper, but it seemed to go faster. 'We're going down hill a bit,' said Julian at last. 'Perhaps we are getting near to where it pours out of the hill.'

They were! Some distance ahead of him Julian suddenly saw a dim light, and wondered whatever it could be. He soon knew! It was daylight creeping in through the water that poured out of the hole in the hillside – poured out in a torrent into the sunshine.

'We're almost there!' cried Julian. 'Come on.'

20 More excite-ment

It was a very sad and disappointed little company that made their way back to the cave. Along the tunnel they went, painfully and slowly, for it was not so easy against the current. Julian shivered; he was wet through with trying to swim.

At last they were back in the cave through which the stream flowed so swiftly. 'Let's run round and round it to get warm,' said Julian. 'I'm frozen. Dick, let me have one of your dry jerseys. I must take off these wet ones.'

The children ran round and round the cave, pretending to race one another, trying to get warm. They did get warm in the end, and sank down in a heap on some soft sand in a corner, panting. They sat there for a little while to get their breath.

Then they heard something. Timmy heard it

With light hearts the children waded along in the water. Now they would soon be out in the warm sunshine. They would find Pongo, and race down the hill in the warmth, catch the first bus, and go to the police station.

But nothing like that happened at all. To their enormous disappointment the water got far too deep to wade through, and Nobby stopped in fright. 'I dursent go no further,' he said. 'I'm almost off my feet now with the water rushing by.'

'I am too,' said Anne, frightened.

'Perhaps I can swim out,' said Julian, and he struck out. But he gave it up in dismay, for the torrent of water was too much for him, and he was afraid of being hurled against the rocky sides and having his head cracked.

'It's no good,' he said, gloomily. 'No good at all. All that wading for nothing. It's far too dangerous to go any further – and yet daylight is only a few yards ahead. It's too sickening for words.'

'We must go back,' said George. 'I'm afraid Timmy will be drowned if we don't. Oh, dear – we must go all that way back!'

first and growled. 'Jumping Jiminy, what's up with Timmy?' said Nobby, in fright. He was the most easily scared of the children, probably because of the frights he had had the last few days.

They all listened, George with her hand on Timmy's collar. He growled again, softly. The noise they all heard was a loud panting coming from the stream over at the other side of the cave!

'Someone is wading up the stream,' whispered Dick, in astonishment. 'Did they get in at the place where we couldn't get out? They must have!'

'But who is it?' asked Julian. 'Can't be Lou or Dan. They wouldn't come that way when they could come the right way. Sh! Whoever it is, is arriving in the cave. I'll shut off my torch.'

Darkness fell in the cave as the light from Julian's torch was clicked off. They all sat and listened, and poor Nobby shook and shivered. Timmy didn't growl any more, which was surprising. In fact, he even wagged his tail!

There was a sneeze from the other end of the cave – and then soft footsteps padded towards them. Anne felt as if she must scream. WHO was it?

Julian switched on his torch suddenly, and its light fell on a squat, hairy figure, halting in the bright glare. It was Pongo!

'It's *Pongo*!' everyone yelled, and leapt up at once. Timmy ran over to the surprised chimpanzee and sniffed round him in delight. Pongo put his arms round Nobby and Anne.

'Pongo! You've escaped! You must have bitten through your rope!' said Julian. 'How clever you are to find your way through that hole where the stream pours out. How did you know you would find us here? Clever Pongo.'

Then he saw the big wound on poor Pongo's head. 'Oh look!' said Julian. 'He's been hurt! I expect those brutes threw a stone at him. Poor old Pongo.'

'Let's bathe his head,' said Anne. 'I'll use my hanky.'

But Pongo wouldn't let anyone touch his wound, not even Nobby. He didn't snap or snarl at them, but simply held their hands away from him, and refused to leave go. So nobody could bathe his head or bind it up.

'Never mind,' said Nobby at last, 'Animals' wounds often heal up very quickly without any attention at all. He won't let us touch it, that's certain. I expect Lou and Dan hit him with a stone, and knocked him unconscious when they came. They then shut up the hole and made us prisoners. Beasts!'

'I say,' suddenly said Dick. 'I say! I've got an idea. I don't know if it will work – but it really *is* an idea.'

'What?' asked everyone, thrilled.

'Well – what about tying a letter round Pongo's neck and sending him out of the hole again, to take the letter to the camp?' said Dick. 'He won't go to Lou or Dan because he's scared of them – but he'd go to any of the others all right, wouldn't he? Larry would be the best one. He seems to be a good fellow.'

'Would Pongo understand enough to do all that, though?' asked Julian, doubtfully.

'We could try him,' said Nobby. 'I do send him here and there sometimes, just for fun – to take the elephant's bat to Larry, for instance – or to put my coat away in my caravan.'

'Well, we could certainly try,' said Dick. 'I've got a notebook and a pencil. I'll write a note and wrap it up in another sheet, pin it together and tie it round Pongo's neck with a bit of string.'

So he wrote a note. It said:

'To whoever gets this note – please come up the hill to the hollow where there are two caravans. Under the red one is the entrance to an underground passage. We are prisoners inside the hill. Please rescue us soon.

Julian, Dick, George, Anne and Nobby.'

He read it out to the others. Then he tied the note round Pongo's neck. Pongo was surprised, but fortunately did not try to pull it off.

'Now, you give him his orders,' said Dick to Nobby. So Nobby spoke slowly and importantly to the listening chimpanzee.

'Where's Larry? Go to Larry, Pongo. Fetch Larry. Go. GO!'

Pongo blinked at him and made a funny little noise as if he was saying: 'Please, Nobby, I don't want to go.'

Nobby repeated everything again, 'Understand, Pongo? I think you do. GO, then, GO. GO!'

And Pongo turned and went! He disappeared into the stream, splashing along by himself. The children watched him as far as they could by the light of their torches.

'He really is clever,' said Anne. 'He didn't want to go a bit, did he? Oh, I do hope he finds Larry, and that Larry sees the note and reads it and sends someone to rescue us.'

'I hope the note doesn't get all soaked and pulpy in the water,' said Julian, rather gloomily. 'Gosh, I wish I wasn't so cold. Let's run round a bit again, then have a piece of chocolate.'

They ran about and played 'he' for a time till they all felt warm again. Then they decided to sit down and have some chocolate, and play some sort of guessing game to while away the time. Timmy sat close to Julian, and the boy was very glad.

'He's like a big hot-water bottle,' he said. 'Sit closer, Tim. That's right. You'll soon warm me up!'

It was dull after a time, sitting in the light of one torch, for they dared not use them all. Already it seemed as if Julian's torch was getting a little dim. They played all the games they could think of and then yawned.

'What's the time? I suppose it must be getting dark outside now. I feel quite sleepy.'

'It's nine o'clock almost,' said Julian. 'I hope Pongo has got down to the camp all right and found someone. We could expect help quite soon, if so.'

'Well, then, we'd better get along to the passage that leads to the hole,' said Dick, getting up. 'It's quite likely that if Larry or anyone else comes they'll not see the foot-holds leading up the wall out of that first little cave. They might not know where we are!'

This seemed very likely. They all made their way down the tunnel that led past the hidden store of valuables, and came out into the enormous cave. There was a nice sandy corner just by the hole that led down into the first small cave, and the children decided to sit there, rather than in the passage or in the first rocky and uncomfortable little cave. They cuddled up together for warmth, and felt hungry.

Anne and Nobby dozed off to sleep. George almost fell asleep, too. But the boys and Timmy kept awake, and talked in low voices. At least, Timmy didn't talk, but wagged his tail whenever either Dick or Julian said anything. That was his way of joining in their conversation.

After what seemed a long while Timmy growled, and the two boys sat up straight. Whatever it was that Timmy's sharp ears had heard, they had heard nothing at all. And they continued to hear nothing. But Timmy went on growling.

Julian shook the others awake. 'I believe help has come,' he said. 'But we'd better not go and see in case it's Dan and Lou come back. So wake up and look lively!'

They were all wide awake at once. Was it Larry come in answer to their note – or was it those horrid men, Tiger Dan and Lou the acrobat?

They soon knew! A head suddenly poked out of the hole nearby, and a torch shone on them. Timmy growled ferociously and struggled to fly at the head, but George held on firmly to his collar, thinking it might be Larry.

But it wasn't! It was Lou the acrobat, as the children knew only too well when they heard his voice. Julian shone his torch on to him.

'I hope you've enjoyed your little selves,' came Lou's harsh voice. 'And you keep that dog under control, boy, or I'll shoot him. See? I'm not standing no nonsense from that dog this time. Have a look at this here gun!'

To George's horror she saw that Lou was pointing a gun at poor Timmy. She gave a scream and flung herself in front of him. 'Don't you dare to shoot my dog! I'll – I'll – I'll . . .'

She couldn't think of anything bad enough to do to the man who could shoot Timmy, and she stopped, choked by tears of rage and fear. Timmy, not knowing what the gun was, couldn't for the life of him understand why George wouldn't let him get at his enemy – such a nice position, too, with his head poking through a hole like that. Timmy

felt he could deal with that head very quickly.

'Now, you kids, get up and go into that tunnel,' said Lou. 'Go on – go right ahead of me, and don't dare to stop. We've got work to do here tonight, and we're not going to have any more interference from kids like you. See?'

The children saw quite well. They began to walk towards the entrance of the tunnel. One by one they climbed into it. George first with Timmy. She dared not let his collar go for an instant. A few paces behind them came Lou with his revolver, and Dan with a couple of big sacks.

The children were made to walk right past the shelf on which were the hidden goods.

Then Lou sat down in the tunnel, his torch switched on fully so that he could pick out each child. He still pointed his revolver at Timmy.

'Now we'll get on,' he said to Tiger Dan. 'You know what to do. Get on with it.'

Tiger Dan began to stuff the things into one of the big sacks he had brought. He staggered off with it. He came back in about ten minutes and filled the other sack. It was plain that the men meant to take everything away this time.

'Thought you'd made a very fine discovery, didn't you?' said Lou, mockingly, to the children. 'Ho, yes – very smart you were! See what happens to little smarties like you – you're prisoners – and here you'll stay for two or three days!'

'What do you mean?' said Julian, in alarm. 'Surely you wouldn't leave us here to starve?'

'Not to starve. We're too fond of you,' grinned Lou. 'We'll chuck you down some food into the tunnel. And in two or three days maybe someone will come and rescue you.'

Julian wished desperately that Pongo would bring help before Lou and Dan finished their business in the tunnel and went, leaving them prisoners. He watched Tiger Dan, working quickly, packing everything, carrying it off, coming back again, and packing feverishly once more. Lou sat still with his torch and revolver, enjoying the scared faces of the girls and Nobby. Julian and Dick put on a brave show which they were far from feeling.

Tiger Dan staggered away with another sackful. But he hadn't been gone for more than half a minute before a wail echoed through the tunnel.

'Lou! Help! Help! Something's attacking me! HELP.'

Lou rose up and went swiftly down the tunnel. 'It's Pongo, I bet it's old Pongo,' said Julian thrilled.

21 Dick has a great idea!

'Listen,' said Dick, in an urgent voice. 'It may be Pongo by himself – he may not have gone back to the camp at all – he may have wandered about and at last gone down the entrance-hole by the caravans, and come up behind Tiger Dan. If so he won't have much chance because Lou's got a gun and will shoot him. And we shan't be rescued. So I'm going to slip down the tunnel while there's a chance and hide in the big cave.'

'What good will that do?' said Julian.

'Well, idiot, I may be able to slip down into the passage that leads to the entrance hole and hop out without the others seeing me,' said Dick, getting up. 'Then I can fetch help, see? You'd better all clear off somewhere and hide – find a good place, Julian, in case the men come after you when they find one of us is gone. Go on.'

Without another word the boy began to walk down the tunnel, past the rocky shelf on which now very few goods were left, and then came to the enormous cave.

Here there was a great noise going on, for Pongo appeared to have got hold of both men at once! Their torches were out, and Lou did not dare to shoot for fear of hurting Dan. Dick could see very little of this; he could only hear snarlings and shouting. He took a wide course round the heaving heap on the floor and made his way as quickly as he could in the dark to where he thought the hole was that led down into the first passage. He had to go carefully for fear of falling down it. He found it at last and let himself down into the cave below, and then, thinking it safe to switch on his torch in the passage he flashed it in front of him to show him the way.

It wan't long before he was out of the hole and was speeding round the caravans. Then he stopped. A thought struck him. He could fetch help all right – but the men would be gone by then! They had laid their plans for a getaway with all the goods; there was no doubt about that.

Suppose he put the boards over the hole, ramming them in with all his strength, and then rolled some heavy stones on top? He couldn't move the caravan over the boards, for it was far too heavy for a boy to push. But heavy stones would probably do the trick. The men would imagine that it was the caravan overhead again!

In great excitement Dick put back the boards, lugging them into place, panting and puffing. Then he flashed his torch round for stones. There were several small rocks nearby. He could not lift them, but he managed to roll them to the boards. Plonk! They went on to them one by one. Now nobody could move the boards at all.

'I know I've shut the others in with the men,' thought Dick. 'But I hope Julian will find a very safe hiding-place just for a time. Gosh, I'm hot! Now, down the hill I go – and I hope I don't lose my way in the darkness!'

Down below, the two men had at last freed themselves from the angry chimpanzee. They were badly bitten and mauled, but Pongo was not as strong and savage as usual because of his bad head-wound. The men were able to drive him off at last, and he went limping in the direction of the tunnel, sniffing out the children.

He would certainly have been shot if Lou could have found his revolver quickly enough. But he could not find it in the dark. He felt about for his torch, and found that although it was damaged, he could still put on the light by knocking it once or twice on the ground. He shone it on to Dan.

'We ought to have looked out for that ape when we saw he was gone,' growled Dan. 'He had bitten his rope through. We might have known he was somewhere about. He nearly did for me, leaping on me like that out of the darkness. It was lucky he flung himself on to my sack and not me.'

'Let's get the last of the things and clear out,' said Lou, who was badly shaken up. 'There's only one more load. We'll get back to the tunnel, scare the life out of those kids once more, shoot Pongo if we can, and then clear out. We'll chuck a few tins of food down the hole and then close it up.'

'I'm not going to risk meeting that chimp again,' said Dan. 'We'll leave the rest of the things. Come on. Let's go.'

Lou was not particularly anxious to see Pongo again either. Keeping his torch carefully switched on and his revolver ready, he followed Dan to the hole that led down to the first cave. Down they went, and then along the passage, eager to get out into the night and go with their wagon down the track.

They got a terrible shock when they found that the hole was closed. Lou shone his torch upwards, and gazed in amazement at the underside of the boards. Someone had put them back into place again. *They* were prisoners now!

Tiger Dan went mad. One of his furious rages overtook him, and he hammered against those boards like a mad-man. But the heavy stones held them down, and the raging man dropped down beside Lou.

'Can't budge the boards! Someone must have put the caravan overhead again. We're prisoners!'

'But who's made us prisoners? Who's put back those boards?' shouted Lou, almost beside himself with fury. 'Could those kids have slipped by us when we were having that fight with the chimp?'

'We'll go and see if the kids are still there,' said Tiger Dan, grimly. 'We'll find out. We'll make them very, very sorry for themselves. Come on.'

The two men went back again to the tunnel. The children were not there. Julian had taken Dick's advice and had gone off to try and find a good hiding-place. He had suddenly thought that perhaps Dick might get the idea of shutting up the entrance-hole – in which case the two men would certainly be furious!

So up the tunnel the children went, and into the cave with the stream. It seemed impossible to find any hiding-place there at all.

'I don't see where we can hide,' said Julian, feeling rather desperate. 'It's no good wading down that stream again – we shall only get wet and cold – and we have no escape from there at all if the men should come after us!'

'I can hear something,' said George, suddenly. 'Put your light out, Julian – quick!'

The torch was snapped off, and the children waited in the darkness. Timmy didn't growl. Instead George felt that he was wagging his tail.

'It's someone friendly,' she whispered. 'Over there. Perhaps it's Pongo. Put the torch on again.'

The light flashed out, and picked out the chimpanzee, who was coming towards them across the cave. Nobby gave a cry of joy.

'Here's old Pongo again!' he said. 'Pongo, did you go to the camp? Did you bring help?'

'No – he hasn't been down to the camp,' said Julian, his eyes catching sight of the note still tied round the chimpanzee's neck. 'There's our letter still on him. Blow!'

'He's clever – but not clever enough to understand a difficult errand like that,' said George.

'Oh, Pongo – and we were depending on you! Never mind – perhaps Dick will escape and bring help. Julian, where *shall* we hide?'

'*Up* the stream?' suddenly said Anne. 'We've tried going *down* it. But we haven't tried going up it. Do you think it would be any good?'

'We could see,' said Julian, doubtfully. He didn't like this business of wading through water that might suddenly get deep. 'I'll shine my torch up the stream and see what it looks like.'

He went to the stream and shone his light up the tunnel from which it came. 'It seems as if we might walk along the ledge beside it,' he said. 'But we'd have to bend almost double – and the water runs so fast just here we must be careful not to slip and fall in.'

'I'll go first,' said Nobby. 'You go last, Julian. The girls can go in the middle with Pongo and Timmy.'

He stepped on to the narrow ledge inside the rocky tunnel, just above the rushing water. Then came Pongo. Then Anne, then George and Timmy – and last of all Julian.

But just as Julian was disappearing, the two men came into the cave, and by chance Lou's torch shone right on to the vanishing Julian. He gave a yell.

'There's one of them – look, over there! Come on!'

The men ran to where the stream came out of the tunnel, and Lou shone his torch up it. He saw the line of children, with Julian last of all. He grabbed hold of the boy and pulled him back.

Anne yelled when she saw Julian being pulled back. Nobby had a dreadful shock. Timmy growled ferociously, and Pongo made a most peculiar noise.

'Now look here,' came Lou's voice, 'I've got a gun, and I'm going to shoot that dog and that chimp if they so much as put their noses out of here. So hang on to them if you want to save their lives!'

He passed Julian to Tiger Dan, who gripped the boy firmly by the collar. Lou shone his torch up the tunnel again to count the children. 'Ho, there's Nobby,' he said. 'You come on out here, Nobby.'

'If I do, the chimp will come out too,' said Nobby. 'You know that. And he may get *you* before you get him!'

Lou thought about that. He was afraid of the big chimpanzee. 'You stay up there with him, then,' he said. 'And the girl can stay with you, holding the dog. But the other boy can come out here.'

He thought that George was a boy. George didn't mind. She liked people to think she was a boy. She answered at once.

'I can't come. If I do the dog will follow me, and I'm not going to have him shot.'

'You come on out,' said Lou, threateningly. 'I'm going to show you two boys what happens to kids who keep spying and interfering. Nobby knows what happens, don't you, Nobby? He's had his lesson. And you two boys are going to have yours, too.'

Dan called to him. 'There ought to be another girl there, Lou. I thought Nobby said there were two boys and two girls. Where's the other girl?'

'Gone further up the tunnel, I suppose,' said Lou, trying to see. 'Now, you boy – come on out!'

Anne began to cry. 'Don't go, George; don't go. They'll hurt you. Tell them you're a . . .'

'Shut up,' said George, fiercely. She added, in a whisper: 'If I say I'm a girl they'll know Dick is missing, and will be all the angrier. Hang on to Timmy.'

22 The end of the adventure

No, Timmy wasn't hurt. The bullet zipped past his head and struck the wall of the cave. Timmy went for Lou's legs. Down went the man with a crash and a yell, and the revolver flew out of his hand. Julian heard it slithering across the floor of the cave, and he was very thankful.

'Put on your torch, George, quickly!' he yelled. 'We must see what we're doing. Goodness, here's Pongo now!'

Tiger Dan gave a yell of fright when the torch flashed on and he saw the chimpanzee making straight for him. He dealt the ape a smashing blow on the face that knocked him down, and then tured to run. Lou was trying to keep Timmy off his throat, kicking frantically at the excited dog.

Anne clutched Timmy's collar in her trembling hand. George began to walk back to the cave. But Julian was not going to let George be hurt. She might like to think of herself as a boy, but he wasn't going to let her be treated like one. He began to struggle.

Lou caught hold of George as she came out of the tunnel – and at the same moment Julian managed to kick high in the air, and knocked Lou's torch right out of his hand. It flew up into the roof of the cave and fell somewhere with a crash. It went out. Now the cave was in darkness.

'Get back into the tunnel, George, with Anne,' yelled Julian. 'Timmy, Timmy, come on! Pongo, come here!'

'I don't want Timmy to be shot!' cried out George, in terror, as the dog shot past her into the cave.

Even as she spoke a shot rang out. It was Lou, shooting blindly at where he thought Timmy was. George screamed.

'Oh, Timmy, Timmy! You're not hurt, are you?'

Dan ran to the tunnel – and then stopped in astonishment. Four burly policemen were pushing their way out of the tunnel, led by Dick! One of them carried a revolver in his hand. Dan put his hands up at once.

'Timmy! Come off!' commanded George, seeing that there was now no need for the dog's delighted help. Timmy gave her a reproachful glance that said: 'Mistress! I'm really enjoying myself! Let me eat him all up!'

Then the dog caught sight of the four policemen and yelped furiously. More enemies! He would eat the lot.

'What's all this going on?' said the first man, who was an Inspector. 'Get up, you on the floor. Go on, get up!'

Lou got up with great difficulty. Timmy had nipped him in various places. His hair was over his eyes, his clothes were torn. He stared at the policemen, his mouth open in the utmost surprise. How had they come here? Then he saw Dick.

'So one of you kids slipped out – and shut the boards on us!' he said, savagely. 'I might have guessed. You . . .'

'Hold your tongue, Lewis Allburg,' rapped out

the Inspector. 'You can talk when we tell you. You'll have quite a lot of talking to do, to explain some of the things we've heard about you.'

'Dick! How did you get here so soon?' cried Julian, going over to his brother. 'I didn't expect you for hours! Surely you didn't go all the way to the town and back?'

'No. I shot off to the farm, woke up the Mackies, used their telephone and got the police up here double-quick in their car,' said Dick, grinning. 'Everyone all right? Where's Anne? And Nobby?'

'There they are – just coming out of the tunnel up-stream,' said Julian, and swung his torch round. Dick saw Anne's white, scared face, and went over to her.

'It's all right,' he said. 'The adventure is over, Anne! You can smile again!'

Anne gave a watery sort of smile. Pongo took her hand and made little affectionate noises, and that made her smile a little more. George called Timmy to her, afraid that he might take a last nip at Lou.

Lou swung round and stared at her. Then he looked at Dick and Julian. Then at Anne.

'So there *was* only one girl!' he said. 'What did you want to tell me there were two boys and two girls for?' he said to Nobby.

'Because there were,' answered Nobby. He pointed to George. 'She's a girl, though she looks like a boy. And she's as good as a boy any day.'

George felt proud. She stared defiantly at Lou. He was now in the grip of a stout policeman, and Tiger Dan was being hustled off by two more.

'I think we'll leave this rather gloomy place,' said the Inspector, putting away the notebook he had been hastily scribbling in. 'Quick march!'

Julian led the way down the tunnel. He pointed out the shelf where the men had stored their things, and the Inspector collected the few things that were still left. Then on they went, Tiger Dan muttering and growling to himself.

'Will they go to prison?' whispered Anne to Dick.

'You bet,' said Dick. 'That's where they ought to have gone long ago. Their burglaries have been worrying the police for four years!'

Out of the tunnel and into the cave with gleaming walls. Then down the hole and into the small cave and along the narrow passage to the entrance-hole. Stars glittered over the black hole, and the children were very thankful to see them. They were tired of being underground!

Lou and Dan did not have a very comfortable journey along the tunnels and passages, for their guards had a very firm hold of them indeed. Once out in the open they were handcuffed and put into the large police car that stood a little way down the track.

'What are you children going to do?' asked the big Inspector, who was now at the wheel of the car. 'Hadn't you better come down into the town with us after this disturbing adventure?'

'Oh, no thanks,' said Julian politely. 'We're quite used to adventures. We've had plenty, you know. We shall be all right here with Timmy and Pongo.'

'Well, I can't say I'd like a chimpanzee for company myself,' said the Inspector. 'We'll be up here in the morning, looking round and asking a few questions, which I'm sure you'll be pleased to answer. And many thanks for your help in capturing two dangerous thieves!'

'What about the wagon of goods?' asked Dick. 'Are you going to leave it up here? It's got lots of valuables in it.'

'Oh, one of the men is driving down,' said the Inspector, nodding towards a policeman, who stood near by. 'He'll follow us. He can drive a horse all right. Well, look after yourselves. See you tomorrow!'

The car started up suddenly. The Inspector put her into gear, took off the brake and the car slid quietly down the hill, following the winding track. The policeman with the wagon followed slowly, clicking to the horse, which didn't seem at all surprised to have a new driver.

'Well, that's that!' said Julian thankfully. 'I must say we were well out of that. Gosh, Dick, I was glad to see you back with those bobbies so quickly. That was a brain wave of yours to telephone from the farm.'

Dick suddenly yawned. 'It must be frightfully late!' he said. 'Long past the middle of the night. But I'm so fearfully hungry that I simply must have something to eat before I fall into my bunk!'

'Got anything, Anne?' asked Julian.

Anne brightened up at once. 'I'll see,' she said. 'I can find something, I'm sure!'

And she did, of course. She opened two tins of sardines and made sandwiches, and she opend two tins of peaches, so they had a very nice meal in the middle of the night! They ate it sitting on the floor of George's caravan. Pongo had as good a meal as anyone, and Timmy crunched at one of his bones.

It didn't take them long to go to sleep that night. In fact they were all so sleepy when they had finished their meal that nobody undressed! They clambered into the bunks just as they were and fell asleep at once. Nobby curled up with Pongo, and Timmy, as usual, was on George's feet. Peace reigned in the caravans – and tonight no one came to disturb them!

All the children slept very late the next morning. They were awakened by a loud knocking on Julian's caravan. He woke up with a jump and yelled out:

'Yes! Who is it?'

'It's us,' said a familiar voice, and the door opened. Farmer Mackie and his wife peeped in, looking rather anxious.

'We wondered what had happened,' said the farmer. 'You rushed out of the farmhouse when you had used the 'phone last night and didn't come back.'

'I ought to have slipped back and told you,' said Dick, sitting up with his hair over his eyes. He pushed it back. 'But I forgot. The police went down into the hills with us and got the two men. They're well-known burglars. The police got all the goods, too. It was a very thrilling night. Thanks most awfully for letting me use the 'phone.'

'You're very welcome,' said Mrs Mackie. 'And look – I've brought you some food.'

She had two baskets stacked with good things. Dick felt wide awake and very hungry when he saw them. 'Oh, thanks,' he said gratefully. 'You *are* a good sort!'

Nobby and Pongo suddenly uncurled themselves from their pile of rugs, and Mrs Mackie gave a squeal.

'Land-snakes, what's that? A monkey?'

'No, an ape, Mam,' said Nobby politely. 'He won't hurt you. Hi, take your hand out of that basket!'

Pongo, who had been hoping to find a little tit-bit unnoticed, covered his face with his hairy paw and looked through his fingers at Mrs Mackie.

'Look at that now – he's like a naughty child!' said Mrs Mackie. 'Isn't he, Ted?'

'He is that,' said the farmer. 'Queer sort of bed-fellow, I must say!'

'Well, I must be getting along,' said Mrs Mackie, nodding and smiling at George and Anne, who had now come out of their caravan with Timmy to see who the visitors were. 'You come along to the farm if you want anything. We'll be right pleased to see you.'

'Aren't they nice?' said Anne as the two farm-folk went down the cart-track. 'And oh, my goodness – what a breakfast we're going to have! Cold bacon – tomatoes – fresh radishes – curly lettuces – and who wants new honey?'

'Marvellous!' said Julian. 'Come on – let us have it now, before we clean up.'

But Anne made them wash and tidy themselves first! 'You'll enjoy i t much more if you're clean,' she said. 'We all look as black as sweeps! I'll give you five minutes – then you can come to a perfectly wonderful breakfast!'

'All right, Ma!' grinned Nobby, and he went off with the others to wash at the spring. Then back they all went to the sunny ledge to feast on the good things kind Mrs Mackie had provided.

23 Good-bye, Nobby– good-bye, caravanners!

Before they had finished their breakfast the Inspector came roaring up the track in his powerful police car. There was one sharp-eyed policeman with him to take down notes.

'Hallo, hallo!' said the Inspector, eyeing the good things set out on the ledge. 'You seem to do yourselves well, I must say!'

'Have some new bread and honey?' said Anne in her best manner. 'Do! There's plenty!'

'Thanks,' said the Inspector, and sat down with the children. The other policeman wandered round the caravans, examining everything. The Inspector munched away at honey and bread, and the children talked to him, telling him all about their extraordinary adventure.

'It must have been a most unpleasant shock for those two fellows when they found that your caravan was immediately over the entrance to the place where they hid their stolen goods,' said the Inspector. 'Most unpleasant.'

'Have you examined the goods?' asked Dick eagerly. 'Are they very valuable?'

'Priceless,' answered the Inspector, taking another bit of bread and dabbing it thickly with honey. 'Quite priceless. Those rogues apparently stole goods they knew to be of great value, hid them here for a year or two till the hue and cry had died down, then got them out and quietly disposed of them to friends in Holland and Belgium.'

'Tiger Dan used to act in circuses in Holland,' said Nobby. 'He often told me about them. He had friends all over Europe – people in the circus line, you know.'

'Yes. It was easy for him to dispose of his goods abroad,' said the Inspector. 'He planned to go across to Holland today, you know – got everything ready with Lou – or, to give him the right name, Lewis Allburg – and was going to sell most of those things. You just saved them in time!'

'What a bit of luck!' said George. 'They almost got away with it. If Dick hadn't managed to slip out when Pongo was attacking them, we'd still have been prisoners down in the hill, and Lou and Dan would have been half-way to Holland!'

'Smart bit of work you children did,' said the Inspector approvingly, and looked longingly at the honey-pot. 'That's fine honey, I must buy some from Mrs Mackie.'

'Have some more,' said Anne, remembering her manners. 'Do. We've got another loaf.'

'Well, I will,' said the Inspector, and took another slice of bread, spreading it with the yellow honey. It looked as if there wouldn't even be enough left for Pongo to lick out! Anne thought it was nice to see a grown-up enjoying bread and honey as much as children did.

'You know, that fellow Lou did some very remarkable burglaries,' said the Inspector. 'Once he got across from the third floor of one house to the third floor of another *across the street* – and nobody knows how!'

'That would be easy for Lou,' said Nobby, suddenly losing his fear of the big Inspector. 'He'd just throw a wire rope across, lasso something with the end of it, top of a gutter-pipe, perhaps, draw tight, and walk across! He's wonderful on the tight-rope. There ain't nothing he can't do on the tight-rope.'

'Yes – that's probably what he did,' said the Inspector. 'Never thought of that! No, thanks, I really won't have any more honey. That chimpanzee will eat me if I don't leave some for him to lick out!'

Pongo took away the jar, sat himself down behind one of the caravans, and put a large pink tongue into the remains of the honey. When Timmy came running up to see what he had got, Pongo held the jar high above his head and chattered at him.

'Yarra-yarra-yarra-yarra!' he said. Timmy looked rather surprised and went back to George. She was listening with great interest to what the Inspector had to tell them about the underground caves.

'They're very old,' he said. 'The entrance to them used to be some way down the hill, but there was a land-slide and it was blocked up. Nobody bothered to unblock it because the caves were not particularly interesting.'

'Oh, but they *are*,' said Anne, 'especially the one with the gleaming walls.'

'Well, I imagine that quite by accident one day Dan and Lou found another way in,' said the Inspector. 'The way you know – a hole going down into the hill. They must have thought what a fine hiding-place it would make for any stolen goods – perfectly safe, perfectly dry, and quite near the camping-place here each year. What could be better?'

'And I suppose they would have gone on burgling for years and hiding the stuff if we hadn't just happened to put our caravan over the very spot!' said Julian. 'What a bit of bad luck for them!'

'And what a bit of good luck for us!' said the Inspector. 'We did suspect those two, you know, and once or twice we raided the circus to try and find the goods – but they must always have got warning of our coming and got them away in time – up here!'

'Have you been down to the camp, mister?' asked Nobby suddenly.

The Inspector nodded. 'Oh, yes. We've been down already this morning – seen everyone and questioned them. We created quite a stir!'

Nobby looked gloomy.

'What's the matter, Nobby?' said Anne.

'I shan't half cop it when I get back to the camp,' said Nobby. 'They'll say it's all my fault the coppers going there. We don't like the bobbies round the camp. I shall get into a whole lot of trouble when I go back. I don't want to go back.'

Nobody said anything. They all wondered what would happen to poor Nobby now his Uncle Dan was in prison.

Then Anne asked him: 'Who will you live with now in the camp, Nobby?'

'Oh, somebody will take me in and work me hard,' said Nobby. 'I wouldn't mind if I could be with the horses – but Rossy won't let me. I know that. If I could be with horses I'd be happy. I love them and they understand me all right.'

'How old are you, Nobby?' asked the Inspector, joining in the talk. 'Oughtn't you to be going to school?'

'Never been in my life, mister,' said Nobby. 'I'm just over fourteen, so I reckon I never will go now!'

He grinned. He didn't look fourteen. He seemed more like twelve by his size. Then he looked solemn again.

'Reckon I won't go down to the camp today,' he said. 'I'll be proper set on by them all – about you going there and snooping round like. And Mr Gorgio, he won't like losing his best clown and best acrobat!'

'You can stay with us as long as you like,' said Julian. 'We'll be here a bit longer, anyway.'

But he was wrong. Just after the Inspector had left, taking his policeman with him, Mrs Mackie came hurring up to them with a little orange envelope in her hand.

'The telegraph boy's just been up,' she said. 'He was looking for you. He left this telegram for you. I hope it's not bad news.'

Julian tore the envelope open and read the telegram out loud.

'AMAZED TO GET YOUR LETTER ABOUT THE EXTRAORDINARY HAPPENINGS YOU DESCRIBE. THEY SOUND DANGEROUS. COME HOME AT ONCE. DADDY.'

'Oh dear,' said Anne. 'Now we shall have to leave. What a pity!'

'I'd better go down to the town and telephone Daddy and tell him we're all right,' said Julian.

'You can 'phone from my house,' said Mrs Mackie, so Julian thought he would. They talked as they went along and suddenly a bright idea struck Julian.

'I say – I suppose Farmer Mackie doesn't want anyone to help him with his horses, does he?' he asked. 'He wouldn't want a boy who really loves and understands them and would work hard and well?'

'Well, now, I dare say he would,' said Mrs Mackie. 'He's a bit short-handed now. He was saying the other day he could do with a good lad, just leaving school.'

'Oh, *do* you think he'd try our friend Nobby from the circus camp?' said Julian. 'He's mad on horses. He can do anything with them. And he's been used to working very hard. I'm sure he'd do well.'

Before Julian had left the farmhouse after telephoning to his amazed parents, he had had a long talk with Farmer Mackie – and now he was running back with the good news to the caravans.

'Nobby!' he shouted as he got near. 'Nobby! How would you like to go and work for Farmer Mackie and help with the horses? He says you can start tomorrow if you like – and live at the farm!'

'Jumping Jiminy!' said Nobby, looking startled and disbelieving. 'At the farm? Work with the horses? Coo – I wouldn't half like that. But Farmer Mackie wouldn't have the likes of me.'

'He will. He says he'll try you,' said Julian. 'We've got to start back home tomorrow, and you can be with us till then. You don't need to go back to the camp at all.'

'Well – but what about Growler?' said Nobby. 'I'd have to have him with me. He's my dog. I expect poor old Barker's dead. Would the farmer mind me having a dog?'

'I shouldn't think so,' said Julian. 'Well, you'll have to go down to the camp, I suppose, to collect your few things – and to get Growler. Better go now, Nobby, and then you'll have the rest of the day with us.'

Nobby went off, his face shining with delight. 'Well, I never!' he kept saying to himself. 'Well, I never did! Dan and Lou gone, so they'll never hurt me again – and me not going to live in the camp any more – and going to have charge of them fine farm horses. Well, I never!'

The children had said good-bye to Pongo because he had to go back with Nobby to the camp. He belonged to Mr Gorgio, and Nobby could not possibly keep him. Anyway, it was certain that even if he could have kept him, Mrs Mackie wouldn't have let him live at the farm.

Pongo shook hands gravely with each one of them, even with Timmy. He seemed to know it was good-bye. The children were really sorry to see the comical chimpanzee go. He had shared in their adventure with them and seemed much more like a human being than an animal.

When he had gone down the hill a little way he ran back to Anne. He put his arms round her and gave her a gentle squeeze, as if to say: 'You're all nice, the lot of you, but little Anne's the nicest!'

'Oh, Pongo, you're really a dear!' said Anne, and gave him a tomato. He ran off with it, leaping high for joy.

The children cleared up everything, put the breakfast things away, and cleaned the caravans, ready for starting off the next day. At dinner-time they looked out for Nobby. Surely he should be back soon?

They heard him whistling as he came up the track He carried a bundle on his back. Round his feet ran two dogs. Two!

'Why – one of them is Barker!' shouted George in delight. 'He must have got better! How simply marvellous!'

Nobby came up, grinning. They all crowded round him, asking about Barker.

'Yes, it's fine, isn't it?' said Nobby, putting down his bundle of belongings. 'Lucilla dosed him all right. He almost died – then he started to wriggle a bit, she said, and the next she knew he was as lively as could be – bit weak on his legs at first – but he's fine this morning.'

Certainly there didn't seem anything wrong with Barker. He and Growler sniffed round Timmy, their tails wagging fast. Timmy stood towering above them, but his tail wagged, too, so Barker and Growler knew he was friendly.

'I was lucky,' said Nobby. 'I only spoke to Lucilla and Larry. Mr Gorgio has gone off to answer some questions at the police station, and so have some of the others. So I just told Larry to tell Mr Gorgio I was leaving, and I got my things and hopped it.'

'Well, now we can really enjoy our last day,' said Julian. 'Everybody's happy!'

And they did enjoy that last day. They went down to the lake and bathed. They had a fine farmhouse tea at Mrs Mackie's by special invitation. They had a picnic supper on the rocky ledge, with the three dogs rolling over and over in play. Nobby felt sad to think he would so soon say good-bye to his 'posh' friends – but he couldn't help feeling proud and pleased to have a fine job of his own on the farm – with the horses he loved so much.

Nobby, Barker, Growler, Farmer Mackie and his wife all stood on the cart-track to wave good-bye to the two caravans the next morning.

'Good-bye!' yelled Nobby. 'Good luck! See you again some time!'

'Good-bye!' shouted the others. 'Give our love to Pongo when you see him.'

'Woof! woof!' barked Timmy, but only Barker and Growler knew what *that* meant. It meant, 'Shake paws with Pongo for me!'

Good-bye, five caravanners . . . till your next exciting adventure!